ALSO BY THESE AUTHORS

Smitten
Secretly Smitten

COLLEEN COBLE

Under Texas Stars novels
Blue Moon Promise
Safe in His Arms
Butterfly Palace

The Hope Beach novels
Tidewater Inn
Rosemary Cottage

The Lonestar novels
Lonestar Sanctuary
Lonestar Secrets
Lonestar Homecoming
Lonestar Angel

The Mercy Falls series
The Lightkeeper's Daughter
The Lightkeeper's Bride
The Lightkeeper's Ball

The Rock Harbor series
Without a Trace
Beyond a Doubt
Into the Deep
Cry in the Night

The Aloha Reef series
Distant Echoes
Black Sands
Dangerous Depths
Midnight Sea

❧

Alaska Twilight
Fire Dancer
Abomination
Anathema

KRISTIN BILLERBECK

The Scent of Rain
A Billion Reasons Why
Split Ends

The Ashley Stockingdale novels
What a Girl Wants
She's Out of Control
With This Ring, I'm Confused

The Spa Girls series
She's All That
A Girl's Best Friend
Calm, Cool, and Adjusted

DIANN HUNT

Bittersweet Surrender
(available as e-book only)
Be Sweet
For Better or For Worse
Hot Tropics & Cold Feet
RV There Yet?
Hot Flashes & Cold Cream

DENISE HUNTER

The Chapel Springs series
Barefoot Summer
Dancing with Fireflies

The Nantucket Romance series
Surrender Bay
The Convenient Groom
Seaside Letters
Driftwood Lane

The Big Sky Romance series
A Cowboy's Touch
The Accidental Bride
The Trouble with Cowboys

Sweetwater Gap

Smitten Book Club

THOMAS NELSON
Since 1798

NASHVILLE   DALLAS   MEXICO CITY   RIO DE JANEIRO

Published in Nashville, Tennessee, by Thomas Nelson. Thomas Nelson is a registered trademark of Thomas Nelson, Inc.

Thomas Nelson, Inc., books may be purchased in bulk for educational, business, fund-raising, or sales promotional use. For information, please e-mail SpecialMarkets@ThomasNelson.com.

Kristin Billerbeck is represented by the literary agency of Alive Communications, Inc., 7680 Goddard Street, Suite 200, Colorado Springs, CO 80920, www.alivecommunications.com.

Publisher's Note: This novel is a work of fiction. Names, characters, places, and incidents are either products of the authors' imaginations or used fictitiously. All characters are fictional, and any similarity to people living or dead is purely coincidental.

Library of Congress Cataloging-in-Publication Data

Smitten book club / Colleen Coble, Kristin Billerbeck, Diann Hunt, and Denise Hunter.
    pages cm
  ISBN 978-1-4016-8716-8 (trade paper)
  1. Love stories, American. 2. Christian fiction, American. I. Coble, Colleen. Love by the book. II. Billerbeck, Kristin. Shelved under romance. III. Hunt, Diann. New chapter. IV. Hunter, Denise. Happily ever after.
  PS648.L6S538 2014
  813'.08508--dc23

                        2013029519

Printed in the United States of America

14 15 16 17 18 RRD 5 4 3 2 1

CONTENTS

Love by the Book

Colleen Coble

> *No well-bred lady should eagerly receive the attentions of a gentleman, even if she admires him. And his reputation must be taken into account before you ever entertain letting him escort you anywhere.*
>
> PEARL CHAMBERS, *The Gentlewoman's Guide to Love and Courtship*

CHAPTER ONE

. . . .

*M*ountains of donated boxes teetered against the west wall when Heather DeMeritt entered the Smitten library. The building had been renovated a few months earlier and still held a trace of that new smell in the brown carpet. The oak bookshelves that housed the library's growing collection and the matching tables still shone with newness. Several businesses had donated the bank of computers lining one wall.

Heather spoke to several friends, then turned to eye the job she'd come to do. She was prepared to work, but the sheer number of books surprised her.

Her friend and fellow book club member, Abby Gray, motioned to her. Abby was the Smitten librarian, though she was much too pretty to fit the stereotype, even with her blond hair perpetually up in a bun.

Heather threaded through the throng to reach Abby's side. "This is going to take awhile."

Abby's cheeks were flushed. "Isn't it exciting? So many people want to help Molly."

Their good friend Molly Moore had recently lost her husband in a tragic fire. He was the only volunteer fireman to die in recent memory, and Smitten was still reeling. As was Molly.

Abby waved vaguely. "You can start there."

Heather opened the nearest box and began to lift out the books to put in sale piles ranging from one dollar to five. Five dollars was too much to pay for some of these books, but it was for a good cause, and everyone would feel great about helping.

An hour later her throat was scratchy, and her nose was stuffy from all the dust. But she'd made progress.

"Need some help?" Elliana Burton asked. Lia, as her friends called her, was the kindergarten teacher at the elementary school in town. She usually had a crayon stuck behind one ear and a slash or two of color on her arms or hands from Crayola markers, but today she looked fresh and carefree in a silky blue top over jeans that hugged her slim hips.

"I'll take you up on it," Heather said. "We might finish in time for coffee at Mountain Perks."

There was only one towering stack left. She lifted down the top box and opened it. A cloud of dust wafted out, and she wrinkled her nose.

Lia waved her hand in front of her face. "Some of these are *old*. They might be worth some money."

Heather took out the top book, a thick tome bound in

green leather. The cover was in surprisingly good condition. She eyed the title, then burst out laughing. "Look at this. Have you ever heard of it? *The Gentlewoman's Guide to Love and Courtship.*"

She laughed again as she opened the book. "Look at this opening, Lia. It claims the reader who understands these patterns and uses them will find true love. Pearl Chambers."

"Yes, she was a local author. Pretty famous back in her day. Wasn't she related to Molly's husband in some way? His maternal great-grandmother or something?" Lia peered over her shoulder at the place where Heather's finger pointed. "I could use a little luck like that. How about you?"

Heather's smile faded. "I don't think so. Romance is overrated. And look at this advice." She read it aloud. "'A young lady should not allow a man to address her by her first name.' A bit outdated, wouldn't you say?"

"Maybe so." Lia's eyes went soft. "Honey, don't swear off all men just because you ran into a rat. The right fellow is out there." She tucked the book under her arm. "In fact, I'm going to buy it for you. You like mysteries. This one is about deciphering behavior. It's right up your alley."

In spite of Heather's protests, Lia marched to the library desk and plunked down ten dollars for the book.

Too bad it would take more than a book to turn Heather's love life around. Since her work was done, she carried the book to one of the tables and began to leaf through it. A yellowed envelope fell out. The return address showed it was from a Beatrice Chambers, and there was a paper inside. Curious, Heather pulled it out. Her brow furrowed when she began to read.

Son, as I write this, I know you have no interest in this old book, but I believe when you find this letter, what I have to say will change everything. Your grandmother found a gold mine in the hills, and left the clues to its location in this book. I'm convinced of it. I've never quite figured out all of the clues. I think you can. Be diligent, and use the money wisely when you find it. Give it to someone needy or help fund a good cause. Turn it around for good in some way. Good luck.

Your loving mother

The book club members sat in comfortable chairs around the fireplace in the back of Lookaway Village Books in downtown Smitten. A small fire gave off a welcome glow that chased away the early March chill.

Heather welcomed the group with a smile. "Thank you all for coming. I know we all feel Molly's absence tonight, but I'm glad we're together. Before we start talking about *The Art of Racing in the Rain*, Abby, would you give a report on the upcoming book sale?"

Abby's smile stretched across her face when she stood. Dressed in jeans and a red sweater, she looked fresh and appealing. "The donations have far surpassed what we expected. The sale will be held on Saturday, and if we sell even half the stock we'll make enough to pay for Curtis's funeral." She sat down to a soft wave of applause.

Shelby Majors's iPhone buzzed, and she rose to answer it, her long brown hair falling over her shoulders. "Nick is outside," she reported. "He and some of the other firemen want to talk to us about what we might do to help Molly."

Natalie Smitten paused as she was pouring the coffee she'd brought from her shop, Mountain Perks. "Good, bring them in. There has to be something else we can do." She set down the thermos, then sat back down.

Shelby hurried to the door and pulled it open. The clean rush of cold air dissipated the scent of smoke. Nick Majors stomped the snow from his boots, then removed his hat before leading the group of men to the fireplace. The men were even more somber than the women, if that was possible. But then they'd been there when Curtis died.

Heather clenched her fists when she saw one of the men with Nick. She couldn't breathe, couldn't tear her gaze away from the face that still haunted her dreams, even after nearly four years. Paul Mansfield's gaze swept the group, then stopped when he saw her. His eyes widened when he saw her. Did he still remember the way she'd thrown herself at him the last time he was in town? Of course he did.

"Paul!" Natalie launched herself from the sofa and flung her arms around her brother's neck. "When did you get to town? How long can you stay?"

Paul hugged his sister. The two looked alike, same dark hair and eyes. Paul towered over most men at six foot four, and his shoulders strained the fabric of his oh-so-proper oxford shirt.

Heather forced herself to look away. What was he doing here?

She saw several of the single women eyeing him. Paul

turned female heads wherever he went with his dark good looks and air of competence. The glasses perched on his perfectly chiseled face added to his sex appeal in some indefinable way, as did the lock of hair constantly falling over his forehead.

Natalie released him and stepped back. "I had no idea you were coming."

"You mean you didn't get the memo? Darn, I thought sure I sent it." He grinned. "There's time enough for that later. Let's concentrate on helping Molly."

"You guys have some ideas?" his sister asked.

Nick took the cup of coffee Shelby offered him. "Yeah, we've been talking. We've never lost one of our own before."

Heather's eyes welled, and she dug a tissue out of her pocket. "I was at Molly's today. She's devastated. She said the house is so empty without him." Several of the other women dabbed their eyes too.

"I still don't understand how it happened," Julia Grant burst out. Her favorite Jimmy Choo shoes showcased her long legs. "Why did he even go in there?"

Heather didn't want to look at Paul, didn't want to notice the way he was even more handsome than the last time she'd seen him. "It seems so odd that Curtis would go inside when the firemen had been told everyone was out."

Nick's mouth was grim. "He was rescuing the family dog. He tossed it out the bedroom window, then turned to get out himself."

And didn't make it. The ceiling collapsed on the veteran volunteer fire fighter. The funeral yesterday had been the largest ever seen in town, with the line spilling out the door of the

funeral home and clear down in front of the newly renovated train station. It had taken three hours in line just to get
inside the door.

"So, about helping Molly?" Tess Stevenson prompted.
The bookstore owner turned her blue eyes Nick's way.

He nodded. "Molly still has Smitten Expeditions. She's
got a good guide too. But she's suddenly a single mom with
no idea of how to run a business. She'll need our support in
lots of ways. Money is easy. The town will give generously.
The other things will take dedicated persistence this week,
and the next week, and the next. Babysitting, helping with
figuring out the books, planning the future. You get the picture. The renovations Curtis had started need to be finished.
Some of us can help with that. And we want to be there for his
boy. He's lost his daddy." Nick pressed his lips together.

Reese Parker pulled a pen and note pad from her purse.
"Babysitting, construction work, accounting advice." She
paused and chewed on the end of her pen. "Anything else?"

"She's had a part-time job, but she'll have to quit that. It
will take all her efforts to make a go of the business. So she'll
probably need more financial help than just paying for the
funeral," Lia said.

"I'm not good at the other things you mentioned, but I
could clean her house every week," Ellie Draper said. "I can
bring in dinner once a week too. I'll organize a food brigade
so she doesn't have to worry about that for a while."

"And I'll take up a collection for funeral costs," Abby
said. "Just in case we can't sell enough old books to cover the
expense."

A chorus of offers filled the air, and Reese jotted them

down. "Okay, we'll get this plan put into place. I'll be contacting each of you with your assignment."

Heather's gaze collided with Paul's. He hadn't offered any services. Maybe he was leaving. Again.

A light still shone out of the bookstore windows. Paul blew warm vapor on his hands and stamped his feet on the concrete as he waited for Heather to come out. Better to get this uncomfortable meeting over with. He'd seen the shock in her eyes when she saw him, and he hadn't done a good job of hiding his own consternation. He'd thought she'd be long gone from here, though if he were honest, he had to admit the thought of seeing her had played a role in his decision to move back to Smitten.

The town had changed since he was last here. White lights sparkled along the street like tiny diamonds. Every storefront wore fresh paint of several colors in the "painted lady" tradition. New streetlights lit the sidewalks, and people milled in the town square even at this hour. The romance destination plan had taken root. He'd played a part in that, and he was eager to see how the new lodge had turned out.

The door opened, and a shaft of light hit the sidewalk. Heather stepped out in a lightweight jacket. Her long blond hair gleamed in the lamplight, and her jeans and knee-high boots accentuated her long legs.

He stepped out from the shadows. "Hi."

She put her hand to her chest. "You scared me."

"Sorry. I wanted to talk to you."

Her lips flattened, and she moved toward the curb. "What about?"

He fell into step beside her as she started across the street. "Can we grab some coffee or something?"

She shot him a look from wide blue eyes like a frightened cat. As well she should after the way he'd treated her.

He pushed up his glasses and gave her his best smile. "I figured we might as well get the awkwardness out of the way. Otherwise we're going to be tiptoeing around each other."

She stopped in the middle of the street and stared at him. "Why are you here, Paul?"

"Can we talk? I'll explain then."

She stared at him as though searching his soul. Her way of looking inside him had been the first thing to attract him. And it had been what sent him running scared from town. He still regretted it. "I'll buy coffee."

She shook her head. "I love Nat, but I don't want her watching over our shoulders. You can come to my house for a minute. I promise to keep my distance." She walked across the street and turned left.

He jogged after her and fell into step beside her. "I'll stop off at the coffee shop and grab us a snack. Be there in ten minutes."

"Okay. I'll see you in a few."

He watched her turn the corner and vanish into the shadows. The hard part was still ahead.

CHAPTER TWO

"Night, night, Charlie." Relishing the scent of toothpaste and little boy, Heather kissed her son. "Sleep tight."

"Don't let the bedbugs bite," Charlie said. He wrapped his arms around her and planted a wet kiss on her cheek. "Love you, Mommy." The three-year-old sounded sleepily content.

"I love you, honey. Very much." She tucked his stuffed bear into the covers with him, then flipped on his goldfish night-light and backed out of the room. The gentle knock came as Heather walked down the stairs. Her throat tightened as she opened the door to greet Paul. He had a cardboard drink carrier in one hand and a sack in the other.

Lord have mercy, but the man was handsome. The crisp white button-down collared shirt contrasted with his dark, curly hair and tanned skin. His eyes were brown, but a warm golden color that invited you to trust him. She'd made that mistake once.

His smile widened as he stepped into the house. "Nice."

She nodded. "There's a big yard, and I'm able to have a nice garden."

"Organic food, of course," he said.

"Of course. How odd you remember."

An incredulous expression crossed his face.

He handed her a coffee, then took one for himself before settling on the sofa. "Natalie swears these brownies are the bomb even if they're gluten-free. I'm not so sure. I've tasted some of her concoctions."

"They're delicious," she said automatically before dropping onto the chair as far away from him as she could manage.

He regarded her over the rim of his glasses. "I'm moving back to Smitten, Heather. I thought we needed to clear the air between us."

When she managed to get the elephant off her chest, she inhaled. She gulped, then swallowed. "I see. I appreciate the heads-up, and I'll be sure not to bother you."

He exhaled and leaned forward. "I want to apologize for how I acted."

"I'm the one who should apologize." Her face burned as she remembered that night. "I threw myself at you. You did the right thing showing me to the door."

He pressed his lips together and shook his head. "It wasn't that at all."

She didn't want to hear what it was. The humiliation would be too much to bear. She rose. "Well, you've apologized, and so have I. I think the air is clear. We can nod at one another politely in Nat's coffee shop, and there will be no worries. Is that all you had to say?"

Though she knew it was ridiculous, she held her breath with the faint hope he might say he'd never forgotten her. She shook her head at her stupidity.

"What?" he asked.

"Nothing. I'll show you out."

"There's something else. We're going to be working together."

"What does that mean?"

"The town has been donated a plot of land to develop as an organic farm. I'd like you to help me design the beds and the buildings. We're going to put in a pumpkin patch and have hayrides for the kids. We'll have a petting zoo, too, with goats and sheep. There are all kinds of plans for it. I've already cleared it with your boss at the county extension office."

The thought of working in close proximity with him took her breath away, and not in a good way. Being around him tonight had shown her she'd never gotten over him.

She shook her head. "I don't think so, Paul. It would be awkward. There are others at the office who can help you."

"Let's put our personal issues away for the good of the town. I need you, Heather. And let's be honest, you're the town expert on organic farming."

What did she say to that? She loved Smitten, was committed to her little town. And he was right—no one knew more about this, even in her office, than she did.

"All right."

His eyes lit. "Wonderful. I'll pick you up tomorrow and

show you what I have in mind. I should have some prelimi-
nary sketches by then."

"Mommy?" Charlie stood in the doorway rubbing his
eyes. "I had a bad dream."

"You're fine, little man." She sprang to her feet and
picked up her son. His warm little body relaxed against her.
"Put your head down." She hummed "Amazing Grace," and
his lids began to drift downward again. "Sorry," she mouthed
to Paul. "I'll be right back." She carried Charlie back to bed
and tucked him in. He didn't stir.

She went downstairs and found Paul standing by the window with a pensive expression. "Sorry about that."

"No problem. He's cute. He looks like his daddy?"

It was on the tip of her tongue to tell him her husband
had left her when she was six months pregnant, but she'd had
all the humiliation she could handle tonight. "Yes."

"I'm glad you're happy. I only wish you the best."

She showed him the door, then leaned against it and let
the tears fall.

When she went back to the sofa, she spotted the old book
Lia had bought her. How on earth could she find any clues in
such an obscure text? Leafing through the fragile pages, she
came to a section titled "Encouraging the Male's Attention."
The old language made her smile, but her smile faded when
she read the last paragraph.

It is always wise to ascertain the male's true intentions. Most
men won't be brought to a proposal if the woman is too easily persuaded of his love. A man who is seriously pursuing a

woman with honorable intentions will be quick to introduce her to his family, though he may hide her from his friends if he is the jealous sort.

No wonder her forwardness had sent Paul running for cover. She shook her head and pushed the thought away. She was only reading this old thing to find clues about the treasure.

Heather let herself into Molly's house. "Moll? I've got scones and coffee from Natalie's shop." She went down the hall and through the living room, strewn with Noah's toys, to the kitchen.

Molly was sitting at the table with a blank expression. She was still in her pajamas, lavender flannel ones with frolicking kittens that Noah had bought her for Christmas.

Heather touched her shoulder. "Moll?"

Molly startled and looked up at her with sorrowful brown eyes, puffy from crying. "What am I going to do, Heather? It's all so overwhelming." She put her hands over her face. "I can't stop replaying that huge fight we had before he left that day."

"I know, honey." Heather well knew the pain of a marriage on the rocks.

She pulled up a chair, then slid the coffee across the table to her. "Here, drink your coffee. You can't go back. I know things weren't great between you and Curtis. You were both so young when you got married, and he never grew up. He was a sweet guy, but he acted like he was still in high school without a family to feed."

Molly picked up her coffee, tucked a long brown strand of hair behind her ear, then took a sip. She managed a smile. "You're a good friend."

"Try not to worry. All of us in Smitten are going to help you. The first thing we need to do is take a look at your finances and see what is going on there."

Molly put her coffee back on the table. "It's worse than I ever dreamed." She reached over and clutched Heather's hand with cold fingers. "Promise you won't say a word! I can't stand it if the whole town knows how foolish Curtis was. They have him up on a pedestal now, and at least that's comforting to Noah."

"I promise. What's wrong?"

Molly released her and sat back. "He took out a second mortgage on our house to fund the business. So if I lose the business, I lose our home too. And this little house has been in his family for four generations. His grandmother was born here to Pearl Chambers. His parents started their life together here. Noah loves this place. I can't take that away from him, Heather, I just can't."

Heather exhaled and sat back in her chair. "I'm so sorry. Try not to worry. We'll sort it out. I can go to the bank with you and ask for better terms. Maybe they would suspend payments for a few months until you get on your feet. Brian is a good guy. He'll work with you."

Molly shook her head. "That might help a bit, but the payments will be overwhelming."

It usually took five years to get a business on its feet. Curtis had started Smitten Expeditions a year ago.

"I know what you're thinking," Molly said. "It would take a miracle to turn it around."

Heather smiled and reached over to squeeze her hand. "God is in the miracle business, and remember—this is Smitten. Our little town is used to helping God make the impossible happen."

Molly's gaze locked with hers, then she bit her lip. "You almost make me think it will be all right."

"Everyone wants to help. We'll do whatever you need." Heather released Molly's hand and dug in her purse, then extracted a piece of paper. "Reese sent over a list we can add to or delete." She slid it across the table to Molly. "What needs tending to first?"

"I hate to be so needy." Molly's voice quavered, but she took the list. "This is too much, Heather. The funeral home gave me some time to pay for the funeral. I don't want to take charity."

"It's not charity. It's looking out for our own. The book sale should cover funeral costs. Ellie Draper is going to bring in dinner for you tonight. I'm not sure who is on for tomorrow, but you don't need to worry about grocery shopping either. Ellie is going to bring in some things for your fridge and cupboard."

Molly swallowed hard, then turned her attention back to the list. "The remodeling is going to have to come to a halt. I don't have the money to pay for labor. I called the contractor yesterday, and he's been paid for what he's done so far. Curtis did that much at least."

"Do you have all the materials?"

"I don't know. There might be a few items needed, but it doesn't matter when I can't pay for the labor. I don't know what he was thinking. Maybe he thought he'd do it himself."

"Let me see what I can do." She suspected Carson and Natalie would want to donate any necessary building materials, and she was sure she could find some carpenters willing to do the work for free to help out. Griffen Parker came to mind.

Molly pressed her lips together. "Don't go begging on my account."

"Molly, you don't understand. People *want* to help. You're one of us. We can't just stand by and do nothing. You can't ask that of Smitten."

Molly covered her face with her hands. "I don't know what to do."

Heather took Molly's wrists and pulled her hands down to stare into her face. "You smile and thank the people who want to do something for you. You don't steal their joy. Got it?"

Molly's brown eyes widened, and she slowly nodded. "All right, Heather, if you're sure that's what people really want to do."

"Things will be all right. You'll see. Leave the rest of the stuff to me and your friends." She glanced around the cheery kitchen, decorated in red and yellow. "Where is Noah, anyway?"

"I let him go to school. I thought it was best to let him get back to his routine as quickly as possible. He's taking it hard, poor little guy. Even though Curtis didn't spend a lot of time with him, he idolized his daddy."

Heather's eyes burned, and she nodded. "A little boy needs a father." She chewed on her thumbnail. "Um, guess who came back to town?"

Molly's dull eyes brightened with interest. "Who?"

"Paul Mansfield."

Molly eyes went wide. "Have you talked to him?"

Heather reached for the sugar bowl and stirred two teaspoons full into her coffee. She needed strength to face all this. "I talked to him last night, and he met Charlie. I think he was glad his rejection didn't ruin my life. If he only knew. I didn't tell him I rushed out and married the first man who asked me. I didn't tell him my husband was a player who left me when I was six months pregnant. I also didn't tell him my heart did a flip-flop the second I saw his face." She put down her spoon.

Molly snorted. "He thinks you're still married? How did he act?"

"He congratulated me and told me he hoped I'd be happy. I think he was relieved." Her eyes prickled. He'd been way too happy he didn't have to worry about her. Heather rubbed her forehead. "I can't believe I was so stupid, Molly." She laughed. "I was reading this silly book last night, written by Pearl Chambers. Wasn't she Curtis's great-grandma or something? Anyway, she says you'll chase a guy off if you're too forward. That's exactly what I did."

Heather reached into her book bag and withdrew the old book. "Someone donated it to the book sale, and Lia bought it. You have to read the opening lines." She pushed it across the table to her friend.

"That's some title." Smiling, Molly began to read, and her grin broadened. "I can't believe you're actually reading it."

"It's kind of addicting. I think old Pearl had a good handle on the male species. And it's just kind of fun."

"Look at this one. 'The male thrives on respect. Curling of the lip or the lifting of a brow by the object of his affections is apt to leave him dejected.'" Molly curled her lip in the very picture of disdain. "Try that on Paul and maybe he'll leave town."

Heather burst into giggles. "I just might do that."

At least she'd managed to sidetrack Molly from her worries. "But it's not the real reason the book is important. It holds the clues to a missing treasure. Surely you've heard the old legend about the gold mine Pearl Chambers found?"

Molly frowned. "That old thing? Good grief, Heather, you can't be serious. Even Curtis looked for a while, but the land is gone now anyway. I need solid answers, not some wild goose chase."

"But what if you still own the mineral rights? I bet Curtis didn't let those go."

Molly nodded. "He said something about that." She shook her head. "But it's just a small-town legend, Heather. There's no truth in it."

"I think it's worth checking out. Here, read this." She showed Molly the letter from Beatrice. "She clearly believed her mother had found something."

Molly shrugged. "There are some old family trunks with pictures and things in the spare bedroom. That might tell us something. But really, Heather, treasure? That's a little far-fetched. I think I need to do something much more concrete to save this house and the business."

"We're going to help you too. But it can't hurt to see what we can find here at the house. I'll try to figure out the clues."

Molly's eyes twinkled. "You're sure you're not interested in reading the book for the good-luck-with-love issue?"

Heather sat back in her chair and laughed. "I can see

you haven't read that thing. One particularly pithy piece of advice is to not answer back and to do whatever your husband tells you."

Molly smiled. "I'm sure there's some good advice in there too. Everyone wants love."

Heather bit her lip. "Maybe. There's stuff like dressing up all the time. It did make me wonder if I don't try enough." She tugged on the hem of her T-shirt. "Maybe a nice sweater with jeans instead of this. And I can't even remember the last time I bothered with makeup."

"Your skin is perfect. You hardly need it."

"Ever the loyal friend."

Molly pushed her hair back from her face. "I'd better get to work."

"You run off, and I'll call the girls to see if we can find any clues to that treasure."

"Check the spare room. There are all kinds of things packed in there from when Curtis's parents lived here. But I doubt you'll find anything."

Heather pulled out her cell to call her friends. "Hope springs eternal."

> *The male thrives on respect. Curling of the lip or the lifting of a brow by the object of his affections is apt to leave him dejected.*
>
> PEARL CHAMBERS, *The Gentlewoman's Guide to Love and Courtship*

CHAPTER THREE

*P*aul had always liked Natalie's house. It was warm and welcoming, just like his sister. They sat at the kitchen table, just the two of them. Carson was at work, and Mia was off to school. The delicious aroma of Nat's coffee filled the room. She owned the local coffee shop and roasted her own special blends.

Nat set an omelet in front of Paul, then pulled out a chair and joined him. "You've been avoiding my questions. Why didn't you call and tell me you were coming?"

He grinned as he dug into his breakfast. "I'm moving back." He waited until her brown eyes widened. "I know I said I wanted big-city life, but I've changed my mind."

She rested her chin on her hand and stared at him. "Why?"

He stared back. They'd been through so much together. Raised by their aunts, they'd stuck together through thick and thin. She'd never wanted to live anywhere else, while he'd yearned for big-city lights and a thriving career.

She poured heavy cream into her coffee and stirred as she waited. When she lifted a brow, he grinned and shrugged. "You can't repeat it until the news comes out in the paper. Well, you can tell Carson, but that's all."

"Like I would."

"I'm opening my own architectural business here. My first project is an organic town farm."

Her eyes brightened. "That's wonderful! But what's a town farm, exactly?"

"The town will own it and manage it. They'll grow organic food to sell. There will be a farmers' market out there, a pumpkin patch, and the old house will be restored as it was in the 1800s as an attraction."

"I love the idea! Where will it be?"

"The old Bristol homestead."

"That will be perfect! It's been derelict for years. But it doesn't explain why you're doing this. I'll be glad to have you here, but you're not telling me the whole story."

"True enough." He exhaled. "I'm lonely, Nat. Pretty silly, isn't it? Millions of people around me, but I don't know any of them. None of them look me in the eye and wish me good morning when we pass on the street."

Her eyes softened, and she reached across the table to take his hand. "Have you tried joining in at your church? Maybe doing some community work of some kind."

"I've tried all that. City people are different from my friends here in Smitten. I had a date the other night with a young woman from my church. I tried to talk to her about a family that had lost everything in a fire, but she kept changing the subject to the great deal she'd found on shoes. I realized then I don't belong there like I thought I did."

She released his hand and picked up her coffee cup. "Just be sure you know what you're doing. You've got a great job and you're about to be made a partner."

"The next morning I got that offer," he admitted. "With a hefty raise. But more money wouldn't make me happy. You make me happy. Aunt Rose and Violet and Petunia make me happy." He picked up his fork. "I'm tired of being alone."

She sipped her coffee before she answered, studying him over the top of her cup with a penetrating gaze. "You're ready to settle down, aren't you? Is that what this is all about?"

His face heated, but he held her gaze. "I might if I could find the right woman." For a moment Heather's face flashed through his mind. He'd ruined that, though. "You and Carson have something pretty special. I'm not sure I could ever find that."

Her smile held a joy he could only envy. "We do, yes. But don't settle for just anyone. Wait until you know you've found the right one."

He'd already lost the right one. "I won't rush into anything."

"So what's the plan? Where are you going to live? We have a spare room if you need to stay with us for a while."

"Aunt Rose would have heart failure if I didn't stay with her. I'm in my old room there until I buy a house. But thanks for the offer."

She hiked a brow. "You know, you should talk to Heather DeMeritt about this project. She knows everything about organic farming. And she cares so much about Smitten."

"I'm one step ahead of you. I'm taking her out to see it tomorrow."

"Good. Anything I can do?"

"Keep an eye out for an office space and a big old house for me to buy."

Her expression turned thoughtful. "I have space over my coffee shop. It's undeveloped and has some great potential."

"Hmm, it's a good location too. Right in the center of town. Mind if I take a look?"

"I'd love it. I'd even give you free coffee."

"That's a deal I can't refuse. Can we go over there now?"

Her eyes went wide. "Without finishing your coffee? Are you crazy?"

He grinned. "I've missed you, Nat. Thanks for always being here for me."

Heather opened the windows of the spare room in Molly's house to let the sweet breeze off Sugarcreek Mountain blow away the stale air. Her friends had been quick to join her when they heard the word *treasure*. The room was about fifteen feet square, and every discarded piece of family furniture had been piled in here since before time began. Old end tables and lamps, dolls, toys, boxes of fabric for quilts, several bed frames, and old blankets made walking through the space difficult.

"So what is it exactly we're looking for?" Lia sneezed ferociously three times. She looked downright adorable with her hair up in a bandanna.

Heather moved to the closet and threw open the door. She stepped back at the scent of old mouse. "Any family photos with names on them. Marriage and birth certificates. Christening or baptism records. I'm not looking in here, though. I'm sure a mouse will jump out at me."

"I'm not afraid of mice," Abby said. "I whack the ones in the library with a broom. You take the dresser drawers."

"You're scaring me," Heather said. "Who are you and what have you done with Abby?"

Abby raised her fist in the air. "I am woman, hear me roar. No mouse will scare me from my appointed duties." She burrowed into the closet until all that could be seen were her jean-clad legs and tennis shoes.

Lia looked around the overstuffed room. "You've done some harebrained things, Heather, but this tops them all. That old book can't lead to anything. I doubt we'll find a single clue here."

"Maybe so, but you have to admit this beats working the book sale."

"I don't know about that," Abby said, her voice muffled by the stuffed closet. "I like talking to the people who walk through."

Heather pulled open the top drawer of the chest of drawers. "I'm a sucker for a sob story, and I'd practically give the books away. There will be more money for Molly if I stay away."

Lia dropped to her knees and looked under the bed. "Here are some tubs with old photo albums in them."

Heather joined her, and they dragged out the four plastic tubs. When she lifted the lid of the first one, she winced. "I'm glad Molly isn't here. This stuff isn't that old—here are her wedding pictures." She pushed the tub aside, unable to bear her friend's happy smile, one that said nothing could ever go wrong with this one, perfect love. Even before Curtis's death, things had been far from perfect.

"And look, Hawaii brochures." Abby had come out of the closet to look over Heather's shoulder. "The ones she brought to show us last month. I don't think we'll ever get that girls' week together. Not now."

An hour later they had found nothing. "I have to get going," Lia said. "It was a great idea, Heather, but I don't think there's anything here that will help us find the mine."

As the girls all grabbed their jackets, the doorbell rang.

"Who could that be?" Heather swung open the door to find Paul smiling at her, and took a step back. His smile faded when she said, "What do you want?"

He held out his hands, palms up. "I thought we'd called a truce."

There had to be dust on her face, and these jeans were old and ragged. The T-shirt was hardly flattering either. She wanted him to see what he'd missed and mourn, but he was likely rejoicing at his escape.

She opened the screen door. "Sorry, you startled me. If you're looking for Molly, she's at the shop."

"I saw your car out front. I live right there at the moment." He pointed to the big Victorian down the street. "I wondered if you might want to go see the farm with me this afternoon."

"It's Saturday. My day off."

"I thought you might at least want to take a look. It won't take long."

She wanted to refuse. The less time spent in his presence the better, but she *was* curious. "What time?"

"About two?"

"Okay."

"Pick you up here or at your house?"

He was taking a lot for granted. She could drive herself. "I'm done here. We were just leaving. I'll just meet you there."

"Suit yourself."

Lia and Abby crowded close behind her. "Hi, Paul," Lia said. "We didn't get a chance to talk last night. I'm surprised Natalie let you out of her sight."

"I barely escaped with my life. She was trying out some new kind of gluten-free carrot cake. I made a run for the back door."

The girls all chuckled. "Most of her gluten-free pastries are pretty good," Heather said.

"*Now* maybe. You have no idea what I've endured." Paul pushed his glasses back up on his nose. "Well, I'll let you all get back to what you were doing."

"See you around." Heather shut the door in his face before he could object.

"He's even more gorgeous than he used to be," Abby said. "I never would have guessed a man in glasses could look so hot."

"It's the contrast of those classic good looks with the muscles," Lia said.

"No kidding," Abby said. "Does he know you got married right off? And that you have Charlie?"

Heather's knees felt suddenly shaky. "He knows about both, but he thinks I'm still married."

"You need coffee to clear your brain," Lia said. "I'll make

it." She marched to the kitchen and went to the coffeepot with the other two trailing behind her. As soon as it was brewing, she pointed her finger at Heather. "There's only one reason you'd let him think you're married. You're afraid you still care about him, aren't you?"

Heather's head hurt, and she rubbed it. "How would you feel if you had to admit you ran off and married someone on the rebound and it ended in divorce a few months later? That you have never stopped mooning over him? I do have a *little* pride. I'll tell him I'm divorced when I'm ready. But I need some space first."

"When did he meet Charlie?" Abby asked.

"Last night. He came by the house."

Abby's eyes gleamed. "Oh, do tell! What did he want?"

"To clear the air and apologize for how he acted. Do you have any idea how that made me feel? To have all that humiliation brought up again. I wanted to fall through the floor." Her face burned.

"It's over now," Lia said, her voice soothing. "Put it behind you and move on."

"It's going to be hard. We'll be working together." The girls exclaimed, and Heather told them about the organic farm. "I have to do it. My boss was adamant."

A worried frown crouched between Abby's eyes. "Just be careful, Heather. You could fall hard again. I don't want to see you hurt."

The scent of coffee began to fill the room, and Heather got down cups. "Don't worry, I won't go down that path again. Paul Mansfield is way out of my league."

"Right," Abby said. "You've never gotten over him. Not really."

Heather turned away from their earnest faces. No amount of wishing in the world could change what was. She'd mask her feelings well this time. She'd forge a business relationship and that would be enough.

Men do not appreciate women who are constantly in histrionics. Modulate your emotions, and always speak in a calm tone.

PEARL CHAMBERS, *The Gentlewoman's Guide to Love and Courtship*

CHAPTER FOUR

. . . .

*P*aul lifted a tree branch out of Heather's way. "Sorry, this is a mess." The last thing he wanted was for her to get hurt.

"A mess" didn't quite sum it up. The recent storm had left tree litter everywhere, and the farmhouse had some missing shingles. The barn was more weathered gray than red, and the white-on-green shingles spelling out an advertisement for Smitten Creamery were faded. He'd found a raccoon in the attic yesterday and had called the extermination place. The screens were missing from the back porch, and the shrubs rambled out of their beds.

He glanced at Heather, then looked away. The sunlight gleamed on her blond hair, and her blue eyes matched the sky overhead. She was way too beautiful for his peace of mind, now that he knew she'd married while he was away. "It isn't doing anyone any good going to wrack and ruin out here."

Charlie tugged his hand from Heather's and ran to climb on the old swing set in the side yard. The Bristols were friends of Paul's great-aunt Rose, and he remembered playing on that swing set with his sisters when they were kids. It was crumbling into rust now from age.

"That's not safe," Paul said, and intercepted the little boy, who squirmed in his arms. He'd design a wooden play area, maybe a pirate ship or something here for the kids.

Heather wore a dreamy expression. "I've always loved this place. The building is really old, you know. Late 1700s." She shaded her eyes to stare out at the rolling hills, still brown from the blanket of winter snow. The trees in the distance weren't budding yet, so the landscape was barren. "It's wonderful to have fallow ground to work with. It's had a chance to rest and recover from the chemicals used in the past."

Mud clung to Paul's boots as he followed her a few feet into the field where stubble from a corn crop still mixed with the remnants of knee-high weeds. "What would you do with it?"

She contemplated a moment. "I know this will sound random, but if we put up a hoop house, we could grow organic ginger. It commands a premium price. And I'd love to see us establish a blueberry farm. The soil pH should be perfect, but we need to test it."

"Blueberries. I thought we'd grow things like cucumbers, watermelon, green beans, peas. You know, the normal sorts of things."

Her eyes sparkled when she turned toward him. "Everyone does that. This is prime blueberry land."

"You're the boss."

She lifted a brow. "I highly doubt it." Shading her eyes,

she stared toward the house. "How soon are you getting someone in to fix up the house before it falls down? The barn too. We'll need it for storing supplies. I'd like to see us have a few cows, maybe even a horse. The manure will be beneficial to the land."

"Whoa, hold on. One thing at a time."

Smiling, she started back toward the house. "Can we go in? It's been ages since I've been in there. I want to show Charlie." She motioned to her son, who was still digging in the dirt with his dump truck. "Charlie, want to see the barn and house?"

The little boy nodded and ran toward them. He still had a toddler's figure with a round belly and chubby legs. Cute little guy. Instead of running to his mother, he stopped and looked up at Paul. After a moment he held up his arms.

Paul glanced at Heather, then scooped him up. "Want to ride on my shoulders?" When Charlie nodded, he lifted him into place. "Hang on to my hair." The child's small fingers wound into Paul's thick thatch, and he winced. "Feels like you've got a tight grip there."

He stepped onto the low porch. "Looks solid. Just needs paint." The screen door hung off one hinge. He opened it out of the way and inserted the key into the lock. He had to finagle it before the lock clicked and he could open the door. Paul wrinkled his nose at the rush of stale air.

"It's stinky," Charlie said.

"Sure is." Paul stepped across the threshold.

Heather followed him, and she stepped to the center of the room and twirled, a ballerina in jeans. "I just love this house! There's so much history here. I can imagine the people who built it. Look at the low ceilings and the beams. It's got character."

To him it had always been an old farmhouse with nothing special to recommend it, but he looked at it through clearer eyes now. "Look at these wide pine floors."

She nodded. "You'd never be able to match them with current wood."

He glanced through the fly-spattered window. The real plaster walls rolled like the hills outside, but they made the place feel homey. There was a ton of old furniture sitting around, and even more, he knew, in the overstuffed attic. And more stuff in the barns.

She trailed a finger on the coffee table. "Lovely piece with good bones. Looks like an old chest from the Civil War. We might be able to use it in the new décor."

He warmed at the communal *we*.

She looked around with admiration. "I could do so much with this place."

Charlie began to wiggle, so Paul lifted him down. His eyes wide, the boy wandered around the room. Paul grinned and glanced back at Heather. "What would you do?"

"I'd give these walls a pale wash of light lemon. The floors need refinishing, and I'd give the beams a fresh stain. Don't even get me started."

His smile broadened. "I thought maybe we could fix it like it would have been when it was a working farm in the 1800s. I'll get it solid, and you can have free rein with decorating."

Her blue eyes widened and she squealed, then flung her arms around him. He embraced her automatically and found her so much softer than he'd expected. And so very desirable.

He quickly dropped his arms to his side and cleared his throat. "The carpenter is coming this afternoon. I'll let you tell him what you want done."

On Friday night most of the book group members showed up. Fifteen women packed the room. Heather passed coffee and tea around as the women settled into the comfortable sofas and chairs around the fireplace. The fire snapped and crackled, a homey sound that relaxed her as she settled onto the sofa with a throw on her legs.

The murmur of voices escalated when Molly joined them. Choruses of "How are you doing?" and "What can I do to help?" circled the group. Heather gave her friend's expression a quick once-over and decided she was going to weather the concern fairly well. Her smile was genuine, though sadness still lurked in her eyes. After all, it had only been ten days since Curtis died.

"Thanks for everything," Molly said. "We're managing."

Reese Parker settled a cheese cube on a Wheat Thin. "Griffen wants to finish the work on the storefront, Molly. He's going to get started tomorrow." She popped the snack into her mouth.

Molly sank onto the sofa beside Heather. "B-but I can't pay him."

"And Carson wants to help too. He'll work on the construction, and if there's anything missing, he'll supply it."

"I don't know what to say. I'll never be able to pay you all back." Molly's voice trembled. "Lia stopped by with the money to pay for the funeral yesterday. I was so moved."

"The library sale was all it took," Lia said. "We had a steady stream of people in all week who'd heard about the fund."

Molly blinked rapidly. "I suppose we should move on to tonight's discussion. I have to admit I didn't get a chance to read it."

"Of course not," Heather said. "We're just glad you're here. Did anyone else read it?"

A chorus of voices answered her. Most had read the Mary Higgins Clark novel and seemed eager to discuss it.

"You and your mysteries," Shelby said, groaning. "I was reading it when Nick came into the bedroom. Scared me so badly I screamed and threw the book at him. I'll be glad when we move on to another romance."

The women's reading tastes were hugely diverse, but they gamely tried to keep up. Heather tried to keep her recommendations a bit tame just for Shelby. "It all ends up okay, I promise."

At least they weren't talking about her and Paul. Not that there was anything to talk about.

⚮

Heather's perfume teased Paul's nose as he followed her up the stairs to the office space above Natalie's store.

"Nat said to tell you she'll meet you here after she picks up the replacement espresso machine."

"Thanks for taking her place." He averted his gaze from

37

the slim black skirt that showed off her killer legs. She was a married woman, and he had no business noticing.

He stepped onto a landing illuminated with light from a big window over the stairwell. "Nice and roomy." A door opened to his right. "This the room?"

Heather nodded and unlocked the door. "When I first saw this, I told Nat it would make a wonderful office space. See for yourself." She opened the door and stepped aside.

He poked his head into the space and blinked. The place was huge, with high ceilings. There were no interior walls, just a big expanse of unfettered space. The pale yellow color added to the sense of an unlimited area to design as he liked. A bank of south-facing windows streamed light into the large room. It would easily house at least four architects at work. There was another smaller room off to the side that would suit him for the main office.

Heather's high heels clicked on the wood floors. "This alcove would be perfect for a receptionist's desk. And the floors are in good shape. Basic refinishing and this place would be awesome. The ceilings are twelve feet high."

He pocketed his hands and imagined the room finished. "Great lighting. I think this will be perfect. I know my sister, and she's going to refuse to name me a price. You've lived here all your life. What's it really worth?"

Heather's full lips turned up, and she chuckled. "You're right. Nat's not going to want you to pay much. I bet you'd do the same thing for her."

He tipped up his chin. "That's different."

"No, it isn't. Families help each other."

He had to laugh. "You're clearly as bad as she is."

She didn't answer, but her eyes were lit with a warm glow as she turned away and examined the walls. "The plaster is in good shape too. A little fresh paint and you'll be ready to go."

He longed to question her about her life. Natalie could fill him in, but he wasn't about to let his sister know what had happened between him and Heather four years ago. He didn't like showing his mistakes.

"I have some initial drawings of the farm if you'd like to see them."

She turned back toward him. "I'd love to! We have to move fast if you intend to plant this year. You're lucky nothing has been planted there in several years. The chemicals used will have degraded, but we still need to work in manure and other organic material."

He grinned. "Manure—what a nice topic of discussion."

A delicate blush accentuated her high cheekbones. "I think it's a perfectly fine topic."

Grinning, he pulled a folded paper from his pocket and took it to the window. "See what you think." She stood close enough for their shoulders to touch as he pointed out the blueberry patch and the new structures he planned.

"I like it. When can we get started?"

Once again he liked the idea of that *we*. "We'll do the planting first, then this summer I'll get the buildings done. Want to meet with me on Monday to work the ground?"

"You're doing it yourself?"

"I'll do the work if you tell me what to do."

"Deal." She headed for the door. "I need to get home and fix dinner. I promised Charlie spaghetti."

He must have imagined the admiration in her voice for just a second. "A favorite of your husband's too?"

She stopped, and he nearly ran into her. He took a step back, and she turned to face him. "Um, I need to clear up something, Paul. I'm divorced."

Divorced. He shouldn't feel so elated, but he straightened and tried to look serious. "I'm sorry."

She shrugged, but her color was still high. "He left me for another woman when I was six months along with Charlie. It seems I tend to drive men away."

He reached toward her. "Heather, I—"

She shook her head. "I know, I know. Everyone is sorry for me, but I'm doing fine. I've learned to depend on God alone. Charlie and I have a good life. I've got a great job that sees to our needs, and my friends keep me busy. I don't need your pity."

He wanted to tell her that pity was the last emotion he felt at this news, but she whirled and rushed down the steps.

"I'll let myself out," he called after her. When he heard footsteps he went to meet her, but it was Natalie who stepped onto the landing.

"What did you do to Heather?" she asked, her voice quavering.

"Nothing. I thought she was married, and she told me she was divorced. It seemed a painful subject."

Nat winced. "It is. She's worked hard to make it on her own. And she never complains. When someone is in trouble, she's the first one there to help. She'd give you her last meal."

"I didn't mean to upset her."

"She'll get over it. Just don't bring it up again."

"Is she seeing anyone else?" He tried to put a casual spin on the question, but Nat knew him too well.

She narrowed her eyes at him. "Don't you hurt her, Paul. You went through half the girls in high school before you left town."

There was some truth to his sister's warning. He'd been afraid of commitment, afraid he'd be tied to Smitten for the rest of his life. What an idiot he'd been. Heather would be unlikely to trust him, knowing what she did about him. But he found he very much wanted to see her smile at him like she did that special day four years ago.

He clenched his jaw. Though it might be an impossible dream, he was going to see if she'd ever consider him again.

Make sure your suitor has a sense of humor. Laughing together heals many wounds.

PEARL CHAMBERS, *The Gentlewoman's Guide to Love and Courtship*

CHAPTER FIVE

. . . .

*T*he field behind her was smooth and ready for planting, though they still had much work to do. Heather turned off the tiller and wiped her brow. A hillside started at the back of the field and led up to a rocky outcropping. There were a few wildflowers beginning to poke up through the dead weeds.

"What are you staring at?" Paul asked.

The wind had ruffled his hair so a boyish lock fell over his forehead. Why couldn't she ignore the way his broad shoulders filled out the flannel shirt he wore or the warmth of his eyes? She'd gotten over him long ago. Of course she had.

She pointed to the hilltop. "I was just thinking about all the Chambers land that borders this."

He nodded. "It was a good-sized property back in the day."

Her gaze scanned the area. "I didn't realize."

He stepped closer. "Why are you so interested?"

She edged away until she couldn't smell the spicy scent of his cologne. "Did you ever hear that old legend about a lost gold mine on the Chambers property?"

He grinned. "You're a treasure hunter?"

"Not for me! I found an old book that's supposed to have clues in it to help find the treasure. That property all used to belong to Curtis's family, and Molly still owns the mineral rights."

His smile vanished. "So you're thinking if you could find the gold, her troubles would be over. It usually isn't that easy, Heather. If it were out there, someone would have found it."

"Still, there's no harm in looking, right?"

He grinned again. "Need a break? I'm game. Let me see what our handy-dandy Google search turns up." He whipped out his iPhone. "Hmm, looks like this area is known to have gold in the streams. There's a stream over there." He motioned to their left.

"What would a gold mine look like?" she wondered aloud.

"You know what?" He snapped his fingers and grinned. "I went through a phase when I was looking for lost artifacts with a metal detector. I think it's still buried in the back of my Jeep. Let me check."

She watched him jog to his SUV. Why hadn't he ever married? In high school, he'd gone through girlfriends like a runner goes through Gatorade. Women loved the studious look when matched with his muscles and classic features. Why did he have to come back to town and disrupt her peace of mind? The wind lifted his hair as he got in the back of the Jeep. She steeled herself as he returned with the metal detector and a small hand trowel.

He raised them in the air. "Sometimes it's good to be a pack rat."

"Do you know how to use that thing?"

"Do I know how to use it! Woman, I'm an expert with it. I went through a period when I was sure I was going to find a diamond ring worth millions."

She had to laugh. "Why did you care? It seems out of character."

"It was the sense of adventure. I was going to be the next Indiana Jones." He took her elbow and steered her toward the stream. "Let's start with the water. If we can get a reading, it might lead us somewhere."

She should pull away, but she liked the warm press of his fingers on her arm. What harm could there be in an hour of fun with him? It's not like she was going to let her guard down. She knew he had no interest in her. He'd made that perfectly clear. But she could still enjoy hearing his voice and watching his expressions.

The stream cut a cold, clear path through the soil. The water tumbled over rocks and sent sprays of water into the air as it hit the rapids.

She stopped at the stream bank and pointed. "Paul, I think I see something yellow and shiny there."

He grinned. "Like we could just walk over here and find a golden treasure, huh?" But he turned on the metal detector and hovered the head over the water. Nothing.

"Well, it *looked* like gold." She walked a little ways down the stream and watched for another glimmer.

He followed her with the metal detector on. It went off, and he dropped to his knees and dug with his small shovel.

"Hey, we struck it rich!" He showed her an adjustable Barbie ring. "That has to be worth at least five dollars."

"More like fifty cents." She plucked the ring from his palm and studied it. "I had one of these once. I lost it when I was ten. I wonder if it could be the same ring?"

He laughed. "It's yours as a memento." Shading his eyes, he gazed at the rocky hillside. "You want to look around up there? There might be a cave or two to explore."

She shivered at the thought of being alone with him in a dark place. "No thanks. I think we'd better get back to work. That field isn't going to get ready on its own."

"It's taking longer than I expected too. I think I'll hire a couple more men to help us till it up. We're supposed to get some rain midweek, and I'd like it to be ready before then so we don't have to redo it all."

His return to a businesslike tone made her spirits fall. It was better to keep him at arm's length, though. Much easier on her emotions.

&

On Saturday morning the door of Smitten Expeditions hung open, and Paul saw several men moving around inside. A ladder leaned above the big storefront window, and his brother-in-law, Carson, paintbrush in hand, stood on the second rung from the top. Paul's pulse skipped when he stepped inside and saw Heather spackling holes in the drywall. She looked so cute with a silvery headband around her blond hair. Her jeans showed off the long line of her legs and her tiny waist, and she wore a frilly pink top.

Pink flooded to Heather's cheeks when she saw him. She stood. "Paul, what are you doing here?"

He gestured around the room. "Same as everyone else. I brought my hammer, and I'm ready to work."

Reese popped up from behind the counter. She consulted the clipboard in her hand. "Great! We need someone to hang drywall."

He glanced around. "Wait a minute. Have you had an architect look at this? I think we could use this space more efficiently." He strode to the left of the door, where a small bump-out jutted into the next office. "The reception area would be better right here, out of the way of traffic. Molly could use the center area for stock like thermal socks and fishing gear."

Heather joined him and glanced around. "I see what you mean. Would it cost much to move the counter?"

He eyed the counter, then shook his head. "It looks like it was placed on top of the wood floor, so the flooring underneath should be intact. I think it's just going to be manpower. And we seem to have plenty of that."

Heather adjusted her silver headband. "Tons of people are here to help. Molly was so overwhelmed, she burst into tears and went home. I hope we have a lot done by the time she comes tomorrow. The book club women are all here painting and moving things around. We hadn't thought to ask an architect's opinion."

"Are you in charge?"

She shrugged her slim shoulders. "Sort of. I mean, it was my idea to help."

"I have a feeling it's often your idea to help others."

Her long lashes swept down to hide her expression, and she bit her lip. "I can be a bit of a busybody."

"That's not what I meant. My sister told me you help the single moms at church too. When do you find time to do everything?"

"You make me sound like Superwoman."

He took her arms and turned her around. "I thought for sure there would be a big S on the back of your shirt."

She laughed, a breathless sound full of delight, when he turned her back around. "Sometimes a person just needs a little encouragement. I've been there myself."

He leaned closer to smell her perfume. The light, flowery scent suited her. "You're amazing, Heather. You encourage me every time we're together."

Her smile faded, and she turned away. "We'd better get to work."

What had he said that offended her? He'd thought he was giving her a compliment. Was she thinking of how he'd pushed her away that night? If he could go back and change his behavior, he would. He'd been scared, pure and simple. Scared of how easily he could imagine a life with her. Scared that he wouldn't get in the car the next day and see the outskirts of Smitten in his rearview mirror. Scared she could change his purpose.

What if he'd pulled her closer and kissed her back? What if he'd never left Smitten? Would the two of them be happily married and living in a cozy Victorian cottage? Maybe Charlie would have been his son if he hadn't been so stupid.

It was much too late for regrets. She had a wall around her heart a mile high now.

"Paul?"

He turned at his sister's voice. "I figured you were around here somewhere." He spied the coffee carrier in her hands. "I'll have the first one, thanks. Did you bring a latte for Heather?"

Nat's dark eyebrow lifted. "Of course. How did you know she likes lattes?"

"I've known her a long time." And he'd paid attention for years, even if he didn't want to admit it to himself or anyone else.

Natalie seemed to accept his comment. She turned and waved to Heather, who came toward them with obvious reluctance. He'd messed up for sure.

Nat held up the carrier. "The front right one is a latte with half and half. One scoop of stevia and a sprinkle of cinnamon."

Heather edged away from Paul and took the cup. "Do you remember what kind of coffee everyone likes, Nat?"

"I could ask you the same thing," Natalie said. "I bet you picked out the paint, and this happens to be Molly's favorite color. You probably bought the blinds too, right?"

Heather blinked. "Well, yes. Um, hey, did Paul tell you he had a great idea about moving the counter? We're getting ready to do that now."

"My brother is good at his job. I should have thought to ask him to have a look before we got started. Anything else you'd suggest, Paul?"

He was ready to look anywhere but into Heather's guarded face. "Uh, it might be a good idea to change out this small window for a bigger one. More light will make the place seem bigger."

Heather shook her head. "Molly has no money to spend. She's already overwhelmed at what the town is doing. Carson and Natalie in particular. They donated some missing building supplies."

"Everything else looks good. And a window isn't that big of a deal. I'll buy it myself." When Heather pressed her lips together, he backed down. "But if you think she would be upset, I won't do it."

A tiny smile lifted her full lips. "Yes, I think she'd like that. Thanks."

He watched her turn and go back to her work. How could he get past the walls she'd put up against him?

Don't punish your suitor for past mistakes. Learn to love and appreciate him for his most excellent qualities. You won't change him, so it is futile to try.

PEARL CHAMBERS, *The Gentlewoman's Guide to Love and Courtship*

CHAPTER SIX

. . . .

*H*eather loved the living room when the fire was licking at the logs and twilight had settled in. Her thoughts from the day still churned in her head as she offered Lia a cookie from the tray, then set the snacks on the coffee table. "Well, you're still smiling after a class outing, but I think I see a few clumps of hair missing."

Lia sat curled up on the sofa and took a bite of her cookie. "It was the field trip from Hades. Two little boys got into the fountain. I had nothing to change them into, and the wind picked up after lunch. We had several bouts of tears among the girls when one of them felt left out. So thanks for inviting me over. I needed some adult conversation. What did you do today?"

"Helped out at Molly's business. I spackled the walls."

Lia's eyes widened. "Was Paul there?"

Heather snatched a cookie herself. "Nearly half the town was there. Including Paul."

"How are you dealing with being around him in such close proximity?"

Heather nibbled on the cookie to give herself time to reply calmly. "It's going okay. I think the farm is a great idea, and Paul is super smart about laying out everything."

"I'm surprised he's not married."

"Me too. I'm sure he'll get around to it when he's ready."

"But he's two years older than we are, isn't he?"

Heather nodded and picked up the old book. "I suppose we should see if we can find any clues to where the mine is located. This is harder than I thought it would be. And wading through that advice about love is rather daunting when you're single."

Lia laughed. "What kind of advice?"

"Listen to this. 'If your man appears distracted, do not try to get him to talk. He will work it out on his own.' That's ridiculous! Everyone needs to bounce problems off others."

Lia sat back and shook her head. "I don't know, Heather. My dad always liked working things out on his own. I think it depends on the person."

"It does have *some* good advice. I saw something in here about how men need their jobs to help define who they are. She put it in flowery language, but that was the gist of it."

"What about the treasure?"

Heather flipped a few pages. "There are so many passages marked with ink or a piece of paper. I don't know which are important." She stopped at a tiny arrow pointing to a paragraph. "I wanted you to see this one. It reads, 'The heart is a woman's hidden chamber. She should keep it for the one man who can unlock it and fit into the space therein.' I wondered if that meant the opening to the mine was small."

Lia leaned forward. "Gosh, this is hard. I guess it could mean that. It's marked?"

"With an arrow—like it's important." Heather showed her the mark. "The arrow is teeny, though. Which I thought might mean it was a clue meant to be overlooked by most."

"But where do you look for a small opening to a mine? We need more."

Heather exhaled and leaned back in her chair. "I know. The area is huge, and so many have already tried."

Lia propped her chin on her hand. "What about search dogs? Do we know anyone with trained animals?"

"There's a search dog training center near Stowe. We could ask for their help. But don't they have to have something to sniff?"

"True. I don't suppose a gold necklace would work." Heather laughed and flipped to another page.

Don't punish your dear one for past mistakes. Learn to love and appreciate him for his most excellent qualities. You won't change him, so don't try.

Her thoughts flew to Paul. She'd stiffened today when he commented about the way she encouraged people.

"What are you thinking about? Your eyes got all squinty like you want to hit something," Lia said.

"Or someone. Maybe myself." Heather tried for a laugh and came up with a cough. "I think I messed up today. Paul said I always encouraged him. I remembered that the only time I actually wanted to encourage him was the time he pushed me away, so I froze him out and walked off."

Lia winced. "He probably had no idea what it was all about, did he?"

"Probably not. We were joking around until then."

Lia studied her face. "Does it still matter? I mean, do you have feelings for him?"

Heather looked down at her hands. "Of course not! That was a long time ago, Lia. But remembering it still embarrasses me."

"Uh-huh." Lia swallowed the last bite of cookie, then reached for her tea. "He was your first love, wasn't he? A girl never forgets the first guy she mooned over."

"You make it sound like it was a silly high school crush."

Lia's eyes went wide. "Wasn't it?"

"I—I . . . of course it was." It had started in high school but continued for many years after.

Even before he'd shown up here, Heather had daydreamed about seeing Paul again. In her imagination, his eyes had widened at the sight of her. He'd taken her in his arms and told her how much he regretted that night. Silly, girlish dreams that refused to be banished. She'd told herself over and over again that she'd had a lucky escape. Paul would never settle down.

Lia stirred sugar into her tea. "You've got that expression again. What are you thinking?"

"It's best if I stay on my guard around him. Who knows if he'll even stay around for long? He says he's moving back for good, but I'm not sure I can believe it."

Lia's brow furrowed. "Honey, you love others so unguardedly, but you seem afraid to let someone else love you. I know you've been hurt, but not everyone is like Jack. There are good men out there."

"You're a good friend, Lia. I know you want what's best for me, but I'm perfectly happy with just Charlie and me. I wouldn't want to risk his happiness by falling for some guy who would turn around and leave about the time Charlie got attached."

"Open yourself up to love a little, Heather. You might be surprised what will happen."

Heather wasn't sure she knew how to do that.

The basement of the church was packed, and Paul saw no place to sit down while he waited for his turn. People from all over town had brought in items for a gigantic rummage sale. The proceeds were to go to Molly, who sat looking a little woebegone at the head table.

Heather approached him with her little boy in tow. She was dressed in a gray skirt and pink sweater that made her look like she was still in high school. "Looking for a seat? Nat saved you one."

He'd hoped she wanted him to sit with her. Crazy thought. He inclined his head toward Molly. "Looks like she wishes she were eating popcorn somewhere else."

Heather turned to look. "She hates being the center of attention. And it's never easy accepting help when you're used to being the strong one."

He touched Charlie's head. "Hey, big guy, I brought my soccer ball. Want to go kick it around for a while until the food is ready? We'll stay out of your mother's hair."

The smile in her eyes faded. "I'm not sure that's a good idea. He's not used to being around men."

"All the more reason for him to get in some soccer while he can." Was she afraid to let him be around her son?

Heather shrugged. "It's time to eat right now. Later maybe."

And later she'd probably have another excuse. "What's your problem?" he whispered as they walked toward the food tables. "I'll make sure Charlie is okay. I like the little guy."

The little boy ran off to join two friends, and Heather stopped. "Right now you might take the time to play with him, but he might get attached to you. When you leave, he'll be upset."

Before he could answer, Aunt Rose spied them. She'd recently married her first love, and the bloom of happiness made her look much younger than her sixties. Her salt-and-pepper hair gleamed in the fluorescent lights, and her smile made everyone want to return it.

"There you are, young man. I've got half a dozen people who want to say hello." She offered up a powdered cheek for him to kiss before she turned bright eyes toward Heather. "My dear girl, you and Charlie must come to dinner one night. Paul needs to get reacquainted with his old friends."

Heather's gaze darted from side to side as though she sought an escape. Paul stifled a laugh. He'd been in her spot before. Aunt Rose was like a tank plowing through a flower bed. There was no stopping her when she set her mind on something.

"I think that's a great idea," he said. "I'm free tomorrow night. How about you, Heather?"

"Not tomorrow."

"Next Sunday evening will give her time to schedule," his aunt said without waiting for Heather to reply. "About six?

I'll make fettuccine alfredo. It's Paul's favorite. I make it with cream cheese, and I think you'll love it. Would you like to bring a nice salad?"

"Um, yes, ma'am." Heather's face was as pink as her sweater. When his great-aunt patted her on the cheek before zooming off to corral another hapless victim, Heather grabbed Paul's arm. "You threw me to the wolves!"

"Tsk, tsk. Aunt Rose is hardly a wolf. She's genuinely caring and pretty darn wonderful."

"Well, yes, she is. But you watched her corner me and didn't say a word."

"I didn't want to get in her bull's-eye." He grinned and steered her toward the food table. "Besides, she's right. I need some friends. Will you be my friend, Heather?"

She hesitated. "We'll be working together, and anything more might cause some awkwardness."

"Then you're fired."

She blinked and stared up at him uncertainly. Was he serious? "What?"

"If I have to choose between friendship or business, friendship wins out. So you're fired."

She bit her lip. "But what if I don't want to be fired? I'm excited about the organic farm."

They reached the table, piled high with food from the best cooks in Smitten. "You can keep your job if you come to dinner and at least pretend to like me."

"I like you fine," she muttered.

His lips twitched, but he managed not to smile. "That's been very clear. You like me so much you cross the street to avoid talking to me."

"I do no such thing! Name one time I avoided you." She picked up a plate and ladled a Mexican dip onto it.

"Well, you wanted to. I saw it in your eyes." He grinned and picked up a plate. "Seriously, Heather, you blow hot and cold. One minute you're letting me help you search for buried treasure, and the next minute you won't let me play soccer with your kid. I won't bite, you know. I want us to start over as if we've never met." He put down his plate and extended his hand. "Hi, I'm Paul Mansfield."

She glanced down the length of the table. "Stop, people are looking."

"Better shake my hand then, and let things get back to normal."

She rolled her eyes, and her cheeks went even redder before she barely touched her fingertips to his. "Fine. Hi, I'm Heather DeMeritt." She jerked her hand back before he could hang on to it.

He felt like whistling, but he followed her down the length of the table and piled his plate high. He needed energy to figure out how to win her.

> *To show your suitor you notice his muscles, compliment him on a job well done.*
>
> PEARL CHAMBERS, *The Gentlewoman's Guide to Love and Courtship*

CHAPTER SEVEN

. . . .

"*A*re you sure this dog knows what he's doing?" Heather paused to wipe the moisture from her brow. They'd climbed up at least two hundred feet. The muscles in her legs burned, and her lungs labored. It was entirely too high for her comfort zone.

"His owner said he was a gold-sniffing dog," Abby said.

"A gold-sniffing dog," Lia scoffed. Her cheeks were pink. "That should have been our first clue we were going to be running in circles."

Heather had to laugh, though she wanted to sit down on the moist ground and pout. This had been a wild-goose chase, but when Abby called with the idea it had sounded like a fun lark for a Saturday afternoon. A patron at the library had mentioned that his dog liked digging for gold. That was all it took for Abby to be off and running. Well, all of them had been game.

Abby blew a strand of hair from her eyes. "Hey, it might work." She whistled, and the dog, a golden retriever, came running with his tail wagging. "Good boy." She ran her fingers through his coat and cooed to him like he was a baby.

Charlie ran up to throw his arms around the dog. Heather watched him with a smile. Maybe she should get him a puppy.

"Sorry to break up the party," Molly said, "but I've got to get back. It's nearly time to get Noah from his friend's. It's been fun, girls, even if we didn't find anything."

"I have to go too," Lia said. "I've got to get my lesson plan together for Monday."

"And I rode with you, so I have to leave too." Abby looked crestfallen. "But hey, we had fun even if we didn't find anything." She glanced at Heather. "You coming?"

Heather hesitated, then shook her head. "Charlie and I will tramp around a little while longer. The farm is on the other side of this hill. I might take a peek. I haven't been out since Wednesday." And then it had been by herself. She hadn't seen Paul since last Sunday. "Thanks for coming out. See you all later."

She watched her friends hustle down the steep embankment. Their vehicles were a faint smudge of color in the distance where they'd parked along the road. The dog's happy bark faded with their excited chatter.

She took Charlie's hand. "Want to go see how our organic farm is coming?"

He stared at her with somber blue eyes. "I like Paul."

"He's very nice," she agreed.

Something rustled behind her, and she turned to see Paul step on top of the ridge. He wore washed-out jeans, a red jacket, and hiking boots. "I thought I heard you all up here. Where'd everyone go?"

"They had things to do. Where'd you come from?"

"I was out for a drive to look at houses and stopped to look at the fields."

His stare was intense, and heat sprang to her cheeks. "What? I have dirt on my face?"

He glanced away and shook his head. "Find anything up here?"

"Nope. And we even had a gold-sniffing dog."

A grin spread across his face. "Is that so? He didn't find a lost Barbie ring? I can do better than him."

"We didn't find a thing but burrs." She brushed two from her pant leg.

Was this the real reason she hadn't left with her friends? She was honest enough to admit she'd wondered if Paul might stop by the farm. It was about time she took herself in hand and eradicated the feelings she still had for him. It was attraction *only*. And it had to stop.

"Any clues to look for?'

"I ran into something that suggested the opening to the mine might be small. A small cave or something in the hillside. There's so much vegetation, though. We didn't see anything."

Charlie danced around beside her. "Mommy, I have to potty."

"Oh dear, can you wait? There's no potty here."

He squirmed and shook his head, his expression a mask of panic. She bit her lip. It seemed awkward to let him water a bush right in front of Paul.

Paul seemed not to notice her discomfort. "I can handle this, man-to-man." He took Charlie's hand. "Come with me, bud."

Heather watched him lead her son to some bushes. He bent over to help Charlie, and she smiled at his solicitude for the boy. He'd be a good daddy someday. Her smile faded. Just not with her child. She had to keep her guard up.

Paul seemed to stumble on a patch of loose rock. "Whoa, look out!" His arms flailed, then he pitched over the side of the slope.

Charlie started to approach the edge too. "Stop, Charlie!" She ran to grab his arm and pull him out of danger. "Stay here. Let me look."

She stepped to the edge and peered over. Paul was sprawled on his back about twelve feet down. "Are you all right?"

"I'm fine." He struggled to his feet and turned to wave. "It would have been more fun if I had a sled."

The blood rushed back to her head when his voice sounded so strong. "Need help getting up?"

"I might go on down. It would be easier than coming back up there. The slope flattens out in about five feet."

"That's fine. I'll see you tomorrow." Her disappointment was only because she hadn't found the mine. She turned to head down the path to the road, but he called her back.

"You have to see this, Heather. Can you get down here?"

"Only by sliding on my backside. And it's not safe for Charlie. What is it?"

He bent over and removed a loose bush that had been dislodged in his fall. "An opening about three feet in diameter. I can't see inside, though. I have a flashlight in my Jeep.

Let me go get it. I think you can access this hillside if you come down where I first came up, then cut over where it flattens out."

Her heart slammed into her ribs. Could he have found the mine?

"Hold the light steady." Paul wasn't about to show his fear of close spaces in front of Heather, but he needed good light in order to manage the tightness in his chest. He touched her hands and guided them into position. "Right there."

Getting onto his hands and knees, he crawled into the cave. It suddenly opened into a much larger space, easily twenty feet in diameter. "Hey, it's huge in here!" There were pick axes and buckets around. The ceiling had been reinforced with beams. "It's a mine! Let me take the light." His fingers closed around the flashlight.

Heather squealed behind him. "I want to see!"

Though she couldn't see him, he grinned. "I'm not sure it's safe, and there's Charlie."

"This has to be it! Do you see any gold?"

He glanced around. "Nothing visible. I'll come out and you can take a peek." He squeezed back through the opening and stood to face her. Charlie lay on the grass with his head on his arm. "Looks like someone has been mining for sure. This might be it, Heather."

Her hands flew to her cheeks. "I have to call Molly!" She did a little dance, then flung her arms around his neck. "You're a genius, Paul. Thank you, thank you."

She leaned up to kiss his cheek, but he turned his head, and her lips landed on his. He'd kissed plenty of girls in his life, but nothing prepared him for the jolt that ran through him. His hands went around her waist of their own accord, and he pulled her closer. She didn't fight him but melted against his chest. Her lips were soft and warm, and her breath smelled sweet and fresh. Her fists clutched his shirt, and the passion simmered between them like heat on a summer day.

Then it was over. She leaped away like she'd been burned. Her face was white. Her eyes darted to her son, playing with ants twenty feet away. Paul followed her glance. Charlie seemed not to have noticed what the adults were up to.

Paul smiled and tried for a light touch. "I should probably apologize, but I'm not a bit sorry. Don't you think we should explore our relationship a bit more?"

"Relationship?" Heather's voice was wooden. "I have a son, Paul. I can't risk getting close to anyone and having him leave us. You're not the staying kind."

That stung. He'd been that kind of man once, but he'd changed. Why couldn't she see that?

He gave a curt nod. "I'll hold the light. Take a look."

She shot him a glance from under her lashes, then crawled into the mine. He crouched by the opening and listened to her move around inside. "It's huge, isn't it?"

Her voice echoed back. "I never expected it to look this way. Don't most mines branch out? This seems to be just one big room."

He leaned over and tried to peer in, but the opening was too small. "I saw a couple of areas where some probing seemed to have occurred. Maybe all they found was in this one area. Or maybe they found nothing and gave up."

She crawled back through the opening. There was a smudge of dirt on her cheek and a twig in her hair when she stood. "This is on Chambers land, right?"

"Yes, this was all part of the original tract. I suppose it's possible there's more than one mine here, but it's not likely. I could swallow one lost mine, but not two."

Her shoulders slumped. "Molly wouldn't have the money to try to start up the mine again. I hadn't thought about that. I'd hoped we'd walk right in and find it in bags or something." She laughed at herself. "I guess the girls were right. I've been reading too many mystery novels."

He wanted to hear that hopeful tone in her voice again. "Let me take a closer look. We can string up some lights and give it an even better going over if I don't find anything. Call your friends while I check it out."

He crawled back inside and studied the space with the flashlight. There was no obvious hole where anything could be hidden. The couple of offshoots ended within a few feet, and he shone the light up the walls clear to the ceiling. Nothing.

He spent more time combing the bigger area, but still came up empty-handed except for an old axe with a *B* carved into the handle. When he went to the opening to tell Heather, he met her crawling through the hole with a bigger flashlight in her hand.

She looked up at him from her hands and knees. "Lia brought over several more flashlights, and Abby is on her way with a battery-powered floodlight." Her small chin was set with determination. "We'll find it."

He helped her up, but she quickly stepped away from him. The cave felt intimate and warm with her in it. "Did you call Molly?"

She shook her head. "I don't want to get her hopes up in case this turns out to be nothing."

"It's the right cave. Look." He turned and grabbed the axe to show her.

Her fingertips traced the letter on the axe. "You don't think there's any treasure here, do you?"

He shook his head. "I think someone probably took it out a long time ago. This place hasn't been disturbed in ages."

Shouts echoed from outside, and Heather turned toward the opening. "I think Abby is here. Maybe we'll find something with more light."

But an hour later they were still empty-handed. It seemed someone had already mined all the gold.

> *Never be afraid to apologize. It takes great courage to admit you're wrong, and you will only be stronger for it.*
>
> PEARL CHAMBERS, *The Gentlewoman's Guide to Love and Courtship*

CHAPTER EIGHT

. . . .

You look lovely, dear." Rose bustled into the sunroom where Heather sat on the flowered sofa with her hands folded in her lap. "That bright blue suits you."

"Thank you." Heather had taken special care with her appearance today, and the short, form-fitting dress was new. Charlie wore new jeans and a blue T-shirt. She'd washed up his sneakers too. He leaned against her shyly.

The soft tans and comfortable furniture in the bright space should have put Heather at ease, but she wished she'd never agreed to come for dinner. It was going to be so awkward since Paul had kissed her yesterday. Her fingers stole to her lips. She'd remember that kiss the rest of her life.

Rose set a silver tea tray on the table, then lifted the pot to pour the tea into the delicate blue-and-white cups. "Paul will be here shortly. He's out looking at houses to buy. I've told him he can live here as long as he likes, but he's a grown man and finds it off-putting to be living with his great-aunt, I think."

Something inside Heather clenched. "He's buying a house?" Somehow she hadn't really believed he would stay here for good.

Rose nodded. "He seems to be done with city life and wants to settle down here in Smitten. I knew it would happen sooner or later. Paul puts on a front that fools most, but not his old auntie. He asked my David to tag along and give him an unbiased opinion."

Heather smiled. Rose and her long-lost love were the cutest newlyweds she had ever seen.

"A front?" she said. Maybe this was her chance to learn a bit more about Paul.

Rose handed her a delicate teacup. "He's always felt his mother's abandonment. He and his sisters were yanked around from town to town until he was eight. She was an alcoholic, you know. Married five times. I think that's why Paul has always been a little skittish of relationships. I knew God would help him settle eventually, though. It's time." She bent down and smiled at Charlie. "I brought you some cocoa, honey. And cookies."

After a moment Charlie took the mug she offered, then scooted back against his mother.

Heather stirred sugar into her tea. "I never knew that. I just thought his mom died, and you ended up raising the kids."

Rose crossed her legs, amazingly shapely for a woman her age. "That would have been traumatic enough, but those poor children didn't have any stability from the time they were born. I tried to heal the wounds, but some things take God's hand alone."

The front door slammed, and Paul's voice called, "Aunt Rose?"

"In here, honey. Our guests have arrived."

His footsteps came across the wood floors. He looked impossibly handsome and carefree when he stepped into the sun-room. His jeans hugged his hips, and Heather liked the red shirt he wore. His gaze darted to her and lingered on her face before sweeping down to take in the rest of her.

"Hi, Heather." His smile broadened. "I like your dress."

She resisted the impulse to tug at the hem. "Thanks. Did you find a house?"

He shook his head. "Neither house was what I was looking for."

"I can keep an eye out. I'm a house junkie. I like to drive around town looking at what's for sale. What do you want?"

He snagged a cookie, then dropped onto the sofa beside her. "I want at least four bedrooms. Something with character too. I'd really like a fixer, something I can design like I want it. And an attic. Have to have a walk-up attic like here. I used to love going through the boxes up there."

Heather laughed. "I've never been in that kind of attic. Only ones with a pulldown ladder into a space above the garage."

"I'll have to show you the attic after dinner."

Rose shook her head. "You'll do no such thing. She'll get dust all over her pretty dress." She stood. "I'd better check on dinner."

Heather sprang to her feet too, glad to get away from the enticing heat emanating from Paul. "What can I do to help?"

Rose waved her hand. "Nothing, child. It's all in the oven. I just need to take a peek and see if it's ready. It's probably got another few minutes, but you never can tell with my oven. I'll call you when it's ready."

"I could set the table."

"Charlie will help me." Rose took the little boy's hand. "Chat with my nephew while I show Charlie my special silver."

Heather sank back onto the sofa. She wasn't sure what to say. The kiss loomed between them.

He took a cookie from the tray. "Did you tell Molly there was nothing in the mine?"

"I did. She took it well. I don't think she really expected us to find anything. But it would have been nice."

"I'm sorry. I know you want to help her."

She peeked up at his sincere face. "Thanks."

"Anything I can do?"

"Send business her way when you can. The construction will be done soon, and we have to help her build her reputation."

A frown settled on his brow. "Does she know anything about the expeditions she'll be taking guests on?"

Heather waved vaguely. "She doesn't need to. An employee does all that."

"That's quite a bit different from the hands-on work she'll need to be doing. I hope she's ready for this."

She sipped her tea. "I don't think she has a choice."

He put his palms on his knees. His fingers were long and ended in clean oval fingernails. A sensitive man's hand, but she'd never seen a sensitive side. Just like yesterday, he'd taken advantage of a simple kiss of gratitude and turned it into something else.

You wanted it.

She pushed away the voice. Whether she'd welcomed it or not didn't change the way he'd moved in.

"Look, Heather, I know you're a little miffed I kissed you, but doggone it, don't shut me out. I'm not the philanderer you think I am. I'm beginning to care about you, and I'd like to explore where we might go from here. Don't close the door to a chance of happiness because of something that happened four years ago."

His aunt had said he'd changed. Was it possible? She wetted her lips. "What does it mean when you say you care about me?"

He reached over and took her hand, then turned it over and rubbed his thumb against her palm. "I was a jerk that night, Heather. You want to know the truth? I was afraid."

She dared to look up and capture his gaze. It was open, vulnerable. "Afraid?"

"You were different. I thought if I let you get too close, I'd never leave Smitten. I thought real life was out there somewhere, but I was wrong. I want to start over and do this right. I'm not asking for a commitment from you, but can we go out? Maybe see what happens?"

His deep, persuasive voice washed over her. What could be the harm? She could lower her guard just a little. Not all the way, but low enough to peek into his soul and see if he was the man she thought he could be.

"All right," she said. "We can go for ice cream after dinner."

"Ice cream?"

"I have to see if you choose the right flavor. I could never spend time with anyone who ate only vanilla. If we could take a convertible, it would be a perfect ending."

His smile broadened. "I think I'll make you wait to find out."

The beautiful April day lifted Paul's spirits until he got out of the car and saw what awaited him at the organic farm. Flies buzzed around the large brown mound in the middle of the field.

He saw Heather standing at the edge of the field and hurried to join her. He waved his hand in front of his face. "Phew, that stinks."

"But it will grow healthy plants." Heather inhaled deeply. "Nothing like the smell of manure."

"You are one crazy woman." He dropped his arm over her shoulders. "Can we go for more ice cream after we get this done? I promise not to order razzmatazz again. I'll go for something tamer like butter pecan. Or Rocky Road. Am I getting warm?"

"I think they'd run us out when they took one whiff." A dimple flashed in her right cheek.

Whoa, he hadn't seen that very often. Maybe he was making headway. Last night had been a blast as he'd sat with Heather and Charlie, licking their cones and talking about everything from politics to their faith. He'd been right. Heather was one in a million. He found himself fascinated by her mind, her moods, and the way she cared about other people.

She picked up a pitchfork. "We'd better get this done."

"We're doing it ourselves? I thought I'd hire some help."
She poked a finger in his side. "Pansy."

"Masochist." When she smiled and turned toward the manure pile, he took her by the wrist and pulled her close. "I think I need fortification for the task ahead. A lot of fortification. Let me smell your perfume first."

She stopped, and a blush touched her cheeks. "I doubt you can smell it. The, um, fertilizer is too strong."

"Oh, I'd know your scent anywhere." He touched her cheek, then tangled his fingers in her long blond hair. "I've been wanting to do that forever."

She stilled as if she was afraid to move. He wound her hair around his hand. "Your hair is so silky, and it smells like flowers."

He bent down and brushed his lips across hers. Her lashes fluttered down, and she leaned in. Her encouragement was all he needed to snake his other arm around her waist and deepen the kiss. She kissed him back, and he was smiling when their lips finally parted.

"I think you're starting to like me," he whispered.

Her blue eyes darkened. "You think?"

He nodded but didn't release her. "Most definitely. And I'm crazy about you, Heather. You can trust me. We'll move slow, but trust me. I'm not going anywhere."

She pulled away. "If you say so." She was still smiling when she moved toward the manure pile. "This isn't going to get done by itself."

"It's going to take us hours," he groaned. Sighing, he picked up a pitchfork. When was the last time he'd done something like this? Like, never?

She turned back to face him with an impish grin. "You just said you were crazy about me, and now you're objecting to spending hours with me?"

"Well, when you put it like that . . . though I can think of a lot more fun things to do together than shovel manure. But for my girl, I can do anything."

She froze, and her eyes widened. She wetted her lips, then looked down.

Paul stepped to her side. "Yeah, I'm staking my claim. Any objections?"

She peeked up at him, then shook her head. "Don't hurt me, Paul. I can't bear it. Not again."

He tipped her chin and stared into her face. "I swear I won't hurt you, Heather. Let me prove myself to you. And Charlie too."

"I-I'll try."

There was still doubt in her expression and soft voice. What was it going to take before she realized he was sincere?

&

Everyone had left the bookstore except for Lia, Molly, Abby, and Heather—and Tess, who had stepped into her office for a few minutes. They were still talking about *The Light Between Oceans*.

Heather threw away the last of the paper cups. "I *hated* that ending. He could have gotten her convicted, then gotten custody."

Abby shook her head so hard her brown hair whipped around her face. "It's the way it had to end. It was real. I would have hated it if it weren't real."

Heather glanced at Molly. "Did you read it, Moll?"

Molly's brown eyes were still haunted, but she managed a smile. "I skimmed it. Does that count?"

Heather tossed the paper plates in the trash. "Normally I would say no, but we'll give you a pass this week." She wrinkled her nose. "I'm so bummed about the mine. I really hoped we'd find that treasure."

"I haven't given up yet," Abby said. "I want to look through the book and see if there's something you missed. Can I have it for a bit, Heather?"

"Have at it. I'll drop it by."

Lia grabbed her spring coat, a bright green with a big flower on the lapel. "I saw you at the ice-cream shop with Paul. You looked very cozy."

"We have spent some time together. Charlie loves him."

"And what do you think?" Molly asked.

"I like him too. There's something different about him. He's more thoughtful. Quieter too."

Abby smiled and pulled on her coat, a dull brown that did nothing for her complexion. "Well, I think it's wonderful. You deserve a really great guy, Heather. I hope you'll both be very happy."

"They're not getting married," Lia said. "I mean, he hasn't proposed or anything, right?"

Heather's smile was beginning to feel strained. "No, of course not."

"You girls are making her uncomfortable," Molly said. "It's much too early to talk about marriage."

"Much," Heather agreed. She slipped her arms into her

coat and held open the door. "Let's get out of here before Tess comes out to see what we're doing here so late."

The wind ruffled her hair as she stepped onto the sidewalk. A red convertible was stopped at the stop sign, and her smile brightened when she realized Paul was driving it. She started to call to him, then saw the woman in the passenger seat.

Isabelle Morgan. The beautiful blonde turned heads wherever she went. Her perfect features were turned toward Paul in an attentive smile. Before the car left the corner, she leaned over and brushed a kiss across Paul's cheek.

Heather whirled and dashed back inside. Her heart was nearly pounding out of her chest, and she felt faint. *Stupid, stupid.* What had she expected? That the toad out there had really become a prince? Paul hadn't changed. Not one bit. Her eyes burned, and she swallowed hard.

Her friends followed her back inside. Lia touched her hand. "Heather, what's wrong?"

She clutched her shaking hands together. "Didn't you see? That convertible out there. Paul was driving. Isabelle Morgan was with him, and she kissed him."

Molly put a hand on Heather's arm. "It might be nothing. Don't jump to conclusions."

"I'm not jumping to conclusions. I *saw* it with my own eyes."

Abby nodded. "I saw it too. I'm sorry, Heather. I know that had to hurt."

"She kissed him, though. He didn't kiss her," Molly pointed out.

"What is he doing with her in the first place? He's never

even told me he has a convertible, and I told him the other day I'd love to have one. It would have been the perfect opportunity to tell me about his and offer to take me for a ride."

Molly nodded slowly. "I guess you're right. Are you okay?"

"I let my guard down. I'm so stupid!" Heather wanted to slap herself. Hard. She wasn't going to cry over him. Not again.

"What are you going to do?" Lia asked.

"I'm going to let him figure out his own stupid farm. I'm not going to work with him anymore. I can't stand it."

Molly put her hand on Heather's shoulder. "I know you, Heather. You won't be happy abandoning the project until it's finished. This is close to your heart. Talk to him about it. Ask for an explanation."

She shook her head. "I never want to talk to him again. It hurts too much."

"It's not like you to run away from a problem," Abby said. "I might, but you wouldn't."

The vision of Paul with Isabelle had imprinted itself on her eyelids. It was going to haunt her for a long time. "Maybe I can talk about it later. I can't do it tonight."

Maybe never.

CHAPTER NINE

*P*aul gave the red convertible another buff, then stepped back with a smile. He couldn't wait for Heather to see it. She was going to love it. His cell phone rang, and he pulled it out and looked at it. His smile broadened. "Hey, Heather. I was just thinking about you. Want to go get ice cream tonight?"

"No, thanks. I just called to let you know I have turned over the farm project to my coworker, Jessica. She can take it from here."

"W-what? No, I want you."

"I'm afraid my schedule is too packed to let me finish it out." Her voice could freeze an Eskimo.

"What's going on? Has something happened? You sound mad."

"Not a thing I didn't expect. I have to go."

The phone clicked in his ear, and he stared at it. She'd

hung up. He jammed the phone back in his pocket. What could have riled her up like this? Things were moving along nicely, and he had high hopes of putting a ring on her finger one day. She was so skittish and afraid of being hurt. Something had to have made those fears come back.

Wait a minute. Could she have seen him last night with Isabelle? His gut clenched. He'd rebuffed Isabelle's advances pretty effectively, but just seeing him with her might have sent Heather's fears into the stratosphere. He clenched his jaw. Shouldn't she have come to him and *asked* him instead of assuming the worst? Did she care so little she was willing to let go of something that could be very special?

He jumped into the car and fumbled for his keys. She might be afraid of confrontation, but he was going to tell her she was dead wrong.

As he was pulling out of the drive, his Aunt Rose came out of the house dressed in crisp linen slacks and a navy sweater. Her smile faded when she saw his face. "What's wrong, Paul?"

He put the car in park and told her about the call and his suspicions. "It's best I find out now, I guess. If she's going to get upset if I even talk to another woman, it would be a problem forever."

Aunt Rose pursed her lips, a sure sign he was in trouble.

"What? Am I missing something?"

"It's not easy to overcome a past reputation, Paul. You can hardly blame her when she has seen a different person from what you are now. What did you do?"

"What makes you think I did anything?"

She skewered him with a stern look. "You mentioned

another woman, so I assume Heather got the wrong idea somehow."

He sighed. "I bought this car from Isabelle Morgan. She, uh, kissed me. On the cheek," he added hastily when Aunt Rose looked horrified. "I put her in her place."

"And you think sweet Heather saw this?"

"She just told me to go fly a kite, so I'm guessing something caused it." He frowned, remembering her cold tone.

"She's a reasonable girl. Just tell her what happened."

He clenched his jaw. "And she might believe me until the next time. I'm not going to live with that every day."

"Give her some time to believe the new Paul. She's worth fighting for."

His great-aunt was always so wise. He smiled. "You like her?"

"I've always liked her. She's one who gives with her whole heart. You need that after the childhood you had."

"I want someone to love me unconditionally. Not a woman who looks at me with suspicion every minute."

"She's just afraid, Paul. And you have to admit, if you'd seen her with a known ladies' man who kissed her, you'd have been upset too."

He hadn't thought about it that way. "Yeah, I guess so." In fact, he would have wanted to bust the guy's jaw. And he'd have been hurt and mad at her. "I don't really know if she saw me. It could be something totally different. I'm going to find out, though. Thanks, Aunt Rose. You're the best."

He started the car and sent up a quick prayer he'd be able to find her, even if he had to drive all over town looking for her car.

Heather sniffled and wiped her nose. Crying didn't solve anything, but she couldn't seem to stop the leakage ever since she'd arrived at Molly's house. Thankfully, Charlie was playing with Noah and wouldn't be upset by her lack of control. She and Molly sat at the kitchen table with some calming tea.

Molly handed her a tissue. "I'm sorry, Heather."

She took it and dabbed her eyes. "Me too. I should have been prepared for this. I mean, it's not like I don't know his reputation."

"Maybe you should talk to Natalie. She might be able to shed some light on this."

"I don't want anyone to know what a fool I've been."

The doorbell rang. "Stay here in the kitchen. I'll get rid of whoever it is." Molly patted Heather's shoulder as she hurried from the room.

Heather mopped her eyes and squared her shoulders. This was ridiculous. She and Paul had exchanged a few kisses. It was hardly an earth-shattering event that they'd broken up. But it *felt* like her world was ending. She just needed to focus on raising her boy and forget romance.

Footsteps sounded behind her, heavier than Molly's bare feet had been. She turned and tried to pin on a smile, then froze when she saw Paul's face. "What are you doing here?"

His gaze traveled over her face. "Looking for you. Have you been crying?"

"Of course not." The tears had dried up with one look at his face. "If you're here to try to talk me into going on with the project, don't bother. You'll do fine without me."

"I don't care about the project. It's just a job. I came to find out what had happened between us. Did you see me with Isabelle last night?"

She gasped at his direct approach. "I did." She folded her arms across her chest. "You kissed her, Paul."

"I didn't kiss her. She kissed me. I'm not interested in Isabelle or any other woman." He took her hand. "I have something to show you."

She allowed him to pull her to her feet and lead her toward the door. They passed Molly, who mouthed, "Listen to him" at her. Heather blinked at the sunshine when they stepped into the yard. The cherry red convertible she'd seen last night sat parked in the drive. The top was down, and the white leather interior gleamed.

She pulled her hand away. "What's she doing here?"

"She's not here. Just the car. I bought it from her because you said you'd like to go for ice cream in a convertible."

She gasped as the words sank in. "Y-you bought this?"

"Yep. And for the record, when she kissed me, I told her I was seeing you and I didn't want to mess up anything with someone I love."

Tears sprang to her eyes again. A myriad of emotions swept over her. What had she done? She'd been so quick to judge him. "Oh, Paul." She swallowed hard. "I'm sorry, so sorry."

He took a step closer. "You should be. I'm not a philanderer, Heather. I'm asking you to let go of your fears and trust me. Can you do that?"

Could she? She studied his face, the cleft chin with its slight bit of stubble. His brown eyes were earnest. She saw fear there too. He wanted this to work, and so did she, but they had no future if she couldn't trust him. He'd been quick to come here and explain. If they both kept things open and truthful between them, they could work out anything, couldn't they?

She took a deep breath. "I can, Paul. I trust you. I'm going to forget the past and move forward."

His eyes lit, and his hands came down on her shoulders. The warm press of his fingers made her quiver. She tipped her face up to meet his as his lips came down on hers. The promise in his kiss made the last bit of her fear fly away.

Risking wasn't easy, but it was so worth it. She remembered the last thing she'd read in the *Gentlewoman's Guide*. Love runs on forgiveness. Maybe the book wasn't so silly after all.

Shelved Under Romance

Kristin Billerbeck

> *Always maintain an element of hope in your demeanor. A gentleman always appreciates optimism in a young lady.*
>
> PEARL CHAMBERS, *The Gentlewoman's Guide to Love and Courtship*

CHAPTER ONE

*A*bby Gray rushed to get the last of the books shelved in the Smitten Library. Tonight her book group met at Lookaway Village Books, and the evening offered one of the rare occasions she got to be out of the house. She looked forward to discussing the books and to seeing her friends, so when several last-minute patrons entered the library, she frowned.

"We're closing!" she said as cheerily as possible as she stood and peered over the long wooden counter. She never wanted to discourage reading. The other patrons turned and left, but Wyatt Tanner emerged from the group, holding up a stack of books in one hand and grinning. She noted how easily he raised the pile of hardbacks and thought he didn't exactly seem like the reading sort. More like a guy who spent endless hours at the gym. But with the amount of time he spent in the library, there had to be more to him. If he didn't render her speechless every time he sauntered into her domain, she might be able to find out what it was.

Wyatt did a lot of computer work for the library through his consulting business, but he was rugged. Tanned skin and lines etched around his mouth from extensive time outside. Looked as though he could hold his own in a street fight. If ever such a thing happened in Smitten, he'd be the one you'd want on your side. The way he looked at her was . . . smoldering and intense.

Wyatt had been volunteering at the library for the past year, converting their card catalog to digital. But Abby loved that the Smitten Library still had its historic card catalog, and that her library science degree still meant something. The Dewey Decimal system simply wasn't as romantic when plugged into a computer. Any monkey could scan a code, but she adored the backup system; the dusty, aged smell of the cards and wood combination when someone opened a drawer was an homage to the old ways.

"So . . . should I come back tomorrow, then?" Wyatt asked with a disarming smile. He had a small freckle on his bottom lip. When he grinned, it captured her full attention.

She smiled. "For you, I'll make an exception."

She took the books from him, and his fingertips brushed hers. She bristled at his touch. Wyatt may have been an avid reader, but from what her friend Molly told her, he also loved extreme sports and challenged his body in ways she thought foolish. That, combined with his desire to streamline her library, made her feel tongue-tied in his presence. He simply had a dangerous air about him that made her want to cower into the safety of her small life.

"How about if I buy you a cup of coffee to make up for keeping you late?"

She slid each of his books through the scanner. "Not necessary. You're all checked in. If you'll excuse me, I've got to get the lights out and be on my way."

He stood up straight, his eyes wide at her easy rejection.

"Is there anything else?" she asked him.

"Do you want some help with the lights?"

She stammered. "Th-that's nice, but I have a system so that I know I've gotten everything turned off."

"Oh. Gotcha." He made no motion to leave; instead, he followed her as she went to hit the lights in the back. "You know, I read your library picks every month. I thought we might have a great discussion on them. You know, give me your professional viewpoint."

She couldn't help but smile. "I'd hardly call my opinion 'professional.' I'm just a book lover like you."

"Did you notice what I read this month?" He looked down at the books he'd just handed her.

"You read *Persuasion*?"

"I did. 'I am half agony, half hope,'" he said, quoting one of her favorite lines.

She had to admit, he was good. Very smooth.

A red-hot heat rose in her cheeks. "I must give you credit. It's not many men who will read Jane Austen. Unless they have to for school." She still wouldn't look at him directly for fear that he could read her easily—like any book.

"Jane's not so bad. I can appreciate her humor. Her cynicism." He walked alongside her, shortening his long stride to stay beside her as she flicked off more lights. "I took you for

87

a Mr. Darcy girl, because I know how you like things the way they are. But now . . ." He rubbed his chin. "Your reaction makes me wonder if you don't harbor a latent aspiration for risk. Maybe you're a Captain Wentworth fan."

"I'll make it easy for you. I like Captain Wentworth's sense of adventure," she told him, practically bursting to discuss her favorite hero. "It's the antithesis of my life." As soon as she said the words, she regretted them. Why prove what he already knew? That she was the quietest mouse in town. She lived like an eighty-year-old woman. He didn't need to know it. But worse, why did she care if he knew?

He moved closer to her. "I can't believe you're bringing this up. I've been trying to . . . What kind of adventure would you like to have, Abby? It's my specialty, you know. Why don't you come out on one of my outdoor adventures? You'd have a blast. And I'd take good care of you. I'd bring you back in one piece."

She shook her head. "I'll live my adventures through characters, thank you. In fact, I'm late for my book club as we speak." She buttoned the top button on her cardigan. "Your weekend treks that I've seen advertised . . ." She stared across the library at the community board. "They seem like the stuff of Hollywood action movies."

"Only because you haven't tried them. You haven't lived until you've soared off the side of a mountain on a hang glider or climbed a sheer granite cliff with—"

"Actually, I've lived very well doing none of those death-defying stunts." She put a hand to her hip. "Do you know what you need, Wyatt?"

He rested his chin in his hands on the counter. "What is it I need, Abby?"

"To learn to enjoy life without the adrenaline rush of nearly losing it."

"What makes you think I don't?"

She didn't have an answer for that.

"What makes you think that I can't enjoy myself sitting in Mountain Perks and drinking coffee across from a beautiful librarian?"

She lifted a brow and crossed her arms. "What do you want, Wyatt?"

"I want to have coffee with you, Abby."

"No, I mean, really."

"I really want to have coffee with you. There's something I need to discuss with you."

She bent down to unplug the copy machine. "I have a lot of responsibilities at home. Friday night is my one night out, and my calendar is full with my book group."

"Your one night out, and you let loose with the wild book club crowd, huh?"

She didn't know how to take Wyatt. He seemed to have a dry sense of humor, but she never understood if he was teasing or serious. The other librarians always giggled when he was around, but without their reactions for cues, she felt fairly clueless.

"That was a joke, Abby." He grinned at her playfully. "I think it's great you go to a book group. Very cool."

She smiled uncomfortably. "Right." She paused and gathered her thoughts. "I take care of my mother, so I go home early after work and get her dinner. On Fridays I go to book club." *Riveting.* She must sound absolutely riveting.

He stared at her blankly.

"I'm trying to explain why I don't go out very often. I appreciate your offer of coffee, but I've usually got to get home."

"What are you, twenty-five, Abby?"

"It's impolite to ask a woman's age." She gazed down at her feet, noting that they, too, were dressed like an eighty-year-old woman's. "I'm twenty-seven."

"Are you a morning person? What about in the morning, before work? People have coffee in the morning, so it would be perfectly reasonable that we meet then." He paused. "To discuss *Persuasion*. And something else. Something I've been putting off for far too long."

Whatever Wyatt was up to, she felt drawn to him as if someone had attached a winch to her waistline and was cranking it slowly, pulling her out of her imprisoned, muddy bog toward his carefree, sunny escape. "*Persuasion* seems appropriate, since you're using that power to entice me." She dropped her forehead in her hands as she realized that she'd said such a ridiculous thing aloud.

"What's the matter?"

"Nothing." She sucked in a deep breath and exhaled. "I need to go. I'm late for book club."

As she finished her rounds, she faced Wyatt, who was still at her side. Her gaze rose up to meet his eyes, and she allowed herself to drink in their light. She reminded herself that she was content, while Wyatt needed adventure to feel alive. He needed a woman like him. A woman like Anne Elliot, who would sail the open seas to be with Captain Wentworth. Abby, on the other hand, was out of sorts if she had to grocery shop on a different night from her usual one. Besides, her mother would take to the idea of her dating the way a cat takes to being tossed into a swimming pool.

Wyatt lifted her hand and held it in his for a moment. "We're friends, right?" He gave her his trademark sideways grin that should be registered as a lethal weapon. "Friends spend time getting to know one another. It's just coffee, Abby. "

She shrugged. "I guess." Coffee seemed innocent enough. He wanted to talk about a book. She was a librarian. It made perfect sense. She just hoped she could keep her heart from getting involved—because men like Wyatt Tanner didn't stay with their feet on the ground for long, and they didn't seem to realize the effect they had on others. "I should get going," she said and turned away from his outstretched hand to gather her things.

Wyatt felt the loss of Abby's hand immediately as his grasp emptied. Her small hand, with its slender fingers . . . her nails always trimmed short and painted with a natural pink color . . . it felt right inside his, like it belonged there. If only he could find a way to tell her so.

"Maybe Monday morning, before work. Mountain Perks. Is seven too early for you?"

"Seven is fine," she whispered hoarsely.

"Be ready to discuss Austen."

She smiled briefly, and he'd have given blood to know what she was thinking. Rather than risk giving her another chance to back out, he made a hasty exit with a smile he felt to his feet. *Abby Gray is the perfect woman.* With caramel-colored hair, which she always wore up in a studious bun, and deep, soulful brown eyes that hypnotized him. He'd spent the better part of a year trying to get to know her better. Trying to do the thing that he'd planned so long ago.

Casey, one of the other librarians, invariably placed herself between Abby and him, so he'd decided to return his books when he knew only Abby would be on duty and he'd have her to himself. She exuded a sense of warmth that made him want her soft nature—she was like a roaring fire in the fireplace. From the moment he first laid eyes on her, he knew. There was something different about Abby Gray that made him feel as if he'd known her their entire lives. She had a petite, athletic frame, and he wondered what she did to stay in shape. She obviously hid her adventurous side underneath an array of cardigans, which only made him want to uncover that side of her more.

He walked down the street and shook his head. As he stared over his shoulder, he watched her emerge from the library and heard her jangle the keys.

Be ready to discuss Austen. Seriously? Did he really just tell a librarian to be ready to discuss Jane Austen? As if he were some kind of literary hero? He could barely string two words together and sound coherent. At least when he was near Abby. He didn't know what touched him so about her, but when he was beside her, he smiled from within.

Hopefully, Abby didn't think he was a blooming idiot. He hadn't meant to be so pushy, but some part of him wanted to get her out of the house more often and learn what went on behind those gorgeous, mysterious eyes. He'd first seen her in church, but she was always flanked by her mother and seemed so off-limits there. Running into her at the library seemed like fate.

She hiked her book bag over her shoulder, and he watched her hips sway gently as she walked in the other direction. She turned and smiled at him with a wave.

He loved the way she laughed, the way she hung back when the other ladies tried to speak to him. All he'd wanted to do was get to her and pull her out of her quiet reverie, but then someone would ask about his outdoor hobbies and he'd see her visibly flinch at the idea of helicopter skiing in Canada or snowboarding atop Sugarcreek Mountain.

"Someone looks smitten." Ellie Draper stood outside her fudge shop, Sweet Surrender.

Wyatt sniffed the sugary scent of her warm concoctions. "You're just trying to sell me some dark chocolate."

"Maybe." She winked. "Abby likes the peanut butter fudge."

"Does she now?"

Ellie shrugged her rounded shoulders. "You know where to find me." With a jingling of bells she disappeared into her sweet shop.

Abby was out of sight now. Most likely she found his love of extreme sports folly. Nothing more than a death wish. He wanted her to know the truth, that computer consulting was only a means to an end. He wanted to create programs that showed athletes how to move their bodies for optimal performance. He didn't want to be known just as the code monkey of Smitten.

Today he had hope. On Monday morning Abby would meet him for coffee and he would get to ask about her, away from the prying eyes of library patrons and nosy librarians. Now he was the one who was half agony, half hope.

Always maintain a modest yet appealing appearance as is becoming of a woman of God. Your appearance is a calling card.

PEARL CHAMBERS, *The Gentlewoman's Guide to Love and Courtship*

CHAPTER TWO

. . . .

*A*bby hurried down the brick sidewalk of Main Street, past the fire station and town storefronts, until she came to the bookstore at the corner of Lookaway Lane and Main Street. It was a beautiful evening with the sun low in the sky and the streets bustling with tourists. There were horse-drawn carriages in the street carrying diners to the romantic restaurants, and the twinkling lights that lined the downtown trees sparkled.

Abby thought it must be easier for single women to find contentment when they weren't forced to watch fawning couples gazing into one another's eyes on a daily basis. Smitten's being the romance capital did have its downside. Nothing reminded a person of her loneliness like people being paired off as if they were getting on Noah's ark.

As she felt the dwindling sunlight on her face and saw the purple majesty of the mountains in the distance, she hesitated to go inside the bookstore. Smitten, Vermont, embodied every one of God's beautiful creations: deep, glass-like lakes, magnificent mountains, and spring colors. Yet she spent most of her hours inside. Wyatt's mention of Captain Wentworth had given her a nudge toward a more adventurous life. Stepping outside more often might be a simple commitment that she could keep. She definitely needed to get out more.

She pushed through the bookstore's door, and the jangle of bells immediately put her at ease. The group had read *Gone with the Wind,* and to celebrate they were eating barbecue like at Twelve Oaks. Someone picked up fried chicken from Jake's restaurant, and everyone had brought a side dish. Except for her.

She slapped her forehead lightly. "I forgot the potato salad I made this morning," she said.

Lia came to hug her. "Don't worry about it, sweetie. We've got plenty of food. You'd think we were feeding an entire Confederate regiment, from the looks of it. How's your mother?"

"Oh, she's fine. Cathy, our neighbor, is having dinner with her tonight, so I won't have to be home early."

"It sounds like they may have a lot of potato salad."

Abby laughed. The round table in front of the bookshelves, which normally housed the best sellers, was filled with delicacies from an earlier, more genteel time.

"Have some sweet tea," Lia offered with her best imitation of a Southern accent. "It's food for what ails the soul, I do declare."

It wasn't the first time Abby had forgotten. She worried her friends might get tired of filling in the gaps for her, but as Molly approached, she figured they had bigger fish to fry. Curtis's death had left Molly to run Smitten Expeditions alone, and as a true girlie girl, it was almost as if Cinderella had been left to guard the castle in her blue gown and tiara.

Molly wasn't big on reading. She preferred movies to books and tortured herself weekly with all the latest romantic comedies. Every week Abby would check out the latest movies from the library for Molly to watch, and sneak in a romantic classic.

She handed over the bag of DVDs from the library.

"Anything good?" Molly asked as she clutched the bag.

"Not this week. All the movies that came in were more in the horror genre, so I brought you a classic: *Pillow Talk* with Rock Hudson and Doris Day."

Molly frowned.

"You'll like it. Besides, there's going to come a day when you've seen everything there and you'll have to go backward whether you like it or not. They're not making as many romantic comedies as they used to."

It didn't seem to bother Molly that they lived in the romance capital—she still sought the escapism of chick flicks.

"*Safe Haven* is out next week. You should like that one. Exceptionally sappy and heart-tugging."

"Bravo!" Molly shouted. "I've been waiting for that one. Maybe I should have a party. What do you think?"

The other women came around them and laughed. Heather crossed her arms. "Abby, do you have to encourage her by bringing her those movies? This is a book club. How are we going to get her to finish the books if you keep offering her addiction of choice?"

"It's harmless," Abby said. "If I'd had her marriage, I'd want to be reminded of romance too." She looked directly at Molly. "I just fail to see how you need the reminder when it's everywhere in this town."

Molly smiled. "Don't get me wrong. I know you guys love me, but it feels like a hundred years since I felt romantic love. I guess the movies remind me what that feels like."

Abby sighed. She couldn't argue with that. The room got quiet, and Abby realized she'd put her foot in her mouth again by bringing up Molly's husband. "I'm sorry, Molly. I suppose that's why they don't let me out often."

Molly smiled and patted her shoulder. "I knew what you meant. And I like it when people remember Curtis. It's better than when they try to avoid saying his name." Molly walked toward the entrance of the bookstore and began welcoming the rest of the club.

Abby stood alone amidst the circle of chairs set up in front of the bookshelves. Suddenly she felt anxious to get started on the book discussion—a time where she wouldn't say the wrong thing and remind people why she felt more comfortable at work than out in public.

Heather, who looked like a model and seemed to have it all together, pulled her aside into a small corner of the store. Before she could say anything, Abby spoke up. "I'm sorry about what I said to Molly about the movies. You don't think I hurt her, do you?"

Heather shook her head. "Forget that. Molly knows you'd never do anything to hurt her." She handed Abby another book bag. "But I do have a way I think you can help her."

Abby took the book bag and peeked inside. "What's this?"

"It's the *Gentlewoman's Guide*. I'm sure our mystery is nothing more than Smitten lore, but I thought with your research skills, we might at least make sure. Do you mind?"

Abby took the book, an antique leather-bound volume, which appeared crumbly and fragile in its age. "Not at all. I'll see what I can find. Do I know everything I need to?"

"There's not much to tell. I found it at the book fundraiser for Molly's family. It was written by Curtis's ancestor, Pearl Chambers. You know the Smitten folklore about the gold in the foothills below Sugarcreek Mountain?"

Abby scanned the book. "What kind of town historian would I be without knowing that story?"

"Finding this book got me to thinking. By all accounts, Pearl was no dummy."

"No. She was very respected in town."

"It's said that her husband, Otis, forbade her to mine the gold she found. Do you think that's so?"

"I don't know if it's true. I do know if there was a cave on that land, it would have been uncovered by now. When the ski resort was built there was so much excavation."

"But what if the gold was already gone?"

Abby shrugged. "It seems like a long shot."

"You said yourself that Pearl was a respected citizen in town."

"She was, but she had a falling out with her daughter, from what I understand."

Abby opened the book, relishing the feel of the old volume. The romance of a simpler time captured her imagination.

Maybe there would be wisdom for a woman like her who had chosen a life of caregiving over romance. "'Never hang your pantaloons publicly,'" she read. "That's some practical advice. I don't see anything here about the gold legend."

"No, I know. That's the point," Heather said.

"How am I supposed to look something up that's not there?"

Lia and Molly had arrived and were walking toward them.

"What's that?" Molly asked.

Heather shoved the book back into its bag. "Nothing. I just needed a professional opinion on a book I purchased."

Abby didn't understand why the book was a secret, or what it had to do with the legend of Smitten's gold, but she could tell by the way Heather was acting that there was a lot more to the story than she could share at the moment.

"We'll talk about it later," Heather whispered.

"Let's eat, shall we?" Lia held her arm out to the table, and Abby's stomach rumbled as the scent of dinner wafted toward her.

"We have plans for you tonight."

"Me? Yes, we've finally finished *Gone with the Wind*."

Lia shook her head. "We all know Molly didn't read it. It's too long for her."

"I did so!" Molly said before she backed down. "Well, some of it, anyway. But even the movie's too long for me. I have to skip all those boring war parts."

The women all laughed and filled their plates with chicken, mashed potatoes, and corn on the cob, and filled their Ball-jar glasses with sweet tea.

"I think maybe you like this book because it brings out your inner Scarlett."

"I don't think I have an inner Scarlett," Abby said honestly, scooping up a helping of mashed potatoes.

"You might be right." Molly looked at Abby's feet. "You're wearing orthopedic shoes."

"They're not special shoes," Abby protested. "They're just comfortable. I'm on my feet all day."

"It doesn't matter if they actually *are* orthopedic; they look orthopedic," Lia explained. "Look at your gorgeous calves. We know you're on your feet all day."

"The girls and I were talking about you this week," Heather said. "We think maybe it's time we abandoned the librarian look for something more up-to-date."

The women sat down in the chairs, their laps all covered by plates full of the night's dinner.

"When's the last time you went on a date, Abby?" Heather asked.

"Does it matter?" Abby said.

"It's not like you to pick a romance novel," Molly said.

"It's *Gone with the Wind*. It's not really a romance." Somehow she felt whatever her friends were up to, they weren't going to be talking much about the book tonight. "Didn't you like it?" she ventured.

The girls all looked at one another as if they shared some dark secret, and she felt completely alone. The rest of the women were happily eating their potluck and seemed oblivious to what her friends were up to.

"Will someone tell me what's going on?"

"Last week when you couldn't make it to book club and

we were discussing the characters, we thought how much like Melanie you are. Melanie was always doing for everyone else. She saw the best in everyone else and never seemed to take the time to worry about herself."

Abby shrugged. "Melanie's the nice one. Is there a problem with that?"

"Of course not," Lia said. "It's just we worry about you taking care of your mother and how little you're getting out."

"Don't take this the wrong way, but you're too young to *become* your mother," Heather said.

"So after club tonight, we're heading to Sparkle. They're keeping it open just for us. We're going to get you a few new things."

"Why? I don't go anywhere. I don't need anything new." Abby felt like a trapped animal. Did her friends know Wyatt had asked her to coffee? Was he in on their little conspiracy?

"You haven't been the same since your mom stopped driving," Lia continued. "We're worried that if you stay like this, our book study is going to become the highlight of your week."

It *was* the highlight of her week. "What's wrong with that?"

Her friends looked at one another again.

"There's a lot wrong with that. I mean, we love you and all, but we're not exactly party central," Molly said.

"I don't mind that. I'm an introvert."

The way her friends were looking at her, Abby had a feeling that book club as she knew it was over. When those three had an agenda, nothing was going to stop them, and if they'd decided she was Melanie and needed a bit more

Scarlett, she wasn't going anywhere without a touch of red.

"Does this have anything to do with Wyatt?"

"Wyatt Tanner?" Molly asked. "Why? Is there some reason it might?"

"No reason."

"I knew there was something there!" Molly said. "When he works for me, he always brings up the library! He's tried to discuss books with me, but I tell him if it weren't for you girls, I'd exist happily on Dr. Seuss and Captain Underpants with Noah. So go on, spill it!"

"He's just a library patron."

Molly, forever lost in her romantic ideals, wouldn't give up. "I knew we got that message about you and Melanie for a reason. It's as if the road is being paved for romance, and we're your fairy godmothers!"

"It's absolutely nothing like that. He was at the library tonight, kept me late, and offered to buy me coffee. He wants to discuss *Persuasion*."

Her friends giggled.

"Is something funny?" she asked.

"Abby, no man wants to get together to discuss a Jane Austen book unless the librarian is hot." Heather shook her head. "Sometimes you are so naive."

"I must have some wisdom if you're telling me I act too old for my age."

"Wyatt sees what we do," Lia intervened. "The sweet, sexy Scarlett within who needs to be rediscovered after smelling like her mother's Bengay and cornering the market on L.L. Bean sweater sets."

"What's wrong with a sweater set?"

Heather groaned.

"It looks like everyone's about finished with dinner," Lia said. "Let's get started on the book discussion, shall we?"

Abby was delighted at the reprieve. At the mention of Wyatt's name, she'd seen his image flash in her mind and felt the hard thump of her heart. While her mind instinctively knew he was out of reach, her emotions couldn't quite believe it. Scarlett O'Hara she was not.

Her friends sat around her, each of them looking at her smugly. Something told her to be afraid. Very afraid. And besides, she liked the smell of Bengay. It was refreshing.

Always maintain and improve upon one's appearance. Love is not, in fact, blind.

PEARL CHAMBERS, *The Gentlewoman's Guide to Love and Courtship*

CHAPTER THREE

. . . .

*S*parkle was a boutique on Lookaway Lane. The shop only displayed a few select items that dotted what appeared to be a lavender-hued living room. Abby supposed the idea behind the sparsely populated store was for the shop-keeper to assist the patrons in selecting the right items for the individual's needs. That kind of expertise came at a price, and that's the reason she had never entered Sparkle before that evening.

In truth, she didn't particularly have specialized needs, other than comfortable shoes and clothes that allowed her to move freely to shelve books and assist her mother. The collection of fancy slinky dresses seemed more than a waste of money—it was a waste of her friends' time. But she didn't dare water down their excitement.

"I cannot wait to see that figure in something that fits!" Heather said.

"I don't know that this is such a great idea." Abby halted at the door. "I won't have any place to wear any of these dresses."

Heather yanked her inside. "It doesn't matter if you think it's a great idea. You're here now. And it's not about being practical. That's the problem, you're too practical and again, I must remind you that you're not seventy. You're allowed to make a few mistakes yet."

"Too practical? As if there could be such a thing."

"We want our friend to come back to us." Lia said. "The one who is full of light and love—not Epsom salts."

"Why does everyone suddenly think I need a make-over?" Abby looked down at her oversized sweater, skirt with an elastic waistband, and of course her black leather shoes—in the middle of Smitten's summer. "If I had more time in the morning, I'm sure I'd devote more attention to my appearance."

Heather, Miss Health and Fitness, spoke up. "You're underestimating what the outside can do for your insides. Healthy living starts on the inside, but the outside can definitely influence your demeanor. Ever since you lost your father, Abby, we've watched more of you go away. It's like all you are is your mother's caregiver."

"It's a full-time job, and I'm doing my duties at the library too. When would I have time to go out and wear a dress like these?"

"You can wear one of these to work," Heather said. "You'd feel better about yourself, and then maybe you'd have more energy to go out."

"Remember when we used to go to the movies and sometimes dinner after work?" Lia asked.

"That was before Daddy passed. My mom is already home alone all day long. She needs company."

"We know," Molly said. "We don't want you to give up on your duties. We just want you to not lose yourself while you do them. You know, restore yourself a little. Even if you only wore the dress to church, wouldn't it be nice to have something new?"

Abby picked up a tag and whistled at the price.

Julia, who was married to the owner of Jake's Restaurant and owned a spa in town, came out from the back room.

"Julia, what are you doing here?" Abby asked. "Do you work here now?"

"Heather asked Allison if she could keep the store open late tonight, but she couldn't be here. I was there and volunteered," Julia said. "If I didn't have a spa, a shop like this would be my second choice! Jake's working late anyway." She motioned toward the sofa. "Have a seat, Abby. Is there a particular color you like?"

"And don't say brown!" Heather chastised.

"I like navy," Abby answered sheepishly.

"Navy is good, but I see you in more of a peacock blue."

Even the word *peacock* brought up visions of fanning herself and strutting her stuff in the library. It seemed absurd.

Julia had lived in New York City, so she brought a chic vibe to Smitten and to her spa. Abby's vibe was more pragmatic. And to be honest, she couldn't remember the last time she'd gone shopping for herself. Usually she was content to shop the Lands' End catalog and circle what she wanted her mother to get her for Christmas.

Julia brought her a sling-back shoe that rested on a small, inch-tall square heel. "These will be easy to spend the day in, and you'll feel pretty."

Abby stared at Julia. Somehow she doubted that heels of any sort would make her feel pretty. Uncomfortable, yes; angry, maybe; but definitely not pretty. "Julia, I don't want to waste your time when you could be at home. I'm not really a fancy dress person."

"Abby, I've done more than a few makeovers in my day, and I wish I could tell you how they revive the soul. This isn't about what you look like. Your friends know that you're beautiful inside and out. This is them wanting to make you feel your age again." Julia rubbed her tummy, which protruded with a few months' pregnancy.

"Should you be out this late?"

"It's nine o'clock. The restaurant is open until eleven. Come in the back and try on some of the dresses I've pulled for you." As Abby stood, Julia slipped an arm around her waist. "Do you know how I miss a waist? You have to wear a waistline for me!"

Heather interrupted, "You may as well get started. We're not letting you go until you've picked out at least two dresses and one decent pair of shoes—that your mother wouldn't wear."

Would Anne Elliot have been afraid of a new frock? Definitely not.

"But look at these slinky dresses, Heather. These are for honeymooners or couples on romantic getaways. They're not for librarians with no social life."

"Ah, but would the librarian have no social life if she dressed like a honeymooner?" Julia asked. "Did you ever think of that?"

"Wyatt Tanner asked her out," Molly blurted.

"He did not," Abby protested. "He asked me to coffee."

"To discuss Austen." Molly giggled. "We all know that Wyatt Tanner isn't going to come off of one of his cliffs to discuss literature unless he's noticed our favorite librarian's beautiful eyes."

As her friends surrounded her, each with a different dress in her hands, Julia offered her a shoe. Abby turned it over. "Eighty-five dollars!" She swallowed the lump in her throat.

"Abby, we know your supposedly non-orthopedic shoes don't come cheap."

"But there's something to them. They're sturdy! This is a flap of leather, and they want eighty-five dollars for it." She looked down at her black, bulky shoes and in comparison the strappy, elegant red of the sling-back. They may have both been in the same shoe family, but they were entirely different species.

"This is perfect!" Heather held up a slinky violet dress. "It's a Persian blue chiffon. You could pair it with a jacket and wear it to the library, then add a scarf and go out for the evening."

"But I don't go out for the evening, and Smitten isn't exactly the fashion capital of the world. No one cares what I wear to shelve books."

"We do." Heather fluttered the flimsy dress in the air. "This would make your eyes look incredible with some navy eyeliner, and it would highlight the gold in your hair."

"What about this one?" Lia brought out a dress in red that seemed remarkably similar to the choice Heather made.

"Aren't these dresses kind of short?" Abby asked.

"They're cut to the knee. You'll be perfectly covered and able to bend at the library without offering any kind of show," Julia said.

"You're turning into your mother, do you get that?" Heather asked.

"Is that such a bad thing?"

"Your mother is nearly seventy years old. You're twenty-seven."

It was true. Her mother had adopted her late in life, and it always felt more like she had grandparents than actual parents. It wasn't just that they were older—her parents had retired souls. Her mother was a quiet knitter. Her father had loved the kitchen and spent hours perfecting the best soups and stews. If her parents were a restaurant, they would have been a diner with American comfort foods and breakfast served any time of the day. Somehow being in the boutique felt like a betrayal of who they had raised her to be.

"I'm sorry. None of these things are me. I'd feel like I was trying to be you, Heather. Or even you, Julia."

Lia spoke up. "Buying a new dress doesn't make you someone different, Abby. Don't deny us the chance to do something kind for you. We feel like you've just given up on looking forward in life."

"I haven't," she said honestly.

"So is there romance in your future? Or just work?" Molly asked gently.

Abby couldn't answer. She simply didn't see marriage in her future. As she watched all the lovey-dovey couples in Smitten, she just didn't know if she had that essence in her. Surely God didn't expect everyone to marry. "If by looking to the future you mean walking down the aisle in a white dress, no, I don't see that happening."

Lia spoke up again. "Molly, Abby doesn't have to get

married to have a future. We just want her to know that she's allowed to have a little fun in life."

"Sure," Molly said. "Of course."

Abby grinned. Molly saw everything through romantic, pink-filtered glasses and couldn't help but hope that marriage was in all of their futures. "Fine, I'll try them on, but truthfully, I don't know where I'd wear one of these."

"What about to Hawaii?" Heather asked.

Ever since the four of them had become friends, they'd dreamed of taking a girls' trip to Hawaii together. That was an adventure Abby wanted to have. Trying on the dress suddenly seemed reasonable.

She snapped the periwinkle dress from Heather's hand and strode to the dressing room. For a moment she stared at her reflection in disappointment. She touched the tops of her cheeks and saw how sallow the skin under her eyes appeared. Her golden hair was starting to turn brown all over from her lack of sunshine. Taking off her light cotton cardigan, she noticed that her once-muscular arms were softer and paler than she remembered. She finally saw what her friends were telling her.

She slipped the dress on and twisted in front of the mirror. The dress was so light, it felt as if she had nothing on at all. The dress was gathered at the waist and had a convenient snap at the bodice. It was very modest, but as she turned to look at the back, she gasped. There was a giant triangle swath cut out of the back, through which she could see her bra strap. That hole would make her self-conscious even if she wore a sweater over it.

"What's the matter?" Julia asked.

Abby stepped out of the small room and turned her back toward her friends. She heard them gasp as well. "I feel kind of naked."

"We're just not used to seeing you in a dress like that," Heather said. "We're shocked, is all."

"You'd like more coverage, I take it," Julia said. "Okay, completely understand—even though you can totally pull it off."

"I'd like to go home," Abby said. Even though she felt lovely in the dress, it embarrassed her to think people thought of her as an orphan who needed to be cared for. It was just deep in her psyche that someone else needed something more than she did.

"You look fantastic!" Lia said. "But we'll find you something more modest if you wish."

"I wish."

Abby tried on many more dresses, and finally everyone agreed on a cranberry-colored silk with a cinched waist, softly pleated skirt, and a scoop neckline. It made her feel like a princess, and secretly, inside the dressing room, she twisted and watched the dress billow and flow. But in all honesty, she couldn't imagine wearing it outside of the house.

"That's the one," Lia said.

Julia wrapped up the dress, along with silver ballet flats and the red sling-back heels, a gift from Julia herself, in pink tissue paper and a silver-handled bag. "Wear it well."

Abby hugged each one of her friends for telling her a truth that she may have needed to hear. Anne Elliot had a new frock. And all was right with the world.

CHAPTER FOUR

. . . .

onday morning came too quickly for Abby, as the thought of seeing Wyatt weighed heavily on her heart. She toyed with wearing her new dress that morning, but didn't want to explain to her mother the reason for the sudden change in her appearance or why she was leaving early for work that day.

Her hands trembled as she made her way toward the coffee shop and the dangerous and mysterious Wyatt Tanner. She didn't even drink coffee. She halted on the brick walkway of Main Street, tempted to turn around and go back home, but as she looked to her right, she realized that she was standing directly in front of the picture window of Mountain Perks.

Wyatt rose from his chair inside and pushed open the door. His smile made everything all right, and she immediately calmed. They were just two friends having coffee. The only danger Wyatt represented was if she allowed her imagination to make the event more than it was.

"Are you coming inside?" Wyatt asked. He wore a black V-neck T-shirt stretched to capacity over his well-developed pecs and a casual gray blazer thrown over the top. He managed casual chic without even trying.

"Uh, yeah. I'm coming in. I was just . . ." She was just wishing she'd worn the cute sling-back shoes her friends had bought her, or at the very least, the silver ballet flats. She hadn't wanted Wyatt to think she'd dressed up for him. Now she wished she had dressed up a bit, so that they didn't appear so grievously mismatched.

"I was worried you might not make it," he said.

She smiled. Whatever his reason, she believed now that Wyatt did indeed want her there. "I just needed to give my mother breakfast before I left."

"Come inside," he said, a distinctive spark in his eye. "I've got us the best table in the house. What can I get you to drink?"

"I'll get it." She began to walk toward the counter when Wyatt appeared beside her and pulled out his wallet. She smiled inwardly. His presence made her nervous, but in the best kind of way. Could a man like Wyatt really have an interest in her? Was she really meeting him for coffee?

"When you invite *me* to coffee, you can pay," he said and grinned.

Abby hiked her purse over her shoulder, trying to play it as casually as possible. As though his dreamy good looks had no effect on her whatsoever.

"I'll have a chai tea," she told Natalie, the owner.

"Want a gluten-free muffin with that?" Natalie asked.

Abby shook her head and checked her watch.

"Are you in a hurry?" Wyatt asked.

"Uh, no." She glanced at her watch again. "Nervous habit."

He grinned again. "So, you're probably wondering why I was so anxious to discuss that book choice of yours."

"It crossed my mind." She ran her finger along the edge of the counter.

"I'm forgetting my manners. How is your mother?"

"She's fine." That answered her question. He wasn't really interested in her at all. She felt the heat of humiliation rise into her cheeks.

"She has vertigo, right? That's why she doesn't drive?"

"Or walk without assistance, yes. How did you know that?"

"Casey told me."

Casey. Casey was the biggest gossip in the library and looked for any excuse to pass on vital data that couldn't be found on any of the library's shelves. "Why would she tell you that?"

"I asked her about you."

Natalie handed her the chai tea, and Wyatt led them back to his table in the corner by the window.

"Why wouldn't you just ask me?"

"You don't usually pay me any attention. You know, I've developed software that I think might help your mother. Anyone with vertigo."

"My mother isn't great on computers."

"She wouldn't need to be. I've developed programs to help sports enthusiasts get better at their sport, and working on balance was a natural part of it."

"Is that what this meeting is about? Your software?"

He sat at the table and leaned in toward her. "No."

His eyes held so much more than he said. Abby looked down at her cup and tucked a strand of hair behind her ear.

"Do you ever wear your hair down?"

She shook her head. "It gets in my way. I've thought of cutting it off—"

"No! I mean, don't do that, it's so beautiful."

A smile gave her away—how hungry she was for his affirmation, even though she knew Wyatt was probably capable of saying what any woman wanted to hear. His gaze darted about the room, and silence spread between them like spilled coffee.

"Hasn't this weather been fantastic? I love Vermont summers," she offered.

"There's nothing better." He placed his coffee cup on the table and tapped his foot on the ground.

"Is something the matter?" She knew he needed to tell her something. She felt his nervous energy within her, and she wanted to offer him some relief, to tell him she felt the same way.

He drummed his fingers again. "I thought this would be easier."

She braced herself on the chair as all sorts of scenarios ran through her head. Did he know something about the library being computerized? Was he privy to some kind of information about her job? Her breathing became shallow as she waited for some news that might challenge her safe world.

"Your father . . . ," he started.

"My father passed away."

"Last year, I know." He raked his hand across his buzzed haircut. "I've waited too long to do this, but, Abby, I barely knew you. I told him that. I wanted to, but every time I got close to you, you'd move away. Or you'd let Casey come deal with me at the library."

"You knew my father?"

"I was in his men's group at church."

She glanced at her watch again and wondered what that could mean. Wyatt was everything her father warned her against. Was that because he knew Wyatt so well? Knew his secrets? "I never heard my father mention your name."

"They're meeting right now. Mondays at seven," he said. "Are you always so suspicious?"

"Am I?" she asked innocently, but she knew she was suspicious. Men like Wyatt lived their lives without any thought to the future. Life was one big game. A woman needed a serious man to settle down with—not a little boy with a grown exterior. How often had that been the topic at the dinner table?

"This isn't going well," he said as he rubbed his eyebrow. "I feel as though you're accusing me of something, and I'm not sure why."

"I'm not much of a conversationalist, I guess." She wanted to run before he realized his mistake in asking her anywhere. "Really. It was lovely. Thanks for the tea." She started to rise.

"Please don't leave, Abby. That's not what I meant."

She settled back into her seat and decided to lead with the truth. She wasn't like Scarlett. She didn't have the mind-set to play games, and with a man like Wyatt she'd be out of her league anyway. "Wyatt, you make me nervous." She took a sip from her tea and avoided his gaze. She could feel his eyes upon her, and she tapped her foot anxiously.

"I make *you* nervous? You're so beautiful, Abby, and smart too. Why would someone like me make you nervous?"

She looked up at him, wondering how he could possibly ask such a question. Wyatt was all charm and good looks, and his smooth words were most likely well practiced. "You just do."

"Because I said you were beautiful? Or because I said you were suspicious?"

She met his intense chestnut eyes directly. "I need to know what this is about, Wyatt. I feel like there's some ulterior motive that I don't understand and that you're laughing at me behind my back." She wanted to hear him protest, to hear him say he felt the undeniable energy between them, but she prepared for the worst.

His cheek flinched as if she'd struck him, and for the first time she saw that he might not be as rough as his exterior. Maybe her words did have the power to cut him to the quick, and she should be more responsible with them. "Abby, I'd never laugh at you."

His words, the warm way he said them, melted her heart. She was so desperate to believe in him that it automatically sent her guard up.

"It's just you've been around the library for so long. Why now?"

He chuckled. "Abby, I've been trying to get to know you for the past year. I've read dozens of books just to have something to say to you. I've read Jane Austen for you! I've tried to talk to you countless times at church . . . and at work. You think I want to digitize the library? I couldn't care less if

Smitten's library is fully computerized. I'm just drawn to you. When I'm near you, I feel calm and contented."

She swallowed hard and glanced around her—to see if there was a camera pointed at her. Or if her friends were going to pop out of the back room telling her they'd made a video for YouTube. To hear him say the words she wanted to hear seemed too good to be true, and as was her inclination, she waited for the other shoe to drop.

"Why is that so hard for you to believe . . . that I want to get to know you?"

Had he looked at himself lately? Had he seen how the women at church gathered around him like moths to the gaslights? His confident nature, his expression-filled eyes, and his easy warmth all weighed against his being the authentic man her father had been. "I'm a librarian. You're an adrenaline junkie who probably belongs on *The Bachelor*—is it really that hard to wonder why this is uncomfortable?"

He shifted in his seat. "We are different, but what if you looked at it like this? You showed me the benefits of Jane Austen. I, in turn, can offer you more adventure in your life. Isn't that a fair trade?" He leaned into the table, and the way he gazed at her with his intense dark eyes made her squirm. Mostly because she was tempted to kiss those lips as they came close to her. The thought surprised and annoyed her.

She cleared her throat to break her gaze. "You really want credit for reading Austen, don't you?"

"If you jumped out of an airplane, wouldn't you want credit for it?"

"I'm not going to jump out of an airplane, so I suppose it wouldn't matter."

"I haven't exactly been honest with you," Wyatt said.

Finally, she'd hear the truth behind his sudden interest.

"*Honest* is the wrong word," he continued. "I haven't been forthright with you. Like I said, I wanted this to come naturally, but maybe we're too different for that. There is another reason I asked you here. It isn't the whole reason, but it's a part of it."

She'd known it all along. Men like Wyatt Tanner didn't offer such attentions without expecting something in return.

"Your father asked me for a favor before he passed." Wyatt stared off in the distance, and his square jaw tightened.

Abby's shoulders drooped. She didn't want to hear the truth. Basking in the warm glow of Wyatt's honeyed words had made her forget for a moment that she was a librarian whose only excitement was lived in books.

She nodded slowly while her eyes rested on his rugged hands. "I see. Well, consider your promise kept. You gave the librarian some attention."

He shook his head. "No, no, you don't understand. I should have done this a year ago, but I didn't think you were ready, and I didn't want to make your grieving that much worse. But I promised your father."

She sipped her tea and swirled the foam in her cup rather than meet those dark, expectant eyes again. "You can't be held responsible for a promise you can't keep."

"Your father was frantic about you before he passed. He thought you'd become a shadow of yourself, taking care of him and your mother. He said he'd always felt guilty they'd adopted you at such a late age. He thought that held you back in life—made you afraid to take risks."

"My parents never held me back. They were—correction—
they *are* the best, most loving people anyone could be fortunate
enough to know."

"I agree," he said as he stared into his empty cup. Then
Wyatt glanced up at her, his chocolate eyes melting with warmth.
Whatever he was trying to say, it didn't speak nearly as loudly as
his intense gaze. He reached into his jacket pocket and brought
out an envelope and placed it in the center of the table.

Tears welled up in her eyes at the sight of Wyatt's name in
the familiar, oversized script of her father's handwriting. It
seemed like a part of her father had come back to her.

Wyatt looked at her. "Read it."

Her dad was a gentle soul. He was sensitive, but tough
as nails. Easygoing, but volatile when someone did wrong
against his family. Mostly, he was Abby's warrior. A man she
knew she could count on, come famine or high water.

Her heart pounded. Why would her father trust a man
like Wyatt Tanner with his last secret? Wyatt was everything
he'd ever warned her about: a risk taker, a man who worked
when he felt like it, and worst of all, an absolute chick magnet.

"My father never even mentioned you," she said.

"Maybe he didn't talk about me at home, but he spoke of
you often to me. I can't help but see you through his light."

> *When a gentleman expresses himself to a woman, he must do so with absolute sincerity.*
>
> PEARL CHAMBERS, *The Gentlewoman's Guide to Love and Courtship*

CHAPTER FIVE

. . . .

Wyatt stood abruptly and tucked the letter back into his inside jacket pocket. He reached out for Abby's hand, which she offered tentatively. The memory of how well her tiny hand fit into his resonated in his soul. "Come with me."

"Where are we going?"

He felt the fear in her eyes to his soul.

"I owe you an explanation." He shouted to the owner, "Natalie, I'd like to take Abby for a ride to show her something. Will you vouch for me?"

"Abby, I'd trust Wyatt with my daughter," Natalie shouted from across the room.

Abby collected her handbag. "You didn't have to do that."

"You said I made you nervous." His mind reeled with how awkward he'd made this for her. He exited hastily, and she followed him out of the coffee shop. They turned north on Main Street. He led her to his SUV, which was parked along the curb, unlocked the door, and opened it for her. "My lady."

"We're going in your car?" She paused on the sidewalk as if he were driving some kind of windowless white van.

"I think that will help me describe the contents of the letter better. A visual aid, if you will."

She stepped up into his SUV, and he startled at the sight of her there. How natural she looked inside his truck, as if she belonged there beside him. His eyes lingered on the big, black shoes she wore, and he wondered why such a tiny sprite of a woman wanted to dress like a dowager. Was there safety in her get-up? Did she think it would throw men off of her stunning brown eyes that melted him like warmed honey?

Once on their way, Abby looked out the window, and he struggled for a way to make the time less awkward.

They headed toward Sugarcreek Mountain, which in the summer season was used for mountain bike riding and other seasonal activities. As the town grew farther in the distance, she finally spoke. "Will I be back in time for work?"

"I promise," he said.

He passed the Sugarcreek Ski Resort parking lot, and he watched her reaction. She rarely spoke, but he knew there was so much going on inside that pretty little head of hers. He wanted to be the man she shared her secrets with, the one who knew what ran beneath those still waters.

They came to the green river valley beyond the ski lodge, and he pulled off the road onto the gravel shoulder. He hopped out of the truck, rushed around to the passenger door, and opened it for her. He lifted his hand to her and helped her down, resisting the urge to grasp her waist to do so. "The gravel is loose here. Why don't you take my hand?"

"I have my walking shoes on," she said.

"Do it for me." His arm tingled with electricity as he enveloped her hand. Her gaze rose up to meet his and held. She clasped his hand and time stopped. A sense of satisfaction filled him. He walked her to the lower path, gripping her tighter so she wouldn't slip on the gravel. He pointed to the sky. "Do you see that?"

She shielded her eyes and looked up. He whisked out his sunglasses from his pocket and handed them to her. "Here," he said.

She unfolded the glasses and put them on. "Is that a hang glider?"

He nodded.

"Who would do that? Latch themselves to a human-sized kite and trust the wind to carry them?"

"I'm hoping that you will."

She pulled the aviators off and thrust them toward him. "Then you've got a lot more faith in me than I do. I'm ready to get back to town now, but I appreciate the personalized tour."

"Wait a minute!" He grasped her hand as she turned to leave. "This isn't some random tour of outer Smitten, Abby. It has to do with your father's letter."

She ignored his comment. "Have you done that before?" she asked, pointing at the sky.

"Hang glide? I do it all the time. I help your friend Molly out when she's got too many tourists. It's one of the hobbies I'm developing software for, so that people can practice the controls before they get out on the hill."

"Isn't that like the landing-the-plane app? I mean, it's not really worth anything in the real world, is it?"

He was taken aback. "Actually, it's very effective. It teaches people how to work the controls to deal with different situations that might come up so that it's more instinctive when you get the actual controls in your hands. It's like training your brain to react correctly in times of crisis. That's how I started working on the app for vertigo. After Casey told me about your mother."

Abby's brow lifted and she changed the subject. "This is crazy." She arched her neck and looked to the sky. "You realize I'm not going to fly on a kite."

"It will be tandem. I'll have all the controls. All you have to do is enjoy the rush and the view."

The sharp winds danced and blew her hair, freeing some of it from the tight bun that she always wore. Even though she had on giant granny shoes and a skirt that seemed two sizes too big for her, she couldn't hide her curvy figure or the brightness that lit her eyes from within. Her joyful spirit, in its quiet, reserved manner, had captivated him from the very first time he laid eyes upon her. He'd done his level best to garner an invitation from her dad to meet her, but Mr. Gray never made the offer. He'd wondered if her father disapproved of him.

Maybe that's why he'd never pressed too hard . . . the fear of rejection was too great.

"I'm not an adventure tourist by any means," Abby said. "I do plan to visit Hawaii someday. It's been my dream. But getting airborne on a kite, not so much."

"Hawaii. Really?" Wyatt asked. The thought of Abby in paradise sent shivers down his spine. He wanted to take Abby to Hawaii. The very thought of another man seeing her in a swimsuit and flip-flops instead of those giant shoes made him raw with jealousy.

"I hope so. The girls and I have talked about it. We read a book set there once, and I think it stirred all of our imaginations to think of a world without Vermont winters."

He took solace in hearing her speak so easily. For the moment he didn't fear her jumping in the truck and taking off, leaving him alone at the windy fields.

"Why would anyone do that?" she asked. "Jump off a mountain and risk life and limb just for an adrenaline rush? God only gives you one life. Why play with it?"

Wyatt smiled down at her. He took a loose tendril of her hair and pushed it behind her ear. She reached for it, but didn't make any motion to step away from him.

"I mean, that's crazy. One gust of wind and you're dead. Who wants to go that way?" She gazed at the couple hovering overhead.

"They're not going anywhere, trust me. They're having the thrill of what it's like to have wings. They're flying."

"That's not flying. That's falling with brakes. Brakes that can easily fail."

He laughed. "Not all of us can be Buzz Lightyear. I assure you, it makes you feel absolutely alive—and when you land, you will still be absolutely alive. And you don't jump off a mountain. You see that glider plane in front of them? That's called a tug. It lifts you up."

"It lifts *you* up. I'm staying put with my feet on the ground. There are other adventures to be had that don't involve testing gravity. Is that why you brought me out here? To prove to me that I'm unworthy of a Captain Wentworth and his sense of adventure?"

"On the contrary. I brought you out here to prove the opposite." Wyatt pulled the envelope out and handed it to her. "Read it," he said.

She touched the script under her fingers, and a pool of tears formed in her eyes.

Abby turned so her back was against the wind. As she pulled out the contents of the envelope, he watched the tickets flutter to the ground. He swooped them up and gripped them while she read the letter. Her eyes devoured the words, which he now knew by heart.

Here are the tickets I promised. Abby will take warming up to the idea. Please let her know it's for me. It's for her own good, and once she's broken out, it will offer me peace of mind. I need to know that she will not sacrifice her dreams to her duties.

God bless you.

Matthias Gray

"I hardly see how my dreams and hang gliding are related. Did you forge this?" But it was her father's writing, and her father always had a reason for anything he did. "My father knows that I couldn't even drive a stick shift. Do you expect me to believe he'd put me behind the controls of a flying machine?"

She knew it was exactly what her father meant. That was the problem.

Wyatt clasped the letter from her. "Your father wanted you to have adventures. He worried that having older parents stole that from you, and he knew he didn't have the time left to offer it to you. He asked, and I considered the idea a privilege."

She handed him the contents. "Maybe I was just meant to be boring. Did you ever think of that? Born that way?"

"Maybe hang gliding is too much—your father said that. He thought we could start slowly. Fishing."

"Fishing? That doesn't sound much more adrenaline-inducing than reading. How about if you fish and I'll bring a book along?"

"Mountain climbing?"

"Fishing would be great," she said. "I assure you, I never missed out on anything. I can't believe Daddy would suggest I jump from space like Felix Baumgartner to right that wrong. It's not even a wrong. It's just the way life is."

"That might be true, but it doesn't address his desire for you to get outside of the box. What kind of man would I be if I didn't honor his last wishes?"

"I like my box, and it really doesn't concern you."

He grimaced. "Except that it does, because we in your father's men's group made him a promise. But all right, fishing it is. I'm picking you up on Saturday morning at ten. We're going to have an adventure."

"My mother—"

"Will be fine for one morning. Your father said so."

"It took you a year. My mother isn't as healthy as she was then. Why now?"

He didn't dare tell her the truth. If she thought he was nuts for hang gliding, she would have found him certifiable if he told her that someday she'd be his wife.

> It is a young man's duty to make the initial overtures toward
> a closer relationship and romance. A young woman cannot be
> too reserved in this respect.
>
> PEARL CHAMBERS, *The Gentlewoman's*
> *Guide to Love and Courtship*

CHAPTER SIX

. . . .

After coffee and the visit beyond the ski lodge with Wyatt, Abby's day at the library was constantly busy. Story time brought in what seemed like every unruly toddler in the state of Vermont. She didn't work in the children's section, but it was an all-hands-on-deck kind of day when the nonreaders ruled the shelves. She closed up with Casey, carefully just exchanging pleasantries now that she knew her words might be parroted back to Wyatt. Not that she had anything to hide.

Rather than fumble with dinner, she stopped by Jake's Restaurant and picked up takeout. Her mom loved the homemade soup and biscuits, while Abby opted for the ribs. She entered her house and put the plastic bag down on the dining hutch—an old library card catalog. When the steps got too difficult for her mother, the dining room table became her sewing room, and the card catalog was labeled with all of her supplies.

Her mother squealed at the sight of the bag. "Jake's and *Dancing with the Stars*," she said. "It doesn't get any better. It's late, so we'll eat out here in the living room."

Abby laughed. "You're like a second grader on rainy-day lunch, when they get to watch a movie inside the classroom."

Her mom offered a weary grin. "I know that when you pick up takeout from Jake's, it usually means that it's been a rough day for you. Tonight we can be a little lazy and watch TV while we eat."

"Okay. Just let me put these in the kitchen." Abby walked through the small combination living/dining room and entered the open kitchen. "What did you do today, Mom?" she called as she put the bag down.

"I've been sewing costumes for the church Christmas pageant. Today I did two sheep and an angel."

Abby walked back toward the dining room to the old farmhouse table and surveyed her mom's work. She felt the silky gossamer angel wings and noted the glistening sequins that outlined them. Two tiny sheep costumes, complete with velvet noses and felt eyes, lay beside them.

"I imagine a few of the kids I had at the library today might be wearing these at Christmas. I definitely can offer some advice on who *not* to put into the angel costume."

"Oh, Abby! All of them are angels and you know it."

She gave a guilty smile. "I do know it. Mom, these costumes are beautiful. I can't believe you still have the patience to do this at your age. I wouldn't have the patience now."

"I had a good day today. I walked quite a bit without the walker and used the sewing machine all day without a crooked stitch. When you don't have your health every day, you have to make the best use of every good moment."

Abby smiled. Her mother did indeed make the most of every moment. Greta Gray was active in mind and soul, but her constant bouts with dizziness made the days unpredictable. The inability to drive made her dependent on others, and Abby watched her mother struggle with the new reality with grace and hope.

"That's wonderful."

"And how was your day, Abby?"

"Story-time day."

Her mother laughed. "You always have a few stories of your own on that day."

"What did you eat today?" Abby asked.

"I warmed the leftover spaghetti from last night. It was wonderful." Her mother was seated in a recliner and prepared to stand by latching onto an electric-blue walker.

"Stay there, Mom. I'll bring the TV tray."

"Oh, I hope those girls are wearing enough clothes tonight."

Abby laughed. The two of them loved the show, but not the dancers' costumes. Her mother always launched into a tirade on modesty.

"Your friend Heather came by this afternoon. She said she tried to see you at the library, but it was a mob house."

"What did she want?"

"She made a pot of tea for us and talked about that book she left with you. *The Gentlewoman's Guide to Love and Courtship.* Doesn't that sound intriguing? And romantic?"

"Romantic?" Abby asked. "I'm not sure that's the word I'd use. Do you remember that old lore about the gold mine on Curtis's family homestead?"

Abby had become an expert on the buried treasure theme from years of people's interest, but before the link to the book, there'd never been any proof that the story was real. Abby was still skeptical . . . but if the mystery could solve Molly's troubles, or even ease them a bit, they had to try.

"Sure," her mother answered. She flicked the television off, cutting short the newscaster's recital of the seemingly endless troubles of the world.

"Heather and the girls think the answer might be in that old book. Maybe Pearl Chambers left clues as to the treasure's whereabouts."

"Well, that certainly sounds up your alley."

Abby stood in the doorway between the rooms. "I have to admit I'm skeptical, but who would have thought the library sale would have been such a success?"

"God never lets a good deed go unpunished, does he?" Her mother grinned in that way she did—as if she knew some deep truth no one else was privy to.

"It would be great if it proved true. To take the burden off Molly financially would lift us all."

"Heather thinks the answers might be coded in that book. I told her how when you were a small girl you could figure out any mystery. You thought you were Nancy Drew. Isn't this exciting, to get a real mystery?"

"If I knew the treasure actually existed, yes." She walked into the kitchen to grab cutlery for dinner. While her mother may use a TV tray, she wasn't about to eat out of Styrofoam.

The woman had standards, and she'd taught Abby that anything done well was worth doing exceptionally. She always said people noticed details like that.

Abby set the TV tray with a chintz place mat and a linen napkin and carried it to her mother.

"You're the one with the research skills, Abby. Heather said that all of Molly's woes would be fixed if they could find that gold ore."

Her mom's face was alight at the possibility. Abby wished it were true, but an orchard of lost maple trees that grew upside down seemed more likely.

"I wish I had your enthusiasm, Mom, but if there were gold, wouldn't it have been found by now?" Abby opened the china cabinet in the dining room, took out a big ceramic bowl, and poured Jake's minestrone into it. She set it on a plate, tore off a piece of French bread, and served her mother. Walking back to the kitchen, she poured water from the electric kettle. She stirred some instant decaf coffee and sweetened it with real cream. She brought the coffee out and set it on the table alongside her mother's chair.

"There could be gold. Where's your imagination, Abby? This doesn't sound like you."

"I think I lost it with one too many readings of Dr. Seuss's *The Foot Book*."

"You need to do this. Heather said if anyone could find some kind of clue in the book, it would be you."

Abby couldn't have stopped herself if she'd wanted to. She'd do whatever she could to make life easier on Molly and her son. She took the book from the coffee table and studied it. The rugged edges were yellowed with age and the brown leather cover was dark at the edges, but otherwise it seemed in remarkable shape for being so old. She ran her fingers over the title and opened up to the first hint for women from another era finding romance. "Who knows, maybe some of these old tricks work." She raised her brows.

"I was looking at it this afternoon. I might have used a few of them to catch your father, but I'll never admit to it."

Abby read the first bit of advice aloud. "'Prudence and virtue will certainly secure the right sort of husband material, but make sure that passion is present.'"

"What's wrong with that?" her mother said. "It's good advice. It doesn't seem dated to me."

"I've got the prudence and virtue; where's the man?"

"One must be patient, I suppose."

Abby sighed, closed the book, and went back to the kitchen. The only man in town interested in her wanted to hurl her off a cliff—okay, in fairness, he wanted her to get tugged into the air. Did that sound prudent or virtuous? She opened the foil container that held the barbecue ribs with broccoli on the side. Rather than grab a plate, she picked up a fork. She joined her mother in the living room and sat on the sofa, which was safely covered in plastic—as it always had been.

Her mother bowed her head and said a prayer over their takeout, and they began to eat.

"Mom, did Dad ever mention Wyatt Tanner to you?" Abby asked, as casually as she could.

"Not that I can remember. Why?"

"He says that they were in that Monday morning men's group at church."

"Maybe he was." Her mom lifted her small shoulders. "It

was a bit like AA in some ways, I guess. The men prayed for each other and shared, but they kept their conversations to themselves."

"AA? Mom! Dad never had a drink in his life."

Her mother chuckled. "I'm only saying it was a private thing. He wanted to protect the men he prayed for and vice versa, so they felt safe." She sipped her soup. "Otherwise, he told me everything."

"Did he ever tell you that he wanted me to hang glide?"

Her mother dropped her soup spoon. "To do what?"

"Hang glide. It's like hanging on a human-sized kite and floating through the air on the wind."

"Is . . . that safe? Because it doesn't sound safe."

"Getting pulled off the ground by an airplane on a human-sized kite? I'm guessing it's safe if it all works like it's supposed to. Not so much if there's a rogue wind or the like. That's the problem with the idea."

"I do know that your father felt that we gave you too sheltered of a life. We tried to take you camping once, but we were so old by then. I remember telling your father, 'I just can't sleep on the ground at my age.' And he agreed. That was the last of our outdoor adventures. You might as well have been raised in the center of New York City for all the outdoor time you spent."

"Mom, you gave me an incredible life. I wouldn't want anybody else as my mother. I never wanted for anything, so this seems like a non-regret."

"But—"

"But if Daddy wanted me to do it, I feel a responsibility toward him."

"Daddy wouldn't have forced you to do anything. I think it's enough that you've even considered it." Her mother smiled. "That Wyatt is a handsome boy . . . but I wonder that your father never mentioned him."

"Well, if Daddy wanted me to do something so wild, he would have told me so himself, not sent a message through Wyatt. After all, Wyatt is the kind of guy Daddy warned me about."

But if she were honest with herself, the idea of spending more time with Wyatt didn't lack appeal. She just hoped for more days like the one at the coffee shop where they enjoyed the gift of gravity together.

"Doesn't he help Molly out with her business? I'll ask around at church and see what I can find out. Opposites attract," Mom said.

"No, forget it. Don't ask anyone. Wyatt was just saying he wanted to train me, starting this Saturday. You know, to be more adventurous, so that Daddy didn't have to worry about me."

"I see no harm in that. If you decide not to jump, you'll at least know you've made the right choice. Without researching it, how would you know?"

Abby's shoulders slumped. Her mother wasn't going to give her the excuse she was looking for to stay cozied up in her safe little world. The truth was, she wanted to be forced out of the safety without the responsibility of the action. Which was hardly fair. After all, adventurers took responsibility for their choices.

As she gazed around the room, with the scraps of fabric strewn about, the antique furniture, and the piles of medications, she realized that she did need a wake-up call. "Mom," she said after clearing the dishes. "I'm going to make a phone call. Do you need anything before I go upstairs?"

"Will you come back for our show?"

"Of course."

"You go right ahead, dear. We'll watch the dancing when you're finished."

She climbed up the thin stairwell to her room, which contained wall-to-wall bookshelves that her father built her.

Abby needed her life to change. She'd avoided the truth of what she longed for so that she could be what everyone else needed her to be. But if she didn't embrace at least a small part of Scarlett or Anne Elliot, she might cease to be Abby altogether. It was time to attach her own oxygen mask— to take care of herself first so she could better help those around her.

She clasped her eyes shut and cupped her hands in prayer and then made her phone call. She punched the numbers into her cell phone while her heart pounded in her throat as she waited for an answer.

"Hello." Wyatt's deep voice resonated so that she felt the vibration.

"Wyatt, it's Abby Gray."

"Abby, is everything all right?"

She liked the sound of concern in his voice. "I've been thinking . . ." Her voice trailed off.

Wyatt exhaled. "Do you want me to come over?"

"No," she answered, betraying her true desires. "On Saturday. I want to cancel the fishing. I want to go hang gliding. I can go with you, right? I don't have to do it by myself."

"Of course. I won't let anything happen to you, I promise. Your father would be so proud of you. Not that he isn't already."

"Thanks. So you'll make the arrangements?"

"I will. I'll call Molly and ask to borrow the tandem glider."

"Oh—"

"Don't worry, Abby, I won't tell her who it's for, if that's what you're worried about."

She loved how he didn't ask her if she was certain. Nor did he question her motives. He simply did as she asked, and she felt empowered. Besides, the sooner the temptation of Wyatt Tanner and his suntanned biceps were off her radar, the more able she'd be to find contentment in the life God handed her.

Matters of the heart can consume the mind. Don't neglect friendships in the midst of courtship.

PEARL CHAMBERS, *The Gentlewoman's Guide to Love and Courtship*

CHAPTER SEVEN

. . . .

*F*riday morning Abby dressed in her new outfit and slipped into the low heels that her friends had bought her.

With the new dress that fit her curves, but bloused out so that she didn't feel self-conscious, she noticed that her librarian hair needed more attention. So she pulled it down from its bun and straightened it. When she did that, her lips looked naked, so she applied a little lipstick. When she did that, she seemed pale, so she added the slightest dab of blush. By the time she left the bathroom, she looked like a completely different person. Her hair's blond streaks showed up more readily when she left her golden hair down.

Her mother's expression stiffened at the sight of her. "My, my. Is that the outfit your friends bought you?"

"Don't you like it?"

"It's lovely. It looks very expensive."

"It was." She brushed her waist. "It's from that fancy boutique on Main Street. I think that Heather paid for it all. Now that she's found love, she's convinced that all of us need to up our game to find romance in Smitten."

"There can't be many single men at the library in the middle of the afternoon. Maybe you should wait to wear that on Sunday."

"I'm wearing it for myself, Mom, because it was a gift from my friends and because it makes me feel good," she said gently. "Not because I'm trying to snag a man."

"Well, all right. If you say so."

"It's my book club tonight, so Caroline is bringing you dinner. She said she'd come by the library first to pick up a movie. I'll make sure it's something you like. "

"Something with Sinatra, maybe?" her mother asked.

"I'll see what I can find. I'm going to stop by Molly's this morning before I go to work. I found something in the book last night that made me wonder if maybe the treasure could be real."

Her mother clapped her hands together. "Really?"

"Probably not, but what kind of friend would I be if I didn't at least check?"

She kissed her mother good-bye on the cheek and drove the short distance to Molly's house.

Abby knocked on Molly's door, but there was no answer. She was probably out with Noah running errands. Abby reached into the planter and pulled out the spare key and let herself into the old farmhouse.

"What do you think you're doing?" a voice echoed.

She screamed and turned to see Heather. "What are you doing here? You nearly sent me out of my skin!"

"I saw you pull up. Thought it might be fun to surprise you." Heather wore coveralls and was clearly there to do some kind of gardening. "Just wanted to get to some of the weeding here. Molly has enough to do."

"Well, you surprised me, all right."

Heather put down her pruning sheers on the front porch and followed Abby inside. "Look at you in your dress. Don't you look gorgeous."

Abby twirled. "I do feel gorgeous. Thank you, Heather. What you girls did for me was really nice. I'm sorry I was a grump about it. I've been thinking . . . maybe my growing up adopted has made me kind of self-conscious about being in debt to people."

"But it's not debt if it's a gift. And we're your friends. We love you. We wanted to do that for you."

"I think the idea is growing on me. But anyway, thanks."

"Is the idea of Wyatt Tanner growing on you?"

She felt heat rise in her cheeks. "Wyatt?"

"Abby, there's nothing wrong with being human. Wyatt is a respectable, gorgeous, single man. What is wrong with admitting maybe you dressed up for him?"

Abby walked through to the dining room. "I didn't. I'm only trying to feel better about myself, like I'm worthy of a pretty dress like this."

"And a man like Wyatt," Heather said.

"You're impossible."

"What did you find out from the book?"

"Well, a couple of things, actually. First off, gold is mentioned in quite a few places. I think I may have found a pattern. Look here." She opened the book to scraps of paper where

Pearl marked the words of interest. "'Who can find a virtuous woman? For her price is far above gold.' Pearl replaced the word *rubies* with *gold*."

"I don't understand."

"Heather, in Proverbs, the actual text reads 'A wife of noble character is worth more than rubies'—not gold. I can't imagine she'd make a mistake like that. It has to be intentional. Pearl was a woman who knew her Scripture."

"Oh, good catch. Well, she might have just thought gold was worth more. Who knows, maybe back in the day it was."

"That's what I thought too, but then I saw that she flagged something about gold 'saved for the generations.' Maybe the treasure is no longer in the cave. Could she have mined it already and then hidden it?"

Heather looked wary. "Surely one woman couldn't do that."

"Maybe not, but look at this passage that's highlighted. It says a 'golden cord of three' is not easily broken."

"And?"

"In Proverbs it's just a 'strand of three,' not a *golden* strand. She's deliberately misquoting these for some reason."

"This is exciting! You think the treasure is real now, too, don't you?"

"I'm not sure," Abby said. "But yesterday at the library I looked up the old Chambers homestead records to see exactly where the property lines were back when Pearl wrote this book. Turns out Molly's barn wasn't on the property until just a few months before Pearl's death."

"So?"

"So what if the barn was built as some kind of hiding spot? If Pearl mined the gold somehow."

"Abby, we have to check this out."

"I agree. Can we go out back there now, before Molly gets back?"

"You're going to wear your new dress into that barn?"

"I hadn't thought of that. But we don't have time for me to change. I promise not to dig or anything. We'll just look around a bit."

The barn smelled musty and was filled to the rafters with sports equipment, old wood, and wet hay, and sawdust was everywhere. Abby kicked some into her shoe and shook it out.

"Abby, you're ruining your new shoes!"

"Look, Heather!" In the corner of the barn lay a wooden box. Abby kneeled down gingerly to inspect it. "It's a sluice box."

"What?"

"It's a way that Pearl might have mined the gold by herself. She could have had help with the ore and mined it in this sluice box."

"Why would they have kept the mineral rights on the property, then?"

Abby looked up at Heather. "Maybe she didn't get it all. It would have been hard rock mining. If Pearl did it by herself or with a few helpers, she wouldn't have been able to get all the ore. She would have needed dynamite."

"I hate to think of Molly struggling so much financially when Pearl might have left her with everything she needs. Why wouldn't she make it obvious?"

"This was a rough town back in the day. A logging town. A prudent woman like Pearl would have kept it very quiet." She stood and heard a tear.

"Abby, your dress!"

Abby gasped and looked down at her silky skirt, which was in two shredded ribbons, one for each knee. Part of her brand-new skirt was still on the nail that stuck out from the barn wall. "What have I done?"

"Maybe solved part of a mystery," Heather said. "But you've definitely proven your point. You might require some tougher gear. I still don't condone orthopedic shoes, but I'm definitely going to go with rayon over silk."

"I'm sorry, Heather. But I really want to be Anne Elliot, not Scarlett O'Hara."

"You tried to tell us." Heather gave her a hug. "Find Molly's gold and you can be both. Which would Wyatt prefer?"

"It wouldn't concern me regardless," Abby said and fluttered her eyelashes coquettishly. She didn't risk saying anything more. The fact that she'd be flying with the likes of Wyatt Tanner in the morning would lead her friends to believe she had a shot at romance in Smitten. Adventure, not romance, was the most she would hope for.

*The world is a library and those who do not seek adventure,
do not read but a single page.*

PEARL CHAMBERS, *The Gentlewoman's
Guide to Love and Courtship*

CHAPTER EIGHT

. . . .

*A*bby skipped her morning coffee since her heart was already pounding relentlessly at the thought of flying over Smitten without so much as an engine. She drove her own car to the field; just in case she changed her mind, she didn't want to force Wyatt to cancel his plans.

Wyatt called out a greeting and jogged toward her dressed in green khakis and hiking sandals. Even though she felt a little queasy, his outdoorsy appearance aroused her appetite.

"Ready to go up?" he asked.

"Don't I need lessons first?" she asked weakly. This was all happening too fast for her liking. "I thought I'd have time to get used to the idea a bit. To feel the air from a casual three or four feet from the ground."

"Nope."

"We're not going on the practice hill over there?" She pointed to the wide grassy field where several people were gathered around a man she assumed was a teacher.

"Abby, I'll be doing the flying today. You're the passenger along for the ride. You just have to enjoy yourself. "

She bit down on her lip as she watched a glider high in the sky with a single person hanging precariously, like the body of a butterfly.

She grasped Wyatt by his wrist and shook her head. "I don't think I can do this."

His expression softened, and she marveled at just how handsome he looked. "You don't have to do this," he told her.

"The tickets are paid for. I don't want them to go to waste."

He lifted her chin so that she was forced to look into his brown velvet eyes that exuded a warmth she would have sworn she felt inside. "You're so valuable to me, Abby. I wouldn't take you up unless I knew that I could keep you safe."

He really did make her feel safe—as though she could trust someone else to be in charge for a change. Her heart seemed to slow a bit. She felt a little lighter, happier.

"Maybe . . ."

"Abby, really. You don't have to. The last thing I want is for you to resent me because you felt coerced into flying when you weren't ready."

"What happens first?"

"I'll strap you into that little sleeping-bag-looking casing."

"Like a sausage?"

"Like a sausage. I'll get into the one that hangs over you."

"I'm going to be on the bottom? As in, I'm the first to hit the ground?"

"We're not going to hit the ground, Abby. When we land,

we'll both put our legs vertical and we'll start to take a few steps. If you feel weak, pull your legs up and I'll do the work, but it doesn't hurt to land. I'll set us down very easily."

She nodded. "All right, let's go. Before I change my mind."

In the center of the long grassy valley that lined the river stood several hang gliders and their operators. Wyatt took her hand and led her toward the group, then introduced her to three men and one woman. She couldn't remember any one of their names. She was far too nervous at the sight of the oversized kite.

Wyatt unzipped the glider and showed her the aluminum construction underneath the sail. He explained which bar she would hold on to, how she would be strapped into the contraption, and what would happen when the "tug" or the small, light plane pulled them into the wild blue yonder.

"I just want to go up before I have time to chicken out."

The woman in the group, who stood beside a pink-and-turquoise hang glider, told her not to worry. "Last week Wyatt took up a tourist who was here for her hundredth birthday," she said.

"Abby, are you paying attention?" Wyatt asked.

"Oh, sorry. What was that?"

"Your feet will be hanging out of the sleeve. When we land, we'll be in an upright position. You may have to take a few steps, but most likely we'll land upright and you'll be on the ground as easily as we took off. You'll want to keep the pole where I position it so that it doesn't strike you as we land."

Her pragmatic side kicked in. Was her life insurance

premium paid? Who would call her mom if she ended up in the hospital with a broken neck? "No one even knows where I am, Wyatt. Maybe I should have told someone."

Wyatt rubbed her shoulder gently and pointed to her car. There stood Lia, Molly, and Heather, all spectating from the side of the road. Lia waved.

"What are they doing here?" Abby demanded.

"Apparently Casey told Molly why I was borrowing the tandem hang glider today."

"I never told Casey what I was up to."

Wyatt shrugged. "Neither did I, but I think it's great that your friends are here. For once, Casey's eavesdropping seemed to serve a purpose."

"But who would have told her?"

"I'd never underestimate Casey's ability to gain information. I think she may actually work for the KGB."

Abby looked again toward her best friends, shocked that they weren't running to talk her out of the action. After all, they simply thought she needed a new outfit. She felt slightly miffed that no one was running up to tell her not to do it.

"Don't we have to get going?" Her voice started to get shaky.

"We can let the next people go ahead of us if you're not ready."

"Really?"

"It's your day, Abby. I was planning on fishing today." He chuckled.

Abby couldn't help herself; she wrapped her arms around him and squeezed tight. She felt so natural in his arms that rather than pull away, she rested her ear against his chest and heard the steady beat of his heart, so soothing against the blustery wind. "Thank you," she whispered.

Still holding her tight, Wyatt whispered, "You are so welcome." He spoke into his headset. "Take the next team up first. We'll go in five." The low vibration of his vocal cords under her ear connected him to her in a way she'd never experienced before. She'd purposely worn her hair down, and his hand smoothed the back of her neck. She shivered at his soft touch. The shelter he provided against the wind, against her fears, made her believe that she could trust him.

His eyes spoke to her, and her fears melted away like clouds giving way to the sunshine. She'd judged Wyatt harshly, based on a series of opinions she'd formed about "men like him," but Wyatt himself had been steadfast. His adrenaline-seeking hobbies didn't mean he wasn't at work when he said he'd be, nor did he miss church. For now, she had every reason to trust him. She supposed the fact that he held her life in his hands was reason enough.

"Ready?" he asked.

She nodded and pulled out of his embrace, wary.

"Step inside the harness." He handed her a nylon casing that she slipped into like a loose body suit. It went just below her hips.

"Is this long enough?"

"It's a training harness. Your legs will be mostly free for when we land. All these ropes on the back will be attached to a caribiner, and you'll hang horizontally in the air. You're not actually hanging on the pole. How's your helmet fit?"

She nodded. In the distance her friends all waved at her

with their arms high in the air, offering encouragement. She swallowed hard, said a quick prayer, and readied herself for the biggest adventure of her life.

After Wyatt strapped her into the hang glider, he began to strap himself in, and she felt his presence hovering just above her. "Now, before we reach our cruising altitude, there may be a little turbulence. Just expect that, and I'll get you through it as soon as possible."

She turned behind her and smiled. "I know you will."

"You see that plane?" one of the men said beside them. "That's your tug. We're going to wheel you out now."

Another man came to her left, and the woman attached something to the plane in front of them. As the man to her left cranked his arm to the side, they began to gain speed. In no time at all they were airborne.

The blustery wind roared in her ears, and her entire body bounced, but Abby had no fear. All she could see was the beauty before her. Lush green valley beneath her, the snaking river alongside them, striking mountains to their left. She felt peaceful and yet so alive. Every molecule in her body seemed to hum. Their bodies worked together in perfect harmony. Soaring above her beloved Vermont felt so natural. As the glider dipped and turned, she was filled with joyous adrenaline. She was flying. And she never wanted it to end. She was free of life's encumbrances and worries; only God's majesty stretched out before her. The swaying green grass danced beneath her, a lone puffy cloud waltzed past them, and she felt only pity for the poor souls in cars on the highway below.

Wyatt's chin rested on her shoulder, and she smiled in her contentment. She'd remember this moment forever.

Wrapped securely in the nylon sleeve with Wyatt protecting her so that all she had to do was float toward the horizon on her dreamlike journey. She didn't want the magic to end.

Too soon, it was over. She'd become so awestruck that as they lowered their elevation, she never even had time to fear their landing. The ground rose up gently to meet them, and at the first touch they synchronized their steps perfectly as if set down by angels' wings.

She yanked her helmet off and let the wind rush through her hair. Every cell in her body felt fully alive. Wyatt unclipped her, and she climbed out of her harness. Before he could remove his own, she pummeled him with a bear hug. "Wyatt, I did it!"

"You did!"

"I loved it! I love—" She stopped herself from saying what she wanted to say, what too much excitement probably led her to feel.

Wyatt smiled coolly, removed his own helmet, and stepped close to wrap her up into his arms. She lifted her mouth toward him and waited, but at the sound of her friends wailing their excitement, he moved away. She didn't want to lose the moment.

"You were going to kiss me."

He peered over her shoulder. "Your friends . . . " He pointed.

Abby turned and lowered her brow. Her friends turned around as if they understood her meaning perfectly. "They'll wait."

He raised his gaze to her friends and back to her, and then Wyatt planted his lips on hers.

His kiss was firm. His arms enveloped her waist and brought her closer to him. It was as if a thousand bees buzzed within her, and she surmised heaven must be like Wyatt's kiss. She pulled away and he pursued her, his thick, rough fingers clasping her jaw. "Kiss me, Abby. I've longed for you."

His words broke the spell. Wyatt's words were not something that could be easily controlled. They were not safe. She felt perilously close to losing herself to desire. Imagine if they'd been alone.

"I have to go." With every ounce of strength, she left the cozy warmth of his arms and the fire of his kisses, and extricated herself from his grasp. She ran toward her friends.

As she got closer, she saw that a fourth woman had joined them—Casey. Abby felt betrayed. It was in the woman's nature to wiggle her way into every situation and ruin what joy could be found.

"Casey," she said. "What are you doing here?"

Casey stared past her toward Wyatt. Her spindly arms were crossed and her gray eyes narrowed. She wore tight jeans, cuffed at the calves, that left very little to the imagination. Her silky pink shirt rippled in the wind and passed Abby like a rogue breeze.

The green tinge of jealousy rose within Abby.

"You took her hang gliding?" Casey shook her head. "You lied to me. I helped you so that you could tell her about the letter. Did you lie to her too? Did you say that her father gave you the letter?"

Wyatt said nothing, and Abby's stomach sank like a stone in Smitten Lake. She searched Wyatt's expression for some form of denial and the reassurance he'd given her in the air, but he offered none. The warm air turned brisk.

"Is that what he told you?" Casey turned toward her. "That your father left him that letter?"

Wyatt's expression fell, and there was no mistaking the truth.

"The letter didn't come from my father?" Abby asked.

"Yes, it did. Let me explain." Wyatt clenched his jaw. "Casey, I told you about the letter in confidence!"

"I trusted you." Abby's voice sounded hoarse. "It was my father's handwriting," she said, as much to convince herself as Casey.

Heather, Molly, and Lia surrounded her. Heather glared at Casey. "Do you realize that everywhere you go you start something? You're supposed to be Abby's friend!"

"I work with Abby. She's made it perfectly clear that our relationship is strictly professional."

"So what are you doing here?" Heather probed. "This doesn't look like the library."

Casey flipped her long, dark hair and raised her chin. "I'm only trying to protect Abby from the likes of Wyatt."

"That's sweet of you, but Abby can handle herself," Heather said.

"Wyatt," Molly said. "Maybe it's better that you go."

"Where did that letter come from?" Abby implored.

"It's your father's letter, I promise you," Wyatt said.

"That isn't what she asked," Casey said. "Take it from me, Abby. Wyatt says what Wyatt needs to say to get close to women. He did it to me, and he'll do it to you. It's what rakes do. It's in their nature."

"You have to tell her to listen to me," Wyatt said to Abby's friends. "I need the chance to explain. Tell her. Abby, please."

Steps took her closer to the car, but Abby had no recollection of putting one foot in front of the other. Somehow the car just got closer.

"How could he lie to me?" She'd never flown so high nor crashed so low in the span of a few minutes. "This is what happens when girls like me take chances."

Tears filled Lia's eyes. "Abby, that's not all you're here for. God doesn't see you as some kind of sacrifice. You have to know that. I'm sure Wyatt has a good excuse. You just need to be ready to hear it."

"It doesn't really matter, does it? He just wanted to help me find my inner strength. A little adventure. It was one bad date. That's all. Just a bad date. Everyone has them." She tried to reason with herself, but her feelings went deeper—they stuck into the cavern of her heart. Wyatt, in a short time but with close proximity, had embedded himself there like the gold in Molly's ore.

"I wanted to try something new and adventurous. I guess I got what I wanted. I learned that maybe I'm not ready to trust an adventure as big as love." Abby pressed her palm to her heart, shocked at the physical sting that stirred within her.

Prudence and virtue will certainly secure the right sort of husband material, but one must make sure that passion is present.

PEARL CHAMBERS, *The Gentlewoman's Guide to Love and Courtship*

CHAPTER NINE

. . . .

*A*bby awoke groggily. She had cried herself to sleep, and her head pounded. Maybe she didn't have an ounce of Anne Elliot's sense of adventure in her. Perhaps she was only *Sense and Sensibility*'s Marianne, full of romantic idealism without the practicality she needed.

Wyatt Tanner had trusted Casey, and that was immediate cause for concern . . . for sensibility.

She squinted against the light as Lia lifted the shades. "Are you awake, Abby?"

She felt her red, puffy eyes and sniffed the fresh scent of coffee.

"What time is it? Is my mother up?" She bolted upright.

"She's having coffee with Casey now."

"Casey? What's she doing here?" Abby popped up and began to dress. "What does she want from me, Lia?"

"I think she wants to *be* you, Abby. You're very confortable in your own skin, and I think that is something very foreign to Casey. She's always trying to make others like her."

"Maybe if she stopped gossiping . . ." Abby felt guilty at once for her nasty response. "I'm sorry, but I feel like whenever Casey is involved in something, trouble is sure to follow."

"In this case, you'd be right."

"What do you mean?"

"After you left yesterday, I asked Casey how she knew about the letter from your father."

"If it even *was* from my father."

"It was."

Abby leaned toward Lia, anxious to hear that Wyatt may have been telling the truth. "How do you know that?"

"I told you, I confronted Casey."

"You confronted someone? That doesn't sound like you, Lia."

Lia combed her fingers through her hair. "Mess with one of my friends, and you get what you get."

The two of them laughed.

"You're a regular Dirty Harry."

"What Casey said just didn't sound like Wyatt, Abby. He's a good guy. And think about what happened. Casey creates trouble wherever she goes, so I simply had to confront her. Turns out Casey's father was in your dad's men's group too. Along with Wyatt."

A mixture of elation and dread pulsed through Abby's body. "So was the letter really from my father? Wyatt didn't lie?" Abby wanted more than anything to hear that Wyatt had been telling the truth. She slipped on a pair of yoga pants underneath her robe. "I was afraid I just believed him because I wanted to be around him."

"No one would blame you. It's obvious he's sweet on you, and he's not hard on the eyes. But why don't you get dressed and come talk to Casey? It's time she answered for her actions."

Abby nodded and smiled, still stunned to hear the unlikely threat from her friend. Lia was usually all sunshine and light, and her devotion meant a lot.

While Abby dressed, Lia buzzed about her room, picking up the things Abby had thrown off in her fit of emotion the day before. Her heart swelled with how much she loved her friends, how much she could depend on them . . . no matter what Casey had to say to her.

When Abby came down the stairway, Casey rose and set her coffee cup on a coaster. She swallowed visibly. "Abby."

"Good morning, Casey. What brings you out so early?"

"Early? Abby, it's nine thirty. I've already been to early service. I guess you're going to the later service."

"Right! Church." She looked down at her yoga pants and fuzzy slippers. "I guess I am."

"From what Lia tells me, I owe you an apology." Casey rolled her eyes and smirked as if she didn't plan to give any kind of apology at all.

"If you're sweet on Wyatt Turner, I had no idea. I only wanted to do as my father wished of me," Abby said.

"*I* gave Wyatt that letter."

"What?" Abby searched her mind to try and make sense out of it. "Did you write it?"

"It was a misunderstanding."

The doorbell rang. "Excuse me a minute. Grand Central Station this morning."

"We haven't seen this much excitement since the day of Matthias's funeral," her mother said matter-of-factly.

"Mother!"

"Well, we haven't."

Abby opened the door to a bushel of red roses so big that only legs could be seen beneath the deliverer. The familiar paper from the Red Barn greenhouse made her smile. "Delivery for Abby Gray."

"That's me. Did Molly Moore send me these?"

"Would you like me to set them somewhere? It's two dozen. Pretty heavy."

"Set them over there on the table." She patted her yoga pants to see if she could find some sort of tip, but she had nothing— not even pockets.

"Tip has already been taken care of, ma'am." The deliveryman tipped his hat, a small black bowler. "I'll just need your signature. Sorry to disturb you so early, but the sender was adamant they reach you before you were out for church this morning."

"No, that's quite all right. Who could be upset about being awakened by two dozen roses?"

"As I was saying—" Casey continued.

Abby tried to sneak a look at the card without being rude.

"Who are the roses from?" Lia asked.

"I don't know. Probably Molly, for my figuring out that the gold on her property was most likely mined already."

"Molly doesn't have time to watch *Gone with the Wind* all the way through. Surely she didn't send them. Open the card!"

Abby obeyed.

Dear Abby,

Forgive me. I would never do anything to hurt you. Please agree to meet with me one more time and hear me out. I don't deserve it, but I ask you in grace.

Ever hopeful and in love,

Wyatt

Abby slipped the card into the waistband of her yoga pants, unwilling to share that they were from Wyatt with Casey standing before her. She didn't want to lie—so she simply shrugged.

Casey glared at her. "Life goes along swimmingly for you, doesn't it, Abby? You're the librarian everyone wants to have wait on them. You're the woman Wyatt Tanner wants to take up in the sky. You're the girl who gets first dibs on all the movies at the library—"

"So I can give them to my friend Molly! Casey, I live with my mother, and Wyatt was doing a favor for my father. You treat me abominably, and I've always wondered what I'd done to you."

Lia rubbed the back of her neck, obviously nervous over the confrontation taking place.

"The roses are from Wyatt," Casey said. "Just say so already."

"Yes, they're from Wyatt. He's apologizing for yesterday."

"The letter is from your father," Casey said. "I gave it to Wyatt. I figured if he wanted to take you on one of his adventures, you two would see how incompatible you are and that would be the end of it."

"How would you get a letter from my father?" Abby asked.

"My father was in your dad's men's group too. When your father knew his health was taking a turn for the worse, he told the men that he was worried about you, that they'd sheltered you too much. He didn't want you to live like he did and never leave Smitten. He wanted you to see more than just the inside of this house." Casey looked toward her mother. "No offense, Mrs. Gray."

"None taken," Abby's mother answered with brows raised. "Though I rather like the inside of this home."

"Casey, get on with it," Abby said angrily. "How did you get this letter?"

"My father was supposed to deliver it, but he never did because he thought that maybe your father wasn't thinking right. 'Imagine,' he said, 'sending your only child up in the air on a virtual kite.' I saw it as my chance to show Wyatt how wrong you were for him." Casey dropped her head in her hands.

It was the first time, Abby thought, she might be truly regretful of her actions.

"I accused him of lying," Abby said with a sick feeling in her stomach. "When he was telling me the truth."

Casey nodded. "I'm so sorry, Abby. I mean, truly I am. Wyatt was never interested in me, and I had no right—"

Abby went toward her fellow librarian and hugged her. "The important thing is you did the right thing when it mattered. You don't know how much that means to me."

Butterflies took flight in her stomach like a thousand hang gliders. She never would have taken the leap without her father's letter. Without Wyatt's encouragement and his physical presence. With absolute clarity, she knew she wanted him by her side. Always.

She kissed her mother's cheek and then Lia's. "Thank you, Lia. Mom, I have to run out—"

"Abby, darling, you're not fully dressed."

Abby scampered back up the stairs two at a time, like an overeager puppy. She selected her most Scarlett-like dress—a red-and-white polka dot number that was a hand-me-down from Lia—and slipped into her new shoes. She brushed her face with powder, slopped some lip gloss on, and jogged down the stairs. "I'll be back!"

She ran the three blocks to church, stopping every so often to slide her shoes back on until she came to the courtyard, where the entire congregation milled about. She said hello absently to anyone who addressed her until she spotted Wyatt talking to one of the deacons.

"Wyatt?"

He tapped the man's arm twice and came to her side. "Abby! Your father didn't give me that letter."

"I know."

"He didn't give me his blessing to court you either."

"It doesn't matter. "

"Do you think he would have allowed me to court you?"

"I'm twenty-seven, Wyatt. It's up to me who I allow to court me."

"And will you?"

"Yes!"

"Even though you think I'm dangerous?"

"I think you're dangerous in a good way. More importantly, I trust you."

"So that means I only have to convince your mother to trust me."

"I think we can arrange that. Maybe bring her a few tubs of Jake's soup, and you'll have her heart."

"But will I have yours?" He leaned into her and pressed a kiss upon her cheek.

Abby grasped his jawline between her palms and pulled his mouth toward hers. "You already do, Wyatt."

A New Chapter

Diann Hunt

A man doesn't always know what he wants. It's up to the gentlewoman to show him.

PEARL CHAMBERS, *The Gentlewoman's Guide to Love and Courtship*

CHAPTER ONE

. . . .

*O*w." Elliana Burton flipped her auburn hair behind her shoulder and cupped her hand against her cheek.

"What is it, Lia?" her mom asked, carving more turkey on the dining room table.

"The apple walnut salad," she said as though a marble were loose in her mouth. "There was a piece of walnut shell. I think my filling came out." She discreetly eyed the silver filling in her napkin.

Sympathetic groans rippled appropriately around the table. If anyone knew the value of teeth, it was their friends from the Smitten Assisted Living Center.

"You'd better get that taken care of immediately." Mrs. Hobson pointed a gnarled finger at her. "You don't want to end up like me." She pulled down her dentures to reveal her plight.

Lia walked over and settled on the sofa. Her mom abandoned the turkey and grabbed the phone.

"Dr. Sam won't come in on Thanksgiving," Lia said.

"Yes, he will. It's an emergency. Besides, I changed Sam
Oliver's diapers. He owes me." Mom punched in the numbers.

Lia moaned. "What a bummer. Not only do I have to
go to the dentist, but I have to miss turkey and gravy, dressing, mashed potatoes, and rolls. This is awful." She leaned
her head back against the sofa and threw her arm over her
eyes. She could still smell the peach lotion she'd put on after
her shower. The lotion her dad had bought her every year at
Christmas until he died two years ago. She still bought it as a
reminder of him.

Her mother clicked off the phone. "He'll meet you at his
office in half an hour."

"That doesn't give him time to eat."

Mom shrugged. "He didn't seem to mind." She shoved
herself off the sofa and made her way back to the table, shoes
clacking against the hardwood. "You know Sam; he's always
willing to help friends."

"He'll give me that lecture about not coming in on a
regular basis." Lia got up and headed for her bedroom to get
her handbag—and her dog-eared copy of *Anne of Green Gables*.
One last-minute glance in the mirror and she tucked a strand
of baby's breath at the side of her hair.

"Rightfully, he should," Mom whispered to her guests.
"She has white-coat syndrome."

"I heard that," Lia called as she walked out the door.

The noonday sun hung suspended just over Sugarcreek
Mountain, bringing a zest of color to the bare trees and

brown lawns of winter. Even the frigid cold couldn't deter her love for the town of Smitten. Cozy shops and bungalows nestled at the foothills of the mountain. People who had time for each other. Front porch people, Lia called them. Everyone had time for a chat.

As she pulled into the dental practice, she noticed that Sam had a new silver truck. She looked at her little VW Bug—yellow with daisies painted on the side doors. Teaching might not afford the fanciest of cars, but she was quite happy with hers.

Grabbing her handbag and book, she got out of the car and walked up the entrance to the door. She shoved her remote into her bag, thinking how nice it was to live in a town where they didn't have to worry about locking their cars.

The air was crisp, but none of the threatened snow yet. She straightened her navy coat and adjusted her red scarf. After taking a deep breath, she pushed the door open. There was no receptionist to greet her, so she called out tentatively, "Hello?"

"Come on back. I'm just getting things ready."

Lia rubbed her sweaty palms together and tried to keep the room from spinning. If her kindergarten kids could go to a dentist, she certainly should be able to. She would get a free toothbrush, after all. But those smells, medicinal-type smells, needles, chairs that recline so you can't get up, bright lights and a mirror. Like she wanted to see that?

And don't even get her started on having someone's hand in her mouth.

When she reached the room, she saw the back of Sam's white coat as he gathered together the instruments he needed, instruments that made her stomach flip-flop. The room was quiet, since it was Thanksgiving Day, but the sterile atmosphere still made her nervous. Something about latex gloves brought on thoughts of dark movies with murder and blood and autopsies.

Her heartbeat kicked up several notches.

"Go ahead and have a seat," he said.

She swallowed hard. It occurred to her they were alone. If he hurt her, who would know? Her knuckles gripped the armrests. What if he resented the fact that she had missed her teeth cleanings for the last three years? Now was the time he could make her pay . . .

She took two calming breaths and said, "I'm really so sorry to bother you on Thanksgiving Day. I bit down on a walnut that, unfortunately, had part of the shell still attached to it."

"Don't worry about it. We'll get you fixed right up." He grabbed an instrument. "I normally have an assistant help me, but since it's Thanksgiving, I couldn't get in touch with anyone." He turned around and flashed a warm smile.

Lia's mouth involuntarily dropped to her chest.

Joey Oliver blinked. "Elliana, I didn't realize . . . My brother didn't say . . . Well, how are you?"

Lia finally clamped her mouth shut and swallowed hard. Then she laughed. Her heart pounded, but not because she was seated in a dentist's chair—because of Joey Oliver. The man she had given her heart to in grade school and never gotten it back.

If only he knew.

"Boy, it's good to see you. How long has it been?"

Forever.

"Fifteen years? I'll bet you're married with ten kids by now." He kept smiling. "I remember when I used to pull your hair and call you carrottop."

That's when she and Anne of Green Gables had established a lasting bond.

"I see you still read it," he said, pointing to her book.

"Yep. I admit I have white-coat syndrome. The book calms me down."

"No worries here. I'll be gentle."

Something about the way he said that made her stomach leap.

"Listen, how about I get you fixed up here and then we go for coffee and catch up?"

He must have given her a dose of something. She was going to coffee with Joey Oliver? After all this time? If she was dreaming, she didn't want to wake up.

☙

Mountain Perks was closed for Thanksgiving Day, as was everything else. Joey pulled his car in front of it, got out, and walked over to Lia's VW.

"Looks like we're out of luck for today. And my schedule is crazy this week. Maybe next week we could get together for coffee and talk about old times?"

Then she remembered. "I have a teachers' conference next week. I'll be gone to Morristown."

"Well, I'll just have to call you. But we'll do this thing." He shot her another grin over his shoulder as he walked back to his car.

Lia watched him drive off and tried to digest all that had happened. Joey Oliver was back in town. Unattached, evidently, or he wouldn't have been planning coffee with her. Would he? Reality set in. He still thought of her as a good friend from back in the day. Was that all she'd ever be to him?

Or could it be that the meaning of her name, *My God has answered me*, was finally happening?

Joey walked into his brother's house and threw his leather coat across the sofa. "Hey, you didn't tell me the patient was Elliana Burton. That was a nice surprise."

Sam shared a glance with his wife, Suzie, flipped the switch on the remote, and shrugged. "Oh, that's right. You two were best buds when you were little."

"We were, though she'd get awful mad at me when I pulled her pigtails." Joey laughed, grabbed a stick of celery, then sagged onto the sofa.

Sam took a bite of pumpkin pie. "She's a nice gal."

"Married?"

Suzie settled on the side of the chair beside her husband. "Nope. Engaged once, but called it off."

"Really?"

Sam and Suzie exchanged another glance.

"Now, don't you two get any ideas. Elliana is just a friend. A very good friend. We have a history." He winked. "Besides, I'm not ready for another relationship."

"Did you tell her about—" Before Suzie could finish her question, Grace, Joey's five-year-old, stepped into the living room, blond pigtails dangling down her shoulders, blue eyes filled with tears.

I can't find my baby. Her hands, dimpled and petite, awkwardly signed the words. Her mouth puckered, eyebrows drooped. She climbed into Joey's lap.

"I'm sure she's around here somewhere." Joey popped the last bite into his mouth and signed back. He pulled Grace into his arms, smoothed back her bangs, and gave her a kiss on the forehead. He looked up at Suzie. "To answer your question, we really didn't get that far. I just told her I joined Sam's practice and was back in town. She paid her bill and that was that." He decided to keep the promise of a coffee date to himself.

Grace snuggled into her daddy's arms, and her eyelids grew heavy.

"Looks like somebody's ready for a nap," Sam said.

Joey smiled and lovingly stroked the little girl's hair. "I know what you two are thinking."

"What do you mean?" Sam asked.

"You know what I mean. You think I shouldn't encourage her signing."

"Look, Joey, she's your daughter. I'm sure you're doing what you think is right," Sam said.

"I told you. The counselor said it was Grace's way of holding on to her mom. If she lets that go, she's afraid she'll forget."

"She's five years old, Joey. She has no hearing problems. It's strange for her to communicate this way when she's perfectly capable of talking and hearing."

Joey looked away. "That's just it. She's tuned others out for so long, I don't know what she really is capable of hearing anymore."

"You need to get her back to a counselor. Set her up with someone in town, or go to Burlington or Morristown."

"They told me she'd come out of it when she was ready. I can wait till then. She doesn't need more therapy to confuse her." Joey stood from the sofa with Grace cradled in his arms and carried her into her room, glad for the excuse to escape. Once he'd laid Grace down and placed the covers over her, he asked Suzie if he could get some lunch.

Suzie jumped up. "Oh, sure! I saved your plate, and there are plenty of leftovers. Want me to help?"

"No need, Suzie. I know where everything is." He headed for the kitchen, then turned back around. "Listen, I want you and Sam to know how much I appreciate you letting us stay here for a few weeks until I can find something for Grace and me."

Suzie waved her hand. "You know you can stay as long as you like. We love having a little girl around the house. Stay till after your house is built, if you like."

Joey was already shaking his head. "No. We won't intrude on your privacy. Plus, I think Grace and I need some time to settle into the new town and all that."

He pulled his covered plate from the fridge and heated it in the microwave. He couldn't quite get past the feeling this was all temporary. They'd stay in Smitten awhile and see how business worked out, how Grace adjusted, and go from there.

As the microwave heated the food, the smell of turkey and spicy dressing filled the room, making his mouth water. He hadn't realized how hungry he was. The timer went off, and he let the plate sit a minute.

Sam and Suzie were his only family. His parents were

both gone. Though his wife's parents were still living, they spent their days traveling abroad and didn't have time for grandchildren. He and Grace had heard from them just once since McKenzie's death last December.

He carefully pulled his hot plate from the microwave, grabbed some silverware, and sat at the table. Not only did Grace need to be around family, he needed it too. The job opportunity had come at a great time. He hoped things worked out in Smitten.

Thoughts of Elliana popped into his head. He hadn't remembered her eyes being such a deep chocolate brown. And her hair had turned a deep auburn. It suited her. He shrugged and picked up his fork.

She had changed since her school days, that much was certain.

The smell of coffee reached Lia as she entered the bookstore where the book group met. Natalie Smitten never failed to treat them to coffee from Mountain Perks. Lia said her hellos, grabbed a cup of coffee, and found a seat next to her good friend Heather DeMeritt and the warm fire.

"I haven't had a chance to talk to you. Guess who's back in town?"

"Who?" Heather asked, wide-eyed, coffee cup perfectly still in her hands.

Knowing Heather loved a good mystery, Lia looked around the room to make sure no one was listening. She leaned ever so gently forward and mouthed the words *Joey Oliver*.

The surprise on Heather's face satisfied Lia immensely. She eased back in her chair. Then she grew warm waiting on Heather's response. She didn't know if it was from the fire or growing panic. "What am I going to do?" She began to fan herself with her book.

Heather chuckled. "You're going to enjoy it, that's what. How long is he here?" She took a sip from her drink.

"He joined his brother's dental practice."

Heather choked on her coffee.

"Okay, you two, what's going on?" Molly Moore scooted her chair into the inner sanctum.

"Joey Oliver is back in town," Heather offered.

"*The* Joey Oliver?"

"The very one," Abby Gray said as she stepped up to join them, blond hair flipped out Meg Ryan style. "I saw him when I went to the grocery this afternoon."

"Love is in the air." Heather grinned.

"Heather, he's not interested in me and you know it."

"Things change. People grow up. You never know," Molly said with a singsong flare.

Lia shoved back the hope that Molly's words brought on. Could Joey ever think of her in that way?

"Let's talk about something else," she said.

"Well, I brought this for you." Abby handed her *A Gentlewoman's Guide to Love and Courtship* by Pearl Chambers.

"Are you still reading that thing? I thought you gave up any hope of finding clues to the Chambers treasure there."

The girls knew that talk of hidden gold was probably just a Smitten legend . . . but if it did exist, it was Molly's husband, Curtis, who had been the last living descendant—and now Molly could certainly use a gold mine if her business was to survive.

"If you and Heather didn't find anything, I sure won't," Lia continued. "I'm no good at decoding anything."

"Think of it like those hidden pictures you find in children's magazines. Those were so much fun." Heather's blue eyes gleamed. She radiated sheer joy and hope about everything. If the grocery store had no milk left, a huge snowstorm was about to hit, and you didn't get your milk, no worries. With a sparkle in her eye, she would give you half of hers.

"Besides," Abby said, "you never know—it might impact your love life like it did for me and for Heather."

Lia barely managed not to roll her eyes. "I'll give it a try."

"Okay, ladies, time to get started," Natalie said.

Lia opened her copy of *Scarlett: The Sequel to Margaret Mitchell's Gone with the Wind*. She loved this book and wished she could be more independent and daring, like the heroine.

Everyone settled into the discussion, and Lia's mind eventually wandered over to the other book in her hand. She was so clueless about men. Maybe Abby was right . . . maybe she would learn something to help her understand the mind of Joey Oliver . . .

CHAPTER TWO

. . . .

I'd heard you'd moved back to town." Martha Burton followed Joey Oliver back through the dental office maze.

"Yeah. Good to see Elliana last week." He motioned for her to slide into the chair. "So what seems to be the problem, Mrs. Burton?"

"Oh dear, please don't call me Mrs. Burton. I'll think you're talking about my mother-in-law. Besides, we're way past that. So glad you're back, Joey. I always liked you." The look on her face made him think he'd missed something in the conversation.

"Thanks, Mrs.—Martha."

She smiled and settled comfortably in her seat.

"So what's happened with you over the past several years? We lost track."

"Open your mouth, please." He looked thoroughly around her teeth. "So where is the problem?"

"Oh I, ahh, righ' 'ere." She pointed, but struggled to express herself with her mouth so wide open.

Clearly, there was an upside to his business.

"Okay, I see."

Upon further investigation and x-rays, he couldn't see a problem at all. And when he told her, she didn't seem surprised.

She chuckled as she got out of the chair, upholstery squeaking in protest. "I guess I just imagined it. Sure glad you were here to check it out." She patted his shoulder.

Joey made a note in her file.

"So where are you staying?"

"My brother's house. Just till I find a place, though. I need a temporary place for my daughter and me until we can build in the spring."

"Daughter?" Her eyebrows shot up. "Are you married?"

"No. My wife died last year."

Mrs. Burton reached over and grabbed his hand. "I'm so sorry, son."

He could tell she meant it.

She thought a moment. "Hard to find temporary lodging around here unless you stay at one of the inns." Then her eyes widened, and she snapped her fingers. "I know just the place for you. It's an upstairs two-bedroom apartment in a big historic home. Simple furnishings, but very nice. The landlord is very agreeable and easy to work with."

Historic meant old, but he could live with that. It would only be temporary. Could be just what he was looking for. He wanted his own place, where he and Grace could work through their pain of loss together in privacy.

"When can I see it?"

"I happen to know that the current renter is moving out the first of December. You could move in right afterward."

"Is it a rental you're handling?" he asked.

"Something like that." There was a hint of mischief in her smile. "How about you call me on Friday." She pulled a card from her purse and scribbled down her number. "Does your daughter go to school?"

"Yes, kindergarten. I haven't enrolled her yet."

"Great. This place is close to Smitten Elementary."

It was sounding better all the time. "Okay then, I'll give you a call," he said, raising her card with the number on it.

Tuesday morning seemed to move at a snail's pace for Lia. The kids were restless and so, it seemed, was she.

She glanced around the room, thankful for the bright colors and chalkboard paint where she allowed her students to get creative with their artwork. She loved how she'd made the classroom her own.

"And let's spell this color, class?" Lia held up the red card and waited for the class response.

"R-e-d," the children said in unison, legs swinging, fingers fidgeting.

Just then someone knocked on the door and opened it. Principal Hunt stood with Joey Oliver and a petite replica of him, right down to the thick head of blond curls.

"Ms. Burton, this is Grace Oliver. She will be joining your class."

Lia's head began to swirl. Joey was in her classroom. With

his daughter. That meant he had a wife. The fantasy she had been building up in her mind came to a crashing halt.

"Ms. Burton?" Mr. Hunt looked at her as though to ask if she was all right.

"Yes, of course. Nice to see you again, Joey—um, Mr. Oliver." The heat rushed to her face, most certainly staining her cheeks the color of her auburn hair. He had always teased her about that when they were teenagers. She looked at him, and he winked at her.

"No white coat today," he said with a smirk.

She smiled. Then, on shaky knees, she scrunched down in front of Grace. "Nice to meet you, Grace. I'm sure you will like it here."

Grace smiled and signed, *Thank you.*

"Oh." Lia stood to her feet.

"She's not hearing impaired," Joey said, "but it's how she communicates. If you know any sign language, it would mean a lot to her if you tried to communicate with her that way. We can talk more about this after class."

"I know some sign. I'll do what I can." She looked at Grace and signed, *You're welcome.* Now her curiosity was piqued, but she'd have to wait to find out the particulars.

Mr. Hunt and Joey said good-bye and left the room with Grace watching after them.

Knees still a bit wobbly, Lia said, "Class, I'd like to introduce you to our new student, Grace Oliver."

"Hi, Grace," they said in unison, all wiggles and darting attention spans.

Lia pointed her to a seat, and they continued on with their lesson on spelling colors.

She hadn't noticed so much the first time she'd seen him, but Joey hadn't aged much. Still had that mop of thick, unruly blond curls and crinkle lines around his shiny blue eyes. And a smile that could melt the snow off Sugarcreek Mountain. She imagined his life with a family. His laughter, his teasing . . .

Todd, a chubby boy with black glasses and a green-and-yellow shirt bearing the University of Vermont's Catamount logo, asked to get out of his seat for a drink of water, setting off an avalanche of thirsty children. While they shuffled up to the water fountain for their drinks, Lia pondered the fact that Grace appeared to know how to spell all her colors, but only revealed them through sign language. Fortunately, Lia had taken some classes in sign language to help with the hearing impaired ministry at church, so she was able to communicate with the little girl.

Lia continued to watch over her students. "Don't crowd the line, Maddox. Zoe and Abby, no talking, please."

Joey had seemed genuinely happy to see her, if only for a moment. But she couldn't think about that anymore. He was married and had a little girl.

"Okay, class, back to your seats. Please get out your writing tablets. We'll practice writing our names."

One little girl's hand shot up.

"Yes, Mia?"

"Xander said I smelled funny. My mommy got me some perfume," she announced with great pride.

"And it's lovely. You smell like a princess," Lia said, causing Mia to sit a little taller in her seat. "Xander meant to say you smelled nice. Right, Xander?"

Xander's expression seemed to say that all girls have cooties.

"May I sharpen my pencil, Ms. Burton?"

Lia gave a nod and watched Micah, dressed in blue jeans and sneakers, walk politely to the pencil sharpener and set to sharpening.

"I need to go to the bathroom." Macy gave a dramatic sigh. Her long hair looked much like Rapunzel's, contributing to the theatrical look.

Grace got out of her seat.

Lia felt she was losing control of her classroom.

"Macy, you may go to the restroom. Then I want everyone in their seats." She looked at Grace. "What do you need, Grace?"

Grace ignored her and twirled around the room.

"Grace, please sit down."

Grace continued to twirl.

Finally it caused a disturbance with the other kids, so Lia took her aside and signed to her, *You have to sit in your chair unless I give you permission to get up. Do you understand?* Grace nodded and went back to her seat.

If Lia didn't know better, she would say the child was indeed hearing impaired. But she'd wait and see what Joey had to say.

&

The classroom was empty, and yellow buses bulging with children had trundled down the windy road toward home. Lia put away a box of crayons and noticed the light snow falling over Smitten. The snowcapped mountains in the distance made for an enchanting scene.

"Sorry I'm late."

She swiveled around to see Joey standing there. Grace smiled when she saw her daddy, picked up her school bag, and ran to him.

"I had a root canal patient that took longer than expected."

"Couldn't Grace's mother have picked her up?" Maybe she was out of line for asking, but it was out there now and there was nothing she could do about it.

Joey looked surprised. He rubbed the afternoon stubble on his chin. "Wow. That's right. I need to catch you up on a few things."

"Okay. Let me just set Grace up with some coloring books and crayons." Lia could feel Joey's gaze follow her as she walked across the room to the supplies. It was uncomfortable having him here. Back in town. So silly that she should feel that way after all these years.

Once Grace was settled at her desk, Joey took the adult seat beside Lia's desk. He pulled in a deep breath. "It's like this. McKenzie, my wife, was hearing impaired."

"Was?"

"That's how Grace learned to sign. It was the way we communicated with McKenzie."

Lia nodded, hoping to encourage him to continue.

He stared at his hands for a moment. "She was killed last December in a random shooting at the mall."

Lia's breath caught in her throat. "Oh, Joey, I'm so sorry." She was surprised she hadn't heard, the way gossip traveled through their little town.

He swallowed hard. "McKenzie's friend and Grace were with her."

Tears welled in Lia's eyes, though she tried desperately

to hold them in check. She looked at Grace, whose furrowed brow showed her determination to color a beautiful snowman. Lia's heart ached for what this precious child had been through.

And Joey.

"That's why she signs." He nodded toward Grace. "The counselor says it's her way of holding on to her mom."

With her head bowed, Lia nodded and lifted a barely audible whisper. "I'm so sorry."

Joey took another deep breath. "Yeah, me too. I haven't taken her to a mall since it happened." Then with resolve he said, "But it is what it is and we have to move on."

His comment brought back her professional side. "Of course."

"I plan to pick her up on time, but there may be times like today . . . If you could bear with me for a week or two—just till we get settled. "

"The good news is she is in all-day kindergarten. There is plenty of after-school care nearby if you're interested."

"That makes me pretty uncomfortable. I hate to throw her into another situation where she doesn't know the adults in charge."

"The thing is, I won't be here next week. Remember, I'll be attending a kindergarten literacy conference in Morristown. So I can't guarantee anyone would be able to stay after school with her. You'll have to make arrangements before Monday."

"Fair enough. " He stretched out his hand to hers. "Thank you for your time, Elliana. It's so great to see you again."

The way he said her name ribboned through her like

warm cocoa. No one called her by her full name, but the first time Joey met her, way back in grade school, he had declared that Elliana was too pretty a name not to use.

His hand was strong, protective—she didn't want to let go. A weak moment enveloped her, and she wobbled to her chair. "Oh dear, I think I need to eat something," she said, refusing to allow the heat to reach her face.

Joey lifted a sweet smirk as though he wasn't buying her excuse, but handed her a packaged cracker from his pocket. "I keep them on hand for Grace."

"Thank you."

His eyes held hers. Deep in those eyes she got a glimpse of the Joey she had known, the carefree I'll-lasso-the-moon Joey. But only a glimpse. A shadow cast it away. He walked over to Grace.

As they edged toward the door he said, "Thank you, Ms. Burton."

Sadness tugged her heart as she watched him leave the room and close the door behind him.

"You're awfully quiet tonight, Joey." Suzie passed the dinner rolls to Grace, who pulled one apart and smeared on a glob of jelly.

"Yeah, I noticed that too," Sam joined in. "Everything okay?"

"Everything's fine. Just explained things to Grace's teacher today."

Grace stuffed a bite of roll into her mouth and signed, *I like Ms. Burton. She's nice. She lets me color.* She waited a moment and signed again. *She smells good too. Like a happy day.*

"That's right," Suzie said. "I'd forgotten Lia was the kindergarten teacher." She turned to Grace. "Just what does a happy day smell like?"

Ms. Burton, Grace signed with a grin.

Joey laughed. "It's funny; now that she mentions it, Elliana did smell good. Like peaches."

Once Grace was excused from the table, the guys started to get up as well.

"Could you wait a moment?" Suzie asked. "I've already talked to Sam about this, Joey, but we thought we should mention it to you."

Joey studied her. "What's that?"

"If it's all right with you, we want to buy Grace a gym set for the yard."

"Whoa, now hold on."

"Oh, come on, Joey. We don't have any children, and we would enjoy watching her play."

"Suzie, Sam, we're not staying here. I'm going to build a house. And in fact, I'm looking for a place to stay while we build it."

"But you can stay here," Suzie encouraged.

He knew they meant well, but he didn't want Grace confused as to who her parent was. Kids could get messed up with too many bosses. He wanted her *around* family; he just didn't want to live with them.

"I appreciate it, guys, I really do. Ultimately, we won't be staying here. We need to get established in a place of our own and settle down to our new normal, you know?"

Sam nodded.

"I guess," Suzie said with a sigh of resignation.

They cleared the table, and the discussion moved to sports and talk of work. Afterward, the guys settled into TV and Suzie got out her childhood tea set and played with Grace awhile.

Joey walked into Grace's room and saw she was already bathed and in her pajamas. He thanked Suzie and read a story to Grace before she went to bed. Once he kissed her good night, he peeked again before closing the door. They had to find their own place. And soon.

A gentle snow fell, sparkling the tips of the evergreens in the town square as citizens of Smitten gathered for the annual lighting of the large central evergreen tree and service. Park benches were filled as guests waited, sipping hot chocolate, compliments of the ice rink concession stand. Horses and buggies stood nearby waiting to take passengers on an enchanted ride through town on this snowy night. These rides changed the world, according to old Mr. Cleaver, owner of Cleaver Horse & Buggy Service. People fell in love on his rides, and homes were born. He figured he offered a great service to Smitten, and Lia felt indeed he did. She wondered if she should take a ride.

A slight wind caused the chain to clink against the flagpole, and the Garner sisters tuned their stringed instruments in the gazebo. If the weather became too frigid, they'd have to get their instruments out of the cold.

Lia and her mother each got a hot chocolate, decided where they would meet, then meandered through the crowd to greet friends and neighbors.

"Nice to see even dentists get a break once in a while," Lia teased when she stepped up to Sam and Suzie Oliver.

"Are you kidding? If you've grown up in Smitten, you wouldn't dare miss the lighting of the tree. It's all about tradition."

Lia grinned. "That it is." She looked around and tried not to sound overly interested. "So where are Joey and Grace?"

"Oh, uh, they, uh—he said they couldn't come for some reason. I guess once you move away from Smitten, you forget the old traditions." Sam's tone held sadness.

"That's too bad. Grace would have enjoyed this."

"I know," Suzie said, head bent.

"Well, I guess I'd better go find Mom before they leave without us. Good to see you!" Lia waved and headed off, wondering all the while about the mystery of Joey not bringing Grace tonight. No doubt he had his reasons, but what could be more important than building traditions with your children?

Once Joey had a break in his appointments, he decided he'd better call Martha Burton and find out if that apartment was still available. He'd been too busy on Friday to call her.

He punched the number into his cell phone. "Mrs. Burton? This is Joey Oliver."

"Yes, yes, so good to hear from you. The apartment

is available. If you decide you like it, you can move in on Wednesday or Thursday."

He hadn't expected things to move quite that fast, but the least he could do was take a look at it and see if it was a fit for them. He made arrangements to meet Martha after work.

Suzie was happy to take care of Grace for him while Joey went to look at the apartment. Martha showed him through the small but very quaint rooms. Arched entrances, dark woodwork and trim, two bedrooms, clean carpet, older furnishings, but very neat and tidy.

"Here's the other thing. I happen to live nearby, and I know you're in need of after-school care for Grace. I would be more than happy to watch her. The bus comes right by my house."

"Oh?" He liked that idea a lot. That made the place even more enticing. They discussed rental details, and it sounded perfect.

"You won't need to sign a lease. I happen to know the landlord has no problem filling this place." She grinned. "You see, I'm actually the renter." She lifted her eyebrows. "This is Lia's house, and I live upstairs."

To say he was surprised was an understatement. Why would she do this for him?

Martha raised her hand to stop any protests. "I'll just move in with Lia, and you can stay here till your house is built. I'll help with Grace, and then once your home is ready, I'll go back upstairs. Simple as that." With her hands on her hips, she gave a wide grin as though the matter was settled.

"I can't—but I can't—does Elliana know about this?" He

was becoming increasingly suspicious, with Elliana being out of town and all.

"She is always happy to help a friend in need. That's what friends are for." Martha was already ushering him to the door. "Now, my furniture will stay here, so I won't have but a few personal belongings to take downstairs. You said you sold your things before you came here so you could start fresh, so now you can wait and buy furnishings for your house once it's built."

Joey hardly knew what had hit him. It seemed like a crazy idea, but he did need help with Grace after school, and he knew Martha Burton well, and liked her. She would be a good influence on Grace. If Suzie hadn't joined the Smitten work force, he could have left Grace there, but since she was unavailable, where else could he go?

Besides, it would be nice to renew his friendship with Elliana.

CHAPTER THREE

. . . .

*L*ia pulled her car into the driveway, cut the engine, and sat there a moment, rubbing the back of her neck. It had been a long week, and all she wanted to do was kick off her shoes and slip into a hot bath. But she had book club tonight. With a sigh she trudged out of the car, grabbed her suitcase from the trunk, and walked toward the front door. She spotted a truck in the back parking area, so she figured her mother had company. Just as well. Lia was too tired to answer all her questions about her conference.

When she shoved opened her front door, the scent of roast beef and gravy curled through the room and caused her weary body to become alert. She hadn't realized how hungry she was. The afternoon muffin hadn't cut it.

Her mom walked into the room wearing an apron and a smile. "Hope you're hungry." She walked over and gave Lia a kiss on the cheek.

"Mom, you didn't need to do this. I wasn't gone that long."

"I knew you would be tired after a long conference and the drive home, so I thought I'd surprise you. Why don't you go wash up? Dinner's just about ready."

Lia smiled. Her mother was always so thoughtful. She hoped she would be more like her someday. Then reality hit her in the head like a brick. A truck in her mother's parking area. Someone else was here. She was setting Lia up!

Lia groaned and flopped back on her bed. The last thing she wanted was a blind date tonight. Didn't her mother remember her book club commitment? She kicked off her shoes and slowly lifted herself in the bed so she could see herself in the mirror. Hair askew, makeup completely soaked into her skin, exposing her tiny freckles. She groaned again.

A knock sounded at the door. "Lia, dear, dinner is ready."

"Coming." Lia swung into action. She washed her face, touched up her makeup, brushed the auburn strands from her face, and set out to make herself pleasant. She'd deal with her mother later.

She was totally unprepared for what awaited her in the dining room.

Hi, Ms. Burton. Grace waved her hands in happy gestures. She ran over and hugged Lia.

"Elliana." Joey lifted that heart-stopping grin of childhood.

"H-hello."

"I thought it would be nice to have Joey and Grace over for dinner." Her mother placed serving bowls on the table filled with salad, mashed potatoes, gravy, roast beef, green beans, cottage cheese, and dinner rolls. "After all, that's what neighbors do for one another." She gave a sly glance to Lia, lifted a sweet smile, and said, "Shall we pray?"

Lia's voice cracked and just flat-out left her. She couldn't find a word in her head to save her.

Mother said a sweet prayer over the meal, much of it having to do with reaching out to the needy and having a servant's heart. Lia had no idea what that had to do with blessing the food, but assumed her mother was inspired.

Once the prayer was over, Grace signed to Lia that she loved her new room, though she would miss Uncle Sam and Aunt Suzie. *Daddy says we can go visit a lot, though.* She stabbed her fork into a green bean and took a cautious bite, smiled, then took another.

"I thought you were going to build." Lia cut a piece of beef. "Did you decide to buy the Baker house down the road?"

Joey cleared his throat and looked at her mother.

Mental trumpets blared, and every nerve in Lia's body sprang to attention. "What's going on? It's like you all are keeping a secret from me." She gave a nervous giggle. And it grew more nervous by the instant. If someone didn't stop her, she'd soon be a laughing hyena.

"Well, honey," Mom began in her sweetest voice, "Joey needed a place, and my apartment is just up there for the taking. I figured I could come down here and help you awhile, since things have gotten so busy. Joey and Grace can stay upstairs until their home is built in the spring or summer."

Joey Oliver would be staying in her upstairs apartment, and her mother would be staying in the very same living quarters . . . within the very same four walls . . . as Lia. She hadn't seen that one coming. She picked up her glass of iced water and drank it till it was almost empty while everyone looked on.

"It will be like old times, Lia," Joey said, as though they were in third grade.

"Yeah," she squeaked.

Joey reached for a roll. "You're okay with it, right?"

"Don't be silly. I told you Lia would be all too happy to have you stay upstairs. Isn't that right, dear?" Her mother gave her daughter an I've-raised-you-better-than-that look.

"And I'll be paying rent. I've already worked that out with your mom," he said hastily.

Lia didn't want to be rude; she was just trying to digest it all. "That's fine. Really. I just—that's fine." She smiled at Grace.

Her mom gave a sharp nod of her head as though the matter was settled and sank her fork into the gravy and mashed potatoes.

Joey happily went back to his plate, oblivious to her inner turmoil.

Lia tried to continue through the meal as normally as possible, though her stomach twisted. Did she want to live this close to the only man she had ever truly loved? Yes, she had been engaged once, but she realized before it was too late that she could never love anyone but Joey. He had cherished her friendship back in the day, but she had wanted more than that. He couldn't see past her pigtails. She smoothed the linen napkin on her lap and looked over at Grace. The little girl needed help. A woman's touch. More than Lia could offer in a classroom.

Maybe her mom was right. Helping out with Grace could

be just what they were meant to do. Besides, it wasn't like she'd see Joey all the time. They had their own entrance to the house, so they could come and go without ever seeing one another. The more she thought about it, the more she decided it couldn't hurt anything.

Everything would be just fine.

Though she was tired, Lia was happy that she had book club tonight. It gave her a chance to get away from the house and mull over everything that her mother had been up to while she was out of town. She laughed aloud in the car. She might have known that leaving her mother alone in the same town with an eligible male meant an inevitable setup.

The stress began to peel away as she drove through town. Main Street was picture-perfect. Lamplight gave a warm, inviting glow to passersby. Tiny snowflakes fell gently across the cozy town and sparkled against large, glistening snow-flake ornaments that hung from wires draped overhead. The town square boasted the evergreen decorated in an array of colored bulbs and tinsel. In the distance Lia spotted ice skaters. She couldn't tell for sure, but it looked like the Garner sisters were among them. They weren't exactly spry young ladies anymore, but Lia admired their spunk and hoped they wouldn't fall and hurt their hands. They kept the town alive with their chamber music.

A contented sigh escaped her. She loved this place with all its quirky residents and small-town charm. And soon it would be full of the hustle and bustle of the Christmas season, her favorite time of the year. Just the thought of it calmed and excited her all at the same time.

Turning her yellow Bug into the bookstore parking lot, she cut the engine, gathered her things, and went inside.

Jenna Henderson was perusing a book on parenting while she stood with a baby on her hip and a toddler whining and pawing at her legs. Lia smiled and walked on. She waved at Deb Matney, who lifted a knitting book with a smile.

Once Lia had her coffee, she sat beside Abby. Heather and Molly soon joined them.

"Hey, Lia, my mom tells me Joey and his daughter just moved," Abby said with a teasing glint in her brown eyes.

"Yes, I'm aware," Lia said.

The others looked intrigued.

"Well, Mom says"—Abby paused approximately four full seconds for effect—"he moved into your apartment upstairs, right?"

Heather and Molly gasped in unison.

"Scandalous, wouldn't you say?" Abby teased.

One would never guess Abby to be the quiet, shy type. When the four of them were together, she was carefree and ornery.

"Are you reading another one of those books with a snarky heroine?" Lia wanted to know.

Heather laughed. "Seriously, Lia, how did you manage that?"

"One word: Mother." Good-humored laughter rippled around her.

"Well, this certainly has possibilities," Heather said.

"Don't you start, Heather," Lia said.

"Oh, give her a break," Molly said.

"Since when are you going soft?" Abby asked.

Molly winked. "She is tutoring my son, after all."

"It's so sad, what happened to his wife," Heather said.

"I know." Lia stirred her coffee. "Such a random thing."

"Such a senseless act," Molly said. "Do you think he's worked through all that, Lia?"

"I don't know." Guilt nagged at her. She shouldn't have feelings for this man. He was undoubtedly still mourning his wife.

Natalie called the book club to order, and Lia let out a sigh as she settled back into her seat.

$\approx$

"Oh, good. You're home," Lia's mother said when Lia stepped into the kitchen.

Hi, Ms. Burton, Grace signed, causing flour dust to scatter everywhere. Flour smudged her face and lingered in her curls. Red icing peeked from the corner of her mouth, and her tongue searched to find it. She looked completely adorable.

Flour and red, blue, and green icing smeared her mother's apron. She looked frazzled, but the glow on her face told Lia she was having a wonderful time.

The kitchen table and counters held decorated Christmas cookies in various shapes and sizes.

You two have been busy, Lia signed to Grace.

Grace's chest puffed out a bit, and she gave a huge smile, revealing pink teeth. They all laughed.

"We thought it might be fun to get a head start on the

Christmas cookies this year," Mom said, putting the last batch of cookies into the oven. She took off her oven mitts and turned to Lia. "Should be finished just as Joey gets home."

"Well, keep up the good work, you two. I'm going to get some comfortable clothes on." Lia went back to her room and changed into her yoga pants and top. Just as she finished, she heard her iPhone signal a text message.

Sam & Suzie want to see Grace tonight.
Time for Mountain Perks?

She stared at the blinking symbol that awaited her response. Excitement rushed through her, but she struggled to keep her good sense. Friends having coffee. That's all it was. But she couldn't help thinking about what Molly had said. *Things change. People grow up. You never know.*

Sounds like fun. What time? she texted back.

They made the arrangements, and she was all ready to go when the doorbell rang at seven thirty. He actually came to the door and walked her out to the truck.

This is not a date. This is not a date. This is not a date.

Lia climbed into the truck, careful not to slip on the snow beneath her feet. Once inside, she pulled off her thick mittens and woolen scarf. "It's nice and toasty warm in here."

"Yeah, I took Grace to my brother's, so the heat has had time to kick in." He turned the radio to the oldies station. "Remember this song?" He grinned.

She smiled back. "I sure do." Was he trying to live out the old glory days with her or what?

They rode for a few minutes without saying anything. Joey sang along with the radio, his voice making the song almost unrecognizable, and Lia suppressed a giggle. She wasn't sure she'd ever heard him sing before. Now she knew why.

"Thanks for meeting me tonight. Since I've gotten to town, I haven't seen all that many people I know from when I lived here. My brother's okay, but it's nice to see a friend once in a while."

"True." What was the matter with her? She couldn't seem to find anything to say.

"Hey, you remember that girl I had a huge crush on—what was her name?"

"Kristina Windsong." How could she forget? Kristina didn't give a hoot about him, and he had picked her! Life was so unfair.

Joey hit the steering wheel with the palm of his hand. "That's it! Wonder whatever happened to her."

"She married Pete Makon, and they moved out west to care for his parents."

"Pete Makon? That little pipsqueak! What did she ever see in him?"

Lia laughed and shook her head. "They say love is blind."

He looked at her. "So it is."

Lia tried not to gulp out loud.

Joey pulled the truck up to Mountain Perks. The bell on the door jangled when they entered. Coffee blends and chocolate scents sweetened the air. The cappuccino machine whirred and whined until perfect foam capped the dark

brews. People sat at tables or in soft chairs, reading magazines, books, iPhones, computers. Joey went up to the counter
to order drinks, and Lia found two overstuffed chairs to sit in
while they chatted.

Joey handed Lia her cup. "Extra whipped cream for the
lady." His fingers brushed against hers, and she tried to ignore
the thrill of it all. He wanted to be friends. Just friends.

Joey looked around the room, then took a sip from his
cappuccino. "You know, this town hasn't changed much."

"Well, I wouldn't say that. Have you seen the renovations
on the train depot?" Lia felt a bit defensive for Smitten. She
had always felt it was a piece of heaven on earth.

He chuckled. "Yes, I did see that. Very nice. I'm talking
about the flavor of the town. The people, the feel of Smitten,
all that. Pretty much the same."

"Is that a bad thing?"

"No, no, a very good thing." He smiled.

Lia took a drink and hesitated a moment. "I can't imagine
ever leaving this place."

Joey looked at her. "It suits you."

"What do you mean?"

"You sparkle here. You're alive, energetic. It suits you,"
he said again.

A shiver ran through her. "Thanks." Another pause.
"Was it hard for you—when you left, I mean?"

"Nah. I was looking for adventure, ready to get out on the
open road, you know?" He laughed. "Actually, never thought
I'd come back. But when McKenzie died and my brother
asked me to join his practice, it seemed a good thing to do to
get around family again. For Grace's sake especially."

Lia nodded and took a sip. "So tell me about McKenzie."

"We met in college. She was hearing impaired but was great at lip reading, so that helped while I was learning to sign. I loved her enthusiasm for helping others. I couldn't help wanting to go out and accomplish something big when I was with her."

"Are you okay? I mean, I know it's something you never get over, losing a spouse, but, well . . . are you okay?"

"It was hard, but our marriage wasn't perfect. I have regrets. Sometimes I wonder if I ruined her life by marrying her."

"Why would you say that?"

He shrugged. "I'm not the romantic type, in case you haven't noticed. McKenzie was full of passion and needed lots of attention. I disappointed her many times."

"Well, I'm sorry things turned out the way they did, but so thankful to have you and Grace here in Smitten."

He stared at his fingers a moment, then sighed. "I just hope we can get Grace to talk again one day."

Lia didn't know what to say without feeling she was overstepping. "I'm praying about that."

Her comment seemed to surprise him. "Really? Thanks."

"That's what friends are for. Hey, I was wondering why you and Grace didn't make it to the annual lighting of the evergreen."

The look on Joey's face made her wish she hadn't asked.

He shrugged. "How about we change the subject for tonight? I'll tell you some other time."

They talked a little longer about former classmates, catching up on who had gone where and done what. Long after their coffee was gone, Joey glanced at his watch.

"Wow, it's getting late. This has been really fun, Lia, but I'd better go pick up the princess. You ready?"

"Sure." Lia grabbed her things and wondered what this whole thing was about. Guess he really did miss her friendship.

If only his heart could open to her for something more.

> *The most insignificant of times spent with a gentleman may be taking root in the heart.*
>
> PEARL CHAMBERS, *The Gentlewoman's Guide to Love and Courtship*

CHAPTER FOUR

. . . .

*T*hanks for watching the little munchkin, bro." Joey gave his brother a good-natured slap on the back.

"It was our pleasure." Sam picked up toys around the room.

Unfamiliar toys. Joey knew they must have been recently purchased for Grace. His brother and sister-in-law were spoiling his daughter—it was a good thing they weren't staying there any longer. Finding the apartment at Lia's had been ideal timing.

She was a perfect little guest, Suzie signed so Grace could see. Grace smiled.

"So what were you up to tonight?" Sam asked.

"I took Elliana out for coffee. We had a nice chat. It's good to see her again."

Sam's and Suzie's gazes collided.

"Now, hold on," Joey said, holding up his hand. "It's not

like that. Elliana was my best friend all through school. She's special, but not in a romantic way."

Suzie lifted her brows. "Hmm, I wonder if Lia sees it that way."

"Of course she does." Elliana had never given any hint to wanting more than a friendship. He would have seen the signs. Wouldn't he?

"Just don't break her heart," Sam said.

"But—" Joey started to protest, but Sam cut him off.

"That's all I'm saying, little brother."

Joey practically laughed out loud in the truck on the way home. The very idea of Elliana and him—well, it was ridiculous. Not that she wasn't beautiful, with those big, expressive eyes and that long, thick auburn hair that he'd admired since he was a boy. He shook his head. "Doggone my brother, putting those thoughts in my head. We're friends. Period."

Grace signed, *Dad, are you all right?*

"Sure. I'm fine. Just fine."

❧

The day was fresh with promise. Lia stretched and yawned. She loved lazy Saturday mornings. Nothing on the agenda. The softest of pillows cradled her head, and her body sank deep beneath a plethora of down comforters. Morning light slipped through her window blinds, spraying all across her room. Another beautiful day.

She smoothed the quilt that topped her comforters. She had purchased it and matching pillow shams on eBay from a seller who'd gotten it from Anthropologie. Teals, yellows, blues, oranges, a spectrum of colors.

Delicious scents roused her. Reluctantly she peeled off the blankets, eased into her warm chenille robe, and tucked her feet into matching slippers.

"Well, good morning, sleepyhead," Mom said when Lia entered the kitchen. "I've made bacon and eggs, biscuits, and coffee. You just sit down and I'll get you a plate."

"Mom, I'm a grown woman. You don't have to cook for me."

"Sure I do. You're letting me stay with you. I've got to earn my keep."

"Well, thank you. It smells wonderful."

"Thank you, sweetie." Her mother sailed around the kitchen with the ease of a chef. In no time she had the table spread with breakfast goodies, their plates filled, and the prayer of thanks said.

"So what are your plans today?" Lia bit into a crisp piece of bacon.

"Christmas shopping with Anna." Anna Conners was one of her mom's best friends. They both loved to knit—Anna owned the Sit 'n Knit in town—and they spent hours visiting together, catching up on kids and solving world crises.

"Oh, that will be nice."

"I'd invite you to go with us, but since I'll be shopping for you, probably not a good idea." Her mom chuckled.

"Oh, I don't know. That sounds like a great idea."

Mother looked at her as though to see if she was serious, but sighed when she saw the smile on Lia's face. "How about you?"

"I have shopping to do too, but I'm not really in the mood. I think I'll grab a good book and a cup of coffee, tuck myself in a warm blanket by the fireplace, and read all day." She might even explore the gentlewoman's book.

"Sounds marvelous. The temperatures are expected to hover around the twenties today."

"Brrr." Lia heard her cell phone ringing from the living room. "Who would call this early?"

Mother laughed. "Not exactly early. It's nine o'clock."

"Right. For you, early is before roosters have their morning coffee." She hurried to answer the phone.

"Hi, Elliana, this is Joey."

Adrenaline surged through her. "Hi, Joey."

"Hey, listen, Grace wanted to go ice skating this morning, and we thought you might like to join us."

She thought of the warmth of the blanket, the fireplace, the hot coffee, her good book. Then she thought of Joey.

"That sounds like fun. When you leaving?"

"Is an hour too soon?"

"No, that sounds just fine."

"Great. Oh, and bundle up. It's cold out there."

The ends of Lia's scarf trailed to the ground while she strapped her feet into the stiff skates. She shivered and wondered, not for the first time, what had gotten into her to agree to this. She loved snow and winter . . . but from the inside looking out.

"You ready?"

Joey stood tall before her, his broad shoulders casting a shadow while she put the finishing touches on her skates. She rearranged her scarf, wrapping it around her neck once more and tucking it into her jacket, then carefully stood. Joey extended one gloved hand to her and one gloved hand to Grace.

Sounds of laughter filled the air. Children shrieked. Blades cut through the ice with a swooshing sound, leaving ice shavings in the wake. Some skaters fell, looking more like a clump of woolens on the ground than people. After several rounds, Grace spotted a friend from school.

She looked up at her dad. *Can I go skate with Peppermint, Daddy?*

"Peppermint?"

"Yep, that's her name," Lia said. "And it's not a nickname."

Joey smiled. "Okay then." He looked toward Grace. "Don't you want to stop and have some hot chocolate?"

After I get my friend? she persisted.

Joey grinned. "Okay, just stay where I can see you."

Lia and Joey watched her skate toward her friend.

"How does a kid end up with a name like Peppermint?"

Lia smiled. "Maybe they like Christmas. Candy canes, all that."

"Is she in your class at school?"

"Yes. Nice family."

"You want some hot chocolate?"

"I'd love some. Maybe my fingers will have a chance to thaw. The air is so cold, I can't feel my nose." She laughed.

He frowned and reached out to touch her nose gently with his glove. "Poor Elliana. We've turned you into a Popsicle."

His brief touch pushed back the chill. "Why don't you just take a seat on this bench and keep an eye on Grace. I'll go get us some cocoa. Sound good?"

"Sounds great."

He looked at her a moment. Then he took off his glove and brushed the hair away from her eyes. Their eyes met; he said nothing. But his gaze went so deep, she began to feel uncomfortable. She shifted. He blinked.

"Um, I'll be right back."

Lia watched him go, wondering what that was all about.

Joey put his glove back on and headed for the concession stand. He pounded his fist into his other palm. Doggone his brother, putting thoughts in his head about Elliana. He couldn't think like that. It would change their friendship and ruin everything.

Spending time with her deepened their friendship, but it scared him that something more was brewing in his heart. Could Sam and Suzie be right . . . did Elliana have feelings for him? He shook off the notion. She would have said something, shown him in some way. He wasn't that stupid.

Was he?

By the time he got back with two steaming cups of cocoa, he had calmed down and put the matter to rest. Elliana was his friend, and that was the way he wanted to keep things.

"Here you are." He passed her the cup and noticed how the cold had turned her cheeks a rosy red and put a sparkle in her eyes.

"Thanks so much. This is awesome." She took a careful sip. "The girls are over by the tree, still skating."

"Her legs are going to be sore in the morning," Joey said, taking a careful sip from his cup.

"I don't know. Kids are so resilient. Uh-oh, here they come. Looks like you may be making another trip for cocoa."

Joey groaned.

"Hey, there's a young man who goes to our school," Elliana said. She called to him. "Aaron, can you help me out?"

The sixth grader glided up to her with ease. "Hi, Ms. Burton."

"If we give you the money, could you get us two hot cocoas?"

"Sure."

Joey pulled out his wallet. "And get one for yourself too."

"Okay, thanks." Aaron skated happily away.

"Good thinking," Joey said. "We make a great team."

Grace arrived then, skating into Joey and wrapping her arms around his waist. *Dad, can we have cocoa now?* she signed.

"Already taken care of."

Once the drinks were delivered, Joey smiled, watching the girls as they enjoyed their warm cocoa. He was glad they had come.

Just then an old jalopy of a truck trundled down the road, rattling and hissing. All at once it backfired with a loud boom.

Grace screamed, dropped her cocoa, and threw her arms around Joey, her whole body quaking.

"It's all right, honey. It was just a truck."

Grace buried her face into her daddy's coat and gripped him so tightly he couldn't pry her lose.

"What's wrong?" Lia asked. "Is she all right?"

"Her mother," was all Joey had to say. "Sorry, but I need to get her home. Let's go."

One thing was for sure: Grace's hearing was fine. But their fun day was over.

Differences of opinion can separate or strengthen. The wise woman can grow through adversity.

PEARL CHAMBERS, *The Gentlewoman's Guide to Love and Courtship*

CHAPTER FIVE

. . . .

While Lia's class worked on writing letters, she graded papers at her desk. She glanced up at Grace, who seemed to have recovered from her scare the day before. The little girl's pain ran deep. Lia's heart squeezed. If only she could help her.

Stacking the students' papers in a neat pile, she put them in a folder marked *Numbers* and placed it in her bottom drawer. Then she walked over to the blackboard, picked up an eraser, and started wiping down the board, ridding it of names, letters, and numbers. She sneezed for the umpteenth time today. She would like to have blamed it on the chalk dust, but she knew better. Her yearly cold had arrived. Normally it hit during Christmas break, but evidently she'd picked up a virus while ice skating.

By the time the bell rang, she was more than ready to go home. The children gathered coats, hats, boots, book bags, and lunch boxes, then chattered and squealed their way to the buses. Once they were gone, Lia tidied her room for the evening. She turned to leave and spotted Joey in the doorway.

"Joey. What brings you here? You know Grace is already on the bus, right?"

"Right. I just wanted to talk to you. Do you have a minute?"

All she wanted to do was go home, put on her pajamas, and drink hot cocoa. "Sure. Take a seat." She pointed to the chair beside her desk.

"Thanks. I wanted to apologize for ending things so abruptly after our skating on Saturday."

"It's all right, Joey. I understand why Grace was upset."

He nodded. Silence hung between them as he studied his hands. "I'm going to take her away."

"What?"

"Over Christmas."

"But why?"

"To get her away from all the reminders."

"But, Joey, Christmas is everywhere."

"It looks a little different in Florida than it does in Chicago. Or Smitten."

"So you won't celebrate Christmas?" The thought nearly took her breath away.

"A day at Disney World would be a nice replacement, don't you think?"

"But what about the Christmas Eve service at church? The live nativity? Joey, children love that. That's the true meaning of Christmas. Do you really want her to miss out on that?"

Joey shrugged. "The fewer reminders of Christmas, the better."

"Is this for you or for her?"

His eyes narrowed and his jaw clenched. "It's for her. But can't it be for me too? We've been through enough."

"So that's the plan? You'll just shun Christmas every year?"

"I don't know," he snapped. "I haven't thought that far ahead."

"You can't protect her from everything, Joey," Lia said as softly as she could.

"We're leaving on Saturday. Just wanted you to know when you didn't see us around the apartment." He stood and walked toward the door.

Lia couldn't help herself. She called out, "Merry Christmas."

He kept walking and didn't turn back.

"Do you believe this, Heather? No Christmas for that sweet little girl? I'm just beside myself." Lia wrung the napkin between her fingers as they sat at a scrubbed table at the Country Cupboard Café. The room was bright and cheery with white walls and tables, cherry-colored seats, and a cherry-colored counter with glass bowls displaying the day's fresh doughnuts. Hamburgers sizzled on the grill. Fresh coffee was brewing and steamed the air with its aroma. Just being there normally perked Lia's spirits, but not today.

Heather swallowed a bite of hamburger. "I don't know what you can do about it, Lia. He's probably just doing it this year. Once the grieving eases, he'll see the importance of having Grace at home for Christmas."

"But she needs Christmas this year! It's not her fault someone killed her mother. It's horrible to even think about it. That's why she needs to be surrounded with the joy of Christmas."

"I guess we know now why he didn't go to the lighting of the evergreen."

"I guess." Lia coughed and wiped her nose.

"Well, going to Disney World isn't exactly a bad deal either. That's a pretty happy place." Heather took a drink of her iced tea.

Lia's head drooped. "I know. I just wish he'd take her some other time." Lia picked up the ketchup bottle and poured some over her french fries.

"You were hoping to celebrate with them, weren't you?"

Lia's head jerked up. "What? No."

"Lia Burton, I know you. I mean, it makes sense. This is the only guy you've ever cared about." Heather smiled.

"It's not like that. Yes, I care about Joey . . . but I've given up on the idea of the two of us ever being anything but best of friends." She coughed again.

"You're coming down with your yearly cold, aren't you?"

Lia nodded and wiped her nose on a tissue.

"At least you can get better over break." Heather studied her a moment. "Too bad about Joey, though. His return to Smitten seemed so full of possibilities."

"He's just a friend, Heather."

Heather locked eyes with Lia. "Whatever you say."

Lia didn't want to talk about it anymore. It wasn't as though she could do anything to prevent Joey and Grace from leaving over Christmas. It was none of her business.

She'd just have to let it go.

Lia was tutoring Molly's son, Noah. They were reading *Llama Llama Red Pajama* together.

"Okay, time to get to work," Mom announced, carrying in Christmas decoration boxes from the garage. They normally had everything in place way before now, but life had gotten so busy they just hadn't gotten around to it. Now that winter break had begun, Lia was eager to put up the tree.

"All right, Noah, guess we're done for today. Want to help us decorate?"

As they hauled the necessary boxes, Lia told her mother about Joey's plans.

"Florida? Over Christmas?" Mom's voice rose an octave. "He can't do that!"

"That's kind of what I thought," Lia huffed as she dragged the Christmas tree box across the living room floor.

"Why didn't you tell me sooner?"

"You've been at church every night getting ready for the Christmas program, and I've been in bed by the time you got home."

"Oh, that's right." Her mother pulled some candlesticks from a box. "Are you feeling any better?"

"I took some cold medicine. Feeling a little light-headed, but okay." She sneezed, and her mother frowned. "I'll be fine." Lia turned to Noah. "You can watch *The Santa Clause* movie till we get to the ornaments if you want."

Noah seemed to like that idea, so she turned the TV on for him, then went back to helping her mom unpack the boxes.

"That poor child. Oh, Lia, I'm just sick." Mom held her hand to her chest the way she did when things didn't go her way.

The front doorbell rang, and Lia went to answer it.

Suzie Oliver stood at the door, looking frazzled. Grace stood beside her, bundled in woolens and boots. "I'm so sorry to bother you."

"What is it? Is something wrong?"

"Joey went hunting with Sam, so I've been watching Grace, but my mom was just taken to the hospital. They think it's her heart. Could you watch Grace for us?"

"Oh, we would be happy to." Lia opened the door wider. "You go to your mom. Grace will be fine here. We're just starting to decorate the house for Christmas. Noah is help-ing us."

If Suzie knew about Joey's wishes, Lia figured she'd speak up. But it was their home, after all, and they were planning to decorate before Grace arrived.

Suzie let out a breath. "Oh, thank you so much. Call me if you need anything." She gave Lia her cell number and hur-ried down the porch steps to her car.

Lia ushered Grace into the house, where she took off her coat, hat, mittens, and boots and settled into the warmth of the house.

"I think she and Noah had better have some hot cocoa before we get started, so they'll have the energy to help us."

Mom winked at Lia, then promptly prepared the cocoa and placed two cups on the oak table.

"Extra marshmallows, right, Grace?" Lia asked, dropping miniature marshmallows into her cup.

Grace nodded and grinned as the marshmallows bobbed to the surface.

My dad says we can't have a Christmas tree this year 'cause we won't be home for Christmas, Grace signed. She took a careful sip.

"She says she won't be home for Christmas," Lia said, for her mom's and Noah's sakes.

"Where you going?" Noah asked.

Though he didn't use sign language, Grace could obviously hear him.

Disney World, she signed.

"Huh?"

"She said 'Disney World,'" Lia said.

"Wow, that's cool."

I guess. Grace didn't look convinced.

"Don't you want to go, Grace?" Mom asked.

I want to go sometime, but I just want to be home for Christmas.

"Did you tell your daddy that?"

Yeah. But he says it's better if we go. Grace looked across the family room at all the decorations, and her eyes brightened. *Do I get to help put up ornaments? I helped Mommy last year.* Her hands fell to her lap.

Yes, you most certainly do get to help. We need you and Noah. We can't do it all ourselves, Lia's mom signed and gave a broad grin.

Lia was impressed by how quickly her mom had picked up some sign language from being with Grace. Her signs were sometimes off, but since Grace could hear, she understood her just the same. It seemed to please the little girl that others used her mother's language.

Grace's feet swung back and forth under her chair while she and Noah tried to communicate. Mother and Lia went to work, placing wreaths, candles, snowmen, greenery, and ornaments in cozy arrangements around the room. They saved their ceramic nativity scene for the fireplace mantel.

"Well, if you two are finished with your cocoa, how about we put up the tree?"

The kids jumped off their seats and ran to her side.

Mom put on some lively Christmas music and they set to work, putting up the tree stand, adding the skirt, then shaping the limbs. With that done, they placed the boxes of ornaments in rows and let the children put them where they wanted them.

This is the best day ever! Grace signed. She picked up an angel ornament and headed for the tree.

Lia hadn't seen the child this happy before. Her face just glowed.

Just then the doorbell rang.

Lia hoped it wasn't Suzie yet. They were having such fun.

She opened the door, and Joey stepped into the house.

"Sorry you ended up babysitting." He stepped inside the house and looked around. He turned to Lia with a frown. "You know how I feel about Christmas and not wanting Grace around it."

Lia pulled him aside so the children wouldn't hear. "We were already decorating with Noah when Suzie and Grace showed up. What did you expect me to do, drop everything and throw sheets over the decorations? You can't hide it from her, Joey. Christmas is everywhere. I'm sorry something so tragic happened for you during this season, but it's not fair to take it away from Grace. It's a joyous holiday."

"You know nothing of what she's been through. I just want to spare her—"

"Spare her or spare you?"

"Why do you keep saying that?"

"Are you sure you're not just trying to run away yourself?"

His jaw muscle twitched. "I don't run away from anything. I'm just trying to not subject my daughter to more painful memories."

"Then make some new memories. In the Christmas season. Make it a happy time for her again."

He stared at Lia until she thought he'd bore a hole through her head. Then he walked over to Grace and signed that they had to go.

Please, Daddy, can I finish the tree?

"No, Grace. We have to go. Now."

Lia's head started to pound with a headache.

Grace's lower lip jutted out, and she quietly pulled on her outer wraps and followed her dad out the door.

Neither said a word of good-bye.

CHAPTER SIX

. . . .

So glad you and Grace could have dinner with us before you leave for Florida," Mrs. Burton said. "We had hoped to spend more time with her over Christmas vacation. We'll miss her while you're gone." She placed the piping hot pan of lasagna on the pad on the table, then added the serving platter of warm garlic bread.

Grace rubbed her tummy and smiled.

"Somebody's hungry," Joey said with a laugh. "She doesn't get this kind of cooking from me." Before settling in his seat he asked, "Is Elliana going to join us?"

Mrs. Burton sighed. "I don't know. Her pneumonia is getting better . . . the antibiotics seem to be working."

"With her fear of doctors, I'm just glad she agreed to go in." Joey smiled. "If you think she's decent, could I go see her?"

"Sure. Her room is the third door on the right. Just knock on the door and let her know it's you."

Joey made his way down the hall to her room and knocked. "Elliana, it's Joey. May I come in?"

After a moment a hoarse voice said, "Come in."

He stepped inside to find her bundled beneath a mountain of covers, her body propped up on fluffy pillows.

She offered a slight smile. "Hello."

Though she looked better than the last time he had seen her, it frightened him to see her looking so vulnerable. He stepped closer.

"You feeling any better?"

"A little stronger every day. Just don't tell Mom. I'm enjoying the life of luxury with her taking care of me." She coughed. "Joey, you're not mad? When you left with Grace the other night—"

"No, I'm not mad at you." He knew he owed her more of an explanation than that, but she seemed so tired. They'd have to talk about it another time.

"So you're leaving tomorrow afternoon?"

"Yeah." He stared at the floor, suddenly feeling self-conscious. "We're supposed to get a snowstorm tomorrow, but I think we'll be out of here before it hits." He winked at her. "We'll be soaking up sun on the beach while you're digging out of the drifts."

"If I had the strength, I'd throw something at you."

He laughed. "I thought you might." He paused. "Any chance you can join us for dinner?"

"I'm not hungry, but maybe I can come out and sit on the sofa."

"I'd like that," he said.

Something about her eyes. So sincere, warm. Even in her

current condition, she was beautiful. How had he missed that in the past? He had always loved her zest for life, the history they shared . . . but romance? It had never occurred to him.

"What is it?" She ran her fingers through her hair. "I look a mess, don't I?"

"You've never looked more beautiful." His eyes held hers and lingered there.

"Well, I guess you'd better go out so I can make myself presentable for dinner. Tell Mom I'll be right there."

"Great." He took her hand and ever so gently brought it to his lips, then placed it carefully back on her bed. "I'll look forward to it." He turned and walked out the door.

His heart pounded in his chest. What was he thinking? He was going to blow it between them, acting like that. It was a good thing he was leaving. He needed to get out of there, away from Elliana, and think. This was coming out of nowhere. Wasn't it? He hadn't always felt this way, had he? Of course he hadn't. They were friends.

It must be seeing her sick that had thrown him. It sent an urgency through him. He wanted to fix things. Just like with his wife. But some things he just couldn't fix.

He stepped into the dining room. "Elliana is going to come out to the living room and lie down on the sofa."

"Oh good," her mother said. "She's been stuck back there, and I was worried she'd get depressed."

"That's enough talking about me." Elliana entered the room with a weak smile. "You go ahead and eat. I'll just sit over here."

Mrs. Burton said the prayer over the meal, and they began to eat.

"Smells delicious," Elliana said.

"Would you like to try some, dear?"

"No, thanks, Mom. I might have some chicken broth later. That would feel good on my throat."

"I'll get it for you now."

Soon her mother had the mug of broth in Elliana's hands.

After Joey and Grace helped clear the dinner table, he walked over to join Elliana, and Grace settled into a Disney movie on TV with Mrs. Burton.

"So," Elliana said, breaking the silence. "You all packed and ready to go?"

"Almost. We're flying out of Plattsburgh. Flight doesn't leave until three o'clock."

"That's about an hour and a half drive. I hope you don't run into bad weather."

"We may head out early, depending on the weather reports."

Elliana fidgeted with her blanket. "You're sure you have to go?"

She glanced up at him, and the look in her eyes made his heart squeeze. He almost wanted to say no. But he had to do this for Grace.

"Yeah, I'm sure."

It *was* for Grace, wasn't it?

"We'll miss you at the Christmas Eve service." There was no hint of judgment in her voice, only caring.

"Don't tell me you're still going?"

She perked up. "Of course I'm going. The doctor says I'm no longer contagious, no fever. Wild horses couldn't keep me away." She laughed. "I look forward to this all year."

"You really love Christmas, don't you?"

"I really do. It's a magical time of year for so many reasons. People are more charitable—"

"And desperate," he said.

"I'm sorry, Joey. I know you've been through so much."

"Thanks. But you're right. I need to work past it. I just haven't been able to do that yet. To forgive, you know?"

"I understand. It would definitely take the power of God to forgive someone for taking the life of a loved one. I can't begin to understand how that must feel. I only know that God is able."

"I know he is too. I'm just not sure I *want* to forgive the man who did this."

"Holding on to it feels better?"

He ran his hand through his hair. "I don't know. It just doesn't seem right to let him off the hook."

"But they caught him?" She coughed.

"Yes."

"Then justice will be served. Whether you forgive him or not doesn't affect the killer. It affects you. And Grace. Your peace of mind."

Joey sighed. "I know you're right, Elliana. Maybe I'll get there one day. Just not right now."

"You know, Joey, sometimes you just need to be willing to be made willing."

He thought about that a minute. "That's pretty deep, you know?" He smiled. "Thanks."

They talked awhile longer, then when Grace's movie was over they said their good-byes and went upstairs to their apartment—Elliana's words on forgiveness following his every step.

Lia tossed and turned in her bed. She finally threw off the covers and sat up. She couldn't get Joey off her mind. She loved him. That was nothing new. But tonight he'd seemed different toward her. Did she dare hope his feelings toward her were changing?

She worried about his unwillingness to forgive. Nothing could tear a man or woman down faster than allowing bitterness to take root and grow. But she'd said as much as she dared. She couldn't make him forgive the man who had killed his wife.

Opening her Bible, she searched for words on forgiveness and prayed them over Joey. In her mind she pictured a sparkling brook, free of debris and clutter. That's what she wanted for him, a clean heart. If they had any hope for a future, he had to be free of the poison.

And oh, how she hoped they had a future . . .

The next morning the doorbell rang. Mom opened the door, and from her place on the couch Lia could see Joey and Grace standing on the front porch wrapped in woolens, boots, and smiles.

"With three feet of snow dumped on Smitten through the night, it looks like we won't be taking that flight today," Joey announced.

"Oh, I'm so sorry," Mom said.

"We've changed our tickets to Christmas Eve in hopes the

weather will have cleared by then and the planes will be back to full service."

"Well, why don't you come in where it's warm and visit a spell?"

Grace shook her head and tugged on her daddy's coat.

"Thank you, Mrs. Burton, but Grace and I wondered if we could make a snowman in your front yard?"

"Well, you certainly may! Our yard needs a nice, friendly snowman. What can I get for you?"

Joey held up his hand. "Not a thing. We brought a bag full of supplies, in hopes that you'd say yes." He looked over toward Lia. "And how are you this fine morning?"

"Much better, thanks. You're in good spirits despite your flight being cancelled."

He lifted his hands and dropped them. "What are you going to do? I just go with the flow. Besides, snow like this brings out the kid in me. I wish you could join us. We could have a good snowball fight."

"I wouldn't want to hurt you," Lia said.

He let out a good laugh. "I'm worried. How about a rain check . . . or snow check?"

"You're on."

"Well, thanks, Mrs. Burton, for letting us do this. We'll be out front for a while."

"That's fine. And once you're finished, come inside for some hot cocoa and coffee."

Grace nodded enthusiastically.

"You've made us an offer we can't refuse."

Joey and Grace turned and walked back outside. Lia moved herself farther down the sofa so she could watch their progress through the window. Her mother brought in a tray of tea and sat down next to her.

"When are you going to tell him?" Mother asked.

"Tell him what?"

"How you feel about him." Her mother methodically stirred her tea.

"Mom, if he doesn't know by now, he'll never know."

"Men are clueless." Her mother hesitated. "Listen, Lia, I know you've loved him for years. The kind of love you have for him—being willing to let him go when he went off to college, knowing how much it hurt you, and now allowing him to work through his grief when you'd like so much more between you . . . Well, that's a once-in-a-lifetime kind of love, and I'm praying God's best for you both."

"Thanks, Mom. I'm afraid Joey will always think of me as the skinny girl with red braids. A pal to fish, ski, and go hiking with."

Mom looked into her teacup. "I think things are changing between you two."

A faint stirring fluttered in Lia's stomach. She had hoped the same thing, but didn't dare vocalize it.

"I don't want to be one of those women who always dreams of the guy while he goes off with someone else and miss my own life in the process. I just don't know."

"Do you have anyone else in mind?"

"Well, no, not at the present time."

"Then there's no harm in seeing where this relationship goes with you and Joey." She sighed. "He's a good man, Lia. He's been through a lot, but I believe there is something between you. Give him time."

"Thanks, Mom. I know you mean well." She reached over and gave her mom a kiss on the cheek. "Whatever will be, will be."

Her mother smiled and patted Lia's hand.

"I think I'll go get cleaned up. It looks like a beautiful day." She got up and headed toward her bedroom, knowing full well her mother was smiling after her.

But the question remained . . . could she love a man whose heart was filled with unforgiveness?

CHAPTER SEVEN

· ·

*L*ia reached for the *Gentlewoman's Guide to Love and Courtship* on her nightstand. She looked forward to reading a little in it each night. Probably a silly notion, but she couldn't help thinking it was helping her gain insight into Joey's world.

> A gentlewoman longs for a kindly gentleman to sweep her into his arms and offer her the world. At the heart of it all, of course, is her innate desire to have a home and family. For true treasure is found in the heart of the home.

The last line was underlined. Lia reread it. Could it have a coded meaning? Her heart pounded hard against her chest. What if the gold was actually *in* Molly's house? But where? *For true treasure is found in the heart of the home.* What was the heart of the home? The kitchen? The bedroom? Where?

Lia picked up her cell phone and clicked off some numbers. "Molly, are you busy?"

"Terribly. I'm watching *You've Got Mail* on cable."

Lia laughed. "Again?"

"What? I love this movie! Are you feeling better?"

"Good as new. The meds finally did the trick. But listen, I think I've stumbled onto something with the book. Can you gather the girls to meet at Mountain Perks tomorrow evening. Say, seven o'clock?"

"Can't make it then. How about *before* work? Say seven *a.m.*?"

"Sure. I'm a lady of leisure over break. But I have a zillion things to do tomorrow, so the earlier, the better for me."

"Sounds good. I'll call the others and let you know if they can meet."

"By the way, do you want me to tutor Noah over Christmas break, or do you want to give him a rest?"

"We'll let him enjoy his break, then get back at it after the holidays. Does that work for you?"

"That's just fine. Thanks, Molly. See you soon."

Lia got more excited by the minute. What if she had discovered the truth? Then panic set in. What if it meant nothing at all? Would the girls think she was ridiculous? Now she wished she hadn't called Molly. It was probably nothing at all.

Joey couldn't get to sleep. Elliana's words kept running through his mind. *Sometimes you just need to be willing to be made willing.* He wasn't sure he could ever forgive the guy who killed his wife, but maybe, just maybe he could be willing to be made willing. The forgiveness would have to come from God working in him.

He punched his pillow for the hundredth time. "Well, Lord, it's up to you. I'm not trying to be stiff-necked about this. It just hurts too much. I don't want to let him off the hook after what he did."

Let me deal with that. Forgiving him doesn't free him from his consequences. It frees you.

"I offer you the best that I have, Lord. I'm willing to be made willing. Please help me forgive."

Having said that, Joey tried to sleep, but couldn't. Elliana's beautiful eyes seemed to look deep into his soul. His love for her was obvious to him now. And he was almost sure she had feelings for him. The question was where they would go from here . . .

The bell on the door jingled as Lia entered Mountain Perks. She stomped the snow from her boots at the door and walked over to secure a table. While she took off her coat, cloche woolen hat, and thick scarf and mittens, Molly and Abby walked in, with Heather not far behind. Lia's heart did a little flip. She was excited to share her book find, and yet nervous too.

The women got their drinks and settled across from one another at the table.

"This weather is crazy. At least they got the streets cleaned off," Heather said as she took off her coat, settled into her chair, then covered an enormous yawn.

"Yeah, I know, it's early," Molly said. "But you had to get up for work anyway. Might as well meet your best buds for coffee."

Everyone agreed, though Abby seemed a tad reluctant. She must have been up late reading the book group's pick.

"Joey had to postpone his flight until this evening. He had planned on leaving Saturday," Lia said.

"Well, he's lucky to be going, that's all I can say." Abby slumped in her chair. "This cold weather wears me out. Give me the tropics!"

A sharp light caught Lia's attention, and she gasped.

"Abby! Are you engaged?" She reached for Abby's left hand while her friend sat there, smiling mischievously.

Heather let out a squeal.

The girls oohed and aahed over the beautiful ring and congratulated their friend.

"Wyatt will make a great husband," Molly said.

"Goodness, first Heather, now you. Who's next?" The moment the words left her lips, Lia wished she hadn't spoken. The girls all looked at her.

"Uh, so maybe now you'll get to go to Hawaii, for your honeymoon," Heather said, taking the heat off Lia.

"We haven't gotten that far. We haven't even settled on a date yet."

They talked a little longer about weddings and honeymoons before Molly took a slurp from her frappe and reminded them that she couldn't stay long, so they'd better get to business.

Lia felt heat flush her cheeks. She pulled out the book, and the friends exchanged a glance.

"Okay, it's like this," she said. "There may be nothing to this at all. I told you I'm no good at puzzles, but as I was reading this last night I found something that piqued my interest."

"Well, what is it? You've got us all curious," Molly said.

Lia looked down at the book and read the section she had marked. "'A gentlewoman longs for a kindly gentleman to sweep her into his arms and offer her the world. At the heart of it all, of course, is her innate desire to have a home and family. *For true treasure is found in the heart of the home,*'" she finished. "That last line is underlined. I got to thinking it could mean something." She looked up at the others.

Heather fell back into her chair. "Wow. I know there's some silly stuff in that book, but that actually makes sense. It's not just the guy that matters, it's the promise of home, of family, of establishing something meaningful and lasting."

Lia thought of Joey and Grace and her own desire to have them close at Christmas. The book had described what she wanted, it was true. But could Joey offer her that world?

"But that's not the point, Heather. What if the gold is actually at Molly's house? At the 'heart of her home'?" Lia said.

"Oh," Heather said. "You may be onto something."

Lia felt her shoulders relax a little.

"What do you think, Molly?" Abby asked.

Molly fidgeted with the straw in her cup. "It's something to consider. But I can't imagine where it would be."

"Let's all think on that while we go our separate ways. 'The heart of the home.' What that could mean in terms of a hiding place," Lia said.

"Oh, I love a good mystery," Heather said.

They talked a little longer about the possibilities, then

parted ways. Lia hoped Molly would find the treasure. It could change everything.

℮

No sooner had Lia gotten back from coffee with the girls when her doorbell rang. Her mother had already gone to breakfast with Anna.

Joey smiled from the porch. "Can we come in a moment?"

Lia looked down at a sleepy Grace, holding her favorite doll and standing close to her daddy.

"Suzie was supposed to watch Grace today, but something came up. I have some errands to run before we leave for our flight. Could I talk you into keeping Grace for me? Please, please, please?" He gave the grin that curled her toes.

Lia thought of all the things she had planned to do, then she looked down at Grace, and they exchanged a smile. "Of course I'll watch her. But I do have some errands of my own, if you don't mind her going with me?"

"That's fine. How about I call you when I'm ready to pick her up? If you're out, we can meet somewhere."

"Sounds good."

Grace went into the living room and sat on the sofa, leaving them at the door.

"You're the best friend in the world," Joey said. Then without skipping a beat, he bent down and kissed her right on the lips! Short, sweet, to the point, but it was a kiss. From Joey Oliver.

"See you soon," he said, waving as he headed down the porch.

Obviously, the kiss meant nothing to him, but Lia felt as though she were frozen in time. And it had nothing to do with the cold wind blowing through her front door.

One last errand and Lia could take Grace home for hot chocolate and thawing out. She could hardly wait. She was wearing out fast, and she still had the Christmas Eve service tonight. She might have to take a nap.

She had to go to University Mall in Burlington. Their Kohl's store had the curtains her mother had wanted for her upstairs apartment. Knowing she would be moving back up there soon, Lia had ordered them right after her mother had showed them to her online. Once Lia picked the curtains up, her shopping would be done.

After she and Grace stopped for lunch, she finally pulled up to the mall. She hesitated. Surely Joey wouldn't mind if she took Grace into Kohl's. It wouldn't actually be going inside the mall—they'd just be entering a single store from the outside entrance.

"All right, Grace, grab your doll bag and let's go. This is our last stop, sweetie."

Grace smiled and grabbed her things.

Holding hands, they walked through the entrance, and Lia looked at all the last-minute shoppers. "Guess we're not the only ones," she said to Grace with a smile.

Christmas displays still flashed, and the loudspeaker announced special deals as shoppers milled around. Lia took Grace to Customer Service, where she picked up her package of curtains. As they made their way back through the store, Lia watched Grace closely. She seemed perfectly fine.

Can we look at the toys, Ms. Burton? she signed.

"Sure." Lia took her over to the toy section, where Grace reveled in the selection of dolls and playthings.

After a while Grace had had her fill. She looked up at Lia and signed, *Cocoa, with extra marshmallows?*

Lia agreed with a smile and they headed for the door. Just as they were going out to the parking lot, they met Joey coming in. His face turned from shock to anger.

"What are you doing here?"

"I told you I had errands to run."

"This is a mall, Elliana. Don't you care about Grace at all?"

"Joey, of course I do! We just went in and out of Kohl's— we didn't go into the actual mall, so I thought it was okay."

He pulled a wide-eyed Grace to him. "Well, you thought wrong. I thought I could trust you with Grace."

She didn't appreciate how small he made her feel. Incapable. Which also made her furious. "You have no right to talk to me this way. Parents entrust their children to me every day. Grace and I had a great time, actually. And now you're making a big deal out of nothing."

"It may not be a big deal to you, but it's all about trust. I need to be able to trust you with my daughter. It's a deal breaker for me." With that he stomped toward the parking lot with Grace, while Lia watched after them open-mouthed. She hardly knew what had just happened.

❧

The windows on his truck fogged up while Joey sat behind the driving wheel and stewed. The shock on Elliana's face haunted him. What was he thinking? There was no harm done. Grace didn't even seem to notice she was in a mall. So why had he overreacted? And with the woman he knew now that he loved. He'd blown it. Big time.

Grace sat sniffling quietly while he drove home. Tiny snowflakes fell on the windshield, and he had to turn on the wipers. He'd go home, get their bags, and they'd head to Burlington for their flight. Maybe the time apart from Elliana would do some good. Still, he couldn't go away with her thinking he didn't want to talk to her anymore. He had to make things right.

If only there was time.

CHAPTER EIGHT

. . . .

*L*ia tried to stop the tears. She should have thought it through. She knew Joey didn't want Grace at the mall. She shouldn't have rationalized. Had she lost Joey forever?

She couldn't help thinking that the rule was more for him, but then, what was he doing there? When he had asked her to watch Grace, she was glad to help. But he could hardly have expected her to stay home when she had so much to do. The more she thought about it, the angrier she got, and the tears dried up. By the time she got to Smitten Expeditions, Molly's store, she had pulled herself together. But one step inside, and she knew she'd never get Molly alone to talk. What was she thinking? This was Christmas Eve, after all.

"Lia, hi. What are you doing here?" Molly's ponytail bounced with every step.

"I shouldn't have come. You're so busy."

Molly grabbed her arm. "Something's wrong. What is it? Let's go into my office for a sec."

Lia followed her, wishing she hadn't bothered her at such a busy time.

"Molly, are these boots still 30 percent off?" a salesperson asked.

"Yes, the sale is good through today."

They stepped through the door of Molly's office, and Molly turned to Lia. "Now, what's going on?"

Lia told her what happened with Joey.

"Oh, Lia, I'm so sorry." She hugged her friend. "He'll come around. It was just the shock of it all that made him react that way."

"I guess. I shouldn't have been so stupid. What if I've lost him forever?"

"I don't think so. I've seen the way he looks at you. He's a man in love."

"Oh, I so want to believe it."

Molly pulled a couple of tissues from her box on the desk and handed them to Lia.

"It's just that he's leaving for Florida and I won't see him for ten days. I'll go crazy wondering what he's thinking, wondering if he'll meet someone else—"

"Now you stop right there. Just give it some time. I know what it's like for him. He's lost his spouse, and he's raising his kid alone, just like me. It's confusing and overwhelming sometimes. Joey knows you weren't purposely trying to hurt Grace. He'll come around."

Lia let out a long breath, feeling the tension leave with

it. "Thanks, Molly. I'm going to let you get back to work now. Thanks for the pep talk."

"Keep the faith, girlfriend. It will all work out." They walked out the door together, and Lia prayed Molly was right.

The joy of Christmas had been sucked right out of Lia. She wrapped herself in winter wear and headed toward the church, where her mom had been all afternoon helping to decorate the sanctuary. She couldn't stay home and sulk on the most wonderful night of the year. Once her car was heated and she was on the road, she turned the radio on to Christmas music. That always lifted her spirits. But all she could see was Joey and how angry he looked when he was at the mall with her. Grace had looked confused and upset, but her hands were silent.

Lia sighed while another teardrop made a wet track down her cheek. She had to stop. Maybe this was the Lord's way of showing her it wasn't right between them.

But couldn't they work out these issues? They weren't so insurmountable. Challenging, yes. Insurmountable, no.

Still, she wanted to be careful. She didn't want to push this relationship if God had something else in mind. She had always wanted to follow God's will for her life—with or without Joey. And once he moved away, she had accepted that it would be without.

Then he returned to Smitten, and it seemed God had brought them together again for a reason. But only God could help Joey forgive and move forward.

Lia pulled her car up to the church parking lot, shut off the engine, and rested her head on her gloved hands on the steering wheel. *Lord, I need your help to get through this. Please help me focus on you tonight, not my problem with Joey. We are in your hands, and I want your will for our lives. Amen.*

Lia walked by the sheep pen where an angel choir sang nearby and shepherds warmed themselves by a fire. She glanced at her watch. Joey and Grace would be landing in Florida right about now. She hoped they'd have a nice time. Stepping up to the manger scene, she took in the goats, llamas, cow, and Joseph standing by Mary, who cradled a baby in her arms. The cares of the day began to melt off her, and she focused on the gift of Jesus to a lost and hurting world.

By the time the Christmas Eve service began, Lia was back into the Christmas spirit and resting in God's direction for her future.

The church organ played quietly as people stepped into the candlelit sanctuary. A holy hush filled the place, and Lia closed her eyes and basked in the Lord's presence, thanking him for the peace that filled her soul.

"Excuse me, is this seat taken?"

Lia looked up to see Joey and Grace smiling, waiting on her to give the okay to sit down. Lia's jaw dropped. "What are you doing here?" she whispered. "Did your flight get cancelled again?"

"No. We changed our minds." He looked at Grace, who grinned and nodded.

Lia was speechless. Was this God's doing?

"Can we talk after the service?" he asked.

"Yes, of course. You want to come over?"

"That would be great." He grabbed her hand and held it. She didn't know what was going on, but evidently he had forgiven her for the mall incident.

They settled into the music, singing "Joy to the World," "Hark! The Herald Angels Sing," and finally "Silent Night." Lia glanced at Grace and saw the little girl's rapt attention. When the service ended, people quietly filed out.

Once outside, Lia asked, "Did you get to see the live nativity?"

"Only briefly," Joey said. "We didn't want to miss the service."

The three of them walked around so Grace could see the animals. When they arrived at the manger scene, Lia asked Grace if she understood what it meant.

Grace signed her thoughts about it and warmed Lia's heart. The child had heard and understood.

They started walking toward their cars. "You were right about all this," Joey said. "It is special. Just like you." He turned and in the shadows of the night reached down and brushed her lips with his own, ever so lightly, yet holding a promise of more. Her heart was light, and she was sure she could float home.

When they got to Lia's house, her mom offered Christmas cookies and milk to Grace and sat with her at the table so Lia and Joey could talk alone in the living room. They sat side by side on the sofa, and Joey cupped her hand in his own, then turned to her.

"I have two gifts for you. Open this one first."

It appeared to be a rectangular box. Lia carefully pulled away the wrapping paper and opened the box to find a leather-bound complete set of the Anne of Green Gables series.

"Your other books looked a bit tattered from years of use," he said with a laugh.

"Thank you so much, Joey."

"Besides, knowing that Gilbert and Anne finally got together made me think of our story."

Her breath caught in her throat.

"I've been a fool, Lia."

Lia started to say something, but he stopped her.

"Let me finish. What you said the other day made a lot of sense. I'm not able to forgive on my own, but I'm willing to be made willing. So that's what I've been praying. God knows my heart. I don't want to grow bitter. I want God to forgive through me. So that's how I'm praying."

She put her hand on his. "I'm so glad."

He sighed. "Then the thing with Grace today. I obviously overreacted. I didn't know how she would do at a mall for the first time since the tragedy, but I realize she was just fine." He looked up at Lia. "The resilience of children, right? That's what you said the other day."

Lia nodded.

"I've considered you my best friend from as far back as I can remember."

Lia's stomach clenched. She hoped things didn't go south from here.

"But what I didn't realize was that I've loved you that long as well. Remember the day we met? You were all dressed for school, red pigtails down your back. And that new kid—can't remember his name—accidentally tripped, knocking you into a mud puddle. I remember when you stood up, there was mud on the tip of your nose. You were humiliated—"

"Thanks for the reminder." She smiled. "But please, go on." She couldn't take her eyes from his smiling face.

"—but I thought you looked beautiful, and I remember my heart feeling all mushy. I couldn't admit that to anyone because I'd never liked a girl before that. They all had cooties."

She smiled as he covered her hand with his own.

"That's when I started asking you to go fishing. I wanted to be with you. I just didn't understand then that it was love."

"Why did you go off to college and get married?"

"Like I said, I didn't know it was love. I thought you were my best friend—and you were—I just didn't know you were so much more than that. I can be dense sometimes."

"So I've noticed."

"Hey." He squeezed her hand playfully, then brushed an auburn strand from her face. "I love you, Elliana Burton. I always have. I always will."

He leaned over and kissed her with controlled passion, passion that made her lips burn and long for more. Tears welled in her eyes when he pulled away.

"I know you'll need time to think about this. I've only been back since Thanksgiving, and only a few days ago realized my true feelings for you. But since we've known each other most of our lives, I hope it won't come as too much of a shock."

Joey got down on his knees then and took a beautiful diamond solitaire from a black box in his pocket. "Elliana Burton, I realize now that I don't want to be without you, ever. Will you make me the happiest man alive and be my wife?"

Tears spilled down Lia's face, and she wrapped her arms

around him. "I've dreamed of hearing those words from your lips all my life. Yes, yes, a thousand times yes!" She pulled him back to the sofa and offered up her lips again—an invitation he lost no time in accepting. She closed her eyes and reveled in his kiss.

"Does this mean you don't mind the white coat?"

She laughed. "As long as you won't wear it at home."

"Deal."

"Well, looks like we're missing a celebration of some kind," her mother said.

Lia stood and held up her hand. "Joey asked me to marry him."

Her mother clapped her hands together. "I knew it! I just knew you were made for each other! I'm so happy for you." Her mother drew her into an enormous hug, then turned to hug Joey. "I've always wanted a son."

Grace walked into the room and signed, *What's going on?*

When Joey told her, Grace grinned from ear to ear, then ran over to Lia and squeezed her hard. "I love you," she said out loud, and it seemed all the air was sucked out of the room.

Lia could hardly believe Grace had spoken. Three precious words that Lia knew would penetrate to the depths of her soul and linger for a lifetime.

"Grace, you used your words," Joey said.

She smiled up at him. "I love you too, Daddy."

They all gathered around her and hugged and kissed her. When they said their good nights later at the door, Lia told Joey, "I'm so thankful for my name."

"Your name?"

"Yes, Elliana. It means *My God has answered me.*" She

looked into Joey's eyes and down at little Grace's shining face and said, "He certainly has answered me. And I am blessed beyond measure."

"We're all blessed," Joey said. He looked at Grace and said, "Very blessed." He kissed Lia once more, then stepped into the sparkling light of snow.

"The Lord has done this, and it is marvelous in our eyes," Lia whispered into the night air.

Her heart swelled with gratitude. Yes, it was marvelous indeed.

Happily Ever After

Denise Hunter

> *A man in love is in want of an opportunity to prove himself*
> *chivalrous. A clever girl will take him up on it.*
>
> PEARL CHAMBERS, *The Gentlewoman's*
> *Guide to Love and Courtship*

CHAPTER ONE

. . . .

*M*olly Moore's shoes squeaked as she limped toward Smitten Expeditions.

Her legs moved like floppy noodles, her soggy clothes clung to her chilled frame, and there was something slimy tucked between two of her pruney toes. What should've been a triumphant return felt more like a walk of shame.

She flung open the door and slogged across the rustic wood floor toward her office, plucking river muck from her hair.

Heather DeMeritt's blond head popped up from behind the registration desk. She'd spent many hours helping Molly with the financial end of the business this past year. Her blue eyes widened. "What happened to you?"

Molly stopped in her tracks, her arms falling like hickory branches in a windstorm. Wet branches. Soggy, limp, dead branches.

"If anyone ever asks you to go white-water rafting, say no. If they ask you to take a party of six whiny tourists on a four-hour guided white-water rafting trip, say no. And furthermore, if you're ever given the chance to run a stinking expedition business—even if it's handed to you on a silver platter —run like the hounds of hell are on your heels, and don't look back."

Molly fell into the rollaway chair, heedless of the expensive leather. She dropped her head against the cushioned back and closed her eyes. *Please, God. Can you just rewind time for me? Just a tiny little bit?*

"That bad?"

Molly snorted, barely containing the sob that built in her throat. The group had seemed so jovial at first. So friendly. By the end of the trip, they weren't even speaking to her. And that had actually been a relief after being raked over the coals for three hours. Bright side: new vocabulary words. None she'd ever use, however.

Her eyes teared up behind her closed lids as the insults replayed. "They cancelled their activities for the rest of the week."

"Still, today was good. $69.00 times six . . ." Heather paused for two seconds. "$414.00."

Beautiful *and* smart. So not fair. Plus she saw the silver lining in everything. Only this time there wasn't one. "I had to refund their money."

"All of it?"

"It's what you do when you torture tourists for four hours. Besides, that seemed less expensive than the lawsuit they mentioned."

"They should've paid for lunch at least."

Molly sighed. "Lost it."

"What do you mean?"

"I mean I lost it. Down the river. Buh-bye club sandwiches. Buh-bye fruit cups and organic chips. Buh-bye expensive, waterproof cooler, floating down the Green River, keeping my food cool and dry for all of eternity."

Heather wrinkled her nose. "Sorry."

Molly covered her face. "I'm such a loser." Her hands muffled her voice. "Why did I think I could do this?"

"You *can* do this. You just need . . . practice."

"I have a couple scheduled for fly-fishing at ten tomorrow."

Heather winced. "At least it's not rafting?"

"Dwight made it look so easy—leave with a rosy-cheeked batch of tourists and come back best friends. Not a hair out of place. Not a drop of water clinging to his scruffy beard. Limp-free and whistling some happy tune. Show-off."

"Maybe he'll come back."

Molly shook her head. "He's moving to Ohio as we speak. His mom needs full-time care immediately."

"Maybe you can get someone else to teach you the ropes."

Teach her the ropes. She'd been sole owner of the business for a year now, since Curtis's passing. She should know the ropes, all of them.

"Maybe you can get some kind of certification?" Heather asked. "Is there a training program you can attend?"

"Certification isn't required in Vermont. I just need to know what I'm doing so I don't kill anyone. You don't know anyone who can raft, fly-fish, and rock climb, do you?" Molly jerked upright and grabbed the schedule, flipping ahead a couple of days. "Oh my gosh. I have to learn to rock climb by Thursday." She dropped her head to her hands. "I'm gonna kill somebody."

"How about the guy from Explorations? Gage Turner. He could teach you."

"He's my competitor. Besides, he hates me."

Heather laughed. "There's not a soul on God's green earth who hates you, Molly."

"Well, he does. And he made it plenty hard to get this business off the ground." Her late husband had had plenty to say about Gage Turner. She couldn't remember the details, but his name brought up all kinds of bad feelings. There had been some kind of rivalry between him and Curtis in high school that had dragged into adulthood.

"Are you sure? He's on the chamber board with me. He seems nice."

"Nice enough to rescue a competitor? I doubt it. I just need to find someone to take Dwight's place before I chase off all my customers."

Molly had placed a help-wanted ad yesterday, the second Dwight had quit. An outdoorsy college student would fit the bill, but college wasn't out yet. And when it was, Noah would be out of school. She couldn't leave her son for hours at a time. He was only eight. But she couldn't afford to pay much. Then again, she couldn't afford more refunds either. She had to do something and quick, before she lost it all.

"If only we could find that gold," Heather said.

"Really, Heather? You still believe Pearl Chambers hid a treasure?"

"Well, we never really followed through on Lia's idea that it could be right in 'the heart' of your house."

Molly's husband, Curtis, had been the last surviving member of the Chambers clan, and Molly and her son, Noah, still lived in the family's homestead.

"The eternal optimist." Molly smiled at her friend. "You're certainly welcome to do another search."

"Friday after book club?"

"Why not."

"Okay. I'll pass the word to the girls." Heather set her hand on Molly's shoulder. "Don't worry. We are going to find it. I just know it. And when we do, all your troubles will be over."

Gage Turner stepped into Smitten Expeditions and closed the door behind him. He scanned the refurbished space with the eye of someone in the business. Clean, wide-plank floors, good lighting, organized product. Pretty small, but nicely done. Rustic and rugged, visually appealing.

Somewhere a TV or radio was playing. The front desk was unattended, so he followed the noise to the open office door off to the side.

Molly Moore stood in the middle of the cramped office facing her desk, feet shoulder-width apart. Her slender right arm whipped back and forth through the air. She mumbled something to herself, repositioned, and repeated the motion.

"Whip it," she whispered. "Just . . . whip the wrist. Nice and smooth." She followed through the motion again, wiggling her cute little rear end as she repositioned.

Gage's lips turned up. He leaned into the doorframe and cleared his throat.

She spun around, dropping her raised hand casually to run her fingers through her straight honey-colored hair. He'd never been close enough to notice the faint smattering of freckles that dotted her nose or the golden slivers that flecked her brown eyes.

"Nice technique."

A pretty blush bloomed on her cheeks. She opened her mouth. Closed it. Crossed her arms over her chest. He decided he liked her flustered. A lot.

It didn't last long, though. A second later her eyes snapped, and her delicate jaw clenched. She shut off the fly-fishing video playing on her laptop and turned to glare at him. "You could knock."

Hmm. Feisty worked too. "Door was open."

She lowered her chin. "Can I help you?"

He stepped into the office and extended his hand. "Gage Turner. Don't think we've actually met." She knew who he was. Smitten wasn't that large, especially off-season.

She eyed his hand as if it were a snake. A venomous one. An instant later she took it. He'd known she would. Had somehow known she was incapable of being outright rude.

"Molly Moore," she said begrudgingly.

Her hand felt small and delicate in his, but there was strength in the line of her jaw and determination in her eyes, in the set of her slender shoulders. Of course she was strong.

After what she'd been through with her husband's death, there was no doubt about that.

"Can I help you?" she asked again in a tone that belied her words.

"Actually, I was wondering if I could help you."

Her pretty eyes narrowed on him as she pursed her generous lips. "*Heather*," she squeezed out.

"Excuse me?"

She rounded her desk, flipped a book shut, and shuffled a random stack of forms. "Listen. I don't need your"—her fingers formed air quotes—"*help*. I'm perfectly capable of running my business, so thank you very much for the offer, but I told Heather I was handling it, and I am. Good day."

"Heather . . ."

She sighed hard. "DeMeritt? The beautiful woman who coerced you to step in and save the day?"

"Listen, I don't know—"

"I'm sure you mean well . . ." She tweaked a dark brow, calling serious doubt to that claim. "But I've got it covered. So thanks, but no thanks."

She didn't like him much, he'd known that. Seemed pretty unfair, given that he'd never said two words to her before today, but her late husband's dislike had apparently rubbed off.

He should walk away. He should. She didn't want his help. But he couldn't seem to forget the scene in his shop yesterday. "I could take your fly-fishing tour."

Her lips parted. He took the opportunity, knowing he might not get another. "And now that your schedule for the rest of the week has somewhat, ah, cleared up, I can help—"

Her eyes narrowed again. "How did you know that?"

He put his hands out, palms up. "Just trying to help."

"How did you know that?" she asked again.

How did she pull off cute with a foot tap and a glare? "Your rafting group came to my place after they left here yesterday."

She wilted like a week-old daisy, her shoulders sinking, the corners of her lips falling. Her eyes went flat. "Oh."

He wished he could take it back. He hadn't meant to humiliate her. "Hey, happens to the best of us."

She grabbed a stack of trifolds and an inkpad and began stamping them. "It was an . . . unfortunate event. But I'm hiring someone to replace my tour guide, so everything's fine. Thanks for checking." Ink. Stamp. Shuffle.

He'd gone about this all wrong. She'd already accepted help from so many others, but they weren't him.

"Well. If there's anything I can do—"

"There isn't." She gave him a tight smile and tossed her hair over her shoulder. "Thanks anyway."

CHAPTER TWO

. . . .

*Y*ou look exhausted, honey." Lia sank into the stuffed chair beside Molly and blew on her fresh cup of coffee. She had a cobweb hanging from her auburn hair, and dust streaked her V-neck T-shirt.

Molly knew she should check on Noah, but she couldn't seem to get up. He'd been asleep since she'd returned from book club and had somehow slept through their treasure hunt. "I'm fine. Just disappointed."

Abby flopped onto the tweed recliner. "We searched every inch."

"Except Noah's room. I'll do that tomorrow." She looked around the living room. She should get up and turn off all the lights. The place looked like the train depot at noon, and she had her electric bill to think of.

"It has to be here somewhere," Lia said. "There were

house metaphors all the way through *Love and Courtship*. It's the only thing that makes sense."

Heather brushed the dust from her dark hair, setting her hands on her hips. "Well, we've done everything we can for tonight. Don't worry, Mol, we won't give up."

"There's still the barn and outbuildings," Lia said.

"And the well," Abby said. "People used to hide things in wells, didn't they?"

"Yeah, dead bodies," Molly said. The night had left her feeling hopeless. No treasure. No tour guide. No customers. Things were really looking up.

"How are things going at the store?" Abby asked.

Molly nodded. "Fine. Good." Maybe if she kept saying it, it would be true.

"Liar." Heather softened the word with a smile, then perched on the arm of Molly's chair. "She hasn't found a replacement for Dwight yet."

"Oh dear," Lia said. "How's that going?"

Molly gave an indelicate laugh. "Don't ask."

"She got an offer from Gage Turner."

"Wait. What did I miss?" Abby shoved aside the worn copy of *Love and Courtship* and raised her brows at Molly. "What kind of offer?"

"An offer of help," Molly said, then muttered under her breath, "If that's what you call it."

"Isn't he a competitor?" Lia asked.

"Exactly." Molly gave a sharp nod to punctuate the sentiment. "He owns that big tour place on Main Street."

Lia pushed her hair over her shoulder. "It does sound a little fishy."

"Hello . . ." Abby's eyes toggled between them. "Have you *seen* Gage Turner?"

Heather waved her away. "Molly needs help, like, yesterday. Seriously, Molly, you have to consider his offer. Especially after the rafting incident."

"There was an incident?" Lia asked.

Molly groaned. "Don't want to talk about it."

"You should accept his help," Abby said. "Definitely."

Molly looked between Heather and Abby. "Haven't you seen *You've Got Mail*? I'm barely hanging on by a thread. I don't need some Joe Fox putting the final nail in my business coffin."

Abby rolled her eyes. "What is it with you and that movie?"

"Honey." Heather set a hand on Molly's arm. "It can't get much worse."

The words made her chest ache. Curtis had worked so hard to get the business up and running. The whole community had pitched in after his death. It shouldn't be this hard. *I'm floundering here, God. Can't you see that?* Guilt stabbed her at the selfish thought. God had helped her through the most difficult year of her life. Who was she to ask for more?

"Has anyone applied for the position?" Lia asked.

"Not a one."

"But things are okay, right?" Lia tilted her head and gave Molly that look that always melted her resolve. "Financially?"

Molly traded a look with Heather. So she hadn't exactly been forthcoming with the other girls. She was so tired of charity. When would she stand on her own two feet? It was so humiliating.

Not as humiliating as losing everything, though.

"You should tell them, Mol."

Abby frowned. "Tell us what?"

Molly took a deep breath and pried her tongue from the roof of her mouth. "I may lose the business."

"What?" Lia leaned forward. "I thought things were going okay."

"And spring is here," Abby said. "Your busy season."

Heather rubbed Molly's shoulder. "Winter was a little hard on her."

Molly sighed. Might as well get it all out. "Things were worse than Curtis let on."

"Worse as in . . ."

"The business was in the red when he passed. He took a loan against our house to do all that refurbishing at the store. I guess he thought it would draw more tourists. Only it didn't."

Lia gasped.

"And he never told you?" Abby said.

Molly felt the anger building inside again. Her husband had forged her name on the loan documents and swept it all under the rug. Was it any wonder she was lacking in the trust department these days?

"With everyone's help, things started turning around last year," Molly said. "We broke even, which was a miracle."

"But winter took its toll," Heather said. "And now her only guide is gone. So, see, she needs help ASAP. It's not just the business but the house that's on the line."

"Oh no," Lia said. "It's been in the family so long."

"We have got to find that gold," Abby said.

"We will," Heather said. "I just know it."

Lia nudged her shoulder. "Maybe you *should* accept Gage's help."

Molly shot her a look. So much for having Lia in her corner.

"Well, he is kind of cute."

"All I'm saying," Abby said.

"What if he has nefarious intentions?" Molly said. "What then? How can I trust him?"

"Honey," Heather said, "he has lots of guides working for him. Maybe he'll lend you one until you find a replacement. Or have one of them teach you the ropes. You're kind of in a corner here. What's the worst that could happen?"

"With my luck? I'll drown in the Green River."

"And . . . problem solved," Abby said.

Three sets of eyes darted her way.

"Kidding!" Abby set her tea down. "Listen, I think you should take him up on it. You can learn this stuff. Think how much money you'd save if you could do the tours yourself. Office help is cheap."

She was right. Dwight was good, but he hadn't come cheap. Molly had paid for his benefits too. If she could learn all the guide stuff, maybe that would solve her deeper financial problem. Still . . .

"Can you really see me taking on the great outdoors?" Molly asked.

Heather wrapped an arm around Molly's shoulders. "Girl, I can see you doing anything you put your mind to."

Molly stepped into the store, her hands shaking. Somehow this had seemed so much easier the other night after the unfruitful treasure hunt. The girls had left her feeling all Annie Oakley. But now, looking around the huge interior of Explorations, she wondered if she wasn't in way over her head.

It was impossible not to compare Gage's shop with her own. Excitement sizzled in the air. Customers bustled around readying for trips, choosing equipment, signing paperwork.

Upbeat music flowed from invisible speakers somewhere up in the rafters. Employees in khakis and logoed polos greeted customers. The place smelled like adventure and money.

I am so out of my league.

Maybe Gage Turner was underhanded. Maybe he was sneaky and dishonest. But the man obviously knew how to run a business. Or maybe he ran it in a way that she never would.

"Can I help you?" A young blonde beamed a smile, baring a dimple.

"Is Gage Turner in? I mean, if he's busy, that's fine, I don't have—"

"In his office." Suzy Q gestured toward a hallway at the back. "First door on the left."

"I don't want to bother—"

"Go on back. He won't mind." With a parting smile, she peeled off to assist a customer with hiking shoes.

Molly regarded the hallway with a frown. *Now or never, Molly. Just get this over with.*

She skirted customers and racks of expensive outerwear. When she came to the open doorway, she paused. The office ceiling vaulted over a rugged oak desk. Matching cabinets lined the ecru walls, and a masculine rug hugged the plank floor. His window overlooked the scenic river. Of course it did.

Gage was hunched over his desk, pen in hand. He punched numbers on a calculator, wearing a frown surely caused by concentration, not distress.

He was good-looking, she couldn't deny that. His dark, tousled hair looked as if he'd just woken, and his lids covered a pair of blue eyes that probably made women melt into a puddle at his feet. The perpetual five o'clock shadow didn't hurt either, nor did the cleft in his chin. He was rugged, smart, handsome, and probably pretty darn rich too.

She mentally added the list of adjectives Curtis had supplied, none of them good. She'd have to stay on her toes where this one was concerned.

Drawing a deep breath, she tapped her knuckles on the oak doorframe.

His head came up, his brows rising expectantly. Upon seeing her, they fell. His lips slackened before tipping up in a cautious smile.

"Am I interrupting?"

He set his pen down and straightened in his chair. "No. Come on in."

She stepped into the office, leaving the door open. Something masculine with a touch of pine filled her nostrils.

"Have a seat."

Molly perched on the edge of the cushy chair opposite his desk, clutching her bag to her stomach. "Nice place you have here."

"Thanks. It's a work in progress."

If there were any progress required, she had yet to spot it.

"What can I do for you?" His chair creaked as he settled back into it. Waiting.

Suck it up, Molly. She bit the inside of her lip. "So, when you came by last week . . . I wasn't very friendly. I'm sorry about that."

He lifted one shoulder and the same corner of his lip. "You were fine."

He had a really nice voice. Deep and gravelly. It kind of made her chest flutter.

Ulterior motive, Molly. He probably has one, remember?

"Um, that's very gracious." She took a deep breath and met his eyes. They were warm, the color of faded denim.

She had to focus. She needed his help, but she needed to know something else first. He probably wouldn't tell her the truth, but she had to ask. "I was, um, wondering why you, you know, offered to help me."

His brows rose a millimeter. He opened his arms on the desk, his hands palms up. "We're neighbors."

Neighbors. Of course. They were competitors too, but he failed to mention that. Of course, with the state of things, she was hardly even that.

Which brought her back to this little visit. "I'm afraid I may have rejected your offer prematurely." Heat climbed into her cheeks. Was no doubt blooming into a blotchy shade of red. Nice.

"What can I do for you, Molly?"

Her name on his tongue made something warm unfurl in her stomach, a sensation she hadn't felt in years and didn't welcome now. Not good. Not good at all.

"Um, I'm sure you've heard I lost my guide."

He tipped his head forward.

"I haven't been able to find a replacement, and I'm thinking about taking over that portion of the business myself."

"Makes sense."

Only because he didn't know her. She had trouble imagining herself doing all those outdoor things. But she thought of Noah's bright brown trusting eyes and their cozy farmhouse, the only bit of normalcy they'd had since his father passed, and knew she'd scale Everest if she had to.

"Do you have any training?" he asked.

"I was actually wondering if you might know someone who could teach me. I know it's asking a lot. If you can't help, I understand. It's the busy season. Your guides are probably booked."

He tipped his head back, studying her. Probably noting her slight frame and glossy pink fingernails. Visualizing the lame little fly-fishing demo she'd given in her office the week before.

"I'm a quick learner."

"I'm sure you are."

"I could tag along on tours or something? I could . . . I could even pay." *Really, Molly? With what?*

He shook his head. "Leading a group isn't the same as being a participant. You have to learn the skills, yes, but you also need to learn to teach them. Having rock climbing experience would be helpful, for instance, but you need to learn how to belay."

"Oh." What was he saying? Was this a no? *Please, God. A little help here.*

"I'd be happy to give you some lessons, though."

"You?"

He tweaked a brow, making him look ornery. "I do possess the necessary skills."

What was his game? Was this part of his heinous plot to take her down?

"I'm AMGA certified," he added.

Her heart dropped. "I thought we didn't need certification in Vermont." At least, that's what Curtis always said.

"Not necessary, but very helpful—something to work toward. So what do you say?"

"I'm sure you're busy."

"I have some downtime in my schedule. I can have you trained for the basics in a couple weeks, tops."

"Oh." What now? Like she had a choice. It was this or foreclosure. Mother and child out on the streets, business bankrupt, no job. She straightened in her chair. "Great. Thank you. I appreciate it."

They set a time for the next afternoon, and Molly shuffled from his office a few minutes later. Ready or not, she was going to learn to run this business of hers from the bottom up.

CHAPTER THREE

. . . .

ime for bed, sport." Molly gave the Nerf football one last toss and stood, shutting off the TV.

"Five more minutes?" Noah threw a spiral that sailed over her head, ricocheted off the hall wall, and bounced into the spare room. "My bad," he said.

"You already got fifteen extra minutes, and tomorrow's a school day. Get into your pajamas."

Molly followed the ball's trail, frowning as she scoped out the spare room. Okay, junk room. The space had become a catchall for every object without a place. Her mom's piano, her old computer, Curtis's sporting equipment, baby toys and special clothes that held memories too dear to part with.

Leaning over, she spied the ball under the piano bench. She stooped down and scooped it out, then stood, pausing to run her fingers over the dusty piano. How long had it been since she'd played? She couldn't remember. She'd practically forgotten it was even here.

Drawn to the keys, to this joyful part of her past, she propped open the lid. It creaked in protest. She ran a hand along the lid. "Sorry, friend. Guess I've neglected you, huh?"

She used to play all the time. It was her favorite de-stressor. But after she'd married, Curtis had complained about the noise. He liked quiet when he came home.

The bench creaked as she sank onto it. She opened the lid. The instrument was probably out of tune. She was definitely out of practice. But she lowered her fingers over the keys anyway and tried a chord progression in C-sharp minor, followed by a rippling four-octave scale.

Out of tune, yes. But the keys felt good under her fingertips. Familiar and comforting. She began to play the "Moonlight Sonata," pleased when her fingers remembered the deep arpeggiated chords. She closed her eyes and let her hands move over the keyboard as warmth flowed through her.

Ah, she'd missed this. Why had it taken so long for her to play again? After the last melancholy chord died away, she launched into Mozart's happy little *Sonata in C.* Her fingers, catching on, zipped over the keys. She smiled, delighted she could still handle the difficult trills and mordents.

"You haven't played in a long time." Noah appeared at her side, snapping up his football. "I like when you play."

Molly finished the B section, letting the last chords ring through the room. "Thanks, buddy."

"Can you play anything you want?"

"Well . . . not anything. Not unless I have music."

"Can you play 'Best Day Ever'?"

"From *SpongeBob*? If I had the music."

"What about 'Another One Bites the Dust'?"

Molly narrowed her eyes. "Someone's stalling." She smacked his pajama-clad backside and lowered the lid. "Come on, let's tuck you into bed."

He groaned but followed her up the creaky wooden stairs. In his room he hopped into his bed and fell back onto his pillow. His room smelled like dirty socks even though they'd just cleaned it last weekend.

She pulled his Catamounts comforter to his chin. He had his dad's square chin and dark hair, but his brown eyes were just like hers, right down to the golden flecks. Sometimes when she looked into them, she worried. He'd lost his dad so young. What effect would that have on him? Was she doing enough to help him cope? Was she giving him everything he needed?

When Noah finished his prayers, she kissed his forehead and stood.

"You should play more often, Mom."

"The piano?"

"Yeah." He burrowed into his pillow. "It makes you smile."

She scanned his sweet little face. How did she get such a special boy? "I might just do that, buddy."

&

Molly looked up at the cliff face, and her knees went weak. She'd hoped to start with something easy like fly-fishing, but she had a couple scheduled for rock climbing tomorrow.

The morning was perfect, she had to admit. The air

still held a chill, and the sun was just rising over Sugarcreek Mountain against a clear blue canvas. The smell of pine trees and the loamy scent of earth fragranced the air.

Behind her, Gage pulled the equipment from the bag. He'd said she needed to experience climbing before she learned to belay. She was going to be hanging by her fingertips from a sheer cliff face. Never mind that the man holding the rope was a competitor who no doubt hoped to see her fail. A long, hard fall would probably suffice.

If he wondered why the owner of Smitten Expeditions had never rock climbed, he didn't ask. He was about to find out anyway.

"How do the shoes feel?"

She tried to wiggle her toes. "Okay, I guess."

"Fit is critical," he said as he organized the equipment. "They should be comfortably tight. No room for your feet to move around. Your toes should hit the front of the shoe. It's okay if they curl slightly. Take a few steps and make sure your heel doesn't lift."

She took a few steps. "Nope."

"Are you Red Cross certified?"

"Yes, for first aid and CPR." She'd gone through the courses with Curtis.

"Good. Okay, let's get you outfitted."

He had her step into the harness and showed her how to adjust it, his hands brushing her waist and thighs. "You'll want to get familiar with the gear and check it regularly."

She hadn't realized how tall he was. She was no shorty at five foot six.

"A good fit will make the climber feel more secure." A frown marred his forehead as he worked and talked, his eyes flickering up to hers periodically. They sparkled in the sunlight. He had dark lashes that swept down across his tanned skin. His nose had a faint bump just below the bridge. His jaw was clean-shaven today, calling attention to his nicely shaped lips.

"Double back the buckle like this. Make sure it's above the hipbones and good and snug." His light, musky cologne teased her nose as he tugged on the harness.

She watched his hands move over the harness, double-checking. Her heart scuttled across her chest at his touch. *What in the world, Molly?*

"Okay, next we rig the harness. This is the belay ring and tie-in loops. We're going to use a follow-through figure eight." He bent his knees, working the rope, his hands near places that made her cheeks flush.

He worked slowly, making sure she watched each loop. He repeated it, then had her try until she'd successfully completed it twice.

Next he showed her how to rig as the belayer, using his own harness. The rope led from his harness up to an invisible anchor at the top of the cliff and back down to her harness. She would be dangling from some dubious anchor.

After fitting her with a helmet, he led her over to the cliff wall. "You'll want to start beginners on this side, especially if they're nervous. As you can see, the face gets higher as you move that way. It's seventy feet at its peak."

She looked up at the wall of rock in front of her. Only twenty-five feet or so. Doable. Even if she fell, she'd survive. Right?

"The handholds and footholds are more prominent on

this side too. As you move toward the middle, it gets more challenging. Ready to give it a go?"

She wiped her damp palms down her pants. "Uh, sure."

"Go for it." He backed up, and she took a step toward the wall. The first holds were easy. The shoes clung to the rock, and the rope holding her stayed taut, making her feel semi-secure. After a while, the holds became less obvious. She scouted for her next reach, tried a couple of options, but they seemed too shallow.

She felt like she'd come a long way. She looked down to check. Mistake. She fixed her eyes on the jagged rock inches from her face, waiting for the dizziness to subside.

"Try your left hand about a foot up," Gage said. "See the ledge?"

She spotted it and grasped it, the rope staying taut as she moved. Her fingers were starting to ache, and her legs trembled as her toes clung to the shelf. She needed a place for her foot, but her brain was begging for terra firma. She took a calming breath, trying to quell the rising panic.

Why had she thought she could do this? Why was he even making her? She was supposed to be on the other end of the rope. The safe end. Why did he have the easy job?

"Doing great, Molly."

But her feet seemed glued to the ledge. And the trembling in her legs could be spotted from a commercial jetliner.

"There's a nice toe hold for your right foot. See if you can stretch up to it."

She forced her foot off the ledge and felt for the hold. Where was it? She gave up, her quivering calf making the call for her.

"I can't."

"Yes, you can. You're only a few feet from the top. You got this."

She glared over her shoulder. She wanted to be on the ground. Only sheer pride kept her from quitting. She wondered what that said about her. Nothing good, she was sure.

"Okay, just let go," he called.

"Of what?"

"Everything. Just let go. Fall."

"Are you crazy?"

"I've got you. I promise."

Sure he did. He'd let go, and she'd fall to her death. Whoops.

She looked down, regretting it quickly when her heart kicked her hard in the ribs. Okay, maybe not death. A broken leg would fit the bill, though, wouldn't it? Hard to be a tour guide when you were hobbling around on crutches.

"Feel how taut the rope is? Just let go."

No. No way. She took a deep breath. She could find that next toehold. She could do this. But her legs were shaking so hard, and her foot wouldn't move.

"I'll be good," she squeaked, sounding a lot like Noah.

She heard his warm chuckle and wanted to smack him upside the head. Unfortunately her hands were occupied, and he was too far away. Below her. Safe on the ground.

"You can do this. This equipment holds six thousand pounds, Molly. Come on. You can't be a bit over one." There was humor in his tone.

Was he trying to make her relax or make her angry? She was leaning toward the latter. Besides, it wasn't the equipment she didn't trust.

Note to self: earn customers' trust before taking their lives in your hands.

"I want you to see that you're perfectly safe. That even if you slip, you'll be okay. Let go. I've got you. I promise."

He promised. What did that really mean? On the other hand, she was kind of at his mercy. Maybe if she went along, he'd let her come back down. *Please, God.*

She loosened her grip on the ledge one aching finger at a time. Her calves quivered at the extra pressure.

"That's it. You can do it."

She grabbed onto the rope with her free hand. Like that would do any good. *Come on, Molly. Just do it. You're wearing a helmet. A broken leg wouldn't be the end of the world.*

When her second hand peeled away from the rock, her feet lost their hold, and she swung out. A sound squeaked from her throat. Her heart thudded. Her mouth went dry. She closed her eyes tight.

But the rope held. She gripped it tight, not even letting go when she swung back into the wall. Her knee scraped the rough surface.

"You did it. Great, Molly. Catch your breath. Give your legs a chance to rest. When you're ready to continue, find some holds and get started again. You're almost to the top, see? Just a couple more holds and you're there."

She looked up. Almost to the top? It seemed like a mile. *Don't look down. Don't look down.* She stared at the jagged rock in front of her nose and focused on breathing. *In. Out. You're going to be fine.*

The harness cut into her thighs. Her butt probably looked the size of a Volkswagen from below.

Really, Molly? You're dangling midair like a trout on a fishing line, and that's what you're worried about?

She took a moment to catch her breath, forced her grip to loosen from the rope, resting her fingers. She could do this. She was almost to the top, right? The sooner she finished, the sooner she could get down.

She sighted some good holds, making a mental path to the top, then went to work. Gage encouraged her, keeping the rope taut. Her legs still quivered, and her heart still thrashed around her chest, but she made herself finish.

When she reached the top, she'd never been so relieved in her life.

"Great job, Molly." He explained how to rappel down the face. The first push off was scary, and she came awkwardly back to the wall, banging her knee. But there was only one way down. Her limbs were tired, making her movements clumsy. She pushed off again, this time catching her weight with her feet.

"There you go. You got this."

By the time her feet hit the ground, she felt as if she'd scaled Mount Everest. She took a couple of wobbly steps. Gage was beaming at her.

"I think I'd rather have your job."

"Well, that's fortunate for you, because you do."

CHAPTER FOUR

· ·

$\mathcal{M}$olly stood behind her desk, looking over Heather's shoulder as she punched numbers into the calculator. The stack of bills was high, and business had been down last month. This wasn't going to be good.

"Could you maybe stand somewhere else?" Heather said.

"Sorry." Molly backed off. "I just know it's not good."

"Let's just hang on and see where we are."

Heather was right. Besides, what good would worry do? It wouldn't put more money in her account. It wouldn't attract more customers. And it sure wouldn't save her home.

"I just don't know how I got here, to this point where everything's in jeopardy."

"Don't beat yourself up. Curtis, God love him, made some bad decisions, and you're doing your best to rectify them."

The subject of her late husband's dishonesty opened a

hole in her gut. Finding out after he was gone that he'd put their home on the line had been awful. She'd felt confused and betrayed. How could he have hidden such a big thing from her? Forged her name? And she couldn't even confront him for answers. If she hadn't had Heather to talk it through with, she would've gone crazy.

"How are you doing with all that?" Heather had been staring at her, no doubt reading her every thought.

"I've forgiven him and I'm moving on. What choice do I have? He's not here and . . ." She gestured to the financials. "I've got a mess to fix."

Heather studied her another moment. "God has been faithful, and he'll see you through the rest of this."

"You're right." She just had to trust him. That was easier said than done these days.

"Hey, did Lia ever give you Pearl's book to read?"

"Oh yeah." She'd been reading *Love and Courtship* at night after Noah was in bed. "I haven't stumbled across a treasure map, but there's sure some crazy advice in there."

"We've come a long way, baby." Heather shoved the laptop at Molly. "Here. Occupy yourself. It's going to be a little while."

Molly took one of the chairs in front of the desk, her muscles protesting as she lowered herself into it. Even two days after climbing, she hurt. On the bright side, her tour yesterday had gone fabulously. Although, truth be told, the honeymooners hardly noticed her existence.

There had been one moment when she'd guided the woman too far to the left of the cliff, and the rope had gotten hung up on a ledge. She'd been stuck dangling helplessly for a few minutes. But nobody had died. Nobody had even complained or demanded a refund. Things were looking up.

She opened the laptop and checked her e-mail, frowning as she read Abby's. *Did you see this?* When Molly clicked on the link, she landed on a Trip Advisor page.

Smitten Expeditions was in bold black letters with a rating beside it—1 out of 5.

There were two reviews, a two-star and a zero. She hadn't even known a zero was possible. She read the reviews, frowning.

Horrible service . . . bad instructions . . . terrible experience. She read on. *I can't say enough about the guide. Enough bad things, that is. To say she was incompetent would be the biggest understatement of the century. My grandma could've done better. Stay away from this place. It's a joke.*

Molly gasped. *The refund, people! You could've mentioned the refund.* Why did people have to be so mean? So personal?

"What is it?" Heather asked.

"Abby sent me a link to a review. The revenge of the white-water group."

"Oh, for heaven's sake. Those people act like you ruined their lives. It was a tour."

"But it's Trip Advisor. They're my only two reviews, and now I have a one-star rating. Listen to this. 'This trip was so horrible, words aren't adequate. The guide couldn't have rowed her way out of a bathtub.'"

"Ouch."

A knock sounded on the doorframe. Molly looked over her shoulder and found Gage standing in the open doorway. Great. Just great. Of course this was the moment Mr. Success would appear.

Molly pursed her lips. "We're closed." She'd turned the sign but must've forgotten to lock up.

His blue eyes warmed. "I didn't stop by for a guided hike." His gaze drifted to Heather, and he greeted her before turning his attention to Molly. She was reluctantly impressed at how quickly he'd turned away from Heather's beauty.

"How'd the climb go yesterday?"

"Very well. Thanks again for your help."

He took a couple of steps in, bringing his manly smell with him. The room shrank two sizes, and it was already the size of a shoe box.

Conscious of the reviews on the screen, Molly closed her laptop as he neared. He'd already heard enough.

"Any problems?"

"None at all." She wasn't going to mention the rope incident. Could've happened to anyone.

Heather stood, the chair rolling out behind her. "You know, I need to call Abby. She left me a voice mail."

Molly glared at Heather's retreating back as Gage perched on the corner of the desk. Molly's eyes flittered to the financials spread across it. They'd probably taught reading upside down at the fancy college he'd no doubt attended.

"What's next on your schedule? I have some time in the morning if you need more lessons."

She eased around her desk and casually gathered the sensitive material before sitting in her cushy desk chair. "Canoeing tomorrow afternoon. But I think I can handle it." Outside the office she heard Heather greet Abby.

"You've been canoeing?"

She shifted. "Not really. But I've done my research." How hard could it be? A boat, two paddles, a serene stretch of the Green River. She wasn't that lame.

"I'm not trying to be a jerk, but that didn't work out so well with the rafting."

She scowled at him. "Thanks for the reminder."

"Come on, it'll be fun, and it won't take long. Tomorrow's supposed to be a gorgeous spring day."

She studied him. His thick arms were crossed over his broad chest. He tilted his head at her, smirking. Even his smirk was hot. So unfair.

She narrowed her eyes. "Why are you doing this again?"

His lips twitched. "So suspicious."

She colored under his direct gaze and wondered idly when she'd last combed her hair and freshened her lip gloss. She shook the thought away. Pearl Chambers and her stupid antiquated advice.

"You didn't answer the question," she said.

He sighed, his gaze lingering on her until she squirmed in her chair.

"How long have you lived here?" he asked.

"Eight years."

"Where did you come from?"

"Is this going somewhere?"

"Humor me."

She sighed hard. "Fine. Buffalo."

"Nice. Home of the buffalo wing and the Sabres. I'm a hockey fan."

She shook her head, giving him her *And . . .* stare.

"It's a small town, Molly. People here stick together and

help each other. When the log mill shut down, we worked together and made things happen. You were here. You watched Smitten go from a dying town to a thriving tourist destination. And now look, you own your own business because of it. That's what happens when people help each other." He lifted his shoulders. "I'm just being neighborly."

Even though they were competitors? Even though he'd tried to keep Curtis from opening shop to begin with? There was more stuff too. She just couldn't remember it all. But Gage had sure gotten Curtis's ire up.

"I love being outdoors," he said. "It's not exactly a chore. Besides, maybe someday I'll need help, and you'll be there."

Hmm. Did he have something else up his sleeve? Something he wanted from her? She looked down at the blotter before he could read her suspicions.

She'd have to think about that later. Right now she just wanted his masculine self out of her cubbyhole office. "All right. Yes, thank you. Canoeing lessons, tomorrow morning."

They set a time, and when he left, Molly sank in her chair. She hoped she wasn't making a monumental mistake.

CHAPTER FIVE

. . . .

*G*age drew his paddle through the water, his eyes on Molly's back. Her fitted pink T-shirt was tucked into the waistband of her jeans. Her light brown hair was captured in a ponytail, and it sparkled with bronze highlights under the sun. An orange life preserver hugged her frame. They were heading toward a warm day, not a cloud in the sky.

She switched sides with her paddle, and he followed suit, a few drops of frigid water dribbling across his legs. "Nice job, Molly."

"This is pretty easy."

"Relaxing, huh? This is a nice stretch." The river helped them along, but not so much that they couldn't enjoy the scenery. Grassy banks sloped up from the river, and countless trees stretched into the sky on both sides, sheltering them from the world.

"You'll love it in the fall," he said. "The colors are great through here."

"How deep it is?"

"Twelve feet or so here."

"Have you ever tipped over?"

"Oh yeah. Not because of me, though."

"Of course not." She tossed a saucy grin over her shoulder.

"Watch it, or I'll do a demonstration."

"I did not dress for a swim." There was a warning in her tone.

"That's half the fun." He rocked the boat.

She squealed, grabbing the sides, her paddle clanking against the boat. "Don't you dare!"

He chuckled, but did as she said. "Spoilsport."

She was fun to mess with. Her cheeks bloomed with color, and he missed that, sitting behind her. However, this view was nice too.

"I think I've got the hang of this," she said a few minutes later. "Should I take the stern now?"

"Let's switch at the halfway point. It's not far."

They approached a bend. "Very nice," he said after they'd navigated it. "So how is it that you're taking a group out here?" Canoeing was usually a put-in and pick-up situation.

"The couple is celebrating their first anniversary. She broke her arm recently, and they have their hearts set on canoeing, so . . ."

"You're their chauffeur."

"Basically."

He wondered if it was hard being around so many couples after losing her husband. Shoot, Smitten wasn't an easy place to be single, period. He should know. He'd done his share of dating but had yet to meet that someone special.

His eyes drifted back to the woman in the bow, and he wondered if she was dating yet. Wondered if she was still in love with her late husband. How she and her kid were really faring.

"You have a son, right?"

"Noah. He's eight."

"Good age. Maybe you can take him canoeing now. And rock climbing."

She drew her paddle slowly through the placid water and paused, resting. "He'd love that. His dad used to take him. I think he misses it."

He was surprised she'd mentioned something personal. The woman had walls a mile high. Walls he was beginning to think he might enjoy taking down, one stone at a time.

"There you go, then," he said.

She grew quiet, and he had a feeling she'd gone to a place in the past. It had to have been a rough year. After her husband had died, Gage had wanted to offer his help with the business more than once. But every time he'd run into Molly, she'd given him the cold shoulder. Besides, he hadn't wanted to patronize her, and as far as he'd known the business was fine in her capable hands.

"So, how'd you get involved in this business?" she asked after they navigated a dead tree.

"My dad and I used to spend a lot of time outdoors. I loved it. My parents always told me to figure out what I love to do, then find a way to make money at it. I took a summer job in Stowe as a guide and worked my way up there after high school. Saved my money. Then Smitten became a tourist destination, and it seemed providential. So here I am."

"No college?" She sounded surprised.

"Nope, never did. You?"

"NYU. Majored in music. My parents were thrilled about that."

"What do you play? Or are you a vocalist?"

"Piano, mostly. Although I'm fluent in flute and clarinet."

"I'm impressed. I don't have a musical bone in my body." He suddenly wanted to hear her play more than he could say. That wasn't likely to happen. "So did you dream of being in an orchestra, or being a concert pianist?"

"Nothing so grand, just a music teacher. My parents liked your plan better, though."

"So now you're a business owner . . ."

She gave a wry laugh that came out as a snort. "Life does throw unexpected curves. I met Curtis at NYU. You probably know he was a business major. I guess opposites attract. We married and moved here when his mom was still alive. Shortly after that, Smitten became a tourist destination, and he saw the same opportunity you did."

"Do you miss playing?"

She shrugged. "Sure. I have a business to run, though, and a child to support. Maybe someday I'll get back to it."

He got the feeling Curtis hadn't left her in a good financial situation. He hated that for her. Wondered if there was more he could do to help. He remembered the chat he'd walked in on at her office the night before. That ugly review.

"You know, if you ever want to talk things through,

business stuff, I'm glad to lend an ear, offer my opinion. For what it's worth."

He didn't think he imagined the way her spine stiffened.

"Thanks, but I have it under control."

Two stones down, one back up, just like that. They approached the halfway point, a sandbar just before the red covered bridge. "Let's switch here." Maybe after a quick break, he could steer the conversation to safer topics.

"Ugh, it's so thick." Molly frowned at the copy of *The Help*, their next book group selection. The other members of the club were gone, and her friends were gathered around the fireplace, sipping coffee and tea in the quiet bookstore.

"It's good," Heather said. "It was on the best sellers list forever."

"The cover's ugly." Molly scanned the back cover copy. "And it doesn't sound vaguely intriguing."

"Don't you dare just watch the movie," Abby said. "We'll know if you do."

Lia curled her feet under her. "It's really good. You'll like it."

"I'll give it a try. But I have to tell you, time is a scarce commodity right now. Plus, I have another book I'm reading, remember?"

"Have you found any clues yet?" Lia asked.

"I did notice Pearl mentioned stairs a couple of times as a metaphor for relationships. Maybe she hid it under the stairs?"

"We looked there," Abby said. "Just a bunch of old junk."

"Just the same, I might check again. Maybe there's a loose floorboard or something."

"Couldn't hurt," Heather said. "Let me know if you need help."

"Are things any better at the store?" Abby asked.

"She's been taking lessons from Gage Turner the past couple weeks," Heather said.

Molly was now proficient at nearly all the activities they offered. Gage had a wealth of knowledge, and she'd tapped into it as much as she could. She was more grateful than she could say. Maybe she should do something nice for him when this was over.

"Oh, I'm so glad he's helping you," Lia said. "Are things better businesswise?"

Molly shrugged. "Well, I found a girl to run the office—April Campbell. And I know what I'm doing on tours now." Too bad she didn't have many customers to impress with her newfound skills. Or enough money in the bank to pay her bills.

"She sure does," Heather said. "That Gage must be one heck of a teacher." Her eyes sparkled at Molly over the rim of her mug.

Molly gave a mock glare. Heather had been teasing her all week.

Abby's eyes toggled between them. "Okay, what are you not telling us?"

"Nothing," Molly said, frowning. "There's nothing I'm not telling you."

"Just that the man can hardly take his eyes off our little Molly," Heather said.

Heat climbed into Molly's cheeks. "That's ridiculous."

A grin stretched across Lia's face. "Do you like him?"

"I hardly know him."

Heather humphed. "You've spent the last two and a half weeks traversing the great outdoors together."

"Plus he's so yummy," Abby said.

"Don't you have your own man to ogle?" Molly said.

"Oh, I do, but I'm not blind."

"You should see the way he looks at her when she's not watching." Heather sighed dramatically. "I'm telling you, the man's already half gone."

"Hello. My husband just died. I have a son to support and a failing business to save." She was just fine on her own. Too busy to even think about being lonely.

Lia set her hand on Molly's shoulder. "It's been over a year, Molly. It's normal to start having feelings again."

"You're a young, vibrant woman," Abby added.

It was hard to believe a year had gone by. Though, if she were honest, things hadn't been right between Curtis and herself long before that.

Lia was right. Something had been stirring inside lately. Especially around Gage. Or when she was thinking about Gage. Which was way too often. Still, regardless of what Heather said, she wasn't sure about Gage's motives.

"Don't you think it's strange that he's putting in so much time to help a competitor?"

Heather waved Molly's concerns away. "He's being neighborly."

"Does it seem like he's snooping or digging for information?" Lia asked.

"Well . . . no, not really." They hardly talked business at all, except for the instruction he gave. But she couldn't forget that comment he'd made about returning the favor.

Abby brushed her golden brown hair over her shoulder. "If you're attracted to him—and how could you not be?—you should totally go for it."

The thought made her stomach flutter. Not butterflies. More like pterodactyls. "I don't know if I'm ready for that."

"Fair enough," Heather said. "But let's at least pray about it. You never know when God's going to bring the right man into your life, and you wouldn't want to blindly pass him by."

CHAPTER SIX

. . . .

*M*olly drew the football back, winged her arm forward, and released the ball. It wobbled through the air in a sloppy arc and dropped into Noah's waiting hands.

"Mom. That was so ugly."

"Hey, if you want spirals, you're gonna have to stand closer."

The warm sunny day had brought half of Smitten out to the lake. Boats dotted the water, families gathered for Sunday picnics under pavilions, and athletic types jogged nearby on the paved lake trail.

It wasn't long ago Noah begged to come to the lake park to climb on the monkey bars and swing on the swings. Now it was football. And the picnic, of course. He still loved food as much as the next boy.

She was tired today. She'd been up until late rooting

290

under the stairwell. Abby was right, it was filled with junk, but Molly cleared it out to check the floorboards and the walls. All she'd turned up was a head full of cobwebs and an outfit full of dust.

In the middle of her reverie, she didn't see the football until it was sailing through the air. She jogged backward to catch Noah's overzealous throw. Her foot caught on something, and she went over backward. Her head clunked on the ground.

"Ouch."

"Mom!"

She waved her hand in the air. "I'm fine!" She lay there a moment, closing her eyes, assessing. Pain in the head. Nowhere else. Just needed a minute. Wow, that did not feel good.

"You okay?"

She opened her eyes.

Gage leaned over her, silhouetted by the sun, his disheveled hair haloed. He'd seen her clumsy fall. Of course he had.

"I'm fine."

He extended a hand and she took it, letting him pull her to her feet. His hand was big and warm around hers. When he let go, she shoved down a pang of disappointment.

"You sure?" he asked.

Noah jogged up to them. "Sorry, Mom."

Molly ruffled his brown hair. "Not your fault, buddy. This is my friend Gage." *Friend?* "Gage, Noah."

Gage shook his hand. "Nice spiral you got there."

"Thanks. I throw better than my mom."

Gage laughed. "Careful, big guy. She controls the food."

Noah frowned as if trying to decode the comment, then turned to Molly. "We gonna eat soon? I'm starving."

"Sure. You grab the ball, and I'll get the lunch out."

She watched Noah jog away as an awkward pause ensued. She turned back to Gage. He wore a white T-shirt and black basketball shorts. He was breathing hard—must've been jogging around the trail—and staring back at her.

Say something, Molly. "Uh, you're welcome to join us . . ." *What are you doing?* "Lia was supposed to come, but something came up, so there's plenty. I mean, you know, if you need to eat."

Need to eat? Very gracious. How could he refuse such an offer?

"I don't want to intrude."

She shrugged. "It's just sandwiches. Bologna, at that. And these weird hot chips Noah likes. They're actually kind of nasty."

Gage's lips twitched. "Why do I get the feeling you're trying to rescind your offer?"

Busted. She opened her mouth, but her mind went blank. She bit her top lip.

"Actually, I do need to eat." His blue eyes sparkled. "Where's the food? I'll help you unpack."

What had she gotten herself into? "Over there." She gestured toward the picnic table and saw Noah already seated there.

"Hurry up, Mom!"

Gage pulled the bottom of his shirt up to wipe his face. She dragged her eyes from his ripped stomach. Yeowza.

"You heard the kid," Gage said.

They settled in and dug into the picnic. To his credit, Gage took down two bologna sandwiches and dived into the hot chips with as much gusto as Noah. He finished the two water bottles he'd fished from the cooler and managed to make Noah laugh twice with stories only an eight-year-old would find funny.

Halfway through the meal, Molly spotted Heather and Paul walking around the lake. She waved, and they came over to visit for a minute, Heather throwing her a covert wink. Molly rolled her eyes. Her friend would never let her hear the end of this.

By the time they finished, Molly had managed to relax. Noah tossed his trash as she began putting the food away.

"Can I go swing?"

Maybe he hadn't grown up so much after all. "Sure."

Gage helped her repack what was left and sat across from her, arms folded on the plastic tablecloth. He watched Noah jog toward the only open swing. "Seems like a great kid."

"I think so."

"He looks like you."

"You think?"

"You kidding me? Those big brown eyes? Spitting image."

"Well, don't tell him that. Boys don't want to resemble their moms." She was starting to get a headache. She ran her hand over the back of her head, feeling the lump.

"Sure you're okay? You went down pretty hard."

"Just a bump." She fished through her purse. "I think I will take something for this headache, though." After she downed the pills, she regarded him. "I'm surprised you're not at work. Weekends are prime."

"We're closed Sundays. Day of rest and all that."

She took another sip of water. She felt the same. Curtis had kept the business open on Sundays. She'd missed attending church with him that last year.

"How did your outings go yesterday?" Gage asked.

"Pretty good. Not a single unhappy camper since the white-water incident."

"Good for you." He stared in a way that made her stomach knot up, his eyes like warm blue lasers.

She squirmed. "What?"

His gaze drifted over her face. "Nothing. You're just a very capable woman."

She snorted.

"Don't do that. You are. You've been through rough times, but you're holding your own. You're raising a great kid, running a successful business. You're more than capable. Own it."

Successful business? Ha. If he only knew. She was hanging on by a thread, on the verge of losing everything.

"What? What did I say?"

Was her every thought etched on her forehead? She folded her hands on the table, watched Noah pumping higher and higher. "Things aren't always what they seem." Noah leaned back, gliding. He liked to make himself as dizzy as possible.

"What do you mean?"

This was the moment. The one where she had to decide whether to trust him or not. She looked into his blue eyes and saw only warmth and openness. Maybe she was crazy but . . .

"The business . . . it isn't going as well as you think." Her heart thudded at the admission. It was a hard one to make to Mr. Successful. She should've gone on letting him view her as capable. Now he'd think she was a failure.

"Want to talk about it?"

She kinda just wanted to take it all back. Her gaze

bounced off him. Maybe he could help. Maybe some of his magic charm would rub off on her.

Molly sipped her water, turned her face into the sun, and let the rays warm her. She didn't want to denigrate Curtis. He'd been a good husband despite his poor judgment. "Bottom line, I need more customers." She gave him a wry grin. "This seems like a stupid thing to be telling my competitor."

He leaned into the table, his broad shoulders stretching the cotton shirt. "Hey, we're friends, right? I'm happy to listen if you want to bounce anything off me. There's enough business for both of us."

Lately she'd doubted that. Maybe she was fighting a losing battle. "Think so?"

"Absolutely. How can I help?"

What did she have to lose?

Molly asked him about her price structure. Curtis had priced their excursions higher than Gage did. Would lowering them attract more customers, or would it just eat into her profits? From there they moved on to overhead costs, then marketing. He was so knowledgeable. What she'd give to have all his experience downloaded into her brain. But this was the next best thing.

He shared freely, and she found herself more than once pulled into his gaze. He was passionate about what he did. About the outdoor aspects, yes, but also about the business end. His eyes lit as he talked.

She wished she felt so excited about the business. Maybe she would if hers were thriving like his. Or at least surviving.

"Mom, is it time for the movie?" Noah's voice broke into their conversation.

She looked at her watch, surprised that over an hour had gone by. "Oh my goodness. Yeah, buddy, let's get this stuff to the car."

She stood, folding the tablecloth.

Gage grabbed the cooler. "I'll get this."

"Thanks."

He walked them to the car. She wondered idly if he'd want to go with them, then waved the idea away. He wouldn't want to see the latest Pixar film. Besides, she'd taken enough of his time.

Gage closed the trunk of her Corolla and turned to her, smiling. "Thanks for lunch. I'm glad I ran into you."

"I should be thanking you for letting me pick your brain."

He shrugged. "I love talking business. My door's always open."

"I appreciate that."

"Mom, we're gonna be late," Noah called from inside the car.

"I'll let you go." He winked.

Those pterodactyls made another appearance. "See you. Thanks again."

He gave a wave and a smile, turning toward the lake. She watched him a minute, noting the heavy thudding of her heart and the warmth in her cheeks. Maybe Heather wasn't so far off base after all.

CHAPTER SEVEN

. . . .

*T*he next week Molly was on the phone, booking a rock climbing tour for a family of five, when Gage walked through the door. She tossed him a smile as she cradled the phone on her shoulder and wrote the appointment into the book.

"You're all set for the fifteenth at ten a.m." She thanked the customer and hung up. Her gaze wandered to Gage, who stood by the picture window.

"Nice display," he said.

"That was all Lia and Heather. They did a nice job, huh? I don't know where they found fake pine trees this time of year."

"You have good friends."

"I do. I'm very blessed. They've really been there for me, especially this past year."

"I have a feeling they're equally blessed by you."

"I hope so." She'd do anything for them. And as hard as it was to see everyone coupling up last year, she was happy for them. No one deserved happiness more than her peeps.

Gage walked to where she stood behind the counter and leaned an elbow on the rustic wood top. She breathed in the smell of his cologne, drawing comfort from the familiarity. His hair was pleasantly mussed, and his eyes sparkled under the showroom lights. *Be still, my heart.*

"Things are going okay businesswise?"

He'd stopped by the store the week before to brainstorm some marketing ideas. It was a scary leap of faith to spend money, but he'd had some good ideas that fit her miniscule budget.

"I've gotten two customers from the online coupon, and I've been asking customers for reviews like we talked about. I've gotten a couple good ones."

"That's great." He gave her a high five.

"Unfortunately, my copy machine bit the dust yesterday."

"Not good."

She shrugged. "We got it secondhand. It was bound to happen eventually."

"Well, you're welcome to borrow mine. My shop's just around the corner, two blocks, on the left. You might've seen it." His eyes sparkled.

She was growing to like the warmth that flooded her when he teased. She suddenly realized how close he was, just a narrow counter between them. She breathed him in again. "I think I know the place."

He quirked a brow. "I hear the owner's really awesome."

"You don't say."

He gave an exaggerated shrug. "That's what I hear."

"Humble too, I suppose."

"Of course." His lips twitched.

They were nice lips too. Perfectly shaped. Not too thin, not too thick. Just right for kissing.

Whoa, Molly. She cleared her throat.

"So anyway . . ." He set a paperback on the counter, flipping it around so she could see the long business title, complete with subtitle. "This is the book I mentioned. Thought you might like to borrow it."

Ugh. So thick. She could only imagine all the boring pages filled with terms she didn't know and concepts she didn't understand.

"What?" he asked.

She really had to get a better poker face. "I appreciate it. I do. But I'm so busy right now. In my spare time I'm supposed to be reading that old Pearl Chambers book, and I just—"

"Pearl Chambers . . . ? The local author from the turn of the century?"

"Right."

"Why would you be reading her work? It must be so out-of-date."

Her advice on getting and keeping a man wasn't exactly world famous, but proud Smittenites knew of her. Out of date or not, Pearl's advice had spun in her mind a time or two recently, but Gage didn't need to know that.

Her face heated at the thought. "It's the old treasure lore." She waved the words away.

"You're looking for the gold mine?"

"Silly, really. But my friends found this old book and are

convinced that there's treasure waiting to be found. I promised to take a look. On top of that, my book club's reading *The Help* this month—you know how thick that thing is?—and I'm way behind. I don't know when I'd be able to get this back to you."

"They made a movie of that, didn't they?"

"Ha. They'll kill me if I cheat."

"SparkNotes?"

"Still cheating."

He smiled, looking down at her like he—well, like he just might think she was adorable. *Is that even possible?*

"So let me ask . . . if you're not much of a reader—why a book club?"

"I like to read—sort of. When the genre's right and the author's good and the book's not, you know, too thick or boring."

"And Venus aligns with Mercury under a crescent moon?"

She made a face. "Fine. It's not about the books. It's about girl time. Friendships. Community. Happy?"

"Nothing wrong with any of that." He shoved the book toward her. "Take it. I'm in no hurry to get it back. Shoot, keep the thing if you want. And here's a bonus: I highlighted the good stuff."

"Better than SparkNotes!"

"So much better." He stared into her eyes, smiling.

Her breath seemed to have stuck in her lungs. The way he looked at her . . . like he could see down to the core. And liked what he saw. Her mouth was suddenly dry. Her heart went to war with her ribs. She should say something, but her mind was blank.

"Listen, Molly," Gage said, his gaze flickering down to his hands before capturing her eyes again.

Something scary twisted in Molly's stomach at the look in his eyes, at the hopeful tone in his voice. Oh no. She was not ready for this.

Not.

Ready.

"I hope I'm not out of line. But I was wondering if—"

Molly grabbed her phone from her pocket and whipped it out. "Incoming call. I have to take this." She put the phone to her ear and said hello, her heart racing.

Gage's face fell. He closed his mouth, looked away.

Molly turned around, hating the look on his face as she carried on a pretend conversation. Why wouldn't he just leave? She couldn't do this. Not now. Not yet. She wasn't ready. Needed time to think.

The strains of her favorite song, "Smitten," filled the air. Molly paused mid-sentence. Her phone was ringing.

No.

She closed her eyes, not daring to turn around, and hit the kill button on her phone.

There was nothing but silence behind her. A flood of heat washed up her neck, into her cheeks. Her ears felt like fiery flames, and she knew they were turning as red as her T-shirt. She'd worn her hair in a ponytail today, naturally.

The door flew open and April barged in, fresh from her lunch break, wielding her suitcase-sized purse. "Oh my gosh, Molly, you have got to go to Piece of Cake and try the cupcake of the day! Chocolate and raspberry have never tasted so good. Hi, Gage."

Gage straightened, rubbed the back of his neck. "April."

"I would've brought you one, but I didn't know it was

so good—I ate it on the way back. Do I have chocolate on my face?"

"You're fine."

"I should be going." Gage's smile didn't reach his eyes as they flickered to hers. He tapped the counter twice and stepped away.

Part of Molly wanted to reach out and grab him. Pull him into her office and apologize. Make him finish his question. The other half wanted to shove him out the door, the sooner, the better.

He lifted his hand. "See you later, Molly. April."

Seconds later she was watching him slip out the door and wondering if she'd just let opportunity slip out with him. There was no way around it. Gage stirred feelings she hadn't felt in a long time. Good ones. Was it really okay, as Lia had said, to feel this way?

She'd loved Curtis. A part of her always would; he was her son's father. Was there room in her heart for another man? Was it too soon? Had she sufficiently worked through her anger toward Curtis? She didn't want to bring baggage into a new relationship.

Relationship? She snorted. *You're getting way ahead of yourself, Molly.*

Beyond one wink and, possibly, a near date invitation, what did she really have? A nice guy who went out of his way to help a friend.

"Any luck with the stairwell?" Heather asked.

Molly shook her head as she sank into the cushy leather

sofa. It was a busy Friday night at Mountain Perks. She'd only intended to grab a to-go cup before picking Noah up from his friend's house, but Heather was there, having arrived early for her date with Paul.

"I searched every square inch. Maybe we're never going to find it. Maybe someone else already did, or maybe Pearl never had it to begin with."

"I don't believe that. It's in that house somewhere."

Maybe. Or maybe they were on a fool's errand. Maybe it was hidden so well they'd never find it in time. Maybe she'd lose her house, and someone else a hundred years from now would become rich off Pearl Chambers's find.

Heather was talking about some problem at work, but Molly couldn't focus. Her thoughts turned to Gage and their last meeting. They were doing that a lot lately.

"He almost asked me out," Molly blurted. Talk about random.

Heather's coffee mug stopped halfway to her mouth. She caught on quick, her blue eyes sparkling. "Gage? When?"

"Wednesday."

"And you're just telling me? Come on, spill. Did he call? What did he say?"

"He stopped by the shop. We were just talking about this and that. He brought a business book for me to read and then—"

Heather gave a wry laugh at the mention of the book.

Molly shot her a look. "Anyway. He kind of leaned into the counter, and he was looking at me like—I don't know. Like he was interested or something, and he said, 'I hope I'm not out of line, but I was wondering if—'"

Molly's phone rang. She frowned, checking the number.

"Déjà vu," she muttered. Upon seeing a toll-free number, she silenced the phone.

"So . . . go on," Heather said.

This was where it got embarrassing. "When he was in the middle of asking, I panicked. I . . . kind of pretended to get a call."

"Oh, Molly."

"It gets worse." She closed her eyes at the memory. "A call came in right in the middle."

Heather made a face. "Pearl Chambers would not approve."

No kidding. "Then April walked in, thank God, diverting his attention, and he left. But he was going to ask me out. At least I think he was. What am I going to do if he does it again?"

"Do you really think he will after *that*?"

Molly palmed her forehead. "I know, I know. I feel like such a jerk."

Heather shook her head. "Only you, Molly. Maybe he will ask again. Do you want him to? Do you want to say yes?"

"No. Yes. I don't know." Molly ran her hand over her face. "When did I become so indecisive?"

Heather put her hand over Molly's. "You've been through a rough year. I'd be worried if you weren't a little uncertain. But if you're starting to have feelings, maybe it's time to explore them. Are you attracted to Gage? What am I saying? Of course you are."

"It just feels weird, another man. I was with Curtis for nine years."

"That's a long time."

"I do want to fall in love again. I loved being married.

Being a family. I just don't know if I'm ready yet to start thinking about all that."

"I guess you're the only one who can answer that. I've been praying for you. When the time comes, you'll make the right decision."

"If the time comes. Maybe it was just an impulsive thing on his part. Maybe he's reconsidered and decided it's a bad idea. Or maybe I just completely misjudged the moment."

Heather squeezed her hand. "Or maybe you're trying to talk yourself out of something that might feel a little scary."

Molly looked into Heather's warm eyes, then made a face. "I hate it when you're right."

*There are few pursuits the male youth enjoys so much as a
hearty challenge.*

PEARL CHAMBERS, *The Gentlewoman's
Guide to Love and Courtship*

CHAPTER EIGHT

. . . .

*G*age dribbled the ball out and turned to face Griffen.
His friend had lucked out with a basketball pad and
an old two-story just outside of town. Not to mention a beautiful best-friend-turned-wife. Some guys had all the luck.

"Where's your other half?" Gage advanced toward the
basket, winded. They'd been at this almost an hour, and the
afternoon sun was getting brutal.

"Girl time." Griffen blocked the shot, but Gage got the
ball back. "Something about shopping and chocolate."

Gage wondered what Molly was doing. He hadn't seen her
since he'd taken her the book. Okay, the book had been an
excuse to see her, to ask her out. Yeah, that had gone really well.

"You gonna shoot or something?" Griffen asked a minute
later.

Gage spun, put up the ball, and missed.

Griffen rebounded, checking the ball, then he dribbled
back in. Gage wiped his face with the tail of his shirt. His mind

went back to that day in her shop, to his unfinished invitation. He couldn't believe she'd faked a phone call.

"What's with the sour face?"

"Nothing."

"Really? 'Cause your head's not in the game, that's for sure."

It was true. He could usually hold his own with Griffen, but today he was losing by at least six points. Maybe more. He'd lost count.

He defended a couple of Griffen's moves, then dodged the wrong way.

Griffen put up a shot, scoring two more. "At least make it a game, man." He gave a sideways smile as he tossed the ball to Gage.

They played a few more minutes, Gage making a concerted effort to refocus. After a nice series of moves, he put the ball up for what should've been an easy layup. It hit the backboard, sprang off the rim, and dropped into Gage's hands.

Griffen shot him a look. "So what's her name?"

"Whose name?"

"The girl who's got you so hot and bothered."

"I'm not hot and bothered."

Griffen smirked.

Gage pitched the ball at his friend.

Griffen caught it at the chest. "It's that Molly chick, isn't it?"

"You gonna check the ball or what?"

Griffen dribbled out, then turned. "Don't shoot the messenger."

Gage crouched low as Griffen neared. "Yeah, well, doesn't matter. She's not interested."

He blocked a shot, but Griffen got it back easily.

"How do you know?"

"Trying to distract me?"

"I'm up by ten, dude. I could be comatose and beat you today." He put up a shot, and the ball swished through the net, the winning point. Gage wasn't even sorry that he'd lost.

"You should ask her out."

Gage gave a wry laugh, retrieving the ball. "You really want to go there?" He wiped his face with his shirt. "Fine. I started to ask her out the other day, but we got interrupted."

Griffen shrugged. "So what's the problem? Call her up and finish the deed. Wrap it up. Get 'er done."

Gage shook his head, cradled the ball against his side. "She'd only say no."

"And you know this how?"

"When I was asking her out, she faked an incoming phone call." And the look in her eyes just before . . . He could still see them now. Man. The memory slayed him.

Griffen's head tilted back, his face going serious. "Ouch."

Gage dribbled the ball. The patting sound it made on the concrete was loud in the sudden quiet.

Griffen grabbed his water bottle from the sidelines and tossed Gage's to him.

"Her husband died last year," Gage said.

"Yeah, I remember. The fire fighter. Reese watched her kid a couple of times. When was it, late last winter? Early spring? Maybe she's not ready yet."

Or maybe she just wasn't interested. Maybe he wasn't her type. Even though he shared the same interests as her late husband, personality-wise they couldn't be more different. Curtis had kept to himself, Gage enjoyed company. Curtis had been serious, Gage liked to mess around. Curtis had held her heart, Gage couldn't even get a date.

"Maybe she was just nervous or something."

The look in her eyes flashed into his mind again, making his stomach ache. "I don't think so."

Griffen sat on the back porch stoop, and Gage sank down beside him. He took a long swallow of water.

"Reese and I were friends a long time before we finally got together."

"I know." Griffen thought Reese had been in love with Sawyer Smitten, her old flame. Turned out her feelings for Griffen had changed, but she was too afraid to admit it. It had been a long, winding road to happily-ever-after.

"My point is," Griffen said, "there's more than one way to skin a cat."

"Meaning . . ."

Griffen finished his water and capped the empty bottle. "Meaning, you don't have to date to spend time together. If you're that interested, figure it out."

Noah held out the fishing line. "Here, Mom."

"Oh no. I'm not touching that worm. You want to fish, you bait the hook, buckaroo."

With a determined scowl, Noah set to work with the wiggling worm.

Molly stretched out on the sloped shoreline, elbows planted into the grass. The sun was pleasantly warm overhead. Already her skin had colored under the afternoon rays.

Now that Noah was out of school, they needed to get outside on the weekends. Most of the week, he was stuck at the store with her. His only breaks came when she had tours and he went to the sitter's.

"This is hard. Dad always did it for me."

She didn't doubt it. Curtis had found it easier to do things himself sometimes. Especially when Noah had been little. "Keep at it. You can do it."

A few minutes later he was casting the line. It settled about fifteen feet out, the bobber dancing on the surface.

"What did I tell you? You're a pro." Molly grimaced when Noah wiped his hands on his shorts. "Need a wet wipe, sport?"

"Nah."

She smothered a grin and resisted the urge to hand him one anyway.

"Fancy meeting you here."

Molly turned at the deep familiar voice. Upon meeting Gage's warm smile, she couldn't help but offer one of her own. "Hey there."

Gage left the walking trail and flopped down beside her, flat on his back, breathing hard.

"Hey, Noah," he squeezed out between breaths. "How you doing?"

"Good. I'm gonna catch a bluegill."

"I bet you will."

"I'd ask what you're doing here," Molly said, "but it's clear you're trying to kill yourself."

"It's true, I'm a masochist."

Noah reeled in a few inches. "What's a masochist?"

"Someone who likes to jog," Molly said.

Gage smiled, closing his eyes as he caught his breath. "I'm inclined to agree about now."

She stole the chance to take a peek. Sweat dampened his dark hair. His white shirt clung nicely to his chest, falling just to the waist of his black basketball shorts. Her eyes swept up his chest again on the way to his face. To his eyes. His open eyes.

Busted.

She looked away, her cheeks heating. *Way to go, Molly. You've been fretting all week, afraid he'd ask you out, and now you're giving him go-signals. Good job.*

"Most people do that in the morning, you know," she said. "Before the temperature tops eighty."

"I barely made it to church on time as it was."

They talked about their respective church services, transitioning to the topic of mutual friends for a while. Midway through, Noah caught a bluegill, and Gage showed him how to remove the hook, letting him do the work.

All week Molly had wondered what she'd say if Gage asked her out. She had no answers yet, so she was grateful for Noah's presence.

"There's Jordan!" Noah reeled in and tossed his pole aside. "I'm gonna go to the playground, 'kay?"

"Um . . . well, what about lunch?"

"Not hungry yet."

"Okay . . ." She frowned as her buffer ran toward his friend. So much for that.

Gage sat up, and she thought for a moment he was leaving. But no. He rested his elbows on his raised knees, settling in.

Say something, Molly. Something benign. Something random. Anything. "How's business going?"

"Not bad. The weather put a crimp in things last week."

"Tell me about it." Half her tours had been cancelled due to the storms. It was hard to turn things around when everything seemed to be working against her. Another loan payment was due soon, and the money wasn't there. She'd already received a warning letter.

"Don't look so sad. The forecast for this week is sunny with a chance of tours galore."

She tried for a smile. She was sure that'd be the case for Gage. For her it was sunny with a chance of bankruptcy. She didn't know which bothered her more: the thought of letting Noah down or the thought of letting Curtis down. The business had been his baby.

She checked on Noah. He and Jordan seemed to be competing for highest swinger, and Noah was behind. "I don't know, Gage. Sometimes I think I'm fighting a losing battle."

"Hey." His eyes softened, warming her through. "Don't lose faith. Look how far you've come. From fear of heights to scaling mountains." He smiled.

"For all the good it's done. I can stay busy and post fliers and garner reviews, but the numbers don't lie. And I gotta tell you . . . what they're saying isn't good."

He regarded her seriously. "How can I help?"

Her heart squeezed at his willingness to give yet more of his time to her failing business.

"I don't know. I'm at the end of my rope. My overhead is as low as possible, and we just aren't making it."

Was she missing something? Maybe if she gave Gage access to everything, he could figure it out. If anyone could, it was him. That was asking a lot, though. It would be time consuming, and this was busy season. Well. *His* busy season.

On the other hand, if she didn't do something soon, she was going to lose everything.

"What is it?" His eyes were locked on her. Deep pools of blue.

She nearly fell in and drowned and, frankly, drowning had never seemed so appealing. *Focus, Molly.*

"You've been so helpful. I hate to even ask . . ."

He cocked his head. The clouds parted, and the sunlight caught the side of his face. "Tell me."

She looked away. Licked her lips. She couldn't think straight when he was staring at her like that. When his eyes went so soft, she felt like a melted pool of chocolate.

"I was wondering . . . if I were to give you access to, you know, everything . . ." Her heart thudded at the thought. It was scary. It was humiliating. He'd see her bank account. Know her incompetence. "Would you . . ."

"You want me to do an operations audit. Assess where you are, see if I find any problems."

"It would take a lot of time."

"Molly."

She turned at his insistent tone. Those blue eyes. Have mercy, she was powerless against them.

"I'm happy to help. I'll come in this week, and next week

too if I need to. If there's something to find, I'll find it. No worries."

She wasn't a weeper, so she wasn't sure why her eyes were suddenly burning, why a knot formed in her throat. "Thanks."

CHAPTER NINE

. . . .

*T*hings were much worse than Gage had imagined. He'd been analyzing Molly's operations in his spare time for the past couple weeks. He'd examined the price structure, the business's efficiency, the benefits and costs of operations. He looked it all over, then did it again, hoping he'd missed something.

Molly kept asking how it was going, and he'd put her off, hoping to find something encouraging, but the news wasn't good. Her price structure was spot-on. The store was efficiently run. She was frugal in her spending. She was doing everything right.

But the loan was eating up her profits. With that kind of overhead, she needed more business. For customers she needed advertising, for advertising she needed money, and for money she needed more customers. It was a vicious cycle.

There was no money. He looked at the bottom line,

frowning as two customers entered Molly's shop. Gage closed the book and moved around the counter.

He'd insisted Molly take Noah out for their lunch break. Molly felt bad about the kid spending his summer cooped up in the store. Besides, the place was a tomb. They sometimes went hours between customers.

He approached the middle-aged man and woman. "Can I help you?"

"We're looking for a good pair of hiking socks," the man said.

"Nothing too thick, though." The woman tossed her blond ponytail over her shoulder. "My shoes are already snug."

Unfortunately, Molly carried little merchandise. "I'm afraid we don't carry them here. There's a place a couple blocks down, though. Make a left on Main, and it'll be on your right."

"Thanks."

He wondered if he should advise Molly to carry more merchandise. Forty percent of his profits came from product sales as opposed to tours.

"Left on Main?" the man said as he stepped out the door.

Gage nodded. "It'll be on your right."

"Thank you." The woman moved aside to let Molly and Noah past.

Noah darted inside, heading to Molly's office for a computer game, probably.

Molly was looking at Gage oddly, her cute smile nowhere to be found. He realized how what he'd said to the customer might've sounded to her.

"They were after hiking socks," he said.

And that quickly her smile was back. "Oh."

"How was lunch?"

"We got takeout from the Country Cupboard Café and took it to the square. A much-needed break—thank you."

The phone rang. Molly picked it up and began answering questions about rafting tours.

Gage sat behind the counter and opened the book again, staring blankly at the pages. He wondered idly about the loan she was paying off. Wondered what they'd used as collateral. The space was rented and the business was new, so it wasn't valuable—especially in its current condition.

They'd likely put up their home. No wonder she was anxious. If something didn't happen fast, she'd lose her business, her home, and her income. A triple blow.

No wonder she'd asked for his help, as humiliating as that must've been. If something didn't change, the next phase would be ugly and public. It was the last thing she needed.

He had to do something. She needed more customers, which equated to advertising. The most effective advertisement Gage did was a full-page color ad on the back cover of *Explore Vermont*. The monthly magazine was available at every retail store in Smitten and all across the state. Tourists depended on it for entertainment ideas and coupons. He'd gained first right of rescission on the back cover the second year he'd been open, and it had brought him a ton of business—still did.

But the cost had nearly choked him at first. And Molly didn't have the money for anything so grand. Plus, any advertising she did at this point had to be not only effective but immediate. Even if she had the money, even if he gave up his rights to the back cover, next month would be too late.

A customer entered the store as Molly hung up the phone. She went to help them as Gage tapped the pen on the counter.

He'd worked with the designer yesterday on the ad for the current issue. It was going to press in a few days. He hadn't approved it yet, though. Could he swap out his own ad for one for Molly? It wouldn't kill his business to go without the ad for a month.

He watched her across the shop, talking with a young couple about their rock climbing offerings. She was animated and friendly, good with people. Authentic. Adorable. She was beautiful too—no getting around that—with her caramel-colored eyes and light-up-a-room smile.

She'd gotten under his skin quickly. More quickly than he could've imagined. He looked down at the ledger. So quickly he was considering doing something he wouldn't have believed himself capable of.

But he couldn't tell Molly. She had her pride—what was left of it—and she'd never accept this kind of help. It had been hard enough for her to ask him to assess the business.

He closed the book, making up his mind. Molly's business needed saving, and he was going to do everything in his power to make it happen.

"Wow, nice ad, Molly." Abby ran her slender fingers over the glossy back cover of *Explore Vermont*.

"Let me see." Lia leaned over Abby's shoulder. "Ooooh, that's beautiful. I want to go rock climbing now."

Molly and Abby laughed.

"What?" Lia said. "It could happen."

Heather rounded the sofa and settled into the recliner in front of the bookstore fireplace with her steaming mug of coffee. "I'm afraid to ask how much it cost."

"Gage has some pull at the magazine. He said he got a really good deal."

Heather frowned. "You don't know how much?"

A thread of worry wormed through Molly. It had happened so quickly. "I'll find out. I did ask Gage, but that was about the time Noah fell off my office chair and hurt his ankle." She'd dropped everything and gone running at his scream.

"Is he okay?" Lia asked.

"He's fine. Just a sprain." And an expensive ER bill. Molly looked over Abby's shoulder, admiring the ad. She did need to find out how much it had cost. But Gage knew the state of her finances as well as she—probably better. He wouldn't have spent more than she could afford. She made a mental note to call the magazine for an invoice. She didn't feel comfortable calling Gage, though he'd been coming around more often.

Only to help you with the ad, Molly. He'd been a godsend on that. He was really good at marketing.

Molly sipped her lukewarm coffee. "We've gotten calls off the ad already. I booked two tours so far, and it's only been on the stands two days."

"That's wonderful," Lia said. "Just what you needed."

"So now on to the important stuff." One of Abby's brows lifted. "Has he finally asked you out?"

Molly's stomach dropped, but she covered with a smile, her gaze bouncing off Heather. "Nope. I don't think he sees me that way."

Heather gave a wry laugh.

"He's sure coming around an awful lot," Lia said. "And you know what Pearl Chambers says . . . when a gentleman comes calling, a young lady can be certain his heart is engaged."

Molly rolled her eyes. "He's just being thoughtful." But she couldn't help but remember the moments she'd caught him regarding her with a wistful expression. She could smack herself for faking that stupid phone call. He'd never ask her out now.

And it was too bad. Because lately she'd been thinking she just might say yes.

> *There are no words as persuasive as a suitor's arms.*
>
> PEARL CHAMBERS, *The Gentlewoman's Guide to Love and Courtship*

CHAPTER TEN

. . . .

*M*olly's fingers moved over the ivory keys. It had been years since she'd played Tchaikovsky's "Doumka." She'd been afraid her rusty fingers couldn't pull off the challenging piece. But she'd been playing regularly after tucking Noah into bed at night. He seemed to like falling asleep to her music.

She'd even dug her old clarinet from the closet and taught him a couple of easy pieces. The kid seemed to have a natural knack. She felt bad for not discovering it sooner.

She smiled as she reached the *brilliante*. Her fingers embraced the notes as if they were dear old friends. As she finished the piece, her smile widened.

The last chord still rang through the air as a knock sounded at the door. Molly checked her watch. Almost nine thirty. Lowering the piano's lid, she went to answer it.

A quick check through the peephole made her heart stutter. She drew a quick, steadying breath, wondering how he knew where she lived. She rolled her eyes. Everyone knew where she lived. Half the town had been by with casseroles and help in the months following Curtis's death.

Her hands were shaking as she unlocked the door and turned the knob. The porch light made his dark hair shimmer, casting a golden glow across his handsome features. He wore work clothes, khakis and a blue polo that matched his eyes to perfection.

"I hope it's not too late," Gage said. "I planned to stop by the store, but I got hung up at work."

"No, not at all. Come in." She stepped aside, and he brushed by her. She shivered at the contact. "Have a seat. Can I get you anything? Soda, coffee?"

"No thanks. I was just wanting to see how business has been the last couple days since the ad came out. It turned out really nice."

"It did. I've gotten a lot of compliments on it. I've also gotten at least two bookings, and the phones have been a lot busier."

"Good, good."

She was about to ask the dreaded cost question when he spoke.

"How was your book group tonight?" He settled in the corner of her plaid sofa.

She took the armchair across from him, a good safe distance away. "Great. Good discussion." She gave a cocky smile. "I read the whole thing."

One side of his mouth tipped up adorably. "Ah, but have you read the book I loaned you?" He hadn't shaved recently, giving him a rugged look.

She itched to feel the scruff against her palms. She knotted her hand into a fist. *What's gotten into you, Molly?*

She tipped her chin up. "Actually, I did." She dug it out from under the newspaper and slid it over to him. "You can have it back now."

He quirked a brow skeptically. "Really?"

Molly made a face. "Well. The highlighted parts."

He chuckled. "Good enough." His eyes drifted around the room.

She wondered what he was thinking. He'd built a log home—more lodge than cabin—on Sugarcreek Road last year. By comparison, the farmhouse was small and old. But it was cozy. Homey. Theirs—at least for the moment.

"Was that you I heard on the piano before I knocked?"

She wondered how long he'd stood listening. Or if he'd only been waiting for a pause. "It was. Tchaikovsky."

His brows ticked up. "Sounded complicated."

She shrugged. "Well, it's not scaling mountains, but it passes the time."

"So modest. I only play one song, and believe me, you don't want to hear it."

She smiled. "Well, now you have to play it for me."

"Just imagine the worst rendition of 'Chopsticks' you've ever heard, and you'll be close."

"I taught elementary kids through college. Believe me, I've heard bad."

"Oh no, I take bad to a whole new level."

She laughed. "Well, we all have our gifts."

She curled her legs in the chair, tucking her stockinged feet under her. This was nice, the company. Adult company.

Her favorite times with Curtis had been after tucking Noah into bed. They'd sat and talked about their days. Well, mainly she'd talked. But it had still been nice.

Gage entertained her with a story of a hiking trip, making Molly laugh harder than she had in ages. He asked about her family and told her about his own, a close-knit clan on the other side of Smitten. His dad had worked at the log mill before it had gone under, and his mom had taught at the elementary school. An only child, he'd been born when his parents were in their thirties. They were both retired now.

They shuffled easily from one topic to the next, not even touching on work again. He regarded her steadily throughout, smiling at the right times, holding her gaze for long seconds at others. It was as if an invisible wire ran between them. Maybe it was the intimacy of the quiet house. Maybe it was the dim lighting or pleasant conversation. But sometimes, when his blue eyes met hers, a flash of electricity zinged through the wire, stirring the pterodactyls in her stomach.

When she checked her watch, she was surprised to see it was after eleven.

"I'm sorry . . . I'm keeping you up." He scooted to the edge of the couch.

She was suddenly loath to see him go. "No, this was . . . nice." She felt her face heating as she stood with him, biting her lip. Had she said too much, read too much into his visit? Why had he said he'd stopped by? She couldn't remember.

"Don't forget your book." She scooped it off the table and handed it to him as he turned at the door.

His eyes locked on hers, the book suspended between them. She couldn't seem to breathe. Breathing didn't seem to matter anyway. All that mattered were those mesmerizing blue eyes. Eyes that were saying something her heart longed to hear. Have mercy. He was looking at her like he wanted to kiss her.

"Please . . . ," he whispered. "Tell me you don't have an urgent call coming in."

She shook her head. For the life of her, she couldn't make herself speak. Couldn't even look away. How could she when he was looking at her like that? When her lips tingled with wanting?

Time stilled as he leaned into her. His lips brushed hers. Too soft to make her heart flutter. Too gentle to make her heart squeeze. And yet they did. She'd wondered what those lips would feel like. Wonder no more. They possessed the power to shrink the world down to the two of them.

He returned for seconds, his fingertips brushing her face, making every cell jump to life. He pulled away too soon, his warm breath on her lips a parting gift.

Her gaze collided with his. She'd never seen blue smolder. His eyes dipped down to her lips and back. He was still close. She could feel the heat of his body skimming hers. Smell his manly scent, a delicious blend of musk and pine.

"I should probably apologize," he said.

Her eyes fastened on his lips, watching the words form with fascination.

"I would, except . . . I'm not sorry."

Her eyes went back to his as something warm and pleasant welled in her. She wasn't sorry either. Confused, maybe. Intrigued, definitely. But not sorry.

An image of Curtis flashed in her mind, bringing a cloud

of guilt. She pushed it away, not wanting to taint the moment. She'd deal with that later.

Fighting Gage's pull, she stepped back where she could breathe. Where she could think without wanting to lean in for round two.

"This is all out of order," he said. "I was going to ask you out."

She bit the inside of her mouth. "Is that why you're here?"

"Depends."

"On what?"

"What your answer would've been."

He wanted to go out with her. *Her.* Molly Moore. It hadn't been her imagination. Maybe she hadn't lost all her instincts. Maybe there were still good things in store for her. A year ago she wouldn't have believed it. A year ago she'd thought her life was over. At least her love life. Now, looking at Gage—

"You could put a guy out of his misery."

She'd always thought him so confident. But now there was a vulnerability in his eyes that made her want him even more.

"Yes," she said.

His brows disappeared under his messy bangs. "Yes?"

"My answer . . . it would've been yes."

A smile curled his lips. She didn't think he could look more handsome, but she was wrong. His smile lit his eyes, made a little dent in his cheeks that she suddenly wanted to kiss.

"Really?"

She quirked a brow and gave him a playful look. "It still will be . . . if you ever get around to asking."

He chuckled, low and soft. The sound made her heart squeeze.

"Go out with me tomorrow night?"

"Where to?" As if it mattered. She mentally made baby-sitting arrangements.

"Dinner at my place? Music on the square afterward?"

He was full of surprises. "You cook?"

"I'm a man of many talents." Ah, there it was, that confidence.

She teased him with her eyes. "That remains to be seen."

"I look forward to proving myself. I'll pick you up, six o'clock?"

"Sounds like a plan." A very good plan. She had a feeling she'd be counting the minutes.

He opened the door, turning on the threshold with a half smile. "Night, Molly."

"Night."

She closed the door behind him, leaning against it to support her quivering legs. Oh yeah. This week was looking up for sure.

CHAPTER ELEVEN

· ·

Rain pelted the store's rooftop and pattered against the windows. Molly was wet and tired from the rafting trip. She still had to do the bills and order inventory. But she couldn't wipe the smile from her face.

Tonight she had a date with Gage.

She changed into dry clothes in the store's bathroom and settled behind her desk, determined to get through the financials on her own. Heather had gone over it with her numerous times. It wasn't rocket science, but numbers weren't her thing. Still. She was capable. Gage had said so.

Her lips turned up at the thought. It had taken forever to fall asleep last night. Her fingers kept going to her lips. They'd tingled for hours as if still sensing his touch. Would he kiss her again tonight?

Mercy, she hoped so. Her smile widened even as heat

flooded her face. For someone who hadn't known if she was ready to date, she'd sure jumped into that boat awfully quickly. Could she help it if Gage was so tempting?

All right, Molly, time to get down to business. She gathered the bills as she heard April greeting a customer. The store had been busier today—a result of the ad, no doubt.

Speaking of the ad . . .

Molly lifted the phone and dialed the magazine. The bill wouldn't be due yet, but she needed to know what to expect.

A receptionist greeted her and forwarded her to the sales department. Someone finally picked up on the sixth ring, and Molly explained what she needed.

"The sales staff doesn't work Saturdays. This is Kylie, I'm just an intern . . . but let me see what I can do." Her perky voice was like a ray of sunshine.

Molly gathered the stamps and envelopes. Where was a pen? Why were her pens always disappearing?

A few minutes later the intern was back. "Okay, I've got it. It looks like you had the back cover of the July issue? The total was forty-five ninety-eight." A phone rang on Kylie's end. "Oh, listen, I have to go. I'll shoot you an e-mail with the invoice." She double-checked Molly's e-mail address and hung up.

Forty-five ninety-eight? That didn't make sense. Gage had said he'd work out a great deal, but that couldn't be right. She could barely get a place mat ad at the Country Cupboard for that.

A few minutes later she opened her laptop and checked her e-mail. The intern was quick, she'd give her that. Molly opened the attachment and scanned the invoice. When she reached the bottom line, the smile slid from her face.

Her heart skipped a beat, then went into double time. Her lungs caught her breath and held it captive. A small squeak escaped her throat.

Not forty-five dollars and ninety-eight cents. But four thousand, five hundred and ninety-eight dollars.

Four. Thousand. Five hundred. Ninety-eight. Dollars.

Her breath released, and her lungs filled again. Quickly. Coming and going so fast she felt as if she were hyperventilating. It had to be a mistake. That was no great deal. That was her entire flipping advertising budget for a whole year.

A. Whole. Year.

It's a mistake, Molly. A typo or a miscommunication. She called the magazine, asked for Kylie, and waited.

Her voice quivered as she spoke. "Hi, uh, Kylie. This is Molly from Smitten Expeditions."

"Hi, Molly! Did you get the invoice?" Her sunshine voice wasn't so cute anymore.

"I did, but—there must be a mistake." She repeated the invoice total.

"No, I'm sure that's right. It normally goes for closer to five, so you got a great deal."

A great deal? *A great deal?*

"I can have your rep call you on Monday if there's a problem?"

Molly nodded, then realized Kylie couldn't see. "Okay. That's fine. Thank you."

She hung up, numbly. A call from the rep wouldn't solve

anything. She looked at the invoice on the screen. Where was she going to get over four thousand dollars?

Maybe Gage was used to spending that kind of money on his own advertising, but he had to understand that an expenditure like that would put her over the edge right now. She scrimped and saved and budgeted so tightly just to survive, and now, in one fell swoop, she'd lost it all.

There was no getting around it. She couldn't pay it. Molly covered her face with her hands.

Deep breaths. Deep breaths, Molly.

There was no way Gage hadn't known this. Hadn't he pored over her financials for serveral weeks? He knew to the penny how much she had in the bank, how much she owed. What had he been thinking?

An ugly feeling wormed up her spine. Gage was far too savvy to be reckless with money. Obviously he knew how to run a successful business—and you didn't do that by spending money you didn't have.

She shook her head. She didn't want to think it. He'd been so helpful. He'd looked at her with his warm blue eyes. He'd kissed her.

Molly looked back at the invoice, doubts warring with the feelings, the trust, that had grown over the past couple months. She'd trusted him enough to hand over her confidential—and embarrassing—information. Would he do something so terrible? She didn't want to believe it.

And yet.

Those memories of Curtis flashed in her mind. She struggled to remember her late husband's complaints against

Gage. Something about the Chamber of Commerce. Curtis had said Gage had been against the formation of Smitten Expeditions. He'd tried to block their opening. Once in business, Curtis had complained about Gage stealing customers. About Gage badmouthing their business to customers.

And right when it was do-or-die time, Gage had walked into her office and offered to "help." Why would a competitor help her stay in business? Hadn't she seen the red flags? She'd been suspicious. But somehow she'd let her guard down, had let him into her business and into her life.

Molly stood abruptly. Her chair rolled back and hit the wall. *What have you done, Molly?*

She'd trusted a man not worthy of her trust, that's what she'd done. Hadn't she done the same with Curtis? Trusting him to make decisions, burying her head in the sand and letting him take care of all the things she didn't like thinking about?

What was wrong with her? Would she never learn?

And Gage! The nerve of the man, to come into her store and gain her trust, only to chop her legs from beneath her. What kind of person did that?

"Just being neighborly?" she spat. "People here stick together?" Did it not matter to him that this was her livelihood? That she was the sole supporter of a child?

Oh, he'd helped her, all right. Helped her run her business right into the ground. Her mind flashed back to when she'd overheard him directing customers to his own store. How many other customers had he stolen while she'd trusted him here, alone in her shop?

A fire of fury welled up inside. He'd thought he could

walk in here and ruin her, and she'd just lie back and take it. Maybe he thought she was too stupid to see what he'd done.

But she saw it. Oh yeah, she saw it, all right. And she was about to let him know.

She grabbed her keys and headed out, barely acknowledging April on her way past. She was too angry to speak. Too angry to walk the couple blocks. She wanted her say, and she wanted it now.

The diagonal parking slots in front of his store were full. She had to park in front of the bakery, three stores down. Molly marched down the brick sidewalk, steaming inside. Maybe she was going down. But she was going to give him a piece of her mind first. She was going to register a complaint with the Chamber or the Better Business Bureau or whoever she could get to listen.

She stepped inside the busy store and scanned the floor. No Gage. If he was out on a tour, she was going to hunt him down.

"Can I help you?" A short brunette the size of a willow weed stepped up to her.

"Where's Gage?"

The bright smile slipped from her face. "Uh . . . in his office?"

Molly strode across the showroom floor, her eyes trained on his closed office door.

Gage's head snapped up when the door bounced against the wall. "Molly . . ." The beginnings of a smile evaporated from his face. He lowered the pen in his hand. "What's—"

"Don't you dare ask me what's wrong." Her voice quivered with rage.

Gage scooted back from his desk, angling his face away. "Okay . . ."

"How could you, Gage? How *could* you?"

Twin commas formed between his brows. "Molly, I don't—What's going on?" He turned his palms up in a *What did I do?* motion.

Oh, he was good, she'd give him that. All innocence. She ground her teeth together. "The ad in *Explore Vermont*? The *four thousand, five hundred and ninety-eight dollar* ad? Ring a bell?"

His face fell. His eyes found the desk, and in that quick response she saw his guilt. "I'm sorry, Molly. I didn't want—"

"You're sorry? *Sorry?* You deliberately sabotage my business, and you're *sorry?* In what world does that make—"

"Wait . . . what?"

"—any sense? I trusted you! I let you come into my business to help me, and instead you run me into the ground with a bill I can't hope to pay. And you—"

"Molly, no . . ."

"—*knew* that, Gage. Nobody knew that better than you. I've tried to reason this out, make sense of it, but there's only one explanation—you did this on purpose!"

He blinked, shuttering those eyes for an instant. His jaw snapped shut.

He wasn't going to deny it. She didn't know what she'd expected, but it wasn't this. Silence. His hands fell to his lap. Then he crossed his arms.

"Nothing, Gage? No excuses? No random explanations?" She tossed her hands up, waiting.

He settled back in his chair. His jaw clenched. There was something in his eyes she couldn't quite place, then it was gone. His face closed, and his eyes went hard.

She crossed her own arms to hide her trembling hands.

To hide the effect his expression had on her. It hurt. There was no getting around it. She'd thought there'd been some-thing between them. Something special. But all there'd been was betrayal.

"No, Molly. I think you've said it all."

She regarded him steadily. Her heart was racing, adrena-line pumping like mad, the fight or flight thing. She'd fought. Her heart had the battle scars to prove it. But he wasn't fight-ing back. She'd won. That's what she'd wanted, wasn't it? Though an apology would've been nice. A little remorse. But no, she wasn't going to get it. She could see that now.

"I thought you were different. I thought you—" *Cared about me.* A knot in her throat choked off her words. She felt the sting of tears and knew the time had come for flight. Before she completely humiliated herself.

She drew a lung-stretching breath. "Guess I was wrong." Her knees wobbled as she turned to leave.

"I guess we both were," he said.

She didn't pause on the threshold. Didn't stop to wonder what his clipped words meant. He'd gotten what he wanted. She marched through his beautiful store—soon to be the only one of its kind in Smitten.

This chapter of her life was officially over.

❧

The door slammed shut behind Molly, the sudden silence behind it deafening. Gage palmed the back of his neck. What the heck had just happened?

Somehow she'd jumped to the conclusion that he'd

sabotaged her business. That he'd purposely put her over the edge. He would never . . .

He cared about her. That was evidenced by the hollow ache inside, by the painful twist of his stomach that left him feeling like he'd been wrung out hard.

He couldn't believe she thought so little of him. Sure, at first she'd been skeptical. He knew Curtis had probably soured her on him. Between their sports rivalry through high school and their competing businesses, Gage had never been Curtis's favorite person.

But he'd thought he'd earned Molly's trust. He *had* earned her trust. She'd given him access to her finances. She'd agreed to go out with him. She'd kissed him. He let his mind linger there a moment, the thoughts making him go warm all over.

But all too soon the anger returned. What did any of that matter if he didn't have her trust? If she threw him under the bus without a moment's hesitation? One little suspicion, and had she given him the benefit of the doubt? Had she asked for an explanation? No, she'd come in spouting accusations. She'd believed the worst of him. The woman had issues, and it wasn't his job to fix her.

Gage set his hands flat on his desk, scanning the pile of applications he needed to weed through. He had better things to do than stew over a woman who'd set his heart on the floor and stomped all over it.

Love is not for the faint of heart or the weak of spirit.

PEARL CHAMBERS, *The Gentlewoman's*
Guide to Love and Courtship

CHAPTER TWELVE

. . . .

"What are you going to do?" Lia asked Molly.

Heather had called an emergency meeting after church once Molly had filled her in on yesterday's fiasco. The friends were gathered around Molly's kitchen table. Paul and the guys had taken Noah to the park to pass the football.

Molly felt the sting of tears. She'd felt that a lot in the past twenty-four hours. Hiding her feelings from Noah had been difficult. He'd have to know eventually, but not before she had a plan.

Molly shrugged. "Unless Pearl's gold magically appears in front of me, I'll call the bank tomorrow. Let them know I'm defaulting on the loan."

Abby leaned in on her elbows. "Are you sure? What if we did another fund-raiser?"

"That's a great idea," Lia said.

"The guys at the firehouse would help," Heather said. "Maybe a chili cook-off or a barbecue event? We could even auction off items."

Molly shook her head. "Thanks, girls. But even if we raised that kind of money . . . I'm sorry, but it just feels like pouring money down the drain. I have to face it. This just isn't my thing. If I'm honest, it never was."

Lia set her hand on Molly's arm. Silence filled the room as the weight of her declaration sank in.

"I still can't believe Gage did that with the ad," Heather said. "Are you sure you're not mistaken? Remember when I jumped to conclusions about Paul and Isabelle Morgan?"

Molly sank into her chair. "It's not like that. He had every chance to explain. You should've seen the guilt all over his face. He had me fooled, that's for sure." She didn't want to think about Gage. She had enough on her plate. Like being jobless and homeless.

You got my back, right, God? You're going to take care of us? 'Cause right now, this all feels pretty scary, and I'm a little short on trust.

"It's going to be okay," Heather said, as if reading her mind. "We'll all help out."

"I'm going to lose everything. What am I going to do?"

"You're going to pack up your things and move in with Charlie and me," Heather said.

Molly gave her a grateful smile. "I couldn't do that."

"I'd be upset if you didn't. We're friends, that's what we do. Charlie will be thrilled. Besides, what's better than a slumber party?"

"Can I come?" Abby asked.

"Me too," Lia said.

"See?" Heather squeezed Molly's hand. "They're already jealous of all the fun we're going to have."

"Are you sure, Heather? It's a lot to ask."

"Of course I'm sure. Noah will love it. We have a big-screen TV. He and Charlie will be playing Xbox until the cows come home."

Molly eyes ached with unshed tears. "He'll love that. Thanks, Heather."

"Well, that's settled. Let's talk jobs," Abby said. "What kind of work are you looking for?"

"The kind that comes with a paycheck."

"I could ask at the county office," Heather said. "We could use some part-time help."

She was so sweet. "Thanks, hon, but I need full-time and insurance." Noah's recent trip to the ER was a reminder.

"What about something with your music?" Abby asked.

Molly sighed. "I'd love that, but it's not practical. Music on the square isn't going to cut it."

Lia popped up straight. "Hey, Mrs. Willikins is retiring. She's not coming back in the fall because of her husband's health, remember?"

"The music teacher?" Molly asked. Noah loved her. She'd heard about Mr. Willikins's stroke, but not about the woman retiring.

"That's right up your alley," Heather said. "You have the degree, you love music and kids . . ."

It did sound perfect. School would be starting next month. "They haven't replaced her yet?"

"I don't know for sure, but I could check tomorrow."

Molly found herself getting excited about the possibility.

If she could get the job, and it paid enough to support her and Noah . . . She could imagine being happy for many years as a music teacher.

Oh, please, God. This would be such an answer to prayer.

As the girls rattled on with plans, Molly found her mind going a different direction. One that took her to thoughts of a man she'd been falling for. A man who'd sorely disappointed her.

Be honest, Molly.

Okay. A man who'd broken her heart. There. She'd said it. And she didn't know if any job in the world could make up for that.

&

Molly unlocked the store and stepped inside, flipping on lights. She looked around the quiet space, sad at the thought of giving up Curtis's dream.

Curtis's dream. Did you hear that, Molly? Not yours. It was high time she let go and moved forward. Even if it did feel as if she were stepping off a cliff.

Heather had stayed with her yesterday afternoon, digging around online, trying to figure out what would happen after she defaulted. How long she'd have before they repossessed her home. She still wasn't clear on the process, but she kept repeating Heather's words: one step at a time.

Lia was supposed to call the school today and find out if the teaching position was still open. *Please, God . . .* She was actually excited about the idea. It was the perfect fit for her.

Meanwhile, she thought, looking around her quiet office,

she had tours to run, loose ends to tie up, and personal effects needing packed. She was going to do this right. Or as right as she could, and trust God with the rest. There was that word again. *Trust*. God had helped through her difficult year. He'd comforted her in her grief and provided for their needs. *Yes, Molly, but you can trust God.*

Unlike some people.

As Molly sat at her desk, the phone rang. She picked up the extension, realizing suddenly that there was no point in booking more tours.

A male voice asked, for Molly. It was Steve, her sales rep from *Explore Vermont*.

"I have a message from our intern to return your call. She says she sent you the invoice for your ad?"

The bill still had to be paid, so Molly hoped it was a terrible mistake. Or that she could talk him down on the price a bit. Or a lot.

"I know you worked out the price with Gage Turner." She managed to squeeze out the name. "I guess I didn't realize it would cost so much."

"I'm so sorry, Molly. Kylie shouldn't have sent the invoice. It was supposed to go to Gage."

Molly frowned at a blank space on her wall. "What do you mean? Why would my invoice go to him?"

She heard a slow sigh.

"I hope I'm not breaking a confidence here . . . Gage's ad was slotted for July's issue. He said to bill his company as usual."

Molly's throat constricted. She palmed it. "What?"

"I told him he'd retain first right of rescission regardless, but he insisted he be billed for the ad."

A terrible dread leaked into her veins. She swallowed hard. "I don't—why would he—"

"I don't know. I just do as I'm told. As long as the magazine gets paid . . ."

No, this couldn't be. Had she made—

She closed her eyes and reminded herself to breathe. This didn't make sense. Why would Gage pay for her ad? What kind of man shelled out over four thousand dollars to save his competitor?

"Are . . . are you sure about this, Steve?"

"I have his e-mail right here." There was a click on Steve's end. "It says, 'Steve, can you make sure I'm billed for the Smitten Expeditions ad instead of Molly?' Oh—oops. He did ask me to keep it between us. Well, shoot."

Molly's heart pummeled her ribs. "It's okay. It . . . it won't matter now." None of it would. "But don't bill Gage. I'll . . . I'll be paying for it now."

"Well . . . hmm. You'll have to work that out between the two of you, I guess. I'm really sorry. I should call Gage and apologize."

"No, don't—I mean, I'll handle it. It was my fault, and you're not the one who sent the invoice."

"Good point. Let's just blame Kylie." A teasing note had crept into his voice. "It's always the intern's fault."

"Exactly," she said numbly. "Thank you for your help."

"I hope we can work together in the future."

They rang off, and Molly cupped her face in her palms. This couldn't be happening. She flashed back to Saturday when she'd marched into Gage's office. She remembered the look on his face when he'd first seen her. The joy in his eyes at her arrival. Right before his smile had fallen away at the look on her face.

And later, the hardness of his eyes, like ice. The clenching of his jaw.

Oh, God, what have I done? He'd done the sweetest, most generous thing, and she'd turned it into something awful.

And why? Because Curtis had said bad things about him? Because Curtis had betrayed her trust, and now she thought everyone else would too? What kind of excuse was that?

She flopped her head down on her desk, not caring when her forehead smacked it. She deserved to be thumped on the head. Her ugly words played back in her head. She'd been so nasty. And after he'd been nothing but kind. All the help he'd given her . . .

His parting words came back to her. *I guess we were both wrong.* Now she understood the cryptic words. Now, when it was much too late. She groaned.

"If you're trying to see into the drawer, it'll probably be easier if you open it."

Molly lifted her head. She hadn't heard Heather enter the store.

Heather's grin fell. "What's wrong?"

Molly covered her face.

Heather plunked down in the seat across from her. "It can't be that bad."

Molly dropped her hands and proceeded to tell her friend just how bad it was. Her face heated as she described Steve's revelation.

"I'm such an idiot," Molly said when she finished the whole sordid tale.

Wincing, Heather grabbed Molly's hand, which was strangling a stack of Post-it notes. "Well . . . it could be worse . . ." She sighed and a moment later, she sat up straight and nodded once. "We can fix this."

"He kissed me."

Heather's eyebrows popped up. "What? When?"

Molly sank into the memory. "Friday night, after book club. He came over. We talked awhile." Molly gave a little sigh. "It was nice. Then at the door he . . . he kissed me. And he asked me out."

"You went out?"

"No, the next day I went postal on him."

Heather's shoulders slumped. "Oh." She stared into Molly's eyes, a sympathetic look on her face. "Was it a nice kiss?"

Molly groaned, dropping her head to the desk. "The best," she mumbled against the blotter. It had been. She'd relived it a hundred times. Even after her tirade. She couldn't seem to help herself.

"You really like him, huh?"

Like him? She'd been getting dangerously close to—*Don't go there, Molly.* "What does it matter? He's never going to speak to me again."

"You don't know that."

"You didn't hear me, didn't hear the awful things I said or the—"

Heather cupped Molly's head and pulled her up. "You're mumbling."

Molly felt the sting of tears. A knot formed in her throat. "I was awful." She couldn't remember feeling so ashamed of herself. It was so unlike her to go off on someone.

"Maybe he'll forgive you."

Molly shook her head. "You didn't see the look on his face. Those hard eyes." She didn't want to think about it. Didn't want to remember him that way.

It was bad enough she'd never see his warm blue gaze on her again. Never feel the touch of his fingertips on her face. Never hear him chuckle at her like he thought she was adorable. There was nothing adorable about what she'd done. About what she'd allowed herself to believe. And no one knew that better than Gage Turner.

A sensible girl treads the stairs of love carefully and
deliberately.

PEARL CHAMBERS, *The Gentlewoman's
Guide to Love and Courtship*

CHAPTER THIRTEEN

. . . .

*M*om, I'm ready for bed!" Noah called down
to her.

She set aside the copy of *Love and Courtship* and traipsed
upstairs, looking down at the wooden treads for anything she
might have overlooked the last hundred times she'd climbed
the stairwell. Three mentions of stairs in the last three chap-
ters. What was she missing?

Noah was in bed, tossing the football to the ceiling, when
she entered the room.

"Think fast." He pitched the ball at her, but it went wide
right, hitting the wall beside his chest of drawers.

The ball thudded off the plaster and onto the wood floor.

"Sorry," he said.

Something about the thud made Molly frown. Had it
sounded hollow? Maybe there was a safe behind the wall.

Really, Molly?

She was losing it. Thinking too much about this stupid treasure when she should just resign herself to losing their home. Losing the business.

The interview yesterday for the teaching position had gone well. Everything would be fine. Eventually.

Unable to stop herself, Molly knocked on the dingy plaster, then knocked again a few feet away. It did sound different. Could be an air duct or something. Probably was.

"Whatcha doing?"

"Just—" She knocked again all over the wall. There was a space that sounded hollow. It was a few feet wide and stretched from the floor to as high as she could reach.

"Mom, you're acting weird."

Adrenaline flowed through her veins. Was it possible? That plaster had been up there forever. The wall faced the west side of the house. She supposed something could be tucked behind it.

She looked at the plaster and counted the cost: a hole in the wall that she'd never have the time or know-how to fix before she put the place on the market. On the other hand, if there was gold back there, the house would never have to go on the market.

"Be right back."

Molly returned a few minutes later with a hammer and two masks. She fixed one on her face and tossed the other to Noah. "Put that on."

"Uh, Mom, what are you doing?"

"Seeing what's back here."

Noah was looking at her like she'd lost her mind. Maybe she had.

"Stay back, okay?"

She shoved Noah's laundry basket aside and drew back the hammer. *Here goes nothing.* The plaster cracked on contact. A few more swings, and chunks were falling on the floor. Mercy, she hoped there wasn't lead paint in there. Or asbestos.

"Stand over there." She gestured toward the doorway, hoping the mask protected against such things.

She kept going until she'd cleared a space the size of a basketball, then turned the hammer and began prying on the wood slats behind the plaster. They slowly splintered away. A cool draft flowed through the growing hole. Her blood pumped with excitement. She peered through the hole, but it was pitch-black.

"Hey, Noah, grab a flashlight for me."

His footfalls flew down the hall and padded down the stairs.

She kept at the plaster and wood slats. By the time he returned, she had an opening the size of her fist.

She shone the light into the hole and sucked in a breath. An open space. A closet? She aimed the light down.

No—a stairway!

Her hands trembled as she set the flashlight on the chest. A stairway, just like in the book. Maybe she wasn't crazy after all.

"What is it? What is it, Mom?"

She pried a large chunk of plaster away. "An old staircase."

"Sweet! Can I see?"

Another piece of plaster clunked to the floor. "Wait till I'm done. Stay back, sport."

It seemed to take forever to clear a hole big enough to allow her through. By the time she did, sweat was trickling down her back. She shone the flashlight through the pillow-sized hole. The stairs took a turn halfway down, but all she could see were old wooden steps and lots of cobwebs.

"Where does it go?"

"It must lead to the kitchen. The pantry, I think. Maybe the pantry was added on when the stairwell was covered up." Maybe Pearl had made sure the stairwell was covered up.

Molly stuck a leg through the hole. "Stay here."

"Aw, Mom . . . ," Noah whined, but he stayed where he was.

She crouched through the opening. On the other side, her stockinged foot ground century-old dirt into the wooden floor. She emerged on the other side, shivering against the coolness. The beam of light illuminated cobweb-coated plaster walls and plank flooring strewn with dead bugs and dirt.

The steps creaked as she descended them. A web tickled her face, and she cleared it with her hand, hoping there was nothing live attached. At the bend, she made the turn and followed the stairs.

Come on, Pearl. Where'd you put it? It had to be here. It just had to be.

She aimed the light down the staircase, and the beam caught on something at the bottom. A heap of burlap.

"Mom, you okay?"

"Noah, get away from the hole. I'll be up in a minute."

She continued down the remaining stairs. When she came to the bottom, she reached for the burlap and pulled, her heart beating a frantic tattoo in her chest.

She sucked in her breath at the sight. A heap of rocks sat at her feet. The beam of light reflected the shiny chunks of gold woven through them. Molly's mouth fell open. Her heart raced. She couldn't believe it. Right here all this time. All these years.

"Oh my gosh! Oh my gosh, oh my gosh."

"What's wrong, Mom?"

She stared at the knee-high heap. Gold. Treasure. How much was here? How much was it worth? She had no idea, but one thing was certain. It was worth a bundle. And it was hers and Noah's.

She laughed, the sound echoing off the old walls. "Not a thing, Noah. Not a single thing."

CHAPTER FOURTEEN

· ·

The girls gathered around the bookstore fireplace, watching the flames lick at the logs. They crackled and popped in the silence.

"I can't believe you found the gold," Heather said.

It had been the hot topic around town that week. "We found the gold. I couldn't have done it without you girls."

"What did the appraiser say?" Lia had put her in touch with a mineral appraiser from Burlington. He'd come out yesterday to examine the ore and take pictures.

"Nothing final yet, but he confirmed it's definitely gold ore, and plentiful."

"What are you going to do with all that money?" Abby said.

Molly curled her feet under her in the armchair. She'd been giving that a lot of thought. "I don't know. Right now, it's just nice to have options."

"At the very least, the store is saved," Lia said.

That had been at the top of Molly's mind all week. "You know, I don't think that's what I want."

"Really?" Abby asked.

She wanted to get back to her passion, her purpose. The gold, if nothing else, gave her the ability to pursue music. The store had been nothing but a burden.

"Gold or no, I want that teaching job."

Abby arched a brow. "Um, you know you're kind of rich now, right?"

"What good is money if she can't do what she wants?" Heather said.

"Good point," Lia said.

Whatever money came from the gold, Molly wanted to do something meaningful with it. Put some away for Noah's education. Give some to the church. Some of it belonged to her friends too. She couldn't have done this without them.

And she wanted to give back to Smitten. The community had done so much for her, had been there for her and Noah when she'd needed them. Her mind had been awhirl with ways she could invest in the community. The firehouse needed updated equipment. The library patrons had been asking for a new genealogy department for a long time. She liked the thought of investing in the library. Pearl would heartily approve.

"When will you hear on the job?"

"They're making a decision next week."

"You're a shoo-in," Lia said. "I talked to the school secretary yesterday. She said as much."

"Oh, I hope so. After scaling mountains and fishing in waders for hours, sitting behind a piano with a classroom full of beautiful faces seems like a dream."

"Speaking of beautiful faces," Abby said. "Have you talked to Gage?"

She'd told the girls about her misunderstanding. "Not yet."

"You haven't apologized?" There was censure in Heather's tone.

"I'm going to . . . I've been a little busy this week, you know. Thought maybe I'd call tomorrow when his store's swamped. Or after hours . . . leave a message. Maybe a text. Or a note slipped under the door." She was kidding. Okay, half kidding.

"Um, I seem to recall your tirade coming in person," Abby said, then shrugged. "Just saying."

Molly sighed. She'd already put it off four days too long. She'd been so busy, though, with the store, the gold. *Really, Molly? You weren't too busy to tell him off.* She just didn't think she could stand having him look at her that way again. Those cold eyes had haunted her all week.

Heather jumped off the couch and pulled Molly from the armchair. "Come on. It's time."

"I haven't finished my tea."

She reached for her mug, but Abby beat her to it, draining the cup dry.

Molly made a face at her.

"What? Mine was gone."

"Any other excuses?" Heather asked.

I don't wanna was right there on her tongue, but even in her head she knew it sounded childish. Heather was right. It was time to eat crow.

She made one more lame attempt. "I don't know where he is?"

"If he's not at his store, you know where he lives." Heather grabbed Molly's bag and hitched it onto Molly's shoulder, then gave her a small shove toward the door. "Off you go."

Gage straightened the hiking boot display and set the measuring device under the bench. His eyes swept the quiet store. He'd already cleaned out last month's magazines and replaced them with current issues. He'd gone through the clothing, sizing things from smallest to largest. He was running out of things to do.

But he didn't want to go home. Home entailed great spans of quiet and boredom. Too much time to think. Too much time to dwell on subjects that either made his blood pressure soar or rent his heart in two, depending on how he felt at the moment.

News of Molly's gold find had trickled through the Smitten grapevine that week. There'd been a write-up in the *Gazette* about it. He'd read it four times, lingering over Molly's words. He was glad for her. But he was also angry at her. She hadn't contacted him since Saturday. But why would she? She didn't need him anymore, she didn't trust him, and she sure didn't love him.

Thinking of those things left him feeling like he was drowning in a pit of despair. Definitely best to stay busy. He could always find something to do at the store. There were never enough pens around here. He needed to order more. And staples. They were almost out.

A knock sounded on the glass door. Stupid tourists. Couldn't they see the Closed sign? Ridding his face of the scowl, he rounded the display and shook his head at the figure outside the door, getting ready to mouth *Closed, sorry*.

But the sight stopped him in his tracks. Molly stood in a white gauzy top and fitted pair of khakis, the last rays of the day turning the sky behind her a rosy pink.

Upon sighting him, she tilted her head, her brown eyes pleading. He'd always been helpless against big brown eyes.

Sucker.

He clamped his lips shut and approached, unlocking the door and opening it a few inches. "We're closed."

"I'm . . . not here to buy a tent."

He steeled himself against her. Against the innocence of her eyes, the cuteness of her freckled nose, the silky smoothness of her hair. His fingers tingled with the desire to run through the soft strands. Then he remembered the things she'd said nearly a week ago.

"What do you want, Molly?"

"Can I come in?"

He sighed, opening the door. He gave her a wide berth, but the citrusy scent of her shampoo that wafted in with her was nearly his undoing. Maybe his brain knew it was over, but his body tended to forget.

He closed the door and planted his feet. No need to take her into his office. Whatever this was couldn't take long, and the sooner she left, the better.

She seemed to take the hint, shuffling in place, her eyes bouncing off his.

He crossed his arms. "I heard about the gold. Congratulations."

"Thanks. It . . . it's been quite the week."

"I'm sure."

She tried to stuff her hands in her pockets, then seemed to realize she didn't have any. Her hands floundered for a minute before settling at her side. A delicate blush bloomed on her cheeks. Why'd she have to be so stinking cute?

"This won't take long. I just want to—I, um, I owe you an apology."

He raised a brow, waiting. The air-conditioning kicked on, ruffling the hair alongside her face. His fingers yearned to tuck it behind her ears. He knotted his hands into fists.

"I know I was wrong about the invoice." Her eyes darted to his before finding the floor. "I know you were going to pay it for me."

Her eyes found his, big, brown and a little damp. "I said some awful things—jumped to the wrong conclusion, a terrible one. You didn't deserve that, and I'm so sorry." She shook her head, her mouth opening and closing twice before she found words. "I don't know what to say. You were so kind to help me. You spent hours helping me, and I—" She shook her head again. "I'm sorry."

"Why?" The question popped out before he could stop it. *What does it matter, Turner?*

"Why?" She looked down at her feet. At her sandals, size 6-1/2, if he wasn't mistaken. Her cute toes peeked out, her pink toenails glittering under the showroom lights.

"Listen, Gage, there's no excuse for my behavior. The truth is, I thought the worst of you from the beginning. I . . . have some trust issues. After Curtis died, I found out he'd hidden things from me—like that loan. I didn't know he'd put our house up for collateral. He . . . he forged my signature. There were other things too."

Gage's stomach twisted. He bit his tongue before he said something he regretted. Curtis was still her late husband, still the father of her child.

"I trusted him, and finding out he'd hidden things from me kind of made me suspicious. I carried those feelings over to you because Curtis had said some things about you over the years . . ."

"Like . . . ?" Gage could imagine. But he'd rather know the truth.

She winced, then shook her head. "It doesn't matter. It's no excuse. I'd spent enough time with you to know better." She gave a wry smile. "And I should know by now I can't trust everything Curtis said."

He regarded her, his ire having cooled at her explanation. It didn't excuse her behavior, but it made sense now. "We were rivals in high school, he probably told you."

"He said you took his spot on the football team." She shrugged. "Stole his girlfriend."

He gave a harsh laugh. "We competed for the same spot on the football team. I earned that position. And the girl . . . she was never interested in him. They'd been friends, only he wanted more. This was all so long ago."

She bit her lip. "Did you put up roadblocks when we were trying to open our store?"

"What? *No.*" What had the man told her? His ire was building again. He stuffed it down. He wasn't going to denigrate her dead husband.

"And you never stole our customers either, I'm guessing."

He unclenched his jaw. "That's not who I am, Molly. I play fair. There's room in this town for both of us."

Something flashed in her eyes before she looked away. He wondered what that look was about.

She crossed her arms over her chest as if needing a shield. But she met his eyes. "I believe you. And I'm sorry I said all those things. Sorry I believed the worst about you. Clearly I have some . . . issues to work out." Her eyes dropped to the floor. "But that's not your problem. I'll get out of your way." She turned and grabbed the handle. "Thanks for hearing me out, Gage."

The door opened, and she slipped through it, shutting it behind her. The bell tinkled good-bye for him.

His heart hammered in his chest, fast and hard. The store felt quieter, emptier, lonelier than it ever had. Molly filled his world with fun. Laughter. She filled his heart with love. Was he going to let her walk away because she'd made a mistake? Because she'd believed her late husband? Because the man she'd trusted had betrayed that trust? Yeah, she had issues. But didn't they all?

He reached for the door.

Molly blinked against the sting of tears as she left the store. *Well, what were you hoping for, Molly? A proposal?* At least he hadn't looked at her with those cold, hard eyes. Well, at least not by the time she'd left.

Still, she was unsettled. Apologizing had been the right thing to do, but she'd thought it would bring her peace. Why did she only feel hollow inside?

She thought of the gold ore, now sitting securely in a safe. She'd thought money would solve all her problems, but it didn't, did it? The most important things in life were priceless. Love couldn't be bought or sold.

But it could be lost. She swallowed hard against the knot in her throat as she reached for her car door.

"What if I want to?"

Molly spun at the sound of his voice, her sandals grinding pebbles into the pavement. He stopped at the curb, his skin golden in the twilight. A breeze ruffled his hair, mussing it. She got lost in thoughts of straightening it with her fingers.

"What?" she asked when she got her brain back.

He stepped off the curb, took another step. His eyes weren't hard now. They were as soft as warm butter. "What if I want to make it my problem?"

Molly's heart skittered across her chest, slammed into her ribs. Did he mean—?

One more step closed the gap. "I've never met anyone like you, Molly."

She thought of Saturday's tirade. No doubt.

He tipped her chin up, and she fell headlong into his eyes. They were more than soft now. They were warm, simmering, melting her from the inside out.

His thumb traced along her jaw, making her knees go weak.

"You're smart. You're caring. You're beautiful and adorable, and I'm just going to say it . . . I've fallen in love with you."

Her lungs emptied. Her eyes burned. Her throat closed up around any words she may have squeezed out.

"You hear me, Molly? I love you. I've been miserable all week."

"Me too. I'm so sorry—"

He put his finger over her lips. "Forgiven."

Her lips tingled under his fingers. His eyes repeated his words verbatim. He loved her. Despite her goofy ways. Despite her behavior. Despite her distrust.

"We all have issues, Molly. Do you care enough about me to work through them together?"

She nodded, found the courage to speak. "I love you too, Gage."

His lips curled up the tiniest bit. "I was hoping you'd say that." And then they were on hers, moving softly, slowly. They lingered over her, savoring. Her hand found his face, cupped the scruff of his jaw. She'd missed him so much. She drew in his familiar smell, sank into his warmth, lost herself in the melding of their mouths.

He deepened the kiss, and she surrendered to it. He made her feel alive again. Priceless. Her heart raced with pleasure, her blood flooded through her veins, her head spun with desire. Kissing him was like coming home. How could that be?

When he pulled away a moment later, he leaned his forehead against hers. His warm breath fanned her lips, teasing. His arms curled around her, pulling her close.

"I really need to take you on a date," he whispered.

Her arms wound around him, her hands coming to rest on his back. "You owe me a home-cooked meal."

He smiled. "I do, don't I?" He brushed her lips once more, then leaned away, meeting her eyes, his expression growing serious. "Don't be mad, but I took care of the invoice. I know money's no issue now, but you shouldn't have to pay for an expense you didn't see coming."

Molly shook her head. "I'm closing the store, Gage." She'd known it was the right thing as soon as she'd said it to the girls.

The corners of his lips fell. His eyebrows pushed together. "What? No."

She fisted his shirt in her palms. "Yes. It's what I want. The store was Curtis's dream, not mine. I want to find my own dream." She told him about the job at the elementary school and about her interview.

He regarded her, and she watched the news sink in. "This is really what you want?"

"Yes." She'd never been so sure of anything in her life. "Once I made the decision, it was like someone lifted a boulder off my shoulders. I was so busy trying to keep the business afloat, I never even thought about what *I* wanted."

"Music makes you happy."

"It does."

"And now you have the means to pursue it. Sounds like you've got it all worked out."

She trailed a finger down his face, still in awe that he was here. Holding her. "I do now." She couldn't believe she had his heart. That when she'd least expected it, love had seeped back into her life and filled her with joy again.

Gage tipped her chin up. "What's going on behind those big brown eyes?"

She nearly melted at the look in his eyes. She could stare into them for the next fifty years or so. But there were other nice things to look at too. Her eyes trailed down his masculine cheekbones to his scruffy jaw, to the cleft in his chin, finally fixing on his lips. Nice lips. Soft, sexy, and most capable. She was suddenly missing them.

"I was just thinking you should kiss me again."

His lips lifted, his eyes smoldered, pulling her in. "Yeah?" he whispered.

"Yeah . . ." And she felt her own lips turn up as he did just as she asked.

Epilogue

. . . .

A warm breeze drifted across the darkened lake. Overhead, stars twinkled on a black palette that would soon be filled with bursts of color. A crowd had gathered around the lake, a boisterous mix of locals and tourists. Families clustered on blankets, and couples sprawled across the grassy lawn. Children milled around, sparklers flickering from their fisted hands.

The smell of fireworks hung in the air, bringing back memories of holidays past. Occasionally a firecracker popped and a firework or two sizzled and whistled. They were illegal, but that didn't stop people from bringing them.

Molly spread her quilt on the grassy slope between Heather and Paul and Lia and Joey. The fireworks would begin shortly, but she had her own fireworks planned, and she could hardly wait to set them off.

"About time you guys got here." Abby squeezed into a

camp chair with Wyatt. "We had to fight the tourists off with Roman candles."

"Thanks for saving our spot." Gage pulled the quilt corners and eased down beside Molly.

"I'm so full," Molly said. "Those char-grilled burgers should be outlawed." Even now the smell of them wafting over from the picnic area made her want another.

"You only had one," Gage said.

"Gage had three," Noah said as Charlie flopped down beside him.

Gage ruffled his hair. "Shh. That was our little secret, big guy."

"Must be nice." Heather flipped her blond hair over her shoulder. "I have to watch my figure like a hawk."

Paul drew Heather close and planted a kiss on her head. "Never mind that. I'll do the watching."

Lia elbowed Joey. "Men. They can eat as much as they want. It's so unfair."

Joey rubbed his flat stomach. "Hey, what did I do?"

Gage lit a sparkler, and it danced to life in his hands.

"I want one!" Noah reached for the stick.

Gage questioned Molly with a look and she nodded.

"Hold it over the grass, away from your body," she said.

They were spending a lot of time together lately. Gage would come for dinner or they'd go to his house. Noah loved his property. With a pond and acres of hills, it was a little boy's wonderland.

Gage was good with her son. Friendly, but not pushy. So authentic. And he was always good to her. Her thoughts turned to their good-night kisses, and her heart squeezed. She was falling more in love with him every day.

Last night he'd taken them out to eat to celebrate. The principal had called and it was official: Molly was the new music teacher. She settled back on her elbows, gratitude welling up in her, overflowing. *Thank you, God. You've blessed me more than I can say.*

A year ago she was a mess. A year ago she'd sat numbly through the fireworks, feeling as if she'd never be happy or whole again. Today she looked at the people God had put in her life and wondered how he'd returned her joy so quickly and completely.

"Should be a good display," Wyatt said. "Supposedly it's the most we've ever spent."

Gage lit another sparkler and held it out beside Noah's. "The town coffers are pretty healthy these days."

"So are someone else's." Abby gave Molly a look. "What are you going to do with all those riches, Ms. Moneybags?"

"She's already donated half of it," Heather said.

"No, I haven't." She'd been thrilled to turn a hefty check over to the fire department, though. And the library.

"I was over at the firehouse yesterday," Wyatt said. "The guys are really grateful."

"I could never repay them for all they've done."

"Well, we at the library appreciate your generosity, let me tell you. I can hardly wait to get the new genealogy wing up and running. We decided to name it after Pearl Chambers."

"She'd definitely approve," Heather said.

Gage met Molly's eyes, raising his brows. He was as eager as she to share the news.

"There's one more project I decided to fund," Molly said.

Abby gathered her brown hair into a ponytail and slapped a band around it. "Girl, you better keep some of that money for yourself."

"This is kind of for me too. It's for all of us." She looked at the girls one by one, a brow tweaked, enjoying the moment.

"What have you done?" Lia asked.

Abby narrowed her brown eyes. "She's definitely up to something."

"What is it?" Even the waning light couldn't conceal Heather's excitement.

"I just wanted to thank you girls. I never would've found the gold without you."

Lia tilted her head. "Oh, honey, you don't have to—"

"Tell us already!" Heather was ready to pop off her blanket.

Molly met Gage's eyes, and they shared a smile. Then she looked at her friends. "Girls . . . we're going to Hawaii."

"What?" Heather practically screamed.

"No way," Abby said.

"Are you serious?"

Molly pulled the brochures from her purse and handed them to the girls. "Seven days in paradise . . . I was thinking winter break just after Christmas."

"I'm so there!" Heather said.

"Do I get to go?" Noah asked, too mesmerized by the spitting sparkler to spare a glance.

"This is just for the girls, big guy," Gage said. "Maybe you can come to my place. We can go ice fishing on the pond."

Noah watched his sparkler fizzle out. "Sweet!"

They'd already talked it over. Gage was planning to take some time off while she was gone.

"Charlie will be with his grandparents," Heather said. "This is perfect!"

"And we'll both be off school." Lia smiled at Molly.

Heather grabbed Molly into a big hug. "I can't believe we're going to Hawaii!"

Lia joined in. "I can't wait!"

"Oh, what the heck." Abby fell onto the huddle, instigating giggles from them all.

"Thanks, Molly!"

"You girls are the best."

"We're going to have a great time!" Heather said. "Sun, surf, and sand."

"I'm bringing a boatload of books," Abby said.

Lia pulled away. "I'm going to lie in the sun and be lazy for seven days straight."

"Go ahead and leave us," Joey said, waving them away martyr-like.

"Don't worry about a thing," Paul said.

"We'll be just fine."

"Oh, you big babies," Heather said, laughing. "We'll come back rested and happy. That will be its own reward."

A boom sounded and a flare shot up. A red starburst flared over the night sky.

"It's starting!" Charlie bounced up and down on the blanket.

They hushed as patriotic music drifted across the lake, and another loud boom echoed through the night, a cluster of starbursts filling the sky overhead. The crowd oohed and aahed.

Gage lay back on the quilt and patted his stomach. Molly rested her head there as Noah claimed an open spot, mimicking Gage's position, right down to the folded arms and crossed ankles.

Molly felt the booms reverberate through her body as she watched the sky fill with color. Beneath her, Gage's taut stomach moved soothingly up and down with his steady breathing. He reached out and drew his fingers through her hair, and a shiver passed through her.

As excited as she was about the trip to Hawaii with the girls, she was even more excited about her future. About her life, right here in Smitten with the people she loved. Going away was fun, especially when the destination was paradise, but she couldn't imagine a place she'd rather come home to. Or a man she'd rather find waiting.

She turned and found Gage looking at her, those blue eyes reflecting the colors in the sky. His lips tilted in a private smile, and she couldn't stop one of her own. No, her treasure, the real kind, the lasting kind, was right here in Smitten.

Reading Group Guide

. . . .

1. Which heroine (Heather, Abby, Lia, or Molly) could you most identify with? Why?

2. Pearl's book of advice was a bit outdated. If you could write your own piece of advice about how to capture a man's heart, what would it say?

3. Heather guarded her heart from Paul because he'd hurt her once before. How do you know when it's wise to guard your heart? Discuss a time you've found yourself in a similar situation.

4. Have you ever had to rebuild trust in someone? Discuss the process and each person's responsibility in that process.

5. Abby lived an excitement-free life. What's the most adventurous thing you've ever done? What adventures still remain on your bucket list?

6. Abby was a Jane Austen fan. Which of Austen's heroines do you think Abby is most like?

7. Joey needed to forgive the man who killed his late wife. Discuss the process of forgiveness. What does it mean? Who benefits?

8. Joey reached a place where he wasn't willing to forgive, but he was "willing to be made willing." Discuss a time when you've been in that place. What did you learn?

9. Molly's late husband, Curtis, broke her trust and that trickled over into her relationships with Gage and God. Have you ever experienced something similar?

10. Molly came to realize that the most important treasures are priceless. Name some of these things. Is there a treasure you've been searching diligently for?

ACKNOWLEDGMENTS

. . . .

*W*hat a joy it's been to work on the Smitten series! The idea for *Smitten Book Club* was conceived in a beautiful Indiana log cabin (we pretended it was Vermont) and met with much enthusiasm by our publishing team.

As with every book, *Smitten Book Club* is the result of a lot of hard work done by many peiople. We are so blessed to work with HarperCollins Christian Publishing. They've been supportive of the Smitten series from the start, and their enthusiasm has been contagious. Thanks to the entire team led by Daisy Hutton: Ansley Boatman, Katie Bond, Amanda Bostic, Sue Brower, Ruthie Dean, Laura Dickerson, Jodi Hughes, Ami McConnell, Becky Monds, Becky Philpott, Kerri Potts, and Kristen Vasgaard.

A special thanks to our editors Ami McConnell and LB Norton. Their expertise is truly outstanding; we're so glad you have our backs!

We're grateful to our agents, Karen Solem and Lee Hough, who were a huge help with this work and many others.

Denise would like to thank Beth White for her help with all things piano-related. Her husband Kevin assisted her on the business portion of her story, and Gray Stevens (whose name may appear in a future Denise Hunter novel!) from Vermont Outdoor Guide Association answered her questions about becoming an outfitter. Any mistakes are hers alone.

We're thankful for our families, our backbones as we juggle life and career.

Thanks to you, our reader. None of this would've happened without you. It's been a joy to dream up Smitten and its inhabitants together and a special privilege to share them with you!

Our biggest thank-you goes to God, who brought the four of us together in a bond of unbreakable friendship. We're all so different, and yet one, in our love for Christ and for one another.

An Excerpt from
Secretly Smitten

. . . .

*W*rapping paper lay strewn around the floor in a happy crumple of color. Tess Thomas handed her cousin one last gift and suppressed a smile. Nat would blush when she saw the filmy negligee Tess had bought. But Tess knew if anyone would look great in the gown, it was her cousin. It was something Tess would never purchase for herself. But then, what need would she have for a honeymoon gown anyway?

While Natalie began to rip paper with abandon, Tess glanced around the packed parlor of their grandmother's old house. Their friends had all shown up for the bridal shower, and there wasn't space for another chair. A few women even sat on the floor with their backs propped against the wall. That was what Tess loved about the small town of Smitten, Vermont. Neighbors were like family. And they'd all pulled together in amazing ways this past year as they worked to put Smitten on the map as a town based on tourism—a romantic destination, in fact. There were so many new businesses, including a big hotel that had taken over the old lumber mill.

Their great-aunt Violet bustled in with a tray of cookies and tea. "Tess, dear," she whispered. "I'm not sure these gluten-free things are worth eating."

The cookies were as lopsided as Violet's red lipstick. The color of that lipstick had never changed over the years—it was the same orangey red that clashed pitifully with Violet's dyed red hair.

Tess took the crumbliest cookie and took a bite. "They're good, Aunt Violet. And Natalie will appreciate that you went to the trouble."

Her aunt's smile brightened. "I'm so glad, honey. You always were my favorite niece!" She winked dramatically.

Tess's sister Clare took the tray. "Let me help you with that, Aunt Violet." She circled the room with the tray in hand, and to their credit, most guests took a cookie.

Natalie took a break from the gifts to nibble on a cookie and glanced around. "Where's Mia?"

"In the attic," Grandma Rose said. "You girls always loved to play up there, remember?"

This three-story Victorian was special. Tess, her sisters, and their cousins had loved exploring the attic when they came to visit their grandmother and great-aunts. The grand old home's welcome enveloped visitors the moment they stepped onto the polished walnut floors.

Tess turned toward the hall. "You stay here with your guests. I'll check on her, Natalie."

When Tess reached the bottom of the stairs, Natalie's adopted daughter, Mia, was descending. The six-year-old had a purple boa around her neck and wore a red velvet dress, the hem trailing on the hardwood. She'd found some lipstick from somewhere—probably Violet's, judging by the color—and her small white teeth gleamed behind the smear of orange.

Mia reached the bottom of the staircase and twirled. "Look at me, Tess!"

A wave of love swept over Tess. If only she could have a daughter like Mia someday. "Smashing," she said in genuine admiration. "That's an unusual necklace." She leaned down to examine the tarnished metal and realized it held a pair of dog tags. "Where did you get it?"

Mia looked down at her feet and shuffled. "In the attic."

"Was it in the trunk you were allowed to be in?"

"No." Mia peeked up at her. She held up her arm to show a bracelet. "My bracelet fell off and went down a hole. I put my hand in to get it and found the necklace too." Red stained Mia's cheeks. "Should I put it back?"

Tess put her hand on Mia's soft hair. "No, it's fine, honey. I just wondered where you found it. I've never seen it before."

Natalie appeared in the doorway from the parlor. "Is something wrong?" She glanced at her daughter.

"Not really. I was looking at something Mia found in the attic."

A frown crouched between Natalie's eyes. "Are those dog tags? What on earth . . . There haven't been any soldiers in our family, have there, Tess?" She held out her hand. "Let me see them, Mia."

Mia's lower lip quivered, but she took off the dog tags and handed them over. "I didn't hurt them."

"It's okay, sweetie. I'm sure you didn't." Natalie reached

out a reassuring hand to embrace the girl. Lifting the tag to the light, she studied it. "David Hutchins."

Tess's grandmother spoke from behind them. "David Hutchins? Where did you hear that name?"

Tess turned to see the color leave her grandmother's face. "On these dog tags Mia found upstairs in the attic." Beyond Grandma Rose, she saw Aunt Violet turn pale and reach out to steady herself on the wall.

Grandma Rose grabbed the door frame. "With David's name?"

For a moment Tess thought her grandmother might faint. She rushed to her side. "Grandma, are you all right?"

Her grandmother wetted her lips. "I'm fine. I'm just trying to understand this. David died in the Korean conflict. As far as I know, his dog tags were never recovered. Neither was his body."

"See for yourself," Natalie said, joining them, hand outstretched.

Grandma Rose clutched the dog tags, then held them to the light. "Mia, where did you find these?"

"In the attic." Mia's voice wobbled. "I'm sorry."

Tess embraced her. "You're not in trouble, honey. Grandma is just surprised they were there." She stared at her grandmother, who was as pale as the white blouse she wore. "Who was David Hutchins?"

Her grandmother was staring at the dog tags. She blinked rapidly. "My fiancé."

Natalie frowned. "I'm confused. What about Grandpa Martin?"

Grandma Rose bit her lip. "I loved him, of course, but he wasn't my first love." She hesitated. "First love is special." Her face took on a dreamy expression. "He used to call me his Betty Boop."

Though it hurt even to imagine her grandmother loving another man before her own grandfather, Tess loved a good mystery, and this smelled like the best kind. "If he died in the war, then how did these dog tags get in your attic?"

"I don't know. It makes no sense."

"Could the military have sent them back to you?" Natalie asked.

"They didn't. I would have kept them close. They wouldn't be in the attic."

"You're sure he died?" Tess asked.

"Of course. The army notified his parents. I was there when they told us of his death." She looked down. "It was the darkest day of my life."

Darker than the day Grandpa died? Tess studied her grandmother's face but didn't ask the question.

"Did he live here in Smitten?" Natalie asked.

Grandma Rose nodded. "Over on Green Valley Road. In that big house where Ryan Stevenson lives now."

Tess's pulse kicked at Ryan Stevenson's name. The handsome widower was a Saturday morning patron at her bookstore. Not that he'd ever noticed *her*.

"David's family moved away after his death." Her grandmother's voice broke, then she recovered her composure and managed a smile. "We'd better get back to our guests."

Tess followed her to the parlor, but her brain was whirling. What did it all mean?

The story continues in *Secretly Smitten*.

About the Authors

· ·

Photo by Clik Chick
Photography

RITA-finalist Colleen Coble is the author of several best-selling romantic suspense novels, including *Tidewater Inn* and the Mercy Falls, Lonestar, and Rock Harbor series.

Photo by Michael
Hawk Photography

Kristin Billerbeck is a Christy Award finalist and two-time winner of the American Christian Fiction Writers Book of the Year award. Her books include *A Billion Reasons Why* and *What a Girl Wants*.

Photo by Clik Chick
Photography

Diann Hunt writes heartwarming stories with a rose-colored view of the world. The author of 25 books, many of them award winners, Diann lives in Indiana with her husband, Jim. Visit her website at diannhunt.com.

Photo by Amber
Zimmerman

Denise Hunter is the best-selling author of many novels, including *The Trouble with Cowboys* and *Barefoot Summer*. She lives in Indiana with her husband, Kevin, and their three sons.